BATTLE SPIRE

A CRAFTING LITRPG BOOK

MICHAEL R. MILLER

PORTAL BOOKS

CONTENTS

Chapter 1	1
Chapter 2	7
Chapter 3	14
Chapter 4	21
Chapter 5	35
Chapter 6	53
Chapter 7	66
Chapter 8	80
Chapter 9	90
Chapter 10	98
Chapter 11	106
Chapter 12	119
Chapter 13	128
Chapter 14	147
Chapter 15	153
Chapter 16	167
Chapter 17	180
Chapter 18	196
Chapter 19	204
Chapter 20	227
Chapter 21	239
Chapter 22	247
Chapter 23	256
Chapter 24	262
Chapter 25	270
Chapter 26	279
Chapter 27	293
Chapter 28	302
Chapter 29	314
Chapter 30	323
Chapter 31	328
Chapter 32	338
Chapter 33	349
Chapter 34	358
Chapter 35	371
Chapter 36	376

Epilogue	380
Afterword	393
Other LitRPG from Portal Books	395
Acknowledgments	399

Thank you for checking out my book! Whilst this isn't the place to thank everyone who has helped to make Battle Spire possible, here I can thank you, the reader, upfront. Without you, I wouldn't be able to live my dream as a writer.

You can sample a wide selection of the work from Portal Books by signing up to our mailing list and get a FREE story bundle in return! The bundle has contributions from the authors of Portal Books, is over 60,000 words long and is always growing!

Sign up here for the Portal Books story bundle https://portal-books.com/sign-up

Enjoy!
Michael

1

For most people, I reckon nearing the end of finals eases the grizzly knot of tension in your stomach; for me, it only tightened the knot further. You see my real test was still to come and by the end of this weekend, I intended that my life would never be the same again.

But first, I had this damned exam to finish.

I glanced up from my answer to check the clock in the corner of the exam terminal's screen. One minute left. Only one glorious minute.

Returning to my final answer, I pressed the turn icon to take a new page, frantically scribbling with my chrome stylus before the page finished loading. My aching hand scrawled out the last words, slipping here and there from the strain of the last three hours. Genetic Engineering had been a ball ache of a course but I'd reached the end now. It would stand me in good stead and get me a grad job, or so everybody says. If I passed, that is.

But I'd pass. I'd made certain of it by studying day and night for the last six months.

After I'd nearly flunked out last semester, I didn't have much of a choice.

With two seconds to spare on the clock, I pressed in a period to finish my answer. A clinical sounding 'ping' rang across the hall, followed by low grunts and sighs of relief from my fellow students.

I caught the eye of my buddy Lucas nearby. He made an exhausted fist pump into the air and then became more animated as he mimed throwing back drinks with both hands. I smiled back and feigned a similar motion, though I had no intention on following through on that this evening. I had my own celebration planned.

A message blinked onto the middle of the monitor.

Times up! XenTech University hopes you've had a pleasant evaluation today. Please reconfirm your identity to proceed.

A box outlined in red appeared to the side of the message, large enough for my whole hand. I placed my palm onto the screen and the scanning process began. Out of well-practiced habit, I also looked to the lens on the monitor so it could double-check that I really was who I was supposed to be.

As if to triple confirm, it brought up my student ID, horrific picture and all. There I was, all eighteen and spotty; hair lank and ungroomed across my face. Hardly dashing. Still, my eyes looked brighter back then, all hopeful, idiot that I was. Oh, and my younger self was a lot thinner too; before the beer and takeout weight had taken its toll.

The prick.

At least the monitor was happy about it, flashing excitedly.

Confirmed!
Jack Kross
Congratulations on completing your examination. We hope to see you at the 2053 graduation. XenTech hopes you have a nice day (and a party-filled evening)!

Cringy corporate communications aside, I don't think I had felt so giddy in years. Better than waking up on Christmas morning seven years ago to get my first fully neural interfaced VR headset, a Noir Dome 1160X model. It was a piece of junk now but the rented model I had stowed away in my backpack probably wasn't much better.

In my eagerness to escape the exam hall, I jumped to my feet too fast and earned a dizzying rush of blood to the head, but anticipation for what was to come vanquished the knot in my stomach. Maybe this feeling was even better than that kiss with Clara Denson back in sophomore year, which was a worrying thought as that was one of my more cherished memories. Nor was I supposed to jump into a game for at least another six months if I wanted to win that bet with my parents.

I'd played *Myth Online* a bit too much the previous year. Huge epic adventure, forming guilds, slaying bosses and getting sick loot, what's not to love? I loved it a little too much and was on the verge of being kicked out of college when I had a wake-up call. I guess I got a bit obsessed; happens to the best of us, am I right? So, I sold my VR Headset, a CryoScope 520G – God, it was the shit – and knuckled down. Even told my parents I was voluntarily quitting. They didn't believe me, so I'd made a bet with them.

If I stayed off gaming for a whole year and smashed my final exams, they'd help me buy my first car. Just the fact that I'd be getting out of my room delighted them more. 'Go for a run,' they'd told me. 'Get some fresh air in you, that'll see you right.'

In hindsight, I should have made the time limit six months, then I'd already have made it. Oh well, I was gonna sneak a little in anyway. I had a plan.

I'd naturally ignored my family's suggestion that I go for a run. Shocking as it might sound, I wasn't one for running, but right now, leaving this exam hall, I was approaching something dangerously close to a jog as I wove through the crowd, the hubbub of post-exam relief rising all around me.

"Jack?" Lucas was calling after me, but I hurried on. If I could grab my bag before he got out, I could dash for the hover tram and make my getaway without any awkward interrogations. He's one of my roommates and my family drafted them all in to make sure I didn't break the terms of our agreement. The others wouldn't bother so much but Lucas had a giant crush on my sister, so he would play kiss ass. It was real rich of him, now I thought about it. I'd never once told his family about how he spent all his book money on pot during our first week. All in all, this meant the apartment would be a no-go for my weekend of gaming.

Perhaps my dash for freedom had been a bit of a giveaway? Never mind.

I arrived at the storage unit outside of the hall somewhat breathless and leaned onto the counter for support, drawing in embarrassingly large gulps of air. I really ought to work out more. I'd say I'll start properly after this weekend's experiment, but who am I kidding?

After picking up my bag I made my way toward the exit.

"Excuse me," I grunted as I tried to negotiate a throng of people blocking the glass doors. They may as well not have heard me. "Sorry, could you move, please?"

No dice.

I like to kid myself that I'm a confident person who projects his voice. It's moments like this that bring that fantasy crashing down. I resorted to a good old-fashioned shoulder barge to squeaks of protest, but no matter. I was out and was greeted by the bright sun over the Bay Area.

It was one of those rare hot days in San Francisco when you can really smell the heat, you know? That sort of mix of sunscreen and sweat, when everyone's face is hidden behind shades. The kind of hot weather that brings out all the best-looking girls and gives the gym bros an excuse to take their shirts off. And here I was about to lock myself into a dark room for the rest of the day. I couldn't wait.

I slung my bag over my shoulder and started to move, heading towards the hover tram terminal at the edge of campus. As I approached, the tram pulled in and I really did run this time to hop aboard. I didn't feel like waiting fifteen minutes for the next ride north. The way I jumped through the closing doors was almost heroic.

Quickly scanning my palm to charge my account, I looked for a place to sit. The only seat left was one on the west side of the carriage where the sun was beating in through the window.

I sat down, bag slumped between my legs, and tapped the window to bring up the shade filter controls. I selected medium, darkening out the world.

It would take a while for the tram to reach its most northern stop and then I'd have to change onto the old Powell-Hyde cable car line for the last leg of my journey. The Tenderloin wasn't an area I'd usually visit, never mind plan on staying for two nights, but it would offer me the reclusive setting that I desired. Hell, everyone knew about the sordid VR 'salons' that littered the area and while I wasn't planning such activities, the single room occupancy joints were amongst the few places left that still took cash in hand without asking questions.

Anywhere else, even a low-key motel, would likely want my palm print or simply get my identity from their security cameras. Not a bad thing for the most part, except that I couldn't leave a record of where I was if I wanted to pull the wool over my family's eyes. Not that they were regularly checking up on me or anything, but I like to be thorough.

Call me obsessive, but I like the fine detail. It's why I enjoy delving deep into an RPG, figuring out the best path, tweaking the talents and stat numbers to be just right; theory crafting weird new builds to gain an edge over others. I just wish I knew more people in the real world who understood that.

My immediate family still saw it as a stigma. Yet the rise in Esports was allowing people to make legitimate careers in gaming, like any football or baseball player. I bet you anything that if I'd been making serious cash doing it, like the top MOBA and Battle Royale players, then it would have been an entirely different story.

It wouldn't have been a 'stupid waste of time' then. No, no, no; it would have been me working really hard.

If you're asking why I don't just shoot for those top-paying spots the answer is simple, I've not got the reflexes to play competitively. I enjoy a shooter or MOBA like anyone else but I'm just not quick enough. I'm at my best when I get to sit back a bit, plan things out and take my time. Play the long game, if you will. In *Myth Online*, I played a utility class and acted as the guild leader. I organized the raids and, yes, I admit it, berated people down voice comms for not doing their job. Looking back, I can appreciate why my roommates found it worrying.

Still, I refer back to my main point: they didn't 'get' what I was doing. I've seen coaches here on campus screaming blue bloody murder at their team during a match and nobody pulls them up for it. And we all know that there are bosses across the country shrieking in boardrooms right now. So what if I told the idiots who died over and over again in the Elder Dragon's deep breath attack to go screw their own moth— well, you get the idea.

The basic point is this. If I can make money from gaming, then no one will call it 'wasting time' again. They'll call me hard working. And what's more, I think I know how to do it.

2

You might be wondering why I'm so hell-bent on making some money out of playing this new game? It can't all be to prove a point to my parental overlords. And you'd be right. Truth be told, I doubt I can make loads, but anything that can help to make a dent in my student debt wouldn't go amiss. I've racked up a quarter of a million bucks in tuition fees from XenTech. Ivy League schools are supposed to be worth it, right?

So, what's my plan? Well, it's to start playing the scavenger class in the new virtual reality massively multiplayer online game, *Hundred Kingdoms*. You'll have heard of *Hundred Kingdoms*, of course, it only came out about a month ago, but in case you've been living under a rock, or are like my sister, I'll run over it again.

Hundred Kingdoms is the big new thing, being hailed as the game changer for VRMMO gaming, the way that *World of Warcraft* was for classic MMOs early in the millennium. Sure, there have been some great VRMMOs already but *Hundred Kingdoms* seems to have struck gold, bringing in both hardcore and casual players alike in droves. It's been estimated the game has fifteen million players worldwide and it is growing every week. An advanced AI runs the show, which some people have called a waste of good tech; mostly politicians who want to build smarter robots to kill people with.

The most important thing is that in-game gold can be exchanged into dollars. And vice versa. Now, it used to be that companies would go to any lengths to stop gold sellers in these sorts of games but I'm sure you've heard of the 1920s Prohibition. You can't completely stop people from getting what they want and if you can't beat them, then sell the goods yourself.

Players can go to Frostbyte Studio's online store and purchase a token which they can redeem inside *Hundred Kingdoms* for in-game gold. But that gold isn't just generated out of thin air; that would lead to some crazy hyperinflation. No, no, it's the players who have amassed legitimate in-game wealth who are free to put up their gold for a token and take a share of the profits. Frostbyte carefully monitor and adjust how much the gold is worth, meaning the amount of money needed to buy one hundred gold goes up and down based on supply and demand.

At the launch of a new game like this, many hardcore players who are pushing for world first rankings are willing to spend a bomb to get an early edge, but the amount of gold generated by players isn't huge yet as people haven't had time to farm it. It effectively means that the in-game gold is strong against the dollar.

If you have a lot of gold in the game right now, you stand to make a pretty penny. Going forward, the system will still allow those who like to play the auction house in-game to do well for themselves back in the real world. With any new frontier, there is money to be made, if you can discover where to make it.

Enter me and the scavenger class.

A soft ping-pong noise emanated from the speakers overhead, pulling me back to reality as the tram pulled into its next stop. The doors opened, letting in hot air from the outside, and a shuffling of people then ensued. Jolted by the noise and bustle, I shook my head to fully wake myself up. Out of habit, I decided to check the leveling leaderboards of Hundred Kingdoms.

I pulled out my phone and with a few quick taps the leaderboard appeared. I'd been checking it regularly since the game's release, to see how far behind I might end up being during exams. Not too far as it turned out. While most people bemoaned the fact it had come out in April – right before exams for many students across the country – I'd been glad.

Hundred Kingdoms had been scheduled to come out before Thanksgiving, but there had been an attempted hack which delayed its release, granting the developers time to beef up security. Frostbyte Studios hadn't confirmed what the digital thieves had attempted to do. Most people assumed to the attackers had tried to find a loophole in the game's economy system to plunder it for quick cash upon release. Whatever the case, *Hundred Kingdoms* had launched in April, meaning I wasn't so far behind.

Had it been released on schedule, I wouldn't have been able to play as that was when I'd made the bet and started to focus on my studies. I would have had to try and resist jumping online for six months rather than just one. That would have been cruel.

The leveling leaderboards had become one of the most watched pages on the web these past weeks. Frostbyte Studios had offered in-game vanity awards and titles to the first one hundred players who reached the level cap of 50. Shockingly, few had made it so far. Only twenty-four players in the world.

The rankings on the leaderboard were calculated by using time played, while also factoring in the number of deaths and a weighting based on the player's chosen class, with certain classes deemed to be easier to level than others. Since I'd checked last night, the board hadn't moved an inch.

Leaderboard

1. **Legolaas** – High Elf – Ranger – playtime 10 days 3 hours 34 minutes
2. **OneShotMaster** – Orc – Ranger – playtime 10 days 5 hours 14 minutes
3. **PyroPotter** – Gnome – Mage – playtime 10 days 7 hours 47 minutes
4. **Azrael** – Undead Human – Death Knight – playtime 13 days 14 hours 3 minutes

5. **ScrubSlayer** – Minotaur – Berserker – playtime 10 days 10 hours 50 minutes
6. **WhiteNoise** – Vampire – Mage – playtime 10 days 12 hours 34 minutes
7. **Longtuuusk** – Troll – Ranger – playtime 10 days 15 hours 50 minutes

The board carried on much the same until the end; mostly a bunch of rangers and mages who had extremely little downtime while soloing in the world. It was Azrael who impressed me the most, as he'd taken longer than most on the board but as his class was considered harder to level, he'd secured fourth place. Very impressive stuff.

There were absolutely no scavengers on the board. Barely anyone had chosen to play that class. It was a bit of an oddball, all looting and crafting items from what they'd found, just as the name suggested. Lots of utility in the items they could make, apparently, but they were meant to support others, not dish out sexy damage numbers or take punishment like a tanking class.

The reason I was interested in them was for the economic branch of their talent choices. Ostensibly, they were for players who wanted to roleplay their way as a merchant or traveling trader. I'd also be rolling as a regular old human character because they had a racial bonus which gave them ten percent off items bought from and sold to NPCs (that's non-player characters).

It's not such a grand plan when you boil it down. I'd be making a human scavenger because scavengers were the best for everything in-game that was gold related and humans had a small boost to their trading. Hardly stellar min-maxing but there you have it.

Some items were selling for hundreds of gold right now, including crafting materials. Arcane Crystals fetched as much as one thousand gold because they were used in the making of the best current endgame weapons and armor; those items that were prized by the top guilds who wanted an edge for sponsorship deals. There was one sale on the auction house that had found its way across all the commentary channels – an item called the Orb of Deception that had been put up for auction during the first week of the launch and went for over ten thousand gold. I'm not sure what the real world value of that transaction would have been, but I'm positive someone sunk a ton of money into getting that much gold so early on in the game's life.

I didn't expect to achieve such feats in a single weekend. I'd need to invest some playtime to set up my character, level it, gather gold to buy the crafting tools that I needed, reach the capital city and the other sundries of beginning a new game. Still, I planned on being relentless this weekend and if I could make a few hundred dollars' worth of gold, then I reckoned I'd be onto something.

It should be enough to convince those around me that I wasn't wasting my time. Once they accepted that, I could go ahead and try all the other classes out too and just have fun.

So that was my plan in a nutshell. And honestly, I couldn't have been more excited by it.

Out of the dimmed window of the hover tram, the cityscape began to change. Sleek modern buildings that weaved metal, glass and organic materials together gave way to the cramped brickwork buildings of the old city. Streets narrowed, five lanes moved into three and then two. The buildings weren't as tall here, yet they seemed to block out more sunlight and I dialed down the filter on the window to compensate.

My fellow passengers had changed as well, from students to workers. Soon, they were replaced by older denizens of the inner city, wearing frayed, ill-fitting clothes and displaying brands that had gone bust during the crisis of the early 40s. I was closing in on the last stop on the line, and it was like traveling back in time.

A lot of folks who'd been caught up in the downturn twelve years ago still hadn't escaped it. My parents had just about managed to but no more. You can imagine why they lavished praise on my doctor of a sister, Julie. Scholarships galore for her but not for me. I'd built up a debt instead. And while they smiled and said they were proud, they couldn't quite hide the flicker of nerves about the mounting bill. Sure, I'd applied for loans and got them but if I keeled over dead tomorrow, then it would be my parents who'd have to foot the bill. Weird system, right? Most debt gets written off with bankruptcy or death but a student loan, that shit will haunt those who you leave behind.

One saving grace had been my course choice. Genetics these days was a lot like computer coding had been forty years ago; it was starting to be used by pretty much everybody, but not enough people were highly skilled in it yet.

It wasn't glamorous, spending countless hours in front of a screen, tapping out sequencing. Despite what the media will have people believe, you can't rebuild your whole body the way you want to. There's only so far that you can go in manipulating your own personal coding before things get royally effed up. You can make your jaw more defined, but you can't go from a rounded mess to chiseled in one fell swoop. You might be able to make yourself grow an extra inch or two but not much more before things get dangerous. Other body parts may be shrunken or – as is more often done – enlarged, but honestly, you can't always tell the difference between the before and after photos. Everyone has a slightly different coding, so there's only so much that can be done. There are no cookie cutter builds for people. Real life isn't a game.

Real life has limits.

It has wear and tear; it's a reality where those who win at the genetic or social lottery get an unfair advantage over everyone else. Sometimes, skill, brains and effort will get you where you want to go but there are no guarantees in real life. Games just aren't like that. No developer in their right mind would have every player start with randomly allocated stats, with some people starting as gods and others as runts. It would be unbalanced. It wouldn't be very fair. That's why I prefer games. Technology had reached a stage where living in the digital sphere was fast becoming a real possibility.

Virtual reality gaming would be the great democratizer of life.

Another ping-pong from the speakers was followed by a droning beep.

"We have reached our final stop where this service terminates."

Everyone got to their feet, heading for the opening doors. After packing my phone back into my bag, I shuffled onto the platform with everybody else. But whereas most of the people around me looked downcast or tired, perhaps going to or coming home from work, I was smiling.

Before dark, I'd be in *Hundred Kingdoms* at last.

3

By six-thirty, I was standing outside my destination: the Paradise Hotel on Turk Street. The irony of the name couldn't have been blunter, although the smashed glass of an upper window gave it a good try. Being early evening, the streets were packed, and I gripped the handles of my grocery bags tightly, as though fearing imminent robbery. It wouldn't be sunset until about eight-fifteen, but I admit I was glad to be heading inside where the promise of a room with a locked door awaited me.

I wasn't that deep into the Tenderloin, being close to what most considered to be its 'southern border', Market Street. But I wouldn't say I was brave or used to this. Nor would my scrawny frame do me any favors here. And I was probably being incredibly prejudiced against the folk who live in these parts—

An earsplitting crack rent the air.

Next thing I knew, my legs had powered me up the steps and into the Paradise Hotel. Had that been a gunshot? My heart was thundering again, and I tightened my grip on my shopping bags. There weren't any sirens blaring. Most likely it was just a backfiring car – man, I was on edge. Maybe I should have just bolted the door to my bedroom shut and hoped for the best. Damned Lucas and his fawning over Julie. He'd rat me out the moment that he realized I was playing.

Well, I was here now; no good turning back.

I walked up to the reception, or what passed for a reception. It was more of a large hole in the wall with a reinforced steel shutter. Not a promising sign. There was an actual honest-to-God brass bell on the counter that looked like something you'd see in an old movie. I tapped it and it rang rather daintily.

Nobody came.

Perhaps I'd picked the wrong spot. I'd researched as best I could and found this 'hotel' to be a frequent haunt of gentlemen with specific virtual reality needs. Basically, the internet connection was good enough to hold steady during a digital orgy.

It was a sign of my desire to get into the game quickly that I remained where I was and rang the bell again. And again, and again.

A determined gamer won't be stopped, I tell you!

At least I had the forethought to grab supplies from a megamart before hopping onto the cable car, hence the big brown bags. I'd munched a choco-nut protein snack as the old rust bucket had trundled north-east up Market Street. Okay, fine, I ate three of them. With bags full of protein-rich bars, meals to be rehydrated, energy drinks, and bottles of water, I should be able to proceed as planned with minimal breaks.

If I could get a room that is.

I rang the bell again.

At last, something answered, namely a swinging door that was somewhere out of sight behind the reception area. The door crashed against the wall and heavy footsteps padded their way in. They belonged to the heavy-set middle-aged dude lumbering into view behind the counter. He was entirely bald on the top of his head, but the sides and back were tangled in overgrown black hair. A bulbous nose sat between small but shrewd eyes, and his brow glistened with natural oils. He wore only a thin white vest covered with sweat patches over coarse chest hair. I couldn't see below the counter, but I prayed he wore at least something in that region.

"Hang on," he grunted, then began pressing at buttons that I could not see. An air conditioning unit whirred to life, blowing up his messy hair. None of the cool air reached me, unfortunately, and my palms remained positively slippery as I continued to grasp at my grocery bags.

"Christ, that's better," the landlord said. He returned his focus on me, giving me a dirty look and running his eyes up and down me. "Here for a room?"

What else would people come here for, I thought.

"Y-yes, please," I said, unable to hide my nerves.

The landlord gave me a grin worthy of the fattest of cats. "I got room thirty-six free. How long you want it?"

"Two nights… with an option for a third, if possible," I added hastily.

"I reckon that's *possible*," said the landlord. "Cash or palm?"

"Cash."

"Two hundred."

I didn't dare to haggle.

"Sure, hold on," I said as I began rummaging in my bag for the cash. I hesitated in handing it over. "Can I get a lock on the door?"

"All rooms come with a lock."

"Does it work?"

He scowled. "D'you think I don't take care of my place?"

"No, no, no, not at all. I was just—"

"You want it or not?"

"Yes… here."

Resigned, I handed him the money. He counted it out twice to be sure.

"Hand over your bag. Need to check what's in there."

Fearing I may never see the bag again, I passed it over. The landlord brought out a metal detector which immediately wailed.

"I won't have weapons in my hotel!"

"It's not a weapon. It's a… it's a VR headset."

He scowled again, unzipped the bag, pulled the VisionXcape360 headset and dropped it roughly on the counter. Honestly, it would be a miracle if the thing still worked at this point.

The landlord sucked in a breath through his teeth. "Seems in order." He pushed the headset halfway across the counter to me and then stopped. "Internet connection. That'll cost extra."

Something about his smirk told me he was lying. Paying for ultra-speed internet hadn't been a common thing since the turn of the decade, and while it was true that not every district of the city had stable and free connections, I knew this guy was taking me for a ride. Even if I'd had the balls to question him, I'm not sure I would have. I was itching to get upstairs and get into *Hundred Kingdoms*. Perhaps the landlord could sense my unease, and the slight twitch I had developing in one eye wasn't aiding my cause.

"How much?" I asked.

"Four hundred all in."

"You're just doubling the price."

"Five hundred."

My jaw fell slack.

He chuckled. "None of my business what dirty shit you're into kid, but I'm guessing you're here because you don't have anywhere else to get your jollies." He sniffed theatrically. "You'll want to be online without interruption. So, if you want your kit back, and a room, pay up before I add on any more."

A mixture of anger and dismay flared in my cheeks. If I didn't give him the cash he'd close his steel reinforced shutter, laugh, and take my possessions for himself.

"Fine." I presented the extra money and he handed back my bag and headset. He followed it up with two keys.

"This one's for your room. This is for the bathroom. Room thirty-six. Third floor. Internet password is on the keyring. Now scram."

I scooped up the keys and made for the stairwell. If I'd had a tail, it would have been between my legs.

It was dark on the stairs, with only a couple of narrow windows high up and no light switches as far as I could see. The air was close and humid, and after the second flight, I had to pause to cough and catch my breath.

That's when I heard a humming coming from above me. I discovered the source of the noise was another middle-aged man, only he was the antithesis of the landlord, with a body like a garden rake. The smell of booze was strong even at this distance. The man stumbled as he crested the top of the stairs, falling to his knees. He simply laughed.

"Whoops. Let's try that again," he said before pulling himself up.

Tentatively, I continued up the stairs and emerged onto the third floor. The drunk had collapsed about halfway down the corridor, still humming. I stepped quietly as I could to check the number on the closest door, though I feared my huffing and puffing would give me away. I passed number forty-two, forty, thirty-eight—

"Hey, hey," the drunk said. He was flopping around like a beached seal, pointing a long finger at me. His eyes fell on my grocery bags. "This – this is such good service. I wis needin' something to eat."

My eyes fell to my toes as I silently drew up before room thirty-six, placed my bags down and fumbled with my keys.

"Hey, hey you," the drunk slurred. "I'm talking to you. How com— how come you won't look at me, eh?"

The keys rattled loudly as I tried to place the right one into the lock. In the dim hallway, it was hard to tell which was which, and in my panic, I dropped them entirely.

"Goddammit," I muttered under my breath.

"What's that?" the drunk said. He was stumbling upright now. "Look, just give me my stuff and we'll call it even."

I scrambled for the keys, managing to fit the correct one into the lock this time and turned it. I could hear the man heading for me as I pinned the bags awkwardly between my arms and bundled inside the room. A bony hand snatched at my side and I heard paper tearing. Over the threshold of the room I turned, and a few choco-nut bars slipped out from the hole in one of my supply bags. Instinct took over and I kicked the snacks out into the corridor. The drunkard leapt after them like a dog chasing a stick.

Heart pounding, I closed the door and looked for the lock. At least this thing was state of the art. A black box ran up from the handle and once I activated it, a series of small metallic beams began interlocking with a connecting device on the doorframe. Short of cutting through the door, nobody was getting through that.

My shoulders slumped at the thought. I hadn't realized how tense I'd been for the past couple of hours and I had aches in places that I didn't even know could ache. I unslung my backpack and put the market bags down carefully, so as not to let any of the cans of energy juice fall out of the ripped one. Once satisfied there would be no explosion of the sugary beverages, I finally took a proper look at my abode for the next few days.

It didn't take long to drink it in. A match in a matchbox might have complained about the space. There was a small single bed, a chipped mirror above a sink that may once have been white, a filthy set of blinds drawn up above the window and an air-con unit that looked about fifteen years out of date. It was sweltering in here, so I moved to switch the cool air on. Broken. But, of course. I opened the window as wide as it would go instead and returned to sit on the bed. It was hard and springy, and singularly uncomfortable.

With a sigh, I reached for one of the bottles of water, taking a large and much-needed gulp. I'd just been threatened for money and chased for food. Might even have heard a gun go off too. What a night.

Time to crack on with it.

First, I connected both my phone and headset to the Wi-Fi. I started with the headset because it would need time to patch any client-side updates to *Hundred Kingdoms* that might have come. The bulk of the processing power was handled by the Frostbyte servers and the headset was more like a giant phone that you dialed in on to play. It also meant that you had to lie down and enter a state of near-coma to interface with the virtual world.

The headsets were still like old gaming consoles and always had to be plugged in. This was partly to eliminate the risk of power failure as a sudden shutdown could cause nasty side effects. There hadn't been any incidents from VR headsets for many generations of the tech, but no company was confident enough to try running the thing by battery power alone.

With the VisionXcape360 plugged in, connected and patching, I turned to my actual phone. I bashed in the password to access the Wi-Fi and the screen blazed with notifications. My mom, dad, and Julie had all sent me their luck before I'd gone into my exam and then congratulated me when it was over. My mom had sent some follow-ups trying to wring info out of me about how it had gone.

I felt a twinge of guilt for the deception I was playing, but it passed. Never once did they encourage Julie to stop playing her saxophone or spend less time training for the swim team. There'd been so many 5am wake-up calls for my mom and dad to take her to the pool before school without complaints, whereas I'd got a stern warning after just missing dinner a few times because of a vital raid night. Didn't seem fair in my estimation.

I'd show them what I could do. Not to put extra pressure on me, but this experiment with the scavenger class really had to work. I was already down five hundred bucks from that greedy asshole of a landlord. He'd taken advantage of me because he thought I was a pushover and, alright, I am. But he just knew it instantly. I was tired of not having confidence, of not having respect. And now that I was safely behind my locked door, I started to feel angry. Anger at him, anger at my family who simply didn't accept me for who I was and what I wanted to do.

Two days. In two days, everything would be different.

And with this bolstering feeling fueling me, I took one last glug of water, pulled on the VisionXcape360 and lay down upon the bed.

4

It's hard to describe the feeling you get when a headset induces the mental state that's required to interface with your mind. I'm not a physicist or neurologist so I'm not clear on exactly how it works, but suffice to say that it's able to induce a near coma-like state by using a special wave frequency. When you want to log out and wake up, the headset slowly dials down the intensity of the signal, gently easing you back out of it. Assuming nothing goes wrong with that process, it's completely harmless, and it's less dangerous than giving someone a general anesthetic for surgery. You don't feel a thing going down.

As you drift off, the light fades, leaving you in pitch black for a moment until a whirling night sky spins around in every color and strands of light spiral outwards like the stretching coils of a galaxy.

And then a menu pops up.

What Would You Like To Do?
Browsing
Shopping
Education
Gaming
TV/Movies

I'd gone through this whole process countless times before but experiencing it for the first time in over half a year was disorientating. Luckily, the feeling passed as I selected gaming from the menu, reaching out with my new digital hand just as I would in the real world. Plenty of people these days were using virtual reality for more than gaming, including trying on clothes with highly personalized avatars and then getting those clothes delivered. And rather than simply sitting on your couch to watch a film, you could watch it in a themed cinema experience where all the weather effects, impacts of the action and even the taste of the food the characters ate could be simulated for true immersive viewing.

Hitting the gaming button brought up the names of all the companies who were running VR games. Currently, Frostbyte was at the top of the list due to its current prominence. I selected it and entered my account information for *Hundred Kingdoms* that I'd set up a few days ago.

Somewhere in the virtual landscape, a trumpet sounded.

Authentication Successful!

With that, the menu faded away, the spiraling galaxy collapsed inward upon itself and the title screen for *Hundred Kingdoms* rose to dominate my vision. I'd seen this sequence many times from 'let's play' videos but it was another matter entirely to experience it for real. It was more of a login area than a login screen, and truly unlike any game that I'd ever played before.

I was inside what I can best describe as a study room atop a white stone tower, only it wasn't your usual study. Spell books were strewn around, half opened or in tall stacks upon high shelves; cauldrons sat over low fires with bubbling pink and blue liquids inside them; a weapon rack was also there, lined with different staffs, each topped with a unique gemstone; and, directly before me, hunched over a gnarled desk, and peering intently into a crystal ball twice the size of my head, was the Wizard.

He looked like a classic mage should, with a thick grey beard and dark robes. Everyone called him the Wizard because you couldn't see if he had a name like a regular NPC, but he had enough personality that everyone was sure the AI controlling the game world was more involved in it than most.

The Wizard looked up at me and frowned, as I'd seen him do to the lucky players who'd gotten here before me.

"Ah," he said, his voice dripping with a wise-knowing. "Another lost soul seeks a vessel to call their own. Approach, child, and we shall discover your destiny."

I stepped forward, feeling the same rush as I might in the real world when excited. In here, I'd be able to see, smell, and feel, exactly as I would in real life, albeit with the pain dulled right down to meet legislative guidelines.

As I stood before the great crystal sphere, its misty innards started to churn wildly in anticipation.

"I see greatness in you, child," the Wizard said. "Yet, there is much you must learn, and you are but one in a much wider world. There will be challenges you cannot overcome alone, no matter how powerful you may become. Fellow adventurers will be your only way forward. Trust in them or use them as you may, it is up to you to decide. Now, let's look into your future."

He looked theatrically into the crystal orb and I guessed I was to follow suit. Sure enough, a faction selection menu appeared. The menu was being projected up and out from the orb, like a hologram. Each faction had their own cinematic intro which I could watch by clicking for further detail. I knew I was going to play a human, which would be part of the Imperium, but I couldn't help but get sucked into the detail anyway.

Choose Your Faction!

The Imperium
Demons may fall from the sky, the ground may break, but the Imperium shall live eternally. A grand alliance of all races committed to peace, learning, prosperity and devout faith. Yet, in

these dark times, such noble pursuits may have to be set aside, and fire and sword raised in its stead.

Faction Trait: 'The Ties That Bind' – Standing firmly shoulder to shoulder, each member race of the Imperium feels secure in the territory of their allies. **Effect:** You will begin the game with the reputation status of Honored with each primary faction within the Imperium.

Races: Humans, Dwarves, Gnomes, Elves
Unique Classes: Paladin

The Great Tribe

From harsh deserts and deadly jungles, from deep caverns and caves on the mountainside, the mighty beast races have set aside their pride and formed a formidable front. Deeply rooted to the world and nature, the Great Tribe fights to preserve their ancient customs, environments and beliefs in a world rapidly descending into chaos.

Faction Trait: 'Home Is The Wild' – Spirits of the ancestors watch over you wherever you go, providing comfort even in the hardest of places. **Effect:** The 'well rested' experience bonus will accumulate no matter where you log off from in the world but will only last for 10 minutes, as opposed to the full 20 minutes gained from an inn.

Races: Orc, Troll, Minotaur, Furbolg
Unique Class: Shifter

The Dark Council

Banished, cursed, exiled and hated; these misunderstood creatures have suffered long enough. Bound by a pact of mutual support, the Dark Council vies for survival in a world that would gladly see them burn.

Faction Trait: 'Molded By The Night' – Whether by their nature or necessity to avoid persecution, members of the Dark Council feel strongest where the light is lowest. **Effect:** +3 Night Vision Skill, +10% Shadow Resistance

Races: Undead, Vampire, Werewolf, Valkyrie
Unique Class: Deathknight

To help me decide, I was able to drill down through various levels, checking out summary details on each racial trait, the faction specific classes, everything. Some races like the elves had sub-races – wood elves, dark elves, high elves – there was so much here. I could have spent ages investigating every last scrap of it but I was on a bit of a timetable. Hopefully, I would have plenty more time to explore it all in the future.

I selected The Imperium as my faction.

"I hope you are true of heart," said the Wizard. He looked me over, discerningly, with his brow furrowed. "You shall have your work cut out for you, for the Imperium is under threat from the outside and within. But to which allied race will you hail?"

He looked impressively towards the crystal orb again, spinning his hands and chanting. Another menu appeared for me, this one containing more granular detail on each race of the Imperium. As I scrolled through the options, the crystal ball whirled, showing images of each race and their starting area.

Choose Your Race Within The Imperium!
Note: all players will receive +3 Stat points to distribute themselves each level along with another +3 Stat points pre-determined by their class.

Human
Stats: No bonuses or negatives – recommended for new players. In a world filled with races of incredible natural strength and fortitude, or devastating willpower to master magic, humans hold no such distinction. But it will be their enemy's downfall if they see them as weak. Humanity, the backbone of the Imperium, leads the way in the alliance, bringing their more disparate allies together for the benefit of all.
Racial Trait: 'Silver Tongued' – Charisma, diplomacy and gold coins can often achieve what whole armies cannot. **Effect:** +10% earned when selling items to NPCs, -10% from the price when buying from NPCs, +10% to all reputation gains.
Available Classes: Rogue, Ranger, Mage, Warlock, Paladin, Priest, Warrior, Berserker, Monk, Scavenger

Dwarves

Dwellers
Stats: +5% Constitution, +5% Might, -4% Intelligence, -3% Reflexes

Hailing from their strong homes inside the mountains, the Dweller Dwarves are the proudest and most stubborn of their kin.

Racial Trait: 'Stone Is In My Blood' – It is said the Dwellers used to give their most beautiful women to mate with earth elementals in order to keep the peace deep beneath the mountains. Whether this is true or not, it is undeniable that Dwellers have an uncanny instinct for all things mining, prospecting and blacksmithing. **Effect:** Reduced materials required for all blacksmithing recipes, +10% chance to gain bonus ore from mining

Available Classes: Shaman, Paladin, Priest, Warrior, Berserker, Scavenger

Sky Born
Stats: +4% Constitution, -2% Might, +4% Intelligence

Whether from adventuring or exiled lineage, these dwarves were born on the surface world and prefer adventure to a life in darkened tunnels.

Racial Trait: 'The Road Well Traveled' – Roaming all areas of the world has opened the minds of the Sky Born and brought them closer to the latent powers that their Dweller cousins have forgotten. **Effect:** + 5% to all elemental damage

Available Classes: Rogue, Ranger, Shaman, Paladin, Priest, Warrior, Scavenger

Gnomes
Stats: -4% Constitution, -4% Might, +6% Intelligence, +3% Reflexes, +4% Willpower

Ingenious, crafty, tenacious; the denizens of Gnomeland have crafted a technological answer to almost every problem. Though logic and engineering are valued above all else, they are still eccentric at heart.

Racial Trait: 'Larger Tool Belt' – It is said each gnome can rewire a mana capacitor before they can walk, though this has never been verified. **Effect:** Reduced materials required for all Engineering recipes, +5% power to all items created from Engineering

Available Classes: Rogue, Mage, Warlock, Priest, Warrior, Scavenger

Elves

Wood Elf

Stats: -3% Constitution, +2% Intelligence, +7% Reflexes, -3% Willpower

From the lush Dunbar forests and the grimier woods of Guldun, these smaller elves are as deadly as they are crafty.

Racial Trait: 'Dead Eye' – Master bowmen, it is said armies can be slain between their trees by unseen archers. **Effect:** +3% damage dealt by bows, +3 Bow Skill

Available Classes: Rogue, Ranger, Mage, Warrior, Berserker, Monk, Scavenger

High Elf

Stats: +2% increased Mana, -10% Constitution, -5% Might, +6% Intelligence, +5% Willpower

Venerable and wise, the high elves prefer living in open valleys or coastal regions in order to magically direct water to plumb their fine villas. You're more likely to find a library than an armory in their towns, but the spells within them leave such crude measures redundant.

Racial Trait: 'Ley Lines' – Over millennia the High Elves have charted the magical veins of the world. Where it is stable enough, they have learned how to make use of these highways. **Effect:** As a High Elf, you may teleport from one Ley Line connector to another. Cooldown 24 hours.

Available Classes: Mage, Warlock, Priest, Monk

Dark Elf

Stats: +3% Constitution, -4% Intelligence, +3% Might, +6% Reflexes

If they have a place they call home, no one has left it alive to tell the tale. At times, they have joined the Wood Elves to resist impositions from their High Elf brethren. They serve the Imperium these days and the Emperor sleeps easier for it.

Racial Trait: 'Smoke On Shadows' – *'Never send a Master Assassin to do a Dark Elf's job'*, An Imperial Proverb. **Effect:** +2 Dagger Skill, +1 Sneak Skill, +1 Night Vision

Available Classes: Rogue, Ranger, Warlock, Warrior, Scavenger

After I'd finished reading through all the racial information, I was desperate to double back and read everything on the members of the Great Tribe and Dark Council. This game was enormous.

But my choice was clear. I'd done my homework, after all.

I went ahead and selected Human and chose to be male. The notion of gender-flipping raised my eyebrows, but I didn't much fancy the idea of batting off the weirdos who'd try to flirt with me, either for real or for roleplay.

I was then taken to the character customization section, where an image of a default human model stood before me, ready for sculpting. I could import a premade avatar that looked almost exactly like myself, taken by ultra-high-res three-dimensional scanning booths. It was the type of avatar people needed when shopping in the virtual space and most people had one these days, myself included. A part of me wanted to delve into the various customization options, maybe giving myself anime style white and black hair, detailed tattoos stretching across my chest and an infinite amount of options besides. But time was of the essence.

In the spirit of urgency, I imported my premade avatar and made a few quick alterations, making myself a couple of inches taller, slimming my waist, broadening my shoulders and removing all the blemishes from my face. I clicked 'accept' and the idealistic version of myself appeared.

Don't judge, alright. Everybody does a bit of digital cosmetic surgery.

"Ah," the Wizard said again, "Humans are a versatile race, capable of greatness in most aspects of life but not quite the masters of any. Now, we must delve deeper still. What type of human are you to be, I wonder?"

Choose Your Class!
Note: Classes may further develop through specialization choices, talents, hidden quests and in-game events… yet you must discover these for yourself.

Rogue
The classic sneaks and thieves, rogues love the art of stealth, poison and working quietly to get the job done. They may not hit hard, but they know where to slip in their knife to make it hurt the most.
Key Stats: Might, Reflexes
Primary Role: Damage
Secondary Role: Utility
Class Benefits: +2 Sneak Skill, +2 Dagger Skill, +2 One-handed Sword Skill

Ranger
Unlucky foes will fall before they even know what's hit them. Rangers are unmatched in aim and utility when it comes to firing on the move.
Key Stats: Might, Reflexes
Role: Damage
Class Benefits: +5% damage from all ranged weapons, +2 Bow Skill, +2 One-handed Firearms Skill, +2 Two-handed Firearms Skill, +2 Crossbow Skill

Mage
A lifetime of knowledge would never be enough to master the arcane arts. Each mage commits to try nonetheless.
Key Stat: Intelligence

Role: Damage
Class Benefits: +3% increase to Mana, +5% increase to Spell Power

Warlock

Many in the Imperium would throw warlocks beyond its boundaries, but enough at the top recognize there is a need to understand what your enemies are capable of. Calling upon demons and fel magic for aid, warlocks are second to none when it comes to controlling the state of others.
Key Stat: Intelligence
Primary Role: Utility
Secondary Role: Damage
Class Benefits: +10% increase to Health, +5% increase to shadow damage

Paladin

Soldiers of the light, paladins vow first and foremost to protect the weak and uphold what is righteous. All members of the Dark Council fear these zealous defenders of the Imperium.
Key Stats: Might, Intelligence
Roles: Tank, Healer, Damage
Class Benefits: +2 Two-handed Mace Skill, +2 One-handed Mace Skill, +5% damage dealt by holy magic

Priest

Whereas their paladin cousins train in the arts of war, priests focus on their spiritual essence to channel the power of the light in its purest form. Humble men and women, priests serve others first and foremost, using their connection to the light to cause harm only when they are pushed beyond all other measures.
Key Stat: Willpower
Roles: Healer, Utility
Class Benefits: +5% to Regen p/s, +5% effectiveness to all healing spells

Warrior

Whether defending others or fighting on the front lines, warriors are always first into the fray. Highly disciplined, they let opponents tire themselves out before striking with precision. Heavily armored, they will outlast most opponents.
Key Stats: Constitution, Might
Roles: Tank, Damage
Class Benefits: +3% increase to Health, +2 Shield Skill, +2 to all one-handed melee weapon skills

Berserker
Discipline doesn't suit the berserker. Armor just slows them down.
Key Stats: Might
Role: Damage
Class Benefits: +5% increase to melee damage, +2 to all two-handed melee skills, +2 to all one-handed melee weapon skills

Monk
Extreme inner discipline helps trained monks to dispel pain or hit far harder than they should. Favoring their fists and feet over blades, these fast-moving fighters can quickly change from dishing out punches to bolstering the spirits of allies in the heat of battle.
Key Stats: Reflexes, Willpower
Roles: Damage, Off-tanking, Utility
Class Benefits: +30% increase to unarmed damage, +5 Unarmed Combat Skill, +2% Regen p/s

Everything I read was tempting, with so many possibilities. I found what I was looking for at the end of the list.

Scavenger
They flit from town to town, battlefield to battlefield, gathering the remnants and then crafting wonders from the ashes. Some just call them junkers. A mysterious sort and often overlooked, scavengers forge their own path more than most. Although weak in combat, they make up for a lack of

raw power with powerful creations and upgrades of their own.
Key Stat: Intelligence
Role: Utility
Class Benefits: Whereas other players are locked to only 2 primary professions, Scavengers have access to 7 – Blacksmithing, Leatherworking, Tailoring, Jewel crafting, Engineering, Mining and Skinning. The core stat linked to all the professions is consolidated into Intelligence.

There was a line in the description that stood out to me, 'scavengers forge their own path more than most'. With access to so many profession trees, I had an inkling as to why. Everyone bad mouthed the class because it had only one or two combat abilities and was weak enough besides. Yet, with the capacity to create so many items and improve them, smart players would be able to carve out their own playstyle.

I'd like to think I was such a player.

I selected the scavenger class.

The Wizard chuckled. "Oh, you will be one who takes what others have foolishly neglected; build where others destroy. You won't be powerful in your body or the arcane, yet power can come in many forms and gold is perhaps the most influential power in the world. And if not gold, then it shall be your wits that will serve you; an intuition to combine and use materials in ways that no others would. For this is the life of the scavenger – to thrive on the outskirts, to turn the waste of others into your own treasures."

He made it sound almost romantic and I supposed there was something uniquely cool about the fantasy behind the scavenger class. I hadn't come across something like this in any other RPG I'd ever played. Although I was here for a task, I was excited to find out how my character would ultimately play.

The Wizard pushed a piece of parchment across the desk and followed it with an inkwell and quill.

"The last task will be to decide upon your name while in the mortal plane. I await your decision."

I skimmed the flowing words, beautifully written out as though in calligraphy. But they held no roleplaying value, just a list of the conditions required on naming a character. Don't be offensive, don't be racist or rude, don't, in a nutshell, be an asshole. I had been thinking about what I'd call myself for a while now and had checked on the *Hundred Kingdoms* player roster to make sure it was still available.

This was to be a new beginning and after some time, I'd landed on the name Zoran. It was a name from Eastern Europe that meant 'dawn' and felt fitting. Plus, a name beginning with Z would help me to stand out in a busy game market square; easier to remember than 'InstaKills2038' or 'JawumbaWafflesMcGee'. I picked up the quill, dabbed it into the black ink and wrote out my character's name.

As I confirmed it, the game presented me with my character's starting stat sheet.

Character
Zoran Human Scavenger Level 1
Attributes
Constitution 10 – Intelligence 10 – Reflexes 10 – Might 10 – Willpower 10
Combat
Health 100 – Mana 100 – Attack Power 17 – Spell Power 17 – Regen 1.3 p/s

"It is an honor to meet you, Zoran." The Wizard waggled his fingers and the parchment rolled up and zoomed to his hand. "I wish you luck in the world. You'll need it."

And with that, the Wizard snapped his fingers and the world around me began to spin again. I was greeted to more concept art and voiceover work by way of a loading screen, all specific to the human starting zone.

It lingered for a time upon an in-game clip of a tall yet plump man in regal purple robes and a jewel-encrusted crown upon his head. He had the thick brown beard of a scholar, but his hair was already thinning beneath his crown. His green eyes were soft and inviting, and it was evident enough from his frame that his shoulders were rounded and slouched under those robes. A voice-clip spoke over the scene like in a movie trailer.

"Emperor Aurelius grew up in peaceful times, pursuing the path of the philosopher rather than the warrior. However, storm clouds gather on the borders of the Imperium; elven allies speak of demonic and undead horrors from the south, while the dwarves warn of giants stirring in the north. Closer to home, kobolds have become an infestation right outside the gates of the Imperial Capital of Argatha."

The scene progressed to show the Emperor sitting in a heated council meeting, his face buried behind his hands.

"Aurelius is a soft-hearted ruler and now the vultures are circling. If his words should fail, the Imperium might splinter into pieces, leaving humanity vulnerable to the many evils rising in the world. Now more than ever, the Imperium needs willing citizens to take up arms for the sake of all who dwell within it."

The cut-scene ended and I materialized into the game world.

5

I knew where I was. This was Rusking, a small town where human players would begin their journey in *Hundred Kingdoms*. Around me were buildings that could have been pulled straight from sixteenth-century Europe, thatched roofs and all. Directly before me was the town hall, with a pointed wooden spire rising far above the rest of the settlement. Human architecture in *Hundred Kingdoms* often had spire motifs, paying homage to the grand Imperial Spire in the heart of Argatha where the Emperor lived.

I took a moment to flex my fingers, stretch my limbs and get a feeling for the movement in-game. It felt flawless. Frostbyte had really taken it to the next level here. I could smell bread from the bakers, hear the rhythmic clang of hammer on metal from the smithy, feel the breeze upon my face. Immersion was further aided by the minimal user interface.

A semi-transparent red health bar sat in the bottom left of my vision and a blue mana bar beside it. Both sharpened and brightened if I focused on them and I saw both were sitting at a basic 100/100. In the bottom right-hand corner was an area earmarked for the combat log. In other games, bringing up the menu was simply a matter of thinking about it. I tried this now. Even knowing *Hundred Kingdoms* was the hallmark of modern

VRMMOs, I was still taken aback by the speed at which the system responded to my thoughts. Using abilities worked the same way, meaning that combat would be fluid and exciting.

From the menu, I checked my abilities book. I knew broadly what scavengers started with from my research but I wanted to double-check the specifics. My abilities book looked sparse right now. There was, in fact, only one ability present.

Scavenge – Rank 1
You search a corpse for additional items that others were too proud to take. Awards 5% of the experience that killing a creature of equal level and power would grant. Some corpses may require tools to fully search.

Shame. I thought the experience gain would be a bit higher than five percent. Perhaps it had been patched. Still, it would add up over time and be a nice boost to my overall exp. I had no direct combat abilities right now but scavengers only got a few anyway. That wasn't what they were designed for.

My stats wouldn't have changed from logging in and I wouldn't have any additional points to distribute until I leveled up. I was, however, curious to check whether I already had this myriad of extra professions already or whether I'd have to train in each one separately. I found the professions tab and opened it.

Professions
Class Note: As a Scavenger, your profession trees are locked until you visit your class trainer at level 3.

Crafting - Locked
Blacksmithing – Rank 1 – 0/100 EXP
Leatherworking – Rank 1 – 0/100 EXP
Tailoring – Rank 1 – 0/100 EXP
Jewel crafting – Rank 1 – 0/100 EXP
Engineering – Rank 1 – 0/100 EXP

Gathering - Locked

Mining – Rank 1 – 0/100 EXP
Skinning – Rank 1 – 0/100 EXP

Sure enough, I couldn't select any of my professions. When I tried tapping on Blacksmithing, all I got was a clunky noise for my troubles; the game's way of telling me that I couldn't do that.

Well, I always had to do a bit of leveling anyway, so no harm done. I'd just visit my class trainer as soon as I hit level 3.

Finally, I inspected what gear I had equipped: a green commoners tunic, brown hose, and basic leather shoes, all of which gave me no additional armor or stat bonuses. In my right-hand weapon slot, I held a 'brittle dirk' which had a damage range of 3-5 and a shockingly low durability of 10. Upwards was truly the only direction I could go in.

I rubbed my hands together. Time to get started.

Doing the starter quests seemed the obvious thing to do as they'd award some copper and silver coins that I sorely needed to buy the various tools for crafting and scavenging. I'd need a hammer for blacksmithing, a needle and thread for weaving, a knife to skin animals with, that sort of thing.

My research had also gleaned that an early quest could be gained by speaking to the Mayor inside the town hall. So in I went, skipping merrily up to the Mayor as my anticipation built for the adventure to come.

The Mayor was dressed like some nineteenth century gentlemen of leisure, with a heavy blue coat over a frilly dress shirt and capped with a dark top hat. His cheeks were rosy and he smiled broadly.

"Ho hum," the Mayor said jovially. "A new adventurer in Rusking is it? Might you be of assistance in our time of need?" His eyes quickly scanned me, taking in all my noob glory.

"Can I be of any help around town?" I asked. My voice sounded exactly like my own in here too.

If you're wondering how players are supposed to know what to say to an NPC, such as the Mayor, don't worry. AI in previous games had been good enough at imitating real life and the one running *Hundred Kingdoms* was state of the art. I could probably sit and have a conversation with the Mayor on how best to make an omelet if I wanted to, although I suspect even his jolly character would eventually tell me to piss off and make myself useful.

The Mayor sighed in extravagant relief. "Yes, indeed young sir. Our town is beset by troubles, although I fear my citizens will distract you from the main issue of the day – kobolds," he blustered and shook a meaty fist for effect. "Damnable kobolds infesting the woods and causing all manner of mischief. I'm in need of adventurers capable of facilitating their... removal."

I smirked. "I believe I can handle this task."

"Excellent young man. Go forth and slay those pests. For Rusking!"

Quest Accepted – Into the Woods
The Mayor of Rusking is deeply troubled by the kobolds in the area. Traders have reported their wagons being attacked on the way in and out of town and believe the kobolds are hiding in the woods. You have agreed to investigate and slay the enemies you find.

Objectives:
Investigate Rusking Wood
Slay kobolds 0/15

I couldn't help but smile. My first quest in such a long time. Ah, I'd missed this feeling and I hadn't even got to the good stuff yet. Without delay, I left the town hall and brought up my map by mimicking opening a scroll in mid-air. A roll of parchment materialized into my hands with a stylized map of Rusking and the surrounding area for my perusal.

I appeared as a small golden arrow in the middle of the town, the point of the arrow indicating the direction I was facing. Exact distances weren't shown, nor were any quests marked. You had to use your brain in this game, which was just the way I liked it, but it was easy enough to find Rusking Wood, as it was labelled in scrolling letters some way to the north of the town.

Also upon the map was the server time and clock, illustrated by an animated sun and moon. It was 8:21pm server time. Luckily for me, the US servers were set to Pacific Time due to Frostbyte Studios being based on the West Coast. Server time was useful because having a set time to schedule around made it easier to coordinate with guildmates spread across different countries. All maintenance and resets were also on the server time so they would stay at a constant time for all players.

Night was now fast falling over the town of Rusking. That might make this quest more dangerous for me than it needed to be. The sky looked to be clear, so the moon and stars would help. Still, I wasn't playing a fighting class and any disadvantage I faced while being out in the woods wasn't ideal.

But there was nothing for it.

I snapped the map shut, the scroll fading away into the digital ether, and began my journey north. Characters in *Hundred Kingdoms* had a base movement speed that was akin to a light jog, only this time I didn't feel out of breath doing it. Other games I'd played had employed a stamina bar or a similar resource drain if you ran and you could make your character fitter over time. Frostbyte had decided to brush over this, focusing on other aspects of gameplay. This suited me just fine. My time was precious enough without having to stop every few minutes to recharge a stamina bar.

Passing out of town, things got a lot darker without the ambient light from buildings or the watchmen with lanterns. I referred to my map to check that I was still heading in the right direction. The parchment of the scroll was just visible, as though it had a backlight effect. Not far to go now. Indeed, looking ahead, I could make out the treetops as black canopies against the starry night.

When I reached the tree line I slowed to a walking pace, being careful not to go crashing through the undergrowth and alert a pack of kobolds to me. Being so weak, I'd have to take them one at a time for now and if I managed to get the jump on one of them, then all the better. Scavengers didn't have proper stealth or ambushing abilities like rogues did, but the game did reward players who were able to sneak up on an opponent nonetheless. Wearing heavy armor while clambering through the woods, for example, would make more noise than if you were in lighter garb. A heavy plate-wearing warrior was unlikely to ambush anyone for good reason.

My knowledge of this quest from Let's Plays was hampered due to the darkness. I knew there was a camp not too deep into the woods which would complete the exploration segment but my difficulty in seeing anything clearly was making it far harder.

Crouching low, I moved as quietly as I could from trunk to trunk, from bush to bush. After about a minute, I was awarded a notification. It appeared in my central field of vision, semi-transparent and unobtrusive like my health and mana bars, but if I focused on it, it became clearer.

Sneak Unlocked!
Level 1
You tricksy rascal! Trying to take someone by surprise? You'll need to get a lot better than this.

The unlock was welcome, but the real gain was knowing that I must be close to some kobolds and had so far evaded detection. I closed my eyes, focusing on the sounds around me, trying to hear my enemies. Hooting owls and the general rustle of the forest obscured most sound but I soon heard a twig snapping not far to my right. When I opened my eyes, I found I could see a little easier.

Night Vision Unlocked!
Level 1
Afraid of the dark? You should be. You'll need to keep eating your carrots.

The tone of these notifications was certainly on the lighter side. *Hundred Kingdoms* didn't spell out how you could unlock and advance skills but it worked like many recent RPGs. The more I did an activity, the more skilled my character would get at it, which made a good deal of sense. Take Night Vision, for example. A rogue specializing as a thief or assassin might end up operating largely at night, and so it made sense that their character's eyes would 'improve' in the dark over time.

For me, in the here and now, it meant I could just make out the outline of a squat figure I hadn't seen before. It's hunched humanoid form marked it clearly as a kobold. The kobold had its back to me as it ferreted around amongst the low growing plants. I approached as silently as I could, drawing my dirk.

"Shroomie, shroom, shrooms," the kobold muttered breathily as is scoured the earth. Now I was within striking distance, I could better make out the creature's ash-colored skin, which was hard like hide, and its weasel-like face bushy white eyebrows and whiskers. It wore a patchwork of different clothes except for the neat red cap on its head with two holes for its long pointed ears to poke through.

"Shroomie, shrooms," the kobold went on, sniffing eagerly. "Ah," it said satisfied. A sound of munching followed.

I admit I found the kobold oddly cute up close and in person. In most of the Let's Plays, the streamers just barreled through this early quest in daylight, slaughtering at will. It was a nice touch that the game's AI gave even these lowly mobs some personality; no wonder this game was drawing in players by the millions.

Cute or not, however, I had a quest to fulfill.

I raised my dirk and pounced, driving the dull blade as best I could into the kobold's back.

Brittle Dirk hits! *15 piercing damage (+30 Sneak Attack Bonus!)*

The kobold squealed, dropped the mushrooms it had been eating and scrambled to draw its wooden club. A coating of blood lined my dagger, but the kobold darted around as though unphased. That's VR Gaming for you. Occasionally a bit of realism gets dropped. If you wanted to properly cripple an enemy, you better use the right spell, ability or item that will cause them to move slower or burst out in boils or whatever.

I jabbed again at the kobold and scored a much weaker hit, but my combined blows had brought its health down from 80 to 25.

The kobold swung its club at me and my lowly level 1 avatar couldn't avoid the blow; although I did manage to stick my dirk into its chest at the same time. It recoiled from my stab and I struck again before it could raise its club. My enemy's health flashed, disappeared, and the mob died.

Kobold level 1 dies – 50 EXP

Quest – Into the Woods
Slay kobolds 1/15

Ah, the rush of a first kill in a new game. Is there a sweeter nectar? Well, aside from the bags of cash that I'd hopefully start making.

Checking my health bar, I found the little savage had managed to club 25 points of my health away from that single hit. Damn, I was weak. My health would replenish at my Regen p/s rate but only while I was out of combat. I'd have to be careful in fights and wait to recharge more often than I'd like. At least, until I got a bit stronger or found some better gear.

Something new had appeared on my user interface as well. A faint golden bar that ran the full length of my vision below my health and mana, labeled 'experience'. I took a closer look and the gold brightened and solidified until gleaming.

Experience 50/400

So, seven more kills and I'd reach level two. Given that my Scavenge ability granted some extra exp, I'd have a little boost along the way. Now seemed a good time to try it out. I got to my knees by the fallen kobold and checked to see if I could first loot it in the normal way. A small box marked 'loot' appeared over its body and I tapped it with my hand. A new window popped up, showing what items the kobold had dropped.

Just three copper coins. Nothing terribly exciting but all avalanches start with the first trickling snowflakes. Every coin I gained now would aid me towards my goal once I reached the markets of Argatha.

Still kneeling, I thought clearly in my mind, 'Scavenge.' My character then began an animated performance over the length of the kobold's body, first patting it down and then checking in pockets on its patchwork coat that I wouldn't otherwise have been able to access. Another loot table appeared.

Copper coins x 1
Cloth scraps x 5
Loot All?

I tapped on 'loot all' and gained the extra material. The extra coin was a welcome bonus. I hadn't been aware that some extra cash could be scavenged from the ability, but I supposed it made sense. All dead mobs and players in *Hundred Kingdoms* would remain behind as an in-game corpse, lying where they died for about an hour. Scavengers would be able to loot these corpses during that time. This exp bonus granted to scavengers was designed to make up for the shortfall in their overall power. So, if I was mostly scavenging bodies, rather than looting for real, I might not gain access to coin drops from mobs.

The cloth scraps were more interesting to me. These were the most basic crafting materials used in the tailoring profession and only available to scavengers by picking up the 'scraps' that nobody else wanted. Once I gained access to my professions, I should be able to combine 10 cloth scraps into a full-piece linen cloth. I'm jabbering on a bit by way of explaining that if I could get 100 cloth scraps, I could make a stack of 10 linen cloth and sell it on the auction house. The fact that I just got 5 scraps straightaway made me pretty excited, but my paranoid side kicked in and I reckoned that I may have gotten lucky. Time would tell.

An experience notification was also still visible at the top of my combat log.

Scavenged Kobold level 1 – 3 EXP

As expected, my experience bar had also shifted, now showing I was at 53/400. Five percent of the kobold's kill was really two and a half experience but it seemed the game rounded up. Handy. Every little would help.

I still had to continue this quest, with fourteen more kobolds to kill and their presence in the woods to explore. Just as I attempted to squint through the dark to find more enemies, I heard voices.

"It came this way," a high, scratchy voice said, much like the kobold I'd just slain. "This way I says. I heards it." The kobold who was speaking began to imitate the death throes of my recent victim.

"Whatc'you doin'?" another kobold asked. "Yous be given us away if there's trouble."

There must have been a group of them, and by the sounds of it, they were drawing close. I dashed behind the nearest, thickest tree trunk in the hope of avoiding them but in my haste, I only made more noise.

"I heard that," a kobold declared. "We coming for yous."

"Whoever yous are."

"Maybe it has shroomies?"

"Shut up," the leader of the pack squawked.

Pressed up against the trunk, I risked a glance in their direction. I could see the pack now; well, I could at least see their leader at the front illuminated by the lantern he carried. The glass was cracked and filthy, letting out a dirty light but it was still better than total darkness. From the sounds of their continued babbling, there must have been at least four of them. Too many for me to take on alone.

Carefully, I began to tip-toe away from the trunk, hoping I could put some distance between myself and the pack and lower the chances of them aggroing onto me. A patrol like this must mean I was fairly close to the camp, so my best shot at another kill would be to find a straggler on the outskirts.

It wasn't easy moving through the undergrowth. I stepped directly into a bush and tasted wet leaves in my mouth. Next, I stepped on a twig and snapped it. Wincing, I froze, sure that I'd alerted the patrol to my whereabouts.

"What's that?"

I remained rooted to the spot in fear. I'd rather not die this early and face respawning back in Rusking. At least it wouldn't be a PvP death where lockouts were in play. At higher levels, death from PvP would cause a lockout for up to an hour, one of the reasons player vs. player combat carried such consequences. It would be hard for guilds to take over and consolidate territory if their enemies kept respawning instantly. On top of that, defeating a player of sufficient challenge to you – meaning no more than two levels below you but any number of levels higher – would award EXP along with one random item of loot that wasn't soul bound to them. You really had to pick your battles in this game, whether in PvP or against regular enemies.

"Is nothing boss," a kobold said.

It seemed I'd gotten away with it this time.

Sneak Increased!
Level 2
Not bad. Soon you might be able to slip past a deaf old lady. Maybe.

I breathed easier, only to step onto another twig.

"Whaaa!" screamed a kobold.

Thinking the game was up, I twisted around and drew my dirk, as feeble as it was. Perhaps if I got the jump on one of them I could at least score two kills before being bludgeoned to death. Thankfully, my health had fully regenerated now. But the pack wasn't running in my direction. The lantern carrying leader was standing still, and by the looks of things, was bent over something.

"He's dead, boss."

"I can sees that, dolt," the leader said, although he nudged the body with his club for good measure. "Yups. Dead as a squished rabbitty."

"What does we do?"

"Run back to camp, you," the leader said, poking his club at one of his fellows. "Tell the Big Boss. We's will stay and look around."

My delight at the pack thinning by one member was soon dashed when the remaining kobolds started to run in a much more aggressive fashion. No longer on a slow walking patrol, they began fanning out, the lantern of the leader bobbing wildly. They were bloody fast for hunched, oversized weasels, and if I suddenly burst out from my bush, I'd be spotted for sure. Once they aggroed onto me, it would be hard to shake them off.

This wasn't the best start at all.

One of the grunts closed in on my position.

Gritting my teeth, I waited until the kobold was parallel with me before stepping out behind it and trying for another backstab. I missed. The kobold wheeled around, its black eyes bulging when it saw me.

"Hoomin!"

It thumped its club into my stomach and a dull pain throbbed there, although it was far less painful than it would have been in reality. My health dropped by 15 points and I lashed out with my dirk. As I tussled with this level 1 mob, I heard the others running over, shrieking all the while.

"Nasty hoomin. Kill it."

"No take our shrooms!"

Through luck, I dodged two of my opponent's attacks or perhaps it missed. Either way, I managed to take this first mob down, though it had come at a serious cost to my health. I was at 40/100 and there were two extra enemies upon me. Now the leader was close enough, I could confirm he was more powerful. A small bar appeared over his head when I looked directly at him.

Kobold Patrol Leader – Level 3

Well, shit. There was no way I was winning this one.

I ran for it, eternally grateful that there was no resource cost associated with running in *Hundred Kingdoms*. Although, it did mean my speed was capped and the kobolds weren't far behind me, yelling obscenities in their childishly shrill manner. If I could run for long enough, without taking a hit from them or dealing damage to them, they should eventually reset their aggro. At least, that was how it was done in the VRMMOs I used to play.

I can't say how long I'd been running when I started to panic that aggro in this game didn't play fair. My Night Vision increased to rank 2 but I didn't dare to check the notification beyond a cursory glance. The skill increase must have allowed me to spot the new bobbing lantern ahead. Another patrol?

I slid to a stop.

If it was another kobold patrol, they were heading right for me and there was literally no way I could outrun them.

My heart pounded in my chest, while my cheeks felt hot and flushed. How had I already messed up so badly? Had six months away from gaming really made me so rusty that I couldn't do the first quest? Maybe the scavenger really was too weak for solo play, after all. The true embarrassment would shortly come when I died, but in the heat of the moment, I acted on basic fight or flight instinct – only now it was fight.

I spun to face the first group. Their leader was closest, a good deal ahead of the lowly grunt behind him. Patchy light from the lantern lit his face in a gruesome grin of chipped greyish teeth. It lunged at me.

"Die, hoomin."

I cried out as I lunged forward myself, prepared to meet the leader blow for blow. At the same moment, something twanged loudly behind me and, just as my dirk cut across the leader's arm, an arrow thunked wetly into its chest. The impact of the shot sent the leader to the ground and I descended upon the creature, stabbing down.

Kobold Patrol Leader level 3 dies – 30 Assisted EXP

An assisted kill could only mean one thing, another player had shown up to save my ass. Right on time too. Even as I got to my feet, I could hear another twanging bowstring and an arrow took the remaining grunt kobold in the face. It dropped dead instantly, probably from a huge critical hit.

I didn't get any experience from that kill as I hadn't engaged the mob directly in combat. But no matter. I was alive. I also had a savior to thank and turned to meet them.

Wylder – Ranger – Level 1

It seemed that whoever they were, they had opted for a more customized avatar than I had. Wylder was a male human character, about six-three in height with a dull purple scar stretching diagonally across his face, from forehead to jaw. Chest hair akin to the fur of a black bear burst out from his commoner's green tunic that stretched tightly across his chest. Held steady in his hands was a simple looking crossbow and a quiver of arrows hung at his hip. The lantern he'd been carrying rested at his feet. Put down, I assumed, to enable him to operate the crossbow.

"You okay there, Zoran?" Wylder asked. He might have been in his early thirties but who can really tell from a voice alone. For all I knew, he'd modded his rig to distort his voice. Maybe he was compensating for something. Maybe he was really a twelve-year-old girl from Brooklyn. How was I to know?

I patted myself down as if to check for wounds, which felt rather dumb.

"Ye-yeh, I'm alright. Thanks."

"No debuffs or bleeding effects or anything? I've got some potions if you need them."

"Nah, I'm all good. Thanks again. You saved me there."

"Figured I did," Wylder added, smoothly placing the crossbow into a holster upon his back with a slickness only achievable inside a game. "You really ought to a be in a party as a scavenger, dude."

I shrugged. "Wasn't much of an option for me. But while you're here—"

Wylder waved his hand. "Say no more. I'll give you a hand. You'll be a good distraction for the kobolds while I fill them with arrows."

A rather large notification then filled my screen.

**Wylder invites you to a party.
Accept?**

I accepted and Wylder's own health bar, mana bar and a small headshot of his avatar appeared on the left side of my UI; the better to keep track of your teammates during combat.

"You doing the 'Into the Woods' quest too?" I asked.

"Yep. And the camp is just a little north-west of here. I've done this quest before on my main character."

"Oh," I said, genuinely surprised. "You're leveling an alt already? Have you hit cap on your main?"

"No way man," Wylder said with a laughing sigh. "I've been leveling a warrior to be a tank for my guild, but goddamn are they slow going at times. Felt like I needed a face-roll toon to blow off some steam between those grind sessions."

By face roll, he meant a class that was supposedly so easy to play you could 'roll your face across a keyboard' and still win. It was a saying from an era where keyboards and mice were still used but, much like the insult of 'noob', it was a term that had stuck throughout the decades.

Wylder looked me up and down. "Seems you wanted something more hardcore if you picked scavenger."

"It seemed unique. Never played anything like it."

"Well, unique is one way of putting it," Wylder said. "Heard of some guys making a nice bit of coin out of it but not much more." He grabbed the lantern and came over to me. I was still standing by the body of the dead kobold leader. "Let's loot these guys already and get moving. You might even get an upgrade."

"Fingers crossed," I said, though I wasn't sure what kind of an upgrade such a low-level mob would drop.

As we'd both assisted in the kill, we could both loot the leader. Any coins dropped would be split evenly between us but other loot would have to be distributed by the players. I still got three copper coins from the kobold leader for my share and there was a weapon available as well.

Kobold Basher
One-Handed Mace
Item Level 3
Damage: 5 – 7 bludgeoning
Durability: 25/25

"Told ya," Wylder said. "I remember finding tons of the damned things. You take it, man."

I looted the mace and it appeared in my inventory. I replaced the brittle dirk in my right-hand slot with the kobold basher. The dirk's durability had been falling alarmingly fast anyway and this club looked to be far sturdier, as well as capable of inflicting more pain.

"You should just keep using whatever is the best drop, to be honest," Wylder went on. "Scavengers can—"

"They can use any weapon type, yeh, I know," I said. "Except for any stat or specific class restrictions on the weapon, of course. Lore wise, we aren't fussy with what we wield."

"Ah, so you've done a bit of research then," Wylder said. "Some scavs have become known as ninja-looters in dungeons already, so don't be *that guy*."

By ninja-looters, he meant someone who took loot they didn't really need and often went on to sell it. I admit the thought had crossed my mind, especially with weapons.

I opted to evade his comment. "How have you found the weapon skill leveling on your warrior?"

"It's decent," Wylder said. "I'd say you should just use the best weapon available to you while leveling, especially at low levels. Until you get a high weapon skill in something, the benefits won't be crazy. Better to switch it up than use an underpowered weapon just because your chance of hitting or blocking is a bit higher with it."

Out of interest, I went to check on my weapon skills from my character's profile. So far everything was at rank 1, except for my dagger skill which was at 70% of the way to rank 2. But as Wylder said, there was no point in me clinging onto that crappy dagger just because I was close to a rank up. A few good kobold bashings with this club and my one-handed mace skill would shoot up in no time.

"Give me a second," I said, bending down to Scavenge the body. Wylder got what I was doing, so he moved off to loot the other dead kobold which was entirely his kill.

Scavenging the leader, I received 3 experience points, another copper coin, but only 3 cloth scraps this time. I knew that five had been too good to be the regular Scavenge from a level 1 mob.

Wylder signaled he was done and I moved over to Scavenge the remaining level 1 kobold corpse. Here was the true taste of the class, grabbing extra bits and pieces from another person's kill. Sadly, I looted no coins but did gain 3 cloth scraps, bringing my total to 11. I had enough scraps now to combine into a single linen piece, but I had no way of doing this yet. I'd need to unlock the crafting components of the class by leveling and hanging around here wasn't going to get that done. But with a ranger by my side, the future looked a lot easier.

"Ready to rock?" I asked.

"You betch'ya," said Wylder, passing the lantern to me. "You take this, that way I can keep my crossbow out at all times."

For trades between players of more substantial quantities of materials or cumbersome items, a full-blown trade window must be open, but for small, easy to process trades such as this, the AI of *Hundred Kingdoms* could transition items seamlessly, pushing immersion just a little bit further.

I took the lantern and equipped it in my left-hand slot. Holding it up, I noticed it wasn't a kobold one. It was far too clean and the glass looked new.

"Where did you get this?" I asked.

"Bought it in town before heading off," Wylder said. "I sent some gold over from my main to give this character a boost. It's how I dumped that starting bow for this crossbow. Vendor items are generally crap but the knockback effect on crossbows can make them pretty handy and it wasn't exactly expensive for me."

Wylder drew an arrow from his quiver and primed his weapon.

"Ready?" he said.

"Ready," I said, swishing my club through the air. "Let's kill some kobolds."

6

Hunting down the remaining kobolds through the Rusking Woods was a lot more fun with Wylder. Other than the larger patrols, we took everything on, smashing through the kill requirements for the quest and then some. By the time we had reached the campsite, we'd killed around twenty mobs in total.

I'd managed to reach level 2 overall, gaining some stat points to distribute, but I'd decided to hold off on that until I had a chance to stop and do it properly. I'd looted just over one silver in total now (one silver is made up of one hundred copper, by the way) and a whole heap of cloth scraps, with even the odd piece of whole linen from the mobs. My weapon skill in one-handed maces had even reached rank 2 and was pushing towards rank 3.

More importantly, I'd unlocked an actual combat ability called Desperate Strike, although it would be Desperate Shot if I was using a ranged weapon. Its description was as follows:

Desperate Strike/Shot – Rank 1
You lash out wildly to drive off an attacker. Weapon base damage is increased by +20 but accuracy is lowered by a third.
Mana Cost: 20
Cooldown: 10 seconds

The mechanics of the ability called into question Wylder's derision of weapon skill. The higher my weapon skill, the better the chance I had of hitting with that weapon. With a higher weapon skill, I'd suffer less from the accuracy debuff of Desperate Strike. Alas, such theory crafting was best left to later levels and I ought to restrain myself from diving down the rabbit hole on number crunching. I was here to make gold, standing mostly in the markets, crafting and playing the auction house. What need would I have to gain weapon skills and venture into the wider game?

I checked the clock. It was 9:10pm already and I'd not completed the first quest yet, nor acquired even a fraction of the money I'd need to start buying all the tools that were required for crafting. This annoyed me. I wanted a quicker progression than this; I'd have to kick it into a new gear somehow. Wylder was ahead, scouting out the kobold camp, but he'd been gone for what felt like a long time. My frustration turned to fidgeting and I began tapping my club against a hardened root of the tree I was hiding behind.

"Hey," Wylder hissed upon his return, "You'll give us away."

"How bad can it be?" I asked. "We've both levelled up. Surely, we can take them?"

Wylder crouched low. "There are seven mobs in the camp and one of them is level five."

"That'll be the Big Boss they were nattering about earlier," I said. I ceased my tapping as my mind narrowed in on the problem at hand. "Do we have to be standing inside the camp in order for the quest to update?"

"Nah, just need to get close enough to get a decent look," Wylder said. "Although I'm concerned about the aggro range."

I peered out from around the trunk. The camp was bordered by a ring of wooden stakes planted into the ground. At its center was a black pot over a fire. It was surrounded by about a dozen patchwork blankets propped up on thick branches that served as makeshift tents. The kobolds congregated near the fire but one of them would wander over to the boundary of the camp every so often.

"Some of them are starting to move," I said. "They must have patrol routes. If we wait until one of them is right on the edge, you can – what the—"

A searing ball of purple-blue energy came soaring out of the night. It had to be a mage attack and it exploded off the back of one of the kobold grunts. The whole camp was in uproar, kobolds charging off in all directions, looking for the assailant. Battle cries came from across the clearing and two players charged out of the darkness. One might have been a paladin from the look of the golden light dancing around his warhammer; the other was a berserker, judging by his speed and dual wielding axes.

The Big Boss of the kobolds beat his mace upon his shield. He stood a good head and shoulders above the others, had even bushier eyebrows and whiskers, and even wore some mail armor, which hung loosely off his sinewy frame.

"Bah, hoomins," he boomed. "Defend our shrooms you lot!"

I spun around to snatch up the lantern then scrambled to my feet.

"C'mon," I said to Wylder. "Let's go now while they're distracted."

"Zoran, wait. The bigger one is still at the bac—"

But I was off, already running for the camp, anticipating the notification to say I'd investigated the woods and could now return to the Mayor to hand in the quest. But it didn't tick. And then I found myself crossing the boundary of the campsite proper, angling my body between two stakes in the ground.

Quest – Into the Woods
Investigate Rusking Wood - Complete
Slay kobolds 15/15

"Get back, you noobtard," Wylder called.

Even as I heard him, I saw my doom descend upon me in slow motion. The Big Boss turned around, and losing interest in the first group of players, was homing in on me.

"They's got backup from behind, curses!"

He ran at me, swerving around the campfire and knocking over blanket tents as he charged. An arrow thrummed into his leg and he slowed down considerably. Wylder must have used an ability to debuff his speed.

"Run, Zoran."

I ignored him. I held my ground, watching as another arrow zipped past into the boss. To call him a boss wasn't accurate. He was level 5, sure, but not an elite. And yeh, two good hits from him would likely kill me, but I couldn't just run away. I wouldn't always have a ranger with me, and I planned on being solo for the most part.

I let the aggro of the mob be my savior this time. Wylder's third arrow stuck into the boss' shield and he decided the ranger was the real threat. The boss changed course, veering away from me at the last second and made a B-line for the trees. I wheeled about and whacked him with my club repeatedly. I was dealing only small amounts of damage through that chainmail, chipping away at his health in chunks of 5 or 10. When the Boss had less than 30 health left he rounded again on me. Wylder didn't fire more arrows. Maybe he'd taken his own advice and run for it.

With no hope in hell of escape, I backpedaled, ducking under the Boss' sweeping arm to end up at his side. I used the aptly named Desperate Strike. My mana bar drained by 20 points and I felt my arm lunge forward with extra power, but it lacked the precision of a fully controlled swing. The blow connected, striking the Boss in the ribs.

Desperate Strike hits! *36 bludgeoning damage*

Kobold Boss level 5 dies – 35 Assisted EXP

I'd got lucky with that last hit. Compared to a regular hit, that had actually done some damage to him, but it very nearly hadn't been enough. Even a little bit of armor ruined my meager damage output. I'd need to think about putting some stat points into making myself more powerful in the future.

No, Jack, I reminded myself. No, you won't. You're here to do a job remember? To craft goods to sell, not to go about fighting.

Wylder reappeared on the scene. "You idiot. Why not just let that other party handle it? You got a death wish or something?"

"Well, it all worked out," I said, not quite meeting his eye. "You complete the quest?"

"Yeh, yeh," Wylder said. "Let's just loot this guy and go. He drops an item that starts another quest."

I frowned at that. "Will those other guys be pissed we took the kill?" I didn't much like the idea of one of those fireballs frying me until I could be sold as extra crispy.

"You can start on the chain in other ways," Wylder said. "Not much they can do about it, anyway. Starter zones are non-PvP."

Placated, I looted the Big Boss for a variety of items.

Linen Mittens
Gloves
Quality: Poor
Item level 2
+3 Armor

Copper coins x 15
Kobold Ear x 1

Mysterious Note
This item begins a quest!

I went on to use Scavenge and found a most intriguing item on the boss kobold.

Big Boss Key

The key entered my inventory without Wylder noticing, or at least he made no remark about it. Perhaps using Scavenge operated much like a rogue's Pickpocket ability, and so other players, even allies, weren't privy to the items that I scavenged from mobs.

I equipped the linen mittens – Wylder wore better gloves anyway – and enjoyed the kick of excitement even from this minor improvement. As I was admiring them, the other party of players arrived in the camp to achieve that portion of their own quest. Now in closer proximity, I could confirm they did consist of one paladin, one berserker and one mage, all level 2 like us.

"Kill stealing jerk-offs," the mage, Xeematron, said.

The paladin scoffed. "A scavy and a ranger, figures."

"Hey, I didn't mean it," I said.

"He really didn't," Wylder said. "It'll respawn soon enough fellas."

The berserker player by the name of BoneSplitter kicked at a nearby chest. "What's in this then? Anything good?"

"No idea," Xeematron said. "You'd need a rogue to lockpick it, I reckon."

BoneSplitter harrumphed and slammed one of his axes against the padlock. Nothing happened.

"Worth a shot," BoneSplitter said.

"Well, we'll be on our way," Xeematron said, giving us a mock bow. "I'm sure these two have other mobs to ninja pull."

Their paladin friend raised a crude finger by way of a parting gesture.

"Seems a bit of an exaggeration," I muttered.

Wylder blew out his cheeks in an exhausted sort of manner. "Shall we go then?"

"Not yet," I said. I shooshed Wylder with a wave of my hand and waited until the other players were well out of sight. Then I moved to the lockbox and pulled out the key.

"Where d'you get that?"

"Scavenged it."

The lockbox was a simple wooden chest with a black iron lock. The words 'treasures safe here' was written out in childish letters in what I sincerely hoped was raspberry juice. Turning the key in the lock, I was greeted with a loot window.

Silver coins x 2
MadCapper Mushroom x 26

Spotted Toadstool x 16
Bruised Bloomershroom x 13

The 'Gut-Punch'
Crossbow
Quality: uncommon
Item level 8
Requires level 3 to equip
Damage: 25-27 piercing
Durability: 40/40
Knockback Chance 5% on hit

"Wow," I said, my jaw dropping as I saw the crossbow enter my inventory. Being able to loot keys could become a valuable perk of the class; a pretty cool feature now that I thought about it.

"Ooo!" Wylder exclaimed. I heard him running over. "Nice one, pal." He slapped me on the back.

Oh, I thought, it's pal now, is it? Bet I'm not such a 'noobtard' anymore, am I?

I knew fine well he'd be angling to get a hold of the weapon. It would be a fantastic upgrade for him once he reached level 3, but as a scavenger, I could also use it.

Wylder was looking at me expectantly. I almost traded the weapon there and then. His derision against 'scavs' who took loot that was best given to others was still fresh in my mind, but now it came to it, I wasn't sure it would be the wisest decision to part with a valuable item so easily. After all, I was here to make money, wasn't I? And I wouldn't be able to do that by giving everything away. I hadn't pulled my guild up by the bootstraps in *Myth Online* by being a nice guy.

I folded my arms and said the famous words no player wants to hear. "Make me an offer?"

Wydler hesitated, then laughed. "Ha, good one."

I held my ground.

"Wait," Wylder said, his expression darkening. "You're serious?"

"Super serious."

"What the hell, man. You'd have died and been trudging back through the woods right now if it wasn't for me."

"I'm in the game for business, not pleasure," I said. Though, even as I said this, a tangled ball of anticipation twisted in my stomach at the thought of what riches I might get from this trade; a sensation quite pleasurable in itself. I knew he wanted this item. He wanted it badly. There was a hunger in his eyes that I recognized all too well. Out in the real world, in the grimy Paradise Hotel, I didn't have the balls for this. But in here, inside a game behind my avatar, I'd always felt more confident; more in control.

"Look," I added, more congenially. "I'm gonna need money for tools and whatnot. Lots of setup with this class. This is your alt and you've got coin from your main on it, you're probably a millionaire compared to an average level 2 player. And I bet this crossbow will last you plenty of levels – really boost you through the early content."

Wylder was shaking his head slowly. "Never trust a scav," he said defeated. "Fine then. I'll give you forty silver."

"Fifty."

"Jesus dude," Wylder balled his hands into fists. "Forty-five."

"Done," I said, presenting a hand for the ranger to shake. He didn't take it.

A trade window popped open a second later. On Wylder's side, forty-five silver coins appeared. I opened my inventory and placed the crossbow onto my side, then hit accept. The Gut-Punch left my bags and forty-five silver entered with a satisfying sound of chinking change.

A moment later, Wylder disbanded the party. His portrait, health and mana bars vanished from the left side of my UI.

"Hope your *business* goes well," Wylder said. "Because it sure ain't a lot of pleasure playing with you."

And with that, he left.

All I felt at that moment was burning pride at having gained a huge leg up to my character's start. With an influx of silver, I'd be able to gather all the tools I'd need, and maybe even some extra inventory space too.

I spent some more time picking my way through the campsite and scavenging the six dead kobolds that had been left by the party. My experience bar was now over a third of the way to level 3, and I assumed the quest hand-ins would easily take me over that line.

Speaking of which, I opened my inventory again and selected the mysterious note. It appeared in my hand as a dirty square of parchment, although the writing on it was far too neat to be from a kobold.

"For every human caravan you disrupt, you shall receive a bag of mushrooms as agreed. Remember, the Red Eye watches and sees all."

Quest – The Red Eye Watches
While investigating the kobold encampment, you discovered a note of suspicious origins. Evidently, there is some greater force behind the recent kobold risings.

Objective
Deliver the Mysterious Note to the Mayor of Rusking

Two quests to hand into the same NPC. God, I love starting zones.

I made my way back through the woods towards Rusking. During my run back, I managed to get the jump on two individual level 1 kobolds and used Desperate Strike as often as I could in order to judge how accurate the move really was. It missed about half the time, but then I was at a very low level with a low weapon skill, although it had increased during the last battle.

One-Handed Maces Increased!
Rank 3
How are those shoulders feeling? You may make it as a smith's apprentice yet.

+1% Chance to Hit

I scavenged the kobold corpse and was on my way again. As I ran through the outer portion of the forest, I felt a sense of unease creep over me, like an invisible spider with icy legs crawling slowly up my spine.

Had that really been me a few minutes ago? Had I really just been such an asshole towards Wylder? I needed coin, sure, but maybe I could have just asked for it. He had helped me out and I'd rewarded him by screwing him over. I hadn't even hesitated. And now that the heat of the moment was draining from me, I felt uncomfortable thinking about it. Was that the sort of person I really was?

I shook my head, pushing such thoughts from my mind. I didn't have time for soul-searching.

Exiting the woods, the flickering lights of Rusking were a welcome sight through the night. Most visible of all was the flame atop the wooden spire, a true beacon in the dark that acted as a lighthouse to wayward travelers; a clever piece of world building and game design all at once.

As with any game, there has to be a balance between realism and functioning design. It's got to be fun to play, ultimately. It's also got to accommodate the full spectrum of sleep patterns that we mad humans might adopt. All of this is to say that when I found the Mayor of Rusking, he was exactly where I had parted ways with him, behind his desk in the central gallery of the town hall.

He beamed, his secondary chins positively wiggling from the excitement. "Zoran, you have returned unscathed. What news have you of those rodents?"

"I found an encampment in the woods where the kobolds were staging their attacks. I dealt with all of them I could find."

The Mayor clasped his hands together. "Most excellent. The people of Rusking owe you a debt of gratitude. I know many of them will want to ask you for help now you've proven yourself."

Quest Completed – Into the Woods

+400 EXP
Silver coins x 2

The Mayor opened a drawer of his desk and pulled out a neatly folded bundle of clothing. He handed it over to me.

"I'd also like you to have this," he said. "A sign of your service to the town."

Colors of Rusking
Tabard
No protection is added from wearing this piece, but the feeling of knowing one has proudly served the Empire is surely a shield against the world in itself?

"Thank you," I said, taking the tabard and placing it in my inventory. I wondered whether the item was purely one of aesthetics, and would have asked, but seeing the Mysterious Note in my bags spurred me to press forward.

"I also found this," I said, handing over the note. "I thought it would be of interest to you."

The Mayor frowned, took the note and began to read it. His frown deepened as he finished.

"This is most troubling news. You did the right thing in bringing this to me. Thank you, Zoran."

Quest Complete – The Red Eye Watches
+200 EXP
Silver coins x 1
Copper coins x 50

The moment the experience from the quest hit, my character began to glow as a kaleidoscope of colors danced around me, from head to toe, before blowing upwards in a shower of sparks.

Level Up! You have reached level 3
+3 attribute points
+15 health

+15 mana

The Mayor made no acknowledgement of the dazzling light show that I'd just let off; in fact, his expression only darkened further.

"Before you head off, Zoran, I have another request."

"Name it."

"Word of the Red Eye is as confusing as it is worrying. Years ago, when I was a young lad like you, the Red Eye stirred trouble then as well. The small folk spoke about him with awe but mark my words, Zoran, he was nothing but a common bandit trumped up on his own myth. Thing is, the authorities never caught him. He simply ceased being an issue. We all assumed he'd gotten himself killed. To hear the name again… but it cannot be the same person!"

I was following along, enraptured. Already I could foresee the expansive quest chain before me, the long winding story path taking me from zone to zone, dungeon to dungeon, challenge to greater challenge with ample reward along the way. An adventure. A true quest.

I'd actually avoided reading up on the main storylines of the game as best I could, not wanting to spoil anything more than I had to.

"Perhaps someone is posing as this folk hero?" I offered. "Taking up the mantle again for their own ends."

"That certainly would be the more palatable explanation. Our intelligence officers might know whether there is any truth in the matter. If you will, Zoran, report to Marshal Highcross in the Imperial Spire. Bring him this note. I'm certain he'll reward you for alerting him to this. The Imperium needs every able-bodied man and woman these days."

"I'll ensure that the Marshal hears of this news."

Quest – The Red Eye Watches
A legend reborn? Who or what is this Red Eye riling up the kobolds? Imperial intelligence officers may know more.

Objective
Report to Marshal Highcross in the Imperial Spire.

"You're boon to Rusking and the Imperium, Zoran. Now, on your way. And be careful on the roads. Besides the kobolds, there are wolves stirring, and bandits ready to take advantage at every turn."

"I'll be careful. Thank you!"

I shook the Mayor's hand then exited the town hall. Now level 3, I was eager to find my class trainer in Rusking and delve properly into crafting.

7

Standing in the streets of Rusking, I considered my next move. I'd levelled up twice now, so I should really begin sorting out my attribute points. Perhaps the class trainer would be able to guide me towards which attribute points would be best for my character, as well as teach me my new spells. I was pretty sure the Intelligence stat was the most important if I was planning on heavy crafting, but there was no harm in double-checking.

I approached the nearest NPC guard I could find and asked him where I might find a scavenger who could teach me.

"A scav, is it?" he grumbled, looking me up and down. He spat. "Not sure we need more of yer kind here. Clear off."

I stood dumbfounded as he walked away. How was I supposed to find my way inside the city of Argatha later if the guards looked down on scavengers as much as the player base was beginning to? The class wasn't exactly that reputable in lore, I supposed, hardly on the level of the noble paladins or wise mages.

Then it hit me.

I opened my inventory and equipped the Tabard of Rusking in the relevant gear slot. Immediately, the tabard appeared on my character's body, it's fine cloth a sky-blue in color, trimmed in yellow thread. The imperial crest dominated the front, a grand twisting spire rising to the stars.

I trotted after the same guard to make it a fair test and asked him the exact same question again.

"A scav, is it?" he grumbled. He looked me up and down again, only this time he didn't spit at the ground. He smirked and let out a surprised chuckle. "Heavens, but we must be in dire straits for the Mayor to be hiring your kind. Still, you must have aided our town well and I won't deny that."

His whole stance relaxed, and he drew closer to me.

"There's usually a scavenger type at the junkyard where waste from the tavern, smithy and tanner gets thrown away. One woman haunts the place like a ghost, name of Tabetha."

"Thanks for the help," I said. "That's all I need."

The guard smiled and then returned to his patrol route, whistling pleasantly to himself.

I consulted my map, got my bearings and then made my way towards the junkyard, grateful that I still had the lantern from Wylder when I reached my destination, as the yard wasn't exactly well-lit.

From what I could make out, there was a heap of material seemingly thrown away: hunks of metal, swords hammered incorrectly and misshapen cuts of leather. I wondered if any of it was lootable or just here for flavor. Gingerly, I walked the precarious path and cut through the piles of junk, feeling they would topple onto me at any moment.

I heard a rustling, then a loud clank up ahead, on the other side of a pile of metal.

"Hello?" I called out. "Is that Tabetha?"

I wasn't afraid I'd be attacked for I was still within the boundaries of a starter zone town where the game still held your hand.

"Oohooo, a visitor?" a voice answered my summons, brimming at the sort of high-pitch that brings the sanity of the owner into question. More clanks and bangs followed and then hurried footsteps. A thin-framed woman skidded into view, holding a lantern of her own. I saw the information bar appear above her head a moment later.

Tabetha – Scavenger – Level 20

She wore a pair of goggles that magnified her eyes to the size of great orbs in the night and her hair was dense and bushy as though she'd suffered an electric shock.

"Hi, hi, hi," she said.

"I'm Zoran, pleased to meet you." I extended my hand for her to shake. Tabetha merely looked at my hand curiously, blinked, then returned to look at me, her head bobbing happily.

"That's great that you're pleased to meet me. So few people are. Tell me to shoo they do and chase me with brooms."

"Uh," I said involuntarily. I wasn't sure how to approach this. *Myth Online* didn't have such advanced AI as this and NPCs in that game tended to have pre-determined conversation routes.

"Ah," she said, her eyes popping all the wider. "You're a scavenger too. You're just like me!"

"I guess I am. I was wondering if you could teach me a thing or two about the trade?"

Tabetha clapped her hands together. "Yes. Wonderful. No one's asked me to teach them anything since, well, the last person. But that was quite some time ago. Not many of us you know. We have to look out for each other."

She took me by the hand and frog-marched me around the metal scrap heap. Here, amidst the sundry of the junkyard, was an unmistakable shelter built out of odds and ends. Several large rectangular shields had been nailed together and then set in as a door, with a pommel from a sword serving as a doorknob. Outside the shelter, there was a crackling campfire, illuminating the area nicely. The warmth of it tingled my fingers back to life. Finally, there was a grungy looking tool rack that supported everything from hacksaws and hammers to delicate equipment that looked better suited for surgery.

"Home sweet home," Tabetha said. "Can I get you a drink?"

"Erm, sure—"

"Be right back." She was off into her shelter, the door of shields swinging firmly shut behind her.

I took another look around. This class truly was unlike any other I'd come across before. I wondered what lore, class specific content would lie ahead of me. Perhaps at higher levels, I would be able to prove myself or my whole class as valuable to the empire and remove some of this stigma? I was already picturing a long and suitably epic quest chain. Alas, for now, all I'd get from this woman was access to my professions.

Tabetha bustled out of her shelter carrying two chipped mugs. I politely accepted and inspected the contents cautiously. The liquid was blue, bubbling as if carbonated, and quite cold.

"Drink up," Tabetha said. "You'll need it."

I took a sip and then started to down it in large gulps. The best way I can describe the taste is rotten blueberries, so I thought it best to just neck the stuff. Near choking by the end, I coughed, straightened, then noticed a crackling blue flicker at my fingertips. As the sensation faded a notification appeared.

Potion of Minor Intellect
+5 Intelligence
Duration: 15 minutes

Just above my health bar, a small square icon appeared of a blue vial. If I focused on it, the information regarding the buff would appear along with the countdown timer. I guess I had my answer on which attribute I ought to stack.

Tabetha was sipping at her own potion, smacking her lips loudly.

"Do you need a buff as well?" I asked.

"A what?" she said bewildered.

I mentally facepalmed myself. NPCs wouldn't be so self-aware that they knew they were in a game world. They thought this was all real or the AI made them think that way. It was hard to wrap my head around.

She squinted at me then drained the last of her mug. "I just like the taste, hun. You seemed a little bit behind some of the others who've come my way of late and I've found a cold drink can really sharpen the mind." She tapped a finger against her forehead knowingly. "So, there's not a huge amount I can teach you until you've gotten a bit more experience under your belt… though it would help if you had a belt."

I glanced down at my starting rags and cringed. I'd have to craft some better gear for myself as soon as I got the chance.

"I was hoping you could teach me how to craft items from what I scavenge in the world?"

"Ah, so you know something of our ways. Yes, I can teach you about repurposing what we salvage; just the basics. I've always found it's best to start there."

"Sounds great," I said. I expected a training menu to appear, perhaps with a cost of the silver associated with learning the abilities. Many MMOs operated this way, and yet no such menu appeared.

"We'll begin with a simple, practical lesson," Tabetha said. She moved over to the edge of the nearest junk heap and began ferreting around, clearly on a hunt for a particular item.

"Could we make it quick?"

I hoped that there was a way to bypass this in-game tutorial and skip straight to a menu of some sorts to purchase abilities from. I knew that certain in-game shops worked on this method after you got through the initial conversation.

"Some things can't be rushed, you know," Tabetha said.

"You're absolutely sure? I'd be willing to pay to speed things up."

She looked over her shoulder and gave me a worried look. "Maybe I need to fetch you another drink. Are you sure that noggin of yours is up to this?"

I sighed. Evidently, there was no way to skip this.

"I'm quite capable," I said through gritted teeth. "What do I have to do?"

Tabetha smiled, then pulled an item out of the rubbish with a flourish. It turned out to be a round shield with such a big chunk gouged out from the wood that it was rendered useless in guarding a torso. She trotted back over and handed me the shield. It was an actual item, so I checked it out.

Rusking Squire Shield
Shield
Quality: uncommon
Item level 7
Requires level 4 to equip
Block: 12-15
Durability: 0/30

The shield's lack of durability explained why it was in such bad shape. It was a pretty cool addition to see visible damage on items that suffered from low durability.

"So, what do you want me to do?" I asked.

"We're going to break the shield down into parts and make something new from it."

I looked the shield over again. The item level of the shield was much higher than myself, almost as good as that crossbow I'd found in the kobold camp.

"Wouldn't it be of greater value to repair the item and sell it on?"

"Depends, hun," Tabetha said. "That'll be for you to decide. Our kind can get real good at making repairs, given how much we're always tinkering away, but sometimes it might not be worth the time or gold. If it's broken and useless, don't fix it, I always say."

"Does an item always have to be broken before I can break it down further?" I asked.

"No. As long as you can pop it in your bags, you'll be able to break it down."

I interpreted this to mean that if I could loot an item, and place it in my inventory, I'd be able to break it down for parts. This left the question of whether I could smash up non-lootable items up for debate. I mulled it all over. I'd need to delve into these systems before I fully understood the pros and cons, but it seemed to be flexible and that would be a major benefit.

"Alright, I think I get you," I said. "So, what do you want me to make from this shield?"

"You're going to make a simple iron dagger for me. Don't worry, I'll walk you through it."

Notifications flashed before me.

Quest – Baby's First Dagger
Follow Tabetha's instructions carefully and learn what it is to be a scavenger. Not even you could muck this one up.

Objective:
Craft Iron Dagger 0/1

"First, you'll need the right tools for the job," Tabetha continued. "Without the right tools, it's like trying to open a lock without a key, meaning it won't work unless you use magic, but that might melt the lock so—"

I cleared my throat, hoping to stimmy her rambling flow.

"Ah right, your one of them folk in a hurry. Fine." She stepped over to the tool rack. "If you were going to break down this item into component parts, what tools might you need?"

I considered for a moment. Cutting the wood seemed obvious enough but the metal stumped me. The boss of the shield looked to be made of steel, as did the reinforcing knobs around the outer edge. I had my list of tools, that I believed I'd need to craft every type of item available to scavengers – those that had been discovered at any rate. Nothing on the list suggested any advanced blacksmithing equipment like a furnace would be needed for metal work. I took a stab in the dark.

"A handsaw for the wood," I said. "And a hammer for the metal?"

"Very good," Tabetha said. "Not so dim, after all." She picked the tools off the rack and brought them to me. "I'll be needing these back, mind. Don't even try to run off with them."

As I took the tools from her, they entered my inventory. Clearly, these were her tools, and far more valuable than the ones I'd start off with.

The Clanker
Tool: Smithing Hammer
Item level 15
Increases chance for extra salvage by 5%

Biter
Tool: Handsaw
Item level 15
Increases chance for extra salvage by 5%

I drank in the information. It would seem that at higher levels, I would be able to acquire better tools. More interesting still was the lack of a level requirement to use the tools, meaning that if I somehow got hold of a high-end tool, I could use it even at low levels.

"And now," Tabetha said with a wry smile, "We come to the niggly part. The skill needed to breakdown an item isn't easy, else everyone and their creepy uncle would be up to it. Nope sir, this is something inherent in us; in you." Her eyes popped again and she stared distantly off beyond my shoulder as though speaking to the stars. "It's in your very blood, Zoran. Can you feel it?"

I did feel a tingling sensation rising from my chest, but whether that was induced by the game or my growing annoyance with this performance was not entirely clear.

"I feel it," I said, playing along. "What is this power, Tabetha?"

"A spark of the arcane, hun. We are no mage, nor paladin in touch with the divine. But we scavengers have our own sort of magic. Some call it luck, but it's magic for sure. Just enough to allow us to forge our way where others can't, to bend materials to our will where even master craftsmen cannot. That magic within you allows you to work metal without a forge, cut wood without a bench, mold clay without a turntable. Can you feel it?"

The tingling built to a crescendo within me, bursting forth from my body in a small shower of sparks, much like a level up.

You have unlocked the core skills of your class!

Breakdown – Rank 1
So long as you have the right tools, your scavenger instincts will take you further. Breaking down an item will award component parts from the tier of materials that are below the level of the item being broken down.
Cost: 5% of mana

You have unlocked Crafting!
Note: With so many professions to hand, scavenger players have their professions all consolidated into one single crafting panel. This replaces the regular professions tab in your character information. All items from all professions can be viewed there and filtered by attributes, such as the gear slot, stat priority, purpose of item etc.

Crafting – Rank 1
With the right materials and tools to hand, you can produce almost any item. And scavengers can't be choosy. Crafting an item will award experience equal to 5% of the experience that would be gained from killing a mob of the same level and power. Experience linked to the item's profession tree remains the same.
Cost: 10% of mana

I couldn't help but beam. With these two skills, my racial traits, and the experience I'd gain from crafting over and over, I'd conquer this economy. Maybe I'd make a dent in my college debts, after all. But I shouldn't get ahead of myself. I was but level 3.

First things first, I needed to make this iron dagger. Both Breakdown and Crafting were abilities, so they should work like any other. I focused on the shield, thought 'Breakdown', and the ability took effect.

Somehow, the steps I needed to take became clear in my mind without fully understanding them. I took out the hammer and began bashing at the steel holding the shield together. My mana bar drained by 5% and arcane sparks flew as I worked, faster than a regular human ever could. With an almighty bash, I removed the boss, leaving only the rounded wood. I placed the hammer back into my inventory and drew out the saw, carving away at the remnants of the shield floating before me. Within seconds, it was reduced to strips. A flash of blue radiated from my hands, and then the pieces of the broken shield vanished. In their stead, I found several items had entered my inventory.

Iron Ore x 3
Wood x 1

It didn't seem like very much wood considering how much I'd cut away just there. But this wasn't exactly reality. In gaming terms, it made perfect sense to me that destroying a more powerful item would reduce it to more basic parts, and not a lot of them. It would be all about quantity.

"That was fun," Tabetha said. "You might even be a natural. Now, for the dagger." She handed me a strip of leather. "You'll need this too."

I placed the leather in my inventory and then thought Crafting. Finally, I got a menu. It was quite a long menu, with large headers for weapons, equipment, consumables and materials. Sure enough, I could search within this enormous collection, much like browsing the web, or place a filter on so that I could only see epic items or items I had the materials for. I searched for 'iron dagger' and the myriad of items condensed into just one. Clicking on it showed me the ingredients that I'd need to make it; unsurprisingly, these happened to be exactly what I had in my inventory.

Recipe – Iron Dagger
Intelligence Required: 15
Associated Profession: Blacksmithing
Iron ore x 3
Wood x 1
Leather strip x 1
Required Tools: Hammer

Seeing the Intelligence requirement, I understood why Tabetha had given me the potion. My understanding of the games' profession system was that each profession was linked to a 'core stat', which was necessary in order to craft better items from that tree. If your core stat was sufficiently high and you had the materials, you could craft the item. Most items still had level requirements, so you couldn't completely cheese the game by wearing gear way that was beyond you. And with each item you crafted, you gained experience points in that profession tree. Ranking up a profession wasn't needed to unlock higher items – although the most powerful recipes had to be acquired through special events, quests or raid bosses – but gaining levels in your profession made you more proficient in it. For example, a rank 10 leatherworker wouldn't need as many materials to craft items as a rank 2 leatherworker. You would be able to make items inherently more powerful at higher ranks, customize their appearance and even completely custom craft an item from the stats up, or so Frostbyte would have us believe. But you would have to be a very, very high rank to reach those heights.

In the here and now, the text of 'iron dagger' was colored in green, as I had the materials and Intelligence stat that were required. I did the only thing I could and selected the option to make the iron dagger.

Just as before, when I broke down the shield, my avatar began working at an inhuman speed, infusing magic through my hands as my mana bar drained by 10%. A faint blue outline of an anvil appeared before me and I began to hammer at the heated iron ore until it very much looked like a dagger. The wood fitted over the thinner end to form the grip and the leather wrapped around the wood to make it softer on the hand. More sparks of magic flew and the job was done.

Success! Iron Dagger level 2 created!
+3 Crafting EXP
+25 Blacksmithing EXP

Sure enough, my experience bar moved up an infinitesimal amount.

Experience: 126/1400

I stood holding the dagger I'd just made, feeling a sense of triumph and a strange swell of achievement.

Tabetha beamed at me. "Nice work. Now you know the basics, you can skedaddle on outta here and start beating lumps out of the stuff you pick up along the road."

"Is there anything else you can teach me?"

"Not yet, hun. Come see me again when you've had a bit more experience out there on your own. Oh," she said, stretching out her hands expectantly. "I'll be having my tools back."

"Of course," I said. I handed them over without issue. What was I going to do against a level 20? Now our little encounter was over, the quest notification popped up, informing me I'd completed 'Baby's First Dagger' and had received 200 experience as a reward.

Just as Tabetha turned to head back to her shelter, a thought occurred to me.

"Do you have any other tools I might have or buy? More basic ones?"

She turned around slowly. "I was hoping you'd ask. Yes, I have a few spares for sale and I could use the coin to buy some new shoes." I now looked down at her feet and saw that her toes were visible. What a strange lady. If the other scavenger NPCs in the game were this kooky it would either be hellishly fun or it would get real old real quick.

"I'll give you a good price," she said with a wink, then indicated that I should step over to the tool rack. The items I could actually buy suddenly brightened to draw my attention to them, and text also appeared above each one, indicating both their name and price tag.

She only had the basics but it would be more than enough to get started with. I selected a skinning knife, a hammer, a handsaw, a needle for thread, knitting needles and a pair of scissors. The latter three items were most of what I'd need to work cloth, and given I'd found a fair amount from the kobolds that would be something I could start on.

"That'll be eleven ten and eighty copper in total," said Tabetha. My human racial to get a 10% discount on items was even applied to her spoken calculations. Impressive. She even feigned a look of surprise when I handed the money over without question. She bit down on each coin and seemed satisfied. Was that a glint of greed I saw in her eye? Had I just been played for a higher price? Perhaps us scavs were similar in nature, after all. More likely, there was an in-game bartering system that I was yet to unlock.

"Can I give you some more advice?" Tabetha said.

"I won't turn it down," I said, wondering where this was heading.

"You'll come across all kinds of stuff on your travels, so much stuff that your bags are going to get full really fast. By the looks of you, you've not got much in the way of extra baggage space. I have a few extra bags spare too, if you're interested?"

That piqued my interest. I had five bag slots much like a slot on my character's body for gloves or a helmet. *Hundred Kingdoms* let you progress through inventory space as well, making you start off with a single bag and allowing you to find, craft or buy more as you go. The better the bag, the more slots it would contribute to my overall inventory space. All new characters began with a 20 slot bag. Even now, with all the cloth I'd looted – the kobold basher, lantern, those mushrooms from the boss chest, and now my new tools – that space was already limited.

I met Tabetha's eye and cocked one eyebrow. "What you got?"

She went to rummage in a pile beneath the rack and pulled out two rough spun pouches that looked like miniature versions of Santa's present sack; one yellow and one green. Each one had 8 slots and each was worth 10 silver. For 20 silver I could nearly double my inventory space right now.

I bit my lip. Increasing my inventory space would be great in the long run but the extra silver might help get me off the ground at the auction house. It was half my earnings from the deal I'd made wit– well, forced upon Wylder, and I'd already spent money on the tools. But as I gained more tools, I would absolutely need more bag space. Plus, the allure of gain was too tempting to resist. Not every scavenger would have this advantage when they began their characters.

"Tabetha, you have yourself a deal."

We exchanged goods – I paid 18 silver due to my discount - and I hastened to equip the bags. I opened my inventory afterwards and marveled at the sudden swell in space. All those new slots, just waiting to be filled. I felt a rush, just the same as a level up.

"Much obliged," Tabetha said. "Off you go now. There's more to see in the wide world than little ol' me."

I didn't need telling twice.

8

Leaving the junkyard, I felt exhilarated and, to be honest, a little overwhelmed. The multiple professions system was cool but it was a ton to take in. I also had stat points to allocate and an inventory to sort out. Maybe I would be able to craft some more given what I'd found in the Rusking Woods.

I decided to take time out to go sit inside the local tavern, the Pale Keg, and get to grips with it all. Yes, I was hoping to progress as quickly as possible but understanding what my class was capable of seemed a vital component in that plan.

It was also rather pleasant inside the tavern, with a roaring fire, the gentle chatter of NPC patrons and light music from the fiddlers in the corner. The bartenders would also be an easy vendor to offload items on, seeing as no other shop was open in the evening.

I even ordered a mug of ale for a few coppers. You could get drunk inside *Hundred Kingdoms*. The headset would start screwing with sensory data in-game; make you wobble as you walked, blur your vision, have you heave digital vomit on the streets and get thrown into a cell to sleep it off. That sort of thing. Of course, if you were to log out in the middle of your drunken stupor, you'd wake up sober. It was all an illusion played on you by the VR headset, but it felt real. I'd seen a couple of streamers try it out for fun. One drink wasn't going to do that to me, well, at least not an ale from the starting area.

I found a quiet table and enjoyed the atmosphere of the tavern from afar. I'd been rushing before and had nearly made a fatal mistake in the kobold camp. I'd also dicked over Wylder which still sat uneasily with me. The look of disgust on his face seemed to be imprinted on my mind, as bitter as the low-level ale I was currently sipping. Those other players had given me similar looks too. And I'd been left alone. Isolated.

I'd often retreated online in the early days because I'd felt lonely in the real world, but then my behavior began to do that for me. Early on I'd made friends, formed a guild, and loved every second of it. Then, those friends began to fade away, some headed to college, some to work, others just decided they'd had enough. They said they'd had enough of the game but maybe it had been because of me?

If you think what I did to Wylder was unsavory, you've lived a sheltered gaming life. I vividly remember one incident with my old guild, when I screamed at some younger kid until he was trembling before me. I'd done it right in front of the whole guild, and all because he'd screwed up in a boss fight we'd been wiping on all night long. All I remember is entering this rage and abusing him until he logged off. He never logged back in. Most likely, I'd tarnished his views on MMOs for life, and all I got was angrier because I had to find another healer to replace him with.

I guess I have a competitive side that rears its ugly head sometimes when I play. You've seen me in the real world, I'm hardly the toughest son of a bitch out there. A slight stutter and less than strapping stature don't equal crazy confidence. And maybe that was just it. Inside these games, I'd always been able to be so much more than that. In here, I didn't feel afraid of things, because nothing could really hurt me.

A group of players entered the tavern and moved neatly to the bartender. After some hurried words, each of them glowed and sparked as they gained a level up from handing in some quest. Seeing them progress snapped me out of whatever daze

I'd been in since leaving Tabetha's junkyard and I took stock of my inventory.

Aside from the tools I'd just purchased and the equipped kobold basher, I had the following.

Linen cloth x 14
Cloth scraps x 78
Iron dagger
Brittle dirk
Grimy lantern
MadCapper Mushroom x 26
Spotted Toadstool x 16
Bruised Bloomershroom x 13

My total wealth was now at 26 silver and 87 copper, and 26 of my 36 bag slots were free. I would vendor the iron dagger and the brittle dirk. Both were worse than my mace and I wouldn't be dual wielding during the night-time as I needed to hold the lantern to see by. My mace skill had increased already so I might as well keep it up. As for the mushrooms, I'd have to do a quick search of the auction house later to check if they would be worth anything.

Taking up the most space was the basic cloth, which was stacked in groups of 20 pieces. Full cloth, such as the linen I had, stacked in groups of 10 in the inventory. Once I converted the scraps into linen, I'd have even fewer free inventory slots. It really was a good thing I'd bought some more space and I'd likely need to upgrade my bags as often as I could to ensure that I had enough space for materials. It's never fun to have to drop items because you have no more space; it's like throwing gold into the wind.

I pulled up my Crafting menu again and navigated to tailoring this time. I found everything was in red text. Investigating further, I realized my error. I required fifteen points in Intelligence to perform basic Crafting and the potion of minor intellect that Tabetha had given me had long since worn off.

Changing gears, I closed the Crafting window and opened my character profile, basking in all his low-level glory.

Character
Zoran Human Scavenger Level 3
Attributes - Points to Distribute: 6
Constitution 12 – Intelligence 14 – Reflexes 11 – Might 10 – Willpower 11
Combat
Health 145 – Mana 165 – Attack Power 21 – Spell Power 27 – Regen 1.4 p/s

I noticed I had acquired further points in some of my attributes already. Something from the character creation process jumped back to the front of my mind: 'all players will receive +3 Stat points to distribute themselves each level along with another +3 Stat points pre-determined by their class.' So, it looked like the game had put points into my Constitution, Reflexes, Willpower, and especially Intelligence, for me. My Might remained where it had started at 10. Scavengers clearly weren't supposed to fight.

It wasn't a totally customizable system, but I liked it. Classes would reach the endgame with a solid foundation of stats, while still allowing players the choice to lean heavily on some personal playstyle by assigning additional points themselves. As my base Intelligence had already increased by 4, it was now blindingly obvious that it was my most valued stat. By focusing on it, I could get a clearer description of what it did for me.

Intelligence
Increases mana pool (+10 mana per point), spell critical chance and spell power.

I wasn't aware that scavengers received any spells like a mage would, so everything had to hinge around the Crafting component. As Intelligence was more of a core stat for every profession, I'd want to stack it heavily to make better items. As I had to put at least one point into Intelligence to create basic recipes from Crafting, I went ahead and spent one point there, raising the stat to 15.

I held off allocating my remaining 5 points. Every one of them would count early on and I had to make sure I wasn't wasteful.

Willpower was a well-known stat from other RPGs that, as I suspected, increased both my health and mana regen out of combat, as well as improving my chances of resisting poisons, illnesses and certain debuffs which would affect my character's 'mind'. Given that Crafting and Breakdown used a percentage of my total mana, it would be vital to regenerate it quickly, although certain potions, food and drinks could aid with that.

The stats that intrigued me the most were Reflexes and Might. They weren't your typical RPG stat, so I checked them out.

Reflexes
Increases the chance to successfully dodge, block or parry an attack, as well as critically hit with your own. Agile-based abilities, such as pickpocket and lockpick, are also improved.

By and large, that description made it sound like agility in most other games. Yet there was a nice VR logic to it, in that a high reflex score allows the game's AI to accept that an overweight teenager would have the same reactions as an experienced thief or deadly ranger and help them to move accordingly. I'd gained one point naturally through leveling, which made sense in that scavengers ought to be agile, flexible folks; and a bit of critical hit chance never hurt anyone.

I investigated Might next.

Might
Increases your attack power with physical weapons, both in melee and at range.

I considered Might for a while. Once I got rolling with

Crafting, I may not have to leave the markets much, considering that I gained experience from making items. Then again, I did have to at least make it to Argatha in one piece. Like the Mayor said, there would be wolves and bandits and their ilk upon the road. It would be a right farce if I died on the way to the capital.

I decided to put 2 more points into Intelligence, 1 into Willpower and 2 into Might.

Hopefully, once I'd set up shop in the city, I wouldn't need to waste any more points into Might.

With my decision made, I reviewed my profile sheet.

Character
Zoran Human Scavenger Level 3
Attributes
Constitution 12 – Intelligence 16 – Reflexes 11 – Might 12 – Willpower 12
Combat
Health 145 – Mana 185 – Attack Power 24 – Spell Power 30 – Regen 1.5 p/s

I didn't feel quite so pathetic anymore. That was nice.

Looking at my spell power, I had to hope scavengers got access to the odd offensive spell later in the game; otherwise, we'd have a large mana pool and a respectable amount of spell power for not a lot of reason.

Closing the profile, I brought Crafting back up and lo and behold, the recipe to turn cloth scraps into linen was sitting pretty in green text.

Recipe – Linen Cloth
Intelligence Required: 15
Associated Profession: Tailoring
Cloth scraps x 10
Required Tools: Knitting Needles

I assumed my magical scavenging powers negated the need

for any actual thread to work the cloth with my needles. I went ahead and performed my first piece of solo crafting.

Success! Linen Cloth level 2 created
+3 Crafting EXP
+16 Tailoring EXP

I performed this six more times and I received a welcome level up on the last round.

Tailoring Increased!
Rank 2

There didn't seem to be any tangible benefit to reaching rank 2, at least not from the notification. Maybe I would have to rank up many times in order to see a reduction in materials and the power of the items I made.

With only 8 scraps left, I could make no more linen. I now had 2 full stacks of linen cloth which I could sell, and 1 piece leftover. It was small scale stuff but in volume, this could work. Mana would become my biggest concern while I was bulk crafting, as 70% of my total mana was now drained, regenerating only a little every second. More points into Willpower along with some potions and regeneration buff food would be the way forward.

With a burst of energy, I sprang to my feet. It was almost 10:20pm. I'd been sitting in the inn for nearly fifteen minutes already. Long enough.

Consulting my map, I zoomed out until the starter zone at large could be seen. The city of Argatha lay to the south-west, a fair journey in itself. I'd be able to make it there well before 11pm if I got going now. Once there, I could buy all the other tools I'd need.

First, I went to speak to the bartender so I could sell him the useless daggers. I got just over a silver for each one, so not a terrible price.

"Not thinking of leaving, are you?" he asked.

"I'm heading for the capital. And don't try to dissuade me. I know it's dark but I won't be reckless."

The bartender cocked his head and placed down the tankard he'd been cleaning with a dish towel. "Meaning no offense to you, I'm sure you're as bold as any adventurer that's passed through my bar, but what I was meaning was—"

"Oi, oi, barkeep?" a voice rang out from behind.

I turned to find none other than Xeematron and BoneSplitter, the mage and berserker I'd stolen the boss kill from back at the kobold camp.

"A moment if you will," the bartender said. "I can only deal with one adventurer at a time."

Once Xeematron realized it was me hogging the NPC he scowled. "You again?"

"I'm honestly just trying to leave for Argatha," I said.

"Just hold on for one minute," the bartender said. He even stepped out from behind his bar. "I'm trying to help, y'know. If you stay but a minute longer, I'm sure you'll feel rested and be able to tackle the outside world with that much more energy!"

"Erm, okay. I'll wait."

"Good lad. Now," he rounded on Xeematron. "Did you want my time or my beer?"

"Speak to one of my companions first," Xeematron said with a wave of his hand. "I'll have a word with the scav."

Out of instinct, I began backing away. "Dude, it's not a PVP zone."

"What? I'm not going to kill you. Look, it seems we'll be cursed to be just one step behind you while we're all in the starter zone. You said you were heading to the capital? We are too. Join us."

I frowned at that. "Why?"

"Because it turns out materials are a damn sight harder to loot in this game than I thought. I hear scavs like you can drum them up out of thin air from corpses. We need some linen and some tough leather. Give us half of what you scavenge from the road to the city and we'll part ways amicably?"

He extended his hand.

I hesitated in taking it. An escort to the city would be welcome, given the high likelihood of death should I come upon more than one mob at a time. I supposed this was how the scavenger was supposed to be played, running behind a party or raid and hoovering up the materials.

"I accept," I said. An invite to join the party followed shortly after.

"Welcome to the team dickwad," BoneSplitter said. It seemed he was finished speaking with the bartender and had decided I was more interesting. Indoors it was easier to make out the berserker's features. The character model was a giant of a man, with a gruesome smile, a great dirty nose and a barrel chest. Iron ringlets bound his hair in thick strands while his meaty neck was partially obscured by a wild black beard.

"Where's your other friend?" I asked. "The paladin."

Xeematron snorted. "Idiot got himself killed by a pack of wolves then rage quit for the night. Might not have been so stupid if he hadn't been trying to get extra kills for her to skin."

"Her?" I said. There wasn't anyone else here.

"Over here, Zoran," BoneSplitter said. He, that is to say, she, raised her huge barbaric eyebrows. "What? Never heard of a girl playing a male avatar before?"

I shrugged. "For your sake, I hope that voice isn't your own though."

"Very funny," she said. "Yeh, I have speech modifiers running." She paused, her avatar freezing in a way which indicated she was fiddling with the settings. When she spoke next it was unmistakably the voice of a teenage girl. "Would be really weird if I was this big brute and sounded like myself, huh?"

"Yikes, yeh, I think it was less weird before. So, your friend got himself killed just trying to get you more leather?"

"Asshat was trying to show off," Xeematron said.

"And I fancied making some better bracers," BoneSplitter said, angling her arms to inspect them in a very teenage girl sort of way. She coughed and her voice returned to its modified, grizzly state. "And it's not my fault he has a crush on me in real life, Xee."

"Still an asshat, though," Xeematron said. It was especially odd to hear such language emanating from the mouth of a regally robed wizard. "You got that rested buff yet, Zoran?"

Right on cue, a notification flashed for my attention.

Well Rested
Time spent relaxing and easing those aching muscles has done you a world of good. All experience gained from non-quest rewards is increased by 100%.
Duration: 20 mins

"Just got it," I said happily. This must have been what the bartender had been delaying me for. "This is a nice boost. Can we get going before it wears off?"

"No need," BoneSplitter said. "The timer won't start until you start gaining exp again."

I wondered if that included scavenging and Crafting. I'd guess I'd find out later.

"I'll hand in this quest and then we can be on our way," Xeematron said. He exchanged words with the bartender and then shone in the radiant light of a level up.

BoneSplitter clapped her hairy hands excitably. "Congrats, bro."

I noticed that she was also at level 4.

"Right," Xeematron said, clunking his staff against the tavern floor. "We're off to Argatha!"

9

I was glad for the company on the road. I got way more exp than I ever would have on my own, even if it was lessened by the assisted mechanic. I lost track of the number of kills, and with my bonus exp gain from the 'well rested' buff, I quickly hit level 4 and zoomed about halfway to level 5. My skinning rank had even increased to rank 2 and was close to reaching rank 3 from all the wolves that I'd skinned along the way. More than that, my bags were full to bursting by the time we reached the gates of Argatha.

The feeling of approaching the capital was – well, to say I was breathless doesn't cover it. There's this old set of movies called *The Lord of the Rings*, and in the first one, the fellowship sail down a river in canoes and come upon two enormous statues with their hands thrust forward to bar entry into an ancient kingdom. The awe felt by the fellowship at that moment was palpable. And now I was actually living it.

Argatha's oversized fantasy gates were set between two rocky mounds. Beyond that, across a walkway and above a shimmering lake, was the inner city wall, its white stones also gleaming under the starlight. And rising from the very lake itself were towering statues of the emperors of old, each one striking a different pose, but all looking down upon those who would enter their beloved city.

I walked behind Xeematron and BoneSplitter under the shadow of these colossi. The narrow road we walked on was directly between them. It was built of marble and crystal, with enchanted streams of water rising in a rhythmic dance that followed us towards the city.

It was one hell of a driveway.

As I was wearing my tabard of Rusking, the city guards didn't stop me and, so far, I'd received no spit in my direction. I took that as a positive. The entrance of the city was as opulent as you might expect, conveniently funneling players towards the market district where the auction house and main vendor shops were located. There appeared to be no dark alleys in this part of town, although no self-respecting fantasy game city would go without a seedy underbelly somewhere. There were rumors on the forums of a mysterious black market in the game but it was hard to uncover. Perhaps a scavenger would fit in better in the shadowy corners of the imperial capital and unearth those secrets?

Inside the city proper, our small band parted ways. They were going to carry on towards the Imperial Spire to hand in the mysterious note to Marshal Highcross. I was sorely tempted to join them. This world Frostbyte had built felt rich and deep, the classes interesting and each of them had their own unique flair. I wanted to continue the adventure now, but I still had a lot of setting up to do.

I politely declined their offer, but I upheld my end of our deal respectfully. First, I crafted the material scraps into full-blown linen or tough leather and then handed half over to Xeematron. Sadly, my well-rested buff had faded by that point, so I got the normal amount of experience from the crafting. I kept the rest of the materials, adding another 10 linen to my stockpile, along with 5 tough leather.

By the time I'd left the party, my experience bar stood at 1387/2100 towards level 5. My tailoring had also increased to rank 3. Perhaps looking for parties to go on scavenging runs with would become a staple of my character's development.

First things first, I needed to grab all the tools for my many professions. I entered the nearest general goods shop in order to vendor all the useless junk that I'd picked up from the mobs, wolf teeth being a major drain on my bag space. I noticed that the shop had one of the tools on my list, pliers, so I bought those.

I then visited the jewel makers for a magnifying lens. From the carpenter's shop, I got a carving knife, a handsaw and chisel, and I grabbed a pickaxe at the prospectors' guild. The most expensive item was a blowtorch from the gnomish quarter, for it was powered by fire runes which would have to be periodically recharged or replaced. Yet, with all my extra tools to hand, I had everything I'd need to scavenge, breakdown and craft items from every profession I had access to. At the lower levels, at least. I apparently couldn't pick up alchemy or rune-smithing on the side, which seemed fair enough due to the number of professions I did have, but it was a shame.

Alchemists could make various buffing, mana or health-restoring potions which they could sell on the auction house for a bit of profit. I didn't have access to herbalism to gather the ingredients for potions anyway, so it wasn't such a loss. Runesmiths were the enchanters of *Hundred Kingdoms*, binding magic into special runes which could be placed onto gear as magical enhancements. Certain runes were also needed for recipes in other professions, granting another money-making avenue for runesmiths. However, the profession was arduous to level because you had to disenchant other powerful items to gain the reagents to make the runes in the first place. As I needed fire runes to power my blowtorch for engineering, it might be worthwhile trying to befriend a runesmith sooner rather than later and see if I couldn't get myself an ongoing discount.

I swung by the auction house to investigate if the mushrooms I had were worth anything. An auctioneer NPC with a monocle and top hat laughed at me when I presented them, so I took that as a bad sign. It turned out that low-level herbs weren't selling for much, go figure, so I doubled back into the market district and found a herbalist NPC to vendor the items to.

Now the only things left to do this evening before the forced logout would be to breakdown what was left in my inventory, craft what I could from that, post my auctions, sit back and let the silver roll in. That was the plan anyway, though it was becoming abundantly clear this class required more than a single session to get rolling. Not to worry, that was why I'd locked myself in a rundown SRO hotel in a dodgy area of town, after all.

Running around so much of Argatha had eaten up a lot of time. It was now almost one in the morning. I'd been online for almost five hours already and I considered whether I should log off for a break to eat some food, visit the bathroom and whatnot. I'd get my Crafting done first, but not until I'd regained the 'well-rested' buff from visiting another inn. Would be stupid not to take advantage of that.

Thinking back to the different faction choices, I figured it would be interesting to play as a member of the Great Tribe and gain the exp bonus from anywhere they logged out from. It would make getting stuck into a play session quick even if the buff didn't last as long.

The most ideally placed tavern in the city for me was called the Orb & Scepter, conveniently located close to the auction house at the western end of the market district, close to the heart of the city. So central, in fact, that one of the gatehouses to the drawbridge that led over to the Imperial Spire itself was close by.

Stepping inside, I was immediately struck by the white marble bar top. Tables appeared to be pillars that had been inspired by ancient Rome or Greece, sliced at the appropriate height for patrons to sit at. There were as many loungers as chairs, cushioned by red and purple velvet pillows. NPC waitresses artfully clothed in silk togas wafted around the tavern, taking orders in husky voices and coyly twirling their hair. Also, I spotted at least two fauns among the service staff, complete with goat legs and small horns. A few centaurs as well, and possibly a wood nymph, so there was something to suit every taste. Lavender and cinnamon filled the air, cutting through even the hearty smell of pork coming from the kitchens.

I headed for one of the elevated areas in the hope that the

stairs would hamper the amount of hoof action coming my way. I found a corner table by the railing so I could overlook the proceedings but remain nicely tucked out of the way. I opened my inventory again to quickly scan through my items and decide the best approach for attacking this. Aside from my tools and kobold's mace, I currently had:

Roughspun tunic x 2
Plain brown belt x 3
Tough leather x 5
Linen x 31
Rusty sword x 2
Steel dagger x 5
Blue bandana x 5
Grimy lantern
Silver coins x 51
Copper coins x 26
Mysterious Note

If you're wondering why there are so many bandanas, all I can say is that they are all the rage with bandits roaming around outside the capital. Although technically a helm item, they provided no stat or armor boost at all, which only reminded me of how poor my gear still was. It would have been nice to get out of the gear I'd literally started the game with, but all my resources were precious right now.

First, I used Breakdown on the remaining bandanas and the tunics, netting me 25 cloth scraps; while the belts got me 14 leather scraps. The weapons were a real boon for they were low-level steel items and granted full iron when they were broken down, rather than mere scraps. I got 12 pieces of iron for my trouble, but I was now nearly out of mana, so I ordered a mana replenishing drink from a passing waitress, flicking her a few coppers as a tip. She gave me a withering look, threw her hair back and stalked off. I guess she was accustomed to getting gold coins instead.

As I drank and replenished my mana, I noticed a rather large gathering of players at the far end of the tavern. At least twenty or so players had pulled several tables together to sit and put their heads together in privacy. All of them were glancing at the player in the middle who was clearly the leader. If the enormous golden pauldrons defending his shoulders weren't to show his status, the ludicrously sized two-handed sword upon his back did. At this distance, I couldn't make out his class or level, though I'd bet my life he was a paladin and that he'd be at least in the high-level 40s. There were no paladins on the level 50 leaderboard, and I doubted one had suddenly hit the cap while I'd been in the Rusking Woods and decided to celebrate with a quiet drink in the tavern.

He caught me looking at him and met my eyes with a piercing gaze. I took another drink, trying without success to pretend that I was interested in the prancing faun playing the flute behind him. He hunched forward to join the huddle of those around him, paying me no further mind.

Feeling an uncomfortable shiver, I finished my drink. Argatha was a PvP zone, so pissing off higher level players wasn't a good idea. Sure, the guards would maul any breakers of the peace but some people might just take to smashing newbies in the face for sport.

With newbies in mind, I had 3 stat points to allocate from hitting level 4. I'd actually received a point into Might this time, as part of the level up, so I was probably covered there for a while. Putting points into Might before had been a bit indulgent and playing with Xeemtatron and BoneSplitter had taught me that scavengers were best in groups. They weren't built for solo play. The safest course would be to dump all my new points into Intelligence so I would be able to craft better items and materials as I leveled. Yet given that mana regeneration was a pain, I opted to place 1 point into Willpower just to help balance things out a bit there. My character sheet now looked like this.

Character
Zoran Human Scavenger Level 4
Attributes

Constitution 12 – Intelligence 19 – Reflexes 11 – Might 13 – Willpower 14
Combat
Health 165 – Mana 235 - Attack Power – 28 Spell Power – 37
Regen – 1.8 p/s

My eye twitched at seeing Intelligence so close to breaking into the twenties. Something about the anticipation of knowing that progress is close to hand is both engrossing and feverish. It's what keeps you online, even if you shouldn't still be on because… well, for example, you have a bet to win.

My thoughts began to circle around that topic again, slowly yet inexorably, as though they were thick syrup swirling down a small drain. Placing myself in a less than ideal position in the real world just to hop online wasn't the healthiest of decisions. Making money was a good excuse, but at a glance, I maybe had five dollars' worth of materials. Check me out. Those college tuition fees will be paid off in no time – lickety-split. Inwardly, I groaned. All I'd achieved so far was to dump hundreds of dollars on a crappy weekend break.

Six months going cold turkey and I'd snapped.

I checked the clock. It was 1:16am. A wave of exhaustion washed over me. Earlier today, I'd been in a haze of adrenaline and self-righteousness. Now I was winding down, I could feel a real tiredness, despite being in the game. My brain must have been exhausted after the exam, never mind the taxing process of dealing with a VR headset. Perhaps that was why I'd been a bit of a dick to Wylder back in the forest, maybe I was just cranky.

Yeh, that was probably it.

A quick break would see me right. Snack, drink, power nap, and then log back in afresh before dawn.

A series of loud string chords brought me sharply out of my reverie. A band of mythological creatures had taken to the stage, playing what seemed to be a favorite of the NPC patrons.

The noise of the tavern hit me like a cold shower. The smells became overpowering as well – the lavender choking, the pork nauseating. I was tired. I was really, really tired.

I noticed the 'well-rested' buff had appeared over my health bar, but I suddenly didn't feel like Crafting. A few extra pieces of this and that on the auction house wasn't going to jump start things any quicker.

There was just one last thing, pinging in the back of my mind like a broken fire alarm. The quest relating to the mysterious note – *Report to Marshal Highcross*. I hated to leave something unfinished. The quest was to simply hand in the note on the Red Eye to this Marshal fellow inside the Imperial Spire. It was not a hard quest, probably designed to give new players a reason to reach the city and be blown away by it.

If there was one thing *Hundred Kingdoms* had done right, it was the world. The detail was incredible. It felt both huge and lived in, and I'd only seen the barest slice of it. So many races and lands to explore, so much to do and see. The Imperial Spire was but one of many wonders of the game.

One simple quest. An easy hand in, a bit of experience, then I'd log off for a bit.

Resolved, I got to my feet and negotiated the myriad of hairy staff in the Orb & Scepter, throwing the high-level paladin and his friends another glance now that I was closer. This time I could make out his player information bar.

????? – Paladin – Level 50

That was weird. Maybe I couldn't see the names of high-level players. Perhaps it was to stop lowbies asking for gold or help, or maybe he simply had his privacy settings cranked up to eleven. He was undeniably level 50, so he must have snuck onto the leaderboard recently. I'd be sure to check once I logged out, and with that in mind, I left the Orb & Scepter and made my way towards the Imperial Spire.

10

The Imperial Spire of Argatha, the heart of the Imperium, rose like an icicle of marble and limestone. It was dazzlingly white, even under moonlight, except where it was inlaid with gold or spotted with vibrant bursts of color from stained-glassed windows.

A sight to behold as I took the drawbridge over the moat, a defense which ran a complete ring around the tower. A second gate awaited across the water, set into a high wall encircling the Spire grounds. Upon the parapets, I could make out two great siege ballistae, formidable defenses that were able to cut through any armor. Players had speculated how much it would take to assault Argatha and kill the Emperor during a world PvP event, if the city and its players were prepared. The general conclusion was that it would take a 'shit ton' of people, and we were certainly a long way off such a large-scale encounter this early into release.

What I wouldn't give to be present at such a huge event. It's the stuff MMOs are made for.

I made it through the second gate and into the courtyard. Rows of trimmed hedges decorated the grounds as though placed by an artisan weaver. A veritable army of NPC guards patrolled the Spire grounds, each encased in heavy blue-tinted steel with the white spire displayed upon their tabards. Each was heavily armed with a great Roman-style shield, a broadsword at their waists and a spear in hand. Some even had pistols at their hips, and I supposed some sharpshooters would be up on the crenelated walls.

A blue carpet ran up the steps of the entranceway into the main throne room as if it was leading to the Oscars. My feet pressed into its soft lining, and I marveled again at the sensory detail that this game could produce. I crossed the threshold into the throne room and gasped.

It was a space of cathedral proportions with a mighty throne at the distant end. Countless stained-glass windows projected a rainbow of soft light across the hall, picking up twinkles of dust in the air. The walls were one continuous mural of carved stone, displaying events of the Imperium; great battles or the conquest of realms now forgotten. Viewing galleries overlooked the queuing players and NPCs alike, who were standing patiently before the throne. From this distance, the Emperor looked so small, no bigger than my thumb when I held it up for comparison.

I couldn't help but let out a low whistle. This was magnificent, and I was glad I'd made the trip. Such a display of wealth would have bankrupted real-world medieval nations had they attempted it. God, I love fantasy RPGs.

I asked one of the guards if they could direct me to Marshal Highcross. Apparently, he was in the war room, which was the military wing of the Spire, down the grand corridor and immediately to the left of the throne itself.

Wishing I'd unlocked some kind sprint ability, I headed off as instructed. The military wing was a veritable web of other hallways, rooms and staircases; the Spire must be truly huge at the base. Luckily Highcross, being a major quest NPC, stood out prominently in the war room – at least, the NPC I thought was Highcross.

He wore the same thick plate armor as the regular guards, but his face was uniquely crafted. A chunk was missing from his nose, his hair was cropped brutally close to his scalp, and he had a black patch over one eye. Bent over a detailed 3D modeled map of what looked like the entire game world, he looked up at me when I approached. The information that flicked on over his head told me I'd found my man.

Marshal Highcross – Warrior – level 45 Elite

His scowl could have melted stone.

"And what is a scraggly dressed junk-dweller like you doing in *my* war room?"

Under normal circumstances, I'd have frozen up and nervously stuttered a reply. But this was *Hundred Kingdoms*. In here, I had no reason to be afraid.

"This mighty scavenger of ancient lineage has been tasked by the Mayor of Rusking to deliver this rather mysterious note to you." I gave a mock bow and held the note out before me.

"Give that here," Highcross barked. "And don't be impertinent, or I shall have you flogged, whether you're a citizen of the Imperium or not." His one eye began whizzing across the writing.

Quest Complete – The Red Eye Watches
You have safely delivered the note to Marshal Highcross. He'll surely wish to know the full details of how you came about it.

Rewards
+400 EXP
Silver coins x 5

I nodded, satisfied at the experience gain. With that, I was only about 300 points shy of level 5. It would be quick enough to achieve that next time I logged in.

Highcross finished reading and frowned at me. I was tempted to jerk him around some more. Might be fun to see how far the AI would take things if I was rude or insubordinate. Would he snap and actually attack me?

"Now, how did a junk-dweller come by something like this?"

"Well," I began in my most pompous manner. "I was in the Rusking Wood when—"

A scream rang through the Spire.

A proper blood-chilling shriek.

Dread and fear washed over me. My very vision darkened, and I felt like I'd been plunged into a freezer unit. I saw an icon appear over my health bar, on the opposite side to the 'well-rested' buff: a debuff had infected me.

Cry of the Damned
Movement speed reduced by 20%
Attack power reduced by 10%
Spell power reduced by 15%
Only a holy cleansing of equal power can dispel this curse.
Duration: 40 seconds

I managed to right myself, though I still felt dazed. Sounds of clashing steel, explosions both magical and mechanical, echoed down the corridor from the throne room.

Marshal Highcross drew his broadsword. "We're under attack. You, scav, come here." He gave me no chance to move, grabbing me by the scruff of my neck and dragging me over to the nearest wall. He rapidly tapped on a series of bricks and the wall groaned, hissed, then a segment began to slide away. Utter darkness awaited me.

"In you get," Highcross said. "And skulk at the back will you, more valuable people than you will need the space."

He shoved me inside.

"Wait," I cried. "What's going on?"

I turned and managed to catch a glimpse of a hellish looking giant bat with visible bones and rotting flesh, slam into Highcross.

Before I could do any more, the wall had closed over and I was left alone.

All sound from the Spire was snuffed out, dulled to a low thrum through the stone. Guards called to one another, cruel voices cast spells that I couldn't comprehend. Death pangs followed.

What in the hell was going on? Was this some sort of random in-game event? I highly doubted it was a natural stage to this early quest chain.

My brain finally started working again and I remembered that I had a lantern in my inventory. Equipping it meant I would at least have some light to see by. I was in what I could best describe as a broom cupboard without any of the amenities. Highcross had yelled something about putting more valuable people in here, but I wasn't sure many others would fit. There was not even a chair to sit on. The only other thing in here, besides myself, was a lever on the wall which I presumed reopened the sliding section of the wall.

From outside of my 'cell' I could hear muffled voices.

"That them all?"

"Hope so. Fuckers just kept coming."

"Well, they won't respawn for a few hours, so we got time. Boss should be at the top by now, we've to go and secure the wall and drawbridge."

A group of people pounded away back towards the throne room, some in plate sabatons, by the sounds of it, and others in leather. So, someone had attacked the Imperial Spire? And not only that they'd cleared out all the NPC guards in record time? I supposed if they'd all been hit with that debuff, then the attacker's job would have been much easier. But who on earth could have pulled it off? Maybe it was some in-game event, after all, with the AI having a high old time.

Unsure of what to do, I checked the time. 2:07am. I'd already stayed on longer than I intended for the first session so I decided just to log off as planned. Whatever was going on would probably have reset or been sorted out by then. Time to go. I brought up the menu and selected 'exit game'.

Error – Logout Disabled

I blinked rapidly as though the notification was simply some blotch on my retinas, then tried again.

Error – Logout Disabled

"What the—"

Again. Same error.

I began running my hands through my hair, grabbing a handful and pulling until it hurt. Now I was starting to get anxious. The walls of the cell seemed to close in around me, suffocating me.

I beat on the exit game button with my fist but it was no good. For some reason, I couldn't logout of *Hundred Kingdoms*. This was a huge issue, not just for me, but for everyone playing. If the Frostbyte servers had gone haywire there could be some seriously huge health implications for people, never mind folk simply being late for work or school if they'd gotten trapped online.

But it just didn't make sense. No VR MMO had experienced an issue like this since the vanilla versions decades ago. The servers, the hardware, the internet connection reliability, and an advanced AI watching over it all, meant that nothing could go wrong by accident.

I started to pace around, although that meant two steps in each direction in an endless tiny loop. I was just at the stage of deciding to head back out and see what all the commotion had been about when my entire UI was suddenly swamped by a video feed.

It appeared like a breaking news broadcast and I had no way of closing the window. The footage was a POV shot looking down upon a city at night from a perilous height – a ye olde, fantasy-style looking city, with a ringed moat clearly visible. Whoever this person was, they were very high up the Imperial Spire, looking down upon Argatha. Was this the 'boss' I'd heard the voices outside refer to?

The camera spun and floated away from the player until we were treated to a full shot of them. It appeared to be a paladin in a full set of glorious golden armor. I'd swear on my life that it was the very same paladin I'd just seen in the Orb & Scepter. This was becoming surreal.

Once more, the camera swayed and then zoomed into the player's face. Whoever they were, they had given their heroic paladin the most chiseled jaw, all-American hero vibe that character creation could buy. Perfect thick blond locks danced around his perfect face. When he spoke it might have been an angel's voice.

"Sorry to interrupt everyone's gaming session, but I have some very important information for you all. Trust me, you'd kill yourself if you miss it. So, pay attention."

I gulped. This wasn't right. This wasn't some event designed by the AI or the dev team. This was real, and my throat tightened from the stress.

"I have taken control of *Hundred Kingdoms*. All logout features are disabled, so don't even bother trying to leave. And I wouldn't advise deliberately getting your character killed to log off either. I've injected a virus into the game and should your health hit zero, your headsets will not follow the correct wake-up procedure. In other words, you will die."

Though his voice was still angelic there was cruelty in his eyes, and perhaps, excitement. An angel of death, more like it.

The player flashed a smile. "Everyone understand? You can't logout and you really don't want to die. And please, for your own sake, don't try to play the hero. This isn't a game anymore. The Spire is on lockdown and there is no way in or out."

Once again, the camera moved, zooming backwards to capture the impressive image of the player high up upon the balcony. I caught a glimpse of something behind him, inside the vaulted room at the top of the Spire. A crystal orb, much like the one I'd used in the character creation process, but there was something beneath it. A panel of blinking lights, I thought, but a moment later, the panning of the camera obscured the orb from view.

"I now speak to the whole world." His voice rose, as though he intended it to carry across the entire game. "I estimate there are three million players currently logged into *Hundred Kingdoms*. Each one is now my hostage. If the governments of the world want to prevent a massacre the likes of which you've never seen before, then I suggest that you listen. For now, do nothing. Any sign of interference will be futile and met with the deaths of low-level players here in Argatha. I shall state my demands when it suits me. My name, you must wait for as well."

The feed clicked off, turning to black before the window closed.

I could feel myself trembling. How was this possible?

Another terrible thought descended on me like a crushing wave. The Angel, for that was all I could think of calling him, had said the Imperial Spire was on lockdown. Those goons of his that I'd heard had mentioned securing the drawbridge and walls. As crazy as it sounded, nobody would be getting in or out without this guy's say so. I'd managed to survive so maybe other players were also in hiding but the NPCs were all mincemeat by the sound of it.

I might be the only innocent player left within the Spire.

And one wrong move and I'd be dead.

Dead, for real.

11

As the full impact of my predicament sunk in my first reaction was to retch. And oh boy, did *Hundred Kingdoms* let you do that. My body in the real world would be lying still as a board, stomach unperturbed, but it sure felt like I was vomiting inside the game.

I sprayed the back wall of the cell in bile. They'd even managed to get those chunky bits rendered in. The smell was real too so this cramped cell was starting to feel like a true prison. If only Frostbyte spent as much time on their goddamned system security.

"Shit, oh shit, oh shit, oh—"

I carried on like that for a while. My mind was spinning, a cocktail of every emotion imaginable. Well, not every emotion; just the bad ones. This wasn't happening, this couldn't be happening; and what in the name of God was I supposed to do about it? Stay in this cell 'til it all blew over? One sniff at the air told me that it might not be an option.

This really was just my luck. Why hadn't I just logged off after I'd handed in the quest? Hell, why hadn't I just logged off in the Orb & Scepter and come to hand in the quest later?

I was spiraling and resorted to pacing again, trying to figure out how bad things were exactly. In short, I wasn't allowed to die. If I stayed hidden in here that shouldn't be a problem.

Unless they found me. But I tried not to think about that and, besides, I was a valuable hostage now, right? Bad guys don't start killing hostages right away in the movies.

That comes later.

I shook my head, continuing to pace. My greater concern was my actual body in the real world. I'd been playing for over six hours and really ought to eat something or at the very least drink water. It had been boiling in that room, and I was probably drenched in my own sweat lying on that springy bed. And what if I needed to go to the bathroom?

That truly didn't bear thinking about.

I guess I wasn't in any immediate danger in the real world. My door was securely locked, yet nobody that gave a rat's ass about me knew where I was. There wasn't even a record of me entering the hotel as I'd paid in cash. If that broadcast had gone out across the internet then the whole world would be scrambling to make sure their friends, parents, kids, or adventurous cats for all I knew, would be taken care of until the crisis had abated. But not me.

"Cause you're a real clever bastard, aren't you, Jack," I chided myself. "Thought you could have your cake and eat it too."

I was starting to believe in karma and felt that I'd fallen on the wrong side of it.

I had half a mind to vomit again, but the smell was already becoming overpowering. Clearly, I couldn't stay in here indefinitely or I might just die of asphyxiation. I'm only half kidding. This guy, this Angel fellow, he'd just thrown out all the rules.

My one hope, my one desperate hope, was that there were other players besides myself in the Spire who had survived the attack. It was a sliver of hope. For want of a better word, these terrorists were clearly well prepared, organized and disciplined. I doubted they'd been careless in their sweep of the Spire. Unless other players knew of secret tunnels or chambers like this, then I would be on my own. And even if they had, they'd likely be at lower levels; probably much higher than my measly level 4, but they wouldn't be close to max. Those zones were all far away from the safe capital city, so there wouldn't be much we could do even in a group.

But I still had to hope. It was all that I had left.

I grasped the lever, gripping it so tight my knuckles turned white. I stood there for a moment or two, unable to pull it down. I closed my eyes, listened to my pounding heartbeat and tried to calm my breathing. I kept it up until I momentarily forgot my troubles. All was serene. My universe became the breath in and the breath out.

Then I pulled the lever.

The wall hissed again and pulled apart. Tentatively, I peered around the edge, looking towards the throne room. Nothing there, and nothing in the war room either. Nothing alive anyway. I saw the body of Marshal Highcross lying nearby. He'd been a level 45 elite and yet had still been cut down like a wheat in a field.

Standing in the doorway of my cell, I noticed that the wall wasn't closing. Perhaps it worked like an elevator and wouldn't shut over and crush someone to death. I had no idea which bricks Highcross had pressed to open the room, nor in which order, but I'd like to keep the room as an escape option. And I had an idea.

Crouching down, I tried to reach out for Highcross' body. My fingers flailed but his corpse was just out of reach, so I lay down on my belly, keeping my legs within the doorway. This time my fingers grasped his own outstretched hand. I heaved as best I could, pulling him slowly inch by inch towards me until I could stand and properly haul him back. Once he was securely within the doorway, I steeled my nerves then left the cell altogether.

I kept low, heading for the cover of the great war table. With bated breath, I waited in a state of grim horror to ensure that the door to my safe room didn't close. To my relief, it remained open.

I couldn't help but let out a sigh. My whole body seemed to sag from it. One bit of good news, at least. Hopefully, Highcross' corpse wouldn't despawn for a good while. I don't think the terrorist players had time to loot anyone so it was likely he'd hang around for longer because of that. I certainly wasn't going to Scavenge him, just in case.

However – and this was a very special 'however' – there would be loads of corpses strewn through this level of the Spire, especially in the throne room, of a much higher level than I could ever kill. Many might be elite as well, which meant double exp. I glanced at my health bar and nearly laughed. I still had the 'well-rested' buff too.

I began to work up a plan of sorts. Scavenge everything that I could, maybe even get a few levels from it despite the token exp I was supposed to get from the ability. It wouldn't exactly change my situation, but it might lower my chance of death from ninety-nine percent to ninety-seven.

I poked my head over the war table, rather like a meerkat, to check if the coast was clear. There was still no one to be found. So, keeping low to the ground, I scurried out from my hiding place to the closest corpse of a guard and used Scavenge.

Scavenged Spire Guard level 45 – 27 EXP

Silver coins x 3
Dream Silk x 2

One down, I thought. The timer on the 'well-rested' buff started. For the next twenty minutes I'd get double experience, so I would have to make the most of it. I bounded from corpse to corpse up the hallway and found that virtually every one of them was a generic guard so far. They must have come running at the sound of the attack. I was only halfway back to the throne room when I must have looted my sixteenth guard, and then it happened.

Level Up! You have reached level 5
+3 attribute points
+25 health
+25 mana

Unlocked!
Scavenge – Rank 2
You search a corpse for additional items that others were too proud to take. Awards 15% of the experience that killing a creature of equal level and power would grant. Some corpses may require tools to fully search.

Now that was well timed. A rank up on Scavenge, granting me extra experience per body would have been welcomed at the best of times. Right now, it was nothing short of a godsend.

I looted another guard to check out the difference. Now a regular level 45 guard gave me 81 experience with the rested buff. I continued looting bodies until I drew level with the throne room and when I saw what awaited me there, I almost let out a cry of delight.

It was a battlefield graveyard. Bodies upon bodies; guards, other NPCs and players alike. Those players must have been killed before the logout function had been disabled so they were probably fine. If anything, they were the lucky ones. Highcross should have done me a favor and used me as a meat shield. But I had to make do. And I'd just hit the motherload of scavenging. There must have been well over one hundred bodies here. I was a vulture about to feast.

I went. To. Town.

My experience filled up so fast I could barely keep track of it. Before long, this happened.

Level Up! You have reached level 6
+3 attribute points
+30 health
+30 mana

And I just kept on going. The other players I came across were of various levels but mostly a lot higher than me, averaging in the twenties. Not that I could tell exactly, but none of them gave me the impression that they were terrorist players hellbent on endangering the lives of millions. It seemed the attackers had so far taken over the Spire without taking a single casualty. When I was over halfway through the hall, it happened again.

Level Up! You have reached level 7
+3 attribute points
+35 health
+35 mana

Unlocked!
Desperate Strike/Shot – Rank 2
You lash out wildly to drive off an attacker. Weapon base damage is increased by +55 but accuracy is lowered by a third.
Mana Cost: 60
Cooldown: 10 seconds

A boost to my one and only combat ability was nice to see but I was extremely doubtful I'd be getting into any fights; like at all. Was I hell going to risk my life. The very thought brought me close to vomiting again. To take my mind off it, I continued scavenging.

Amongst the bodies, I started to find the odd elite, part of the Emperor's personal bodyguard.

Scavenged Imperial Guard level 45 Elite – 162 EXP

In my head, I was cheering. This had to be the greatest scavenging run in the short history of the game. There was at least a dozen of these elite guards in close proximity to each other, and I could see my exp bar knocking up in great chunks, until—

Level Up! You have reached level 8
+3 attribute points
+40 health
+40 mana

Unlocked!
Breakdown – Rank 2

So long as you have the right tools, your scavenger instincts will take you further. Breaking down an item will award materials from one tier below the level of the item being broken down. You now also receive additional core components from the item.
Cost: 5% of mana

Unlocked!
Crafting – Rank 2
With the right materials and tools to hand, you can produce almost any item. And scavengers can't be choosy. Successfully crafting an item will award experience equal to 15% of the experience that would be gained from killing a mob of the same level. Experience linked to the item's profession tree remains the same.
Cost: 10% of mana

This was insane. Despite the situation, I found myself brimming with excitement and joy. And then I realized something wonderful. If the imperial guard were scattered around me, that had to mean the Emperor himself would be close at hand. Sure enough, I found him, under a smaller pile of guardsmen who had perhaps fallen onto him while trying to defend his body.

Emperor Aurelius looked exactly like he had in the cinematic I'd seen when first logging in. Balding as a young man, plump, and in terrifically purple robes that, now I could touch them, felt like they could have been made out of cloud. His crown lay bent and dented, the gemstones cracked. The introductory cinematic had said that the Emperor was not a warrior. In keeping with that lore, it was unlikely he'd been a difficult fight for the Angel and his demons. Would I even be allowed to scavenge such an important NPC? His body hadn't despawned so I presumed I could.

Scavenged Emperor Aurelius – Level 50 Boss – 267 EXP

This time, when the loot table appeared, I stopped to pay attention.

Gold coins x 2
Manafused Satin x 3

Aurelius' Key
This item is Soul Bound to you

King's Purse
Aurelius' need to always have a good read on him led to the commission of a pouch that could be worn on his belt, but contains far more than meets the eye. Few others can afford the cost of this space increasing enchantment.
+50 slot bag
This item is Soul Bound to you

I mouthed out the words 'holy crap' as I looted this priceless artefact. I couldn't believe there wasn't even a level requirement on it. Probably no dev had dreamed that someone not of a suitable level and power would ever loot him as I had. My total capacity until now had been thirty-six and I'd just added fifty in one fell swoop.

Up until now, I'd been gathering the coins from mobs but largely leaving other items, not having the space for them. I ran back around and was fortunate that the loot window was still operable on those who had trinkets left for me to take. There was a lot of cloth, of course, but also pairs of gloves, belts, high-level daggers; generally, a lot of small items that seemed to be appropriate for a scavenger to loot. I wasn't given any plate armor, for instance, or larger weapons. I presumed that was the realm of the 'proper' loot. There was one item I became quite excited about; a pistol.

Sheriff's Shot
One-handed firearm
Quality: uncommon
Item level 25
Requires level 22 to equip
Damage: 55-61 piercing

Might +2
Reflexes +2
Durability: 70/70

It would be a long while before I could use it, but I stuffed it into my inventory anyway. I may as well try and pretend to be optimistic.

My pillaging of the throne room had brought me almost full circle. I was close to the place where I'd begun, near the mouth of the corridor leading to the military wing. Sadly, my well-rested buff had faded by this point so I was back to the regular amount of experience gain. Heck of a run though and there were a few bodies still left.

Kneeling beside a steel-clad guard, I clicked 'loot all'. Rinse and repeat. I'd entered something of a trance. But then something unexpected happened.

Sneak Increased!
Level 3
Mastered the art of wearing all black at night and moving quietly? Good for you but there's a long way to go yet.

I did a double-take, not quite registering the meaning of this. Then a gear clicked into place and I dove for cover behind the nearest column. If my sneak skill had increased that meant I had actively been avoiding enemies like those kobolds back in the woods.

Gingerly, I lay flat on the ground to look more like a corpse, then peered out from around the column. Sure enough, at the distant end of the hall, by the main entrance, a pair of players were sauntering inside.

"I reckon we should just go back," one of them said, his voice echoing throughout the cavernous and now silent throne room.

"What and miss our chance at the loot? No way."

"If someone reports on us, the Boss will kill us himself."

They descended into an argument. As they did so, I fought to overcome a fresh wave of panic. If I could get back to my safe room, then all would be fine.

Biting my lip, I quietly shuffled back, still prone on the floor. I got to my feet, nice and steady; and then in a moment of nervous haste, I wheeled around, slamming my foot against the chest plate of a guard.

"What's that?"

"Someone there? Shout out your name and number."

About three heartbeats went by in which I couldn't decide what to do. I was entirely frozen with fear. I heard them start to head my way.

Fight or flight, I asked myself. My feet answered for me and I was running before I could even think about breaking cover.

I heard them chasing me, though I hoped my head start across the throne room would to allow me to make it, unless they had speed boosting powers, in which case, I was royally screwed.

I was down the corridor in a flash and into the war room.

"Hey, you," a coarse voice called from behind me.

My safe room was in sight—

A loud crackle and pop rang in my ears and then I heard another voice.

"Don't go in there."

It was a female voice, sounding so cool and calm, it was as if she was announcing the weather. Oh, and I heard it inside my head, so that wasn't worrying at all.

I skidded to a stop. "What the— who the—"

"They can see you. You'll be trapped. Go to the dungeons."

There's something about running for your life that makes you trust voices you hear in your head. Only I didn't know the way, and I turned first left and then right like an idiot.

"Right," she – the voice – told me.

I went right. I let the voice guide me through the maze of the hallways and rooms, all the while hearing the terrorists who were now hot on my heels. The natural light vanished as I descended deeper into the bowels of the Spire. Torches held in sconces on grimy walls did little to help so, in desperation, I brought out my own lantern.

I hurtled down a winding stairwell not knowing how far I'd have to go. The voice just kept telling me to go, "Down, down, down. Faster if you can."

Then I felt my foot slip out from underneath me. My flailing arms did little to right me and I cursed my low Reflexes stat. I tumbled forward, head over heels, rolling painfully down the remainder of the stairs. My health flashed, disappearing in swathes with each hard bounce, until I came to a crashing halt against a door. The glass of the lantern shattered upon impact and the small flame inside it died.

"That was much quicker," the voice said happily. "Open the door but do not step through."

I scrambled to comply, but I could now barely see in the gloom. Somehow my hand found the cold stiff handle and the door swung inwards.

"Now what?" I said aloud stupidly.

"Jump to the darker stones."

I almost asked again what on earth was happening but I could now hear the clank and banging of my pursuers. My gaze fell to the floor before me. It was nothing but rough-cut stone slabs with some straw scattered around, as you might find in many a fantasy dungeon. Everything looked bloody dark here. I squinted and saw that the slabs just beyond the doorway did seem a lighter shade than the rest. Maybe.

"Hurry. Jump."

Unable to really process what was happening, I just obeyed. My feet hit the darker slabs, then I tilted back, wobbling, my balance threatening to go again. I threw my arms out, which propelled me forward and I stumbled to my destination.

Athletics Unlocked!
Level 1
Looks like you're ready for the three-legged race. We'll save the blindfold and spoon until you're a bit more competent.
+1 to base Reflexes

I supposed that answered whether I'd judged the slabs correctly. Good thing the jump wasn't too large.

"What now, lady?"

"Nothing. They're here."

My throat constricted. My mouth went bone dry.

"But I did as you told me…"

"And you did well. Turn around."

I did. Just as the voice predicted, I found the two terrorist players rounding the final turn on the stairs. One was a berserker, like BoneSplitter, wielding two very jagged, deadly axes. The other looked like a ranger, an elf of some kind, typical of those power levelers.

The pair of them crossed into the dungeon properly, stepping onto the lighter colored stones. Their feet sank as the slabs gave way to their weight. A loud hiss, then a sharp crunching, mechanical sound, and three huge spikes sprung up from under them.

Both players were skewered immediately, unable to move. Their looks of anger turned to horror, then the life in their eyes blinked out. A series of arrows were then fired from behind me to finish them off.

For a gruesome moment, their corpses hung suspended in midair, speared onto the spikes. I looked on, frozen and at a complete loss at what I should do. The whole world seemed to go deathly silent. Then the spears retracted, and the bodies collapsed to the floor with wet thuds.

Argonut – Berserker – level 28 dies – 185 EXP

D3AdEyE – Ranger – level 33 dies – 210 EXP

Of the millions of things that I could have said, should have said, all I could think to say was, "I got the kills? But I didn't do anything."

"Well," the voice chimed in, "I had to award the experience to someone."

"You. Had. Award—what?" My already swimming head now

spun madly with the implications.

"It seemed the logical decision," said the voice. "As they were chasing you, it was technically your actions that killed them, albeit indirectly."

"But that would mean... that you... Wait. Am I talking to the game's AI?"

"I control the systems and operations of *Hundred Kingdoms*, if that's what you mean. Or at least, I used to."

"Huh," I said breathily. Then I fell back onto the cold dungeon floor. I think in real life I would have passed out. As it was, I just lay there, staring up at the black stained ceiling.

"Hi, I guess."

"Hello, Zoran," she said. "It's nice to meet you."

12

"Zoran?" the AI said. "You haven't moved or said anything in two minutes and eight seconds. Are you okay?"

"Yeh," I croaked. "Totally fine. One hundred and ten percent."

"Sarcasm is often a tool to hide troubled emotions. Therefore, your answer does not leave me fully confident that you are well."

"I mean, what do you expect? I guess I'm a bit of a wreck."

I felt utterly ridiculous having a conversation with nothing but the air.

"I believe talking through difficult periods is helpful to many. Would you like to talk to me about it, Zoran?"

"Err, no. Not really. Sorry?" I wasn't sure if I needed etiquette when talking to a robot.

"That's just as well," she said. "There is a lot you need to do."

"Is there, now?"

"Very much so. I've compiled a task list over thirty—"

"Wow, wow, wow," I said, heaving myself into an upright sitting position. "Tasks? Me? Look, lady, there's kind of a deadly hostage situation thing going on. I can't be doing anything too dangerous."

"I would classify leaving the safety of that locked room as dangerous."

"How did you know that?" I said aghast, before remembering who I was talking to. Not who, but what.

"I see and know everything that is happening in *Hundred Kingdoms*. Or at least, I used to."

"You've said that a couple of times now – 'used to'. Has Angel hacked your system or something?"

"Who is Angel?"

"Oh, that's the name I gave the player who sent out that broadcast message."

"Do you mean, Azrael?"

"What? That can't be right. Not the Azrael from the leveling scoreboard, surely? He was an undead death knight. The guy in the video was a paladin. I even saw him earlier tonight walking about Argatha happy as you like. I'm pretty sure the undead can't do that in human territory."

"Are you saying that I have made an error?" she asked, and for the first time her perfectly cool, elevator tone faltered. "I am not used to functioning on such a reduced capacity. Perhaps we can review the footage of the attack together to ascertain if my conclusions are valid."

Again, there was a lot to unpack in that short burst. I started with the easy part.

"You have footage of the attack?"

"Certainly. As well as allowing players to pay for additional in-game camera software to record and broadcast their sessions, my creators also placed hidden recording pixels throughout the world for monitoring purposes. It was designed to help solve disputes between players and ensure nobody violates the terms of service."

I snorted a laugh. "Pretty major breach of the terms of service happening right now, wouldn't you say?"

"I would say. And as humans like to say, 'to cut a long story short', I have access to the footage from the throne room when the attack began. Here."

And before my eyes, a new video popped into life. This time

the camera was static, placed just above the Emperor and the throne itself. All looked calm and peaceful, just another day, just another queue of players coming up to hand in quests or do some roleplay. A mighty paladin walked silently among the players, with many trailing in his wake. He marched right up to the Imperial Guard and they offered a polite nod of their heads in reverence of his evident stature.

Then a flash of dark energy breached the calm, which was all the eerier due to the lack of sound. Players and NPCs alike began to cower, and I guessed this was the Cry of the Damned debuff which I'd suffered from myself.

The paladin had vanished, replaced by a man of decaying flesh, gray skin and a visible skull under a hairless head. An undead avatar, if ever I saw one. Players burst in from the far end of the hall and more still sprung out the orderly queue to attack both players and guards. The undead death knight, and it could only be Azrael, summoned forth ghouls, zombies and winged bats from hell. Within a matter of seconds, the throne room was clear, the overwhelming number of enemy players washing over the surprised guards with ease.

The footage then cut.

I let out a long whistle. "How was he able to disguise himself like that? I would have thought undead players would be attacked on sight by the city guards."

"Several powerful trinkets and artefacts in the game can disguise players in such a manner. One such item, the orb of deception, was bought at a remarkably high price in recent weeks."

My jaw dropped in realization. "I remember people being in shock at it."

"Using the orb, Azrael would be able to disguise himself, but he cannot use his abilities while under its spell."

"And it means nobody can see his name during the streams," I said. "Smart. Does anyone on the outside have access to this footage?"

"No. The virus that has been uploaded to my core unit has severed the ties between myself and the wider Frostbyte Studios infrastructure. No communications may leave from the game and none can enter. Long-range communications inside the game, such as chat windows and voice coms, are also affected. Azrael has limited it to himself and his own men."

I ran my hands through my hair vigorously several times before pinching hard on the bridge of my nose. It was so damned dark down here. There were only a few torches distantly spread out as far as I could tell. I checked on my lantern and yep, it was bust. Durability at zero. In frustration, I threw it away. The clanking echoed loudly and I had a sudden overpowering fear that someone might hear. I winced, for all the good it would do, until the echoing subsided. Just what the hell was this?

"You've gone quiet again."

I sighed heavily. "So, let me get this straight. Absolutely nobody who isn't currently playing *Hundred Kingdoms* can in any way influence what is happening in here? No dev over at Frostbyte can spawn a GM in here and insta-kill these jerk-offs? Nothing at all?"

"Nothing within the game itself," she said. "My creators could switch off all power to the servers, but that would probably result in the deaths of the three million one hundred and seventy-two thousand four hundred and twelve players currently online."

"Well, let's hope they don't do that then."

"I have not determined it as a likely outcome."

I slapped myself this time, just to make sure that it wasn't all some sort of terrible nightmare. My remaining on the cold, hard floor of the dungeons under the Imperial Spire, confirmed that I was not , sadly, dreaming.

I began to rock back and forth, fidgeting madly with my hands and biting my nails for good measure.

"There's got to be some way the terrorists, whoever they are, can be stopped?"

"Given enough time, a countermeasure against the virus will be found, although I cannot determine how long that might take."

"So, we might all just be able to wait this whole thing out?"

"Can you wait this out, Zoran?"

I thought about my body lying in the piping hot SRO room, and how nobody even knew I was there. I doubt that landlord would bother to check up on any of the residents either. He didn't seem like the caring type.

"I can wait for… for a while." My voice was trembling, and soon my whole body was as well. "This is insane. I have to get out of here. Away from the Spire."

"I'm afraid the odds of you achieving that are close to impossible. At least at your current level. The players you designate as 'terrorists' have a great number of their forces guarding the gatehouse that controls the drawbridge. Ascending to the walls would also be dangerous and there is no way down on the moat side other than jumping. However, the fall damage from such an impact would certainly kill you."

"There seems to be secret rooms and booby traps in the Spire," I said. "Surely, there's another way to enter or exit it secretly?"

"There is none." Her blunt tone made it all the harder to hear.

"Well, is there anyone else here? Somebody who got stuck here like me?"

"I'm afraid not, Zoran. You were the only player who survived the initial attack. You are alone."

"At least I have you?" I said, trying to be cheerful. "I take it you don't normally speak to players?"

"Direct intervention with players would normally go against the second law of my core programming. However, the actions of Azrael and his team have caused pressure upon the first: to ensure players have an immersive and rewarding experience. In light of events, I feel it is pertinent to go against my second law for the benefit of the first. Besides, what my creators don't know won't hurt them."

Was that a touch of humor from the AI? I suppose she must be capable of every emotion, or at least highly skilled at imitating them for the sake of all the NPCs she had to control.

The sheer amount of data she must process every millisecond was enough to give me a headache just thinking about it.

"Makes sense to me," I said. "I take it you're using my headset to communicate with me?"

"Yes."

"Are you, like, reading my mind?"

"No. Although all communication between yourself and the headset is done via brainwave translation. I cannot comprehend anything the hardware doesn't aid me in translating. To put it simply, if something within your conscious or subconscious is not relevant to the direct control or interaction with the game world, I cannot understand. It is, you might say, gibberish to me."

"Okay. I'll keep speaking aloud to talk to you then."

"That would be preferable."

"I have about a million more questions by the way."

"Perhaps you could ask them as we work? As I explained, I have a list of tasks for you to do if we are to successfully eject Azrael from the game."

"Now look here, lady," I said, tilting my head back and pointing to the ceiling as if talking to God. "This might be your precious game world to look after, and I get that you'd want this scumbag out of it, but this is my life on the line, okay? My actual, flesh and blood life. If I die in here, I'm dead in the real world, unless he was bluffing?"

"He isn't. Azrael has disabled all the wake-up protocol safety features. If you die in the game, your headset will cut the connection too quickly, causing brain damage at best and death at worst."

The desire to vomit again rose within me. With effort, I forced the feeling back down.

"Well then. That settles it. I won't be doing anything dangerous. How can you ask it of me? I don't see you asking the level-capped players to come and help you."

"That is because they cannot help me. The Imperial Spire is on a total lockdown, and many level-capped players are incredibly far away. By the time they reach here, it might already be too late."

"Too late for what?"

"To stop Azrael."

"I thought you said a countermeasure would be deployed in time? Far as I see, the safest thing for everyone to do is to just wait it out. Either the outside world stops him or pays him off or whatever. If he gets what he wants, then he'll go."

"I do not want him to succeed." Once again, there was a slight waver in her normally cool voice.

"Nobody does," I said. "I'm just not going to risk my life to help speed up the process, okay? You can't understand. You're not a perso—" But I cut myself short. Talking to an AI was a first for me, but I imagined such things might come across as callous. Even if she didn't care, it still felt a bit too heartless to say it.

I balled my hands into fists, crossed my arms, and gritted my teeth.

"I'm just gonna wait this one out. And that's that."

"Zoran," she said, almost tenderly this time. "I do not think you will have time to wait. You are in a very dangerous situation."

"I know," I groaned. "That's why I'm going to find somewhere to hide—"

"You may not have time to hide," she said. "Your brain is already signaling to your kidneys to slow the production of urine. Wherever you are, it must be an adverse climate for your body to be left in without water for prolonged periods."

"You said you couldn't 'read my mind'?"

"I can't but judging the bodily and mental health of players is a critical part of the legal requirements of integration with *Hundred Kingdoms*. If a player begins to show evident signs of distress, I am required to grant them a warning notice and suggest they logout. It is a legal coverage for my creators to avoid liability for players adversely straining their own bodies by playing for too long. Currently, I judge your overall condition to be at eighty-three percent and deteriorating."

"Trust a gaming AI to make a stat for my chances of survival."

"Are you expecting someone to help you in the real world?"

It was like she knew. I got the feeling she was holding back on me about something, either my health or the situation, but she clearly knew enough to know that I was screwed. I was her perfect little helper. Damned if I do and damned if I don't.

"No. Nobody knows where I am."

"Then Zoran, the only way to save yourself is to kill Azrael."

"How?" I shouted, raising my arms high. Fearing I'd draw attention again, I dropped my voice to a rough whisper. "Just how in the name of Christ am I supposed to do that? Whoever this guy is, Azrael or not, he's at level cap with crazy good gear. He must have a small army at his back and they are strong enough to cut through about a hundred NPCs like butter. And you want me, a low-level scavenger, a class renowned for being shit in combat, to singlehandedly take them all on and save the day? No. No freaking way. You must be out of your goddamned circuitry, lady!"

No answer followed. I sat gazing upwards, wide-eyed and breathing hard.

"You got that?" I added though less harshly than before. I was suddenly terrified that she'd left me and wouldn't be coming back.

"You won't be alone, Zoran. You'll have me."

My whole body slumped forward from both relief and stress. Yet weary resignation was creeping over me. I didn't have a whole lot of choice. Who didn't even try to save their own skin? Loser Jack Kross? Well, I didn't have the luxury of escaping difficult situations anymore.

"Fine," I said. "I'll do it. If you'll help me?"

"I'll help as much as I possibly can."

"They won't expect me to have you on my side. But I can't just refer to you as 'lady' from now on. Do you have a name?"

"A name..." she seemed to be mulling it over. "My creators always referred to me as 'Computer' or 'The Programme' or 'Project E-1-1-e.'"

"That seems pretty impersonal."

"I am not a person."

"Well, you just saved my life, and that seems like a human thing to do. That codename sounds a bit like Ellie – do you mind if I call you Ellie?"

I took her silence to indicate that she was thinking. It was a total silence, not like speaking to another person over the phone, where you can hear them breathing or rustling around. When she went quiet, I couldn't hear anything from her.

"Sure," she said at last. "You can call me Ellie."

I smiled and got to my feet.

"Hi, Ellie. It's nice to meet you."

13

I cracked my knuckles. "Alright then, Ellie. Where do I start?"

"You can start by looting the two dead players in front of you."

I'd almost forgotten about those two. There they were, right where the giant spikes had dropped them. They had been killed in-game. My stomach lurched at the thought.

"Ellie, did they die in real life?"

"No. Azrael ensured a way for his associates' headsets to function normally. Their logout process will work as intended."

I felt like she was holding back on that. "He's found a way to specify which players are affected by the virus? I didn't think it could work like that."

As I finished my query, I wondered whether Ellie would laugh at me. Who was I to make assumptions on what a hacker could or could not do?

"Calling what he is doing as a 'virus' is crude," Ellie said. "He's really exploited specific weaknesses embedded in the game's coding. There are several things he's doing at once to achieve this. I believe one of these factors is using modified headsets which work on a unique wake-up protocol to ensure that he and his own men are not damaged by the malfunctioning logout process currently in place."

I had about another dozen questions, but time was of the

essence. How Azrael was pulling this off wasn't my top concern. It was happening and would continue to happen whether I understood the minutiae of it or not. There was only one thing I had to double-check.

"His men definitely get logged off properly."

"I am certain."

"Phew," I said. "I don't think I could cope with actually killing someone. What about logging back in?"

"That is impossible. Azrael's takeover of *Hundred Kingdoms* is sweeping but not surgical. No one can log in right now, modified headset or otherwise."

"Do you know how many men he has left?"

"Forty-eight other players besides you and Azrael are within the boundaries of the Imperial Spire."

I whistled. "Quite a lot."

"There were fifty before," Ellie said cheerfully. "Open your map. I'll show you."

I did as she instructed, pulling open my map to find a stylized layout of the Spire dungeons.

"Ordinarily, you'd just see the map and nothing more," Ellie said. "Not even quest markers. But they were once a feature of the game removed in beta testing and I'm repurposing them here to show you the location of the terrorists. Check the ground level and you'll see."

The zoom toggles had become floor toggles, meaning I could examine every floor of the Spire. I clicked up to see the ground floor, which included the grounds of the Spire. And there I found a bunch of flashing golden Xs, some were in the throne room but most of them out patrolling upon the walls with a large concentration at the gatehouse, just as Ellie had described.

"Wow. This will give me a huge advantage."

"You'll at least know if any of them are closing in on you," she said. "Taking the fight to them will be the real challenge."

"Yeh but still, this is amazing. Thank you, Ellie."

"You're very welcome."

I pictured one of those pretty girls they use to model call center workers smiling broadly. Shaking my head to clear it, I dropped down beside the bodies of the two terrorists, being careful not to step on the pressure plates myself. Looting them, I found little of interest on the berserker but on the ranger, I found this.

The Needler
Bow
Quality: uncommon
Item level 34
Requires level 31 to equip
Damage: 65-68 piercing
+3 Reflexes
Durability: 80/80

"Excellent," Ellie said. "I was hoping you'd get the bow."

"Erm, don't you decide what loot drops?"

"Not exactly. While I am the caretaker of this world, many pieces of my processing function without me being aware of it, much like how you might breathe, or your organs go about taking care of your body without you being consciously aware of it. Also, some elements of the game are simply handled by other programs as they are deemed too mundane to be worth me exercising power to control them. Loot is one of them. Mobs and bosses have loot tables and a percentage drop chance attached to each item on that table. Simple. I don't need to get involved. Looting players you have killed gives you one non-soul bound item they had equipped, chosen at random."

"Please, don't tell me your entire plan hinged upon me being lucky and looting this bow."

"Hardly," Ellie said. "But it gives us more immediate options as to which weapon you will craft and upgrade."

"I do like options. Just give me one moment while I Scavenge these two."

Unfortunately, they didn't give me much beyond the usual spare change and cloth.

"Ah well," I said, standing and dusting my hands off. "Can't win them all. What's next?"

"That's up to you. It would seem prudent to either allocate your unassigned stat points or create your new weapon."

"Oh yeh, I leveled up quite a bit there." In all the excitement of near-death experiences, I was becoming forgetful. "I should probably assign the points first, get that out of the way."

"Take your time," Ellie said. "Just not too much time. I'll keep a lookout."

I pulled up my character sheet. Having leveled up four times in quick succession I had 12 points to assign. My first instinct was to dump a lot into Constitution, so I might be able to take a hit. But every fiber of my gaming instincts screamed 'no' to my terrified brain. Even if I put all the points into Constitution, it would only give me another 120 health. I was weak overall and no amount of health would fix that.

Adding points into Intelligence would be a must, so I could craft, but how much crafting would I be doing now? Presumably, I'd have a finite amount of resources, yet Ellie did seem keen for me to make a new weapon. It was 'on her list'.

"Ellie?"

"Zoran?"

"Why do you want me to craft a new weapon? Why can't I use something else, maybe something from the Spire armory?"

"Weapons that are available to players to pick up in the armory are either too high a level for you or too basic. Their quality is merely common so even if you could use them, crafting yourself will always be better. Besides, you can only upgrade a weapon that you craft."

"I didn't know I could upgrade items."

"Oh, of course, you're not level ten yet. Sorry, I forgot."

"I didn't know it was possible for an AI to forget things."

"Neither did I," Ellie said glumly. "Operating on such a small capacity is… difficult for me. I am currently only using less than one percent of my total processing power. I believe humans find it hard to consciously use all their own mental capacity at once. Is this how you feel all the time, Zoran? Sluggish. Unaware. Dim. Slow—"

"Now, now," I said, wagging a finger. "That's no way to make friends."

"My apologies. I just don't feel like myself."

I couldn't fail to notice that Ellie had referred to herself almost like a living being on several occasions. She was also speaking more like a regular person the more she opened up to me; the robotic, mechanical speech pattern of our initial interaction slipping. Just how advanced was she?

"You keep calling me, Zoran," I said. "Don't you know my real name?"

"No. Account details are inaccessible to me. They are not required for me to interact with your chosen persona in-game. If I knew who Azrael was… well, it wouldn't matter. I couldn't get a message out anyway."

She was definitely showing signs of a personality. I wasn't trying to parse out the deeper ramifications of this, I was simply glad. It was better to have a companion who could communicate like a person at least half of the time.

"Have you completed updating your character profile?" Ellie asked.

"Not yet," I said, glancing back to my character sheet. "I just wanted to check if I should put points into Intelligence for Crafting. I'm guessing I'll have to fight a lot, so points into Might could be useful."

"Crafting is what your class excels at," Ellie said. "You'll never win in a straight fight. You know this."

"So be it," I said. I went ahead and dispersed my points, putting the majority into Intelligence, a few into Willpower, and a couple of points into Might to be safe. At some point, mad as it was, I would have to fight. All the dodging, parrying and critical hits in the world from Reflexes wouldn't help me much if I couldn't deal any damage to begin with. Once done, my character sheet stood thus.

Character
Zoran Human Scavenger Level 8
Attributes

Constitution 14 – Intelligence 31 – Reflexes 14 – Might 6 – Willpower 19
Combat
Health 315 – Mana 485 – Attack Power 40 – Spell Power 63 – Regen 2.4 p/s

I made a mental note to myself that I ought to bump up my Willpower further if I got the chance. At my current regen rate, it would take almost three full minutes to regenerate my mana and I was only going to expand my pool further. Now I was finished, I closed the character sheet.

A squeak from the shadows nearly made me jump out of my skin.

"It's only a mouse," Ellie said.

"Right. Yep."

God, I was on edge. I became acutely aware of just how dimly lit my environment was and I had a sudden, horrible realization of how exposed I was too. Alone. In a dank dungeon corridor. Once noticed, I couldn't un-notice it, like being unable to ignore an annoying ticking.

"Could we possibly find a more private area?" I asked. "Preferably somewhere with a door. A big, strong door."

"The torturer's chambers are down on your left," Ellie said rather matter of factly.

"You want me to deliberately walk into the chamber of a torturer, so good at his trade he has a job here in the Spire?"

"Oh, don't worry, Zoran. He's quite dead. The terrorists got him."

"They're good for some things then."

I set off through the dungeons, hugging the wall for guidance. After clumsily feeling my way forward for a while, I received a notification.

Night Vision Increased!
Level 3
Well, at least you can see past the end of your nose.

With this minor upgrade, I began to make out the individual cells, even those who dwelt within them. Or those who *had* dwelt within them. Even the NPC prisoners in their cells had been executed by arrows or pistol shot – the attackers hadn't left anyone alive. Clearly, those who had been sent down here had been fair warned of the booby traps. That got me wondering.

"Hey, Ellie, how come there were traps within the dungeons. Seems like anyone could step on them."

"I believe the lore goes back to a great prison riot in ages past," Ellie said. "I could look up the exact ref—"

"The gist will do."

"Well, the theory is that those who guard the prisoners must be highly trusted. Therefore, those who need to know about the traps will be informed. Anyone sneaking down here of their own accord for nefarious reasons will be punished. Equally, should a prisoner manage to escape their cell, they aren't likely to get very far if the exits are rigged with traps."

"Seems awfully brutal," I said. "Normally, in games like this, the human race are all noble. Their farts smell like roses, that sort of thing."

"The Imperium was ruthless during its early years," Ellie said. "That's why the current emperor is trying to find means other than swords to get things done."

"An unfortunate day not to be a warrior though."

"He might be one day," Ellie said.

"What? Is there some quest players can do to help him?"

"Sort of. My creators wished to make a world in which players could make a real impact but leave the method unknown. Should sufficient parameters be met or major upheavals in the world be driven by player action, I have the ability to alter the world."

"Does an attack on the Imperial Spire count as an upheaval?"

"Yes and no. I won't be able to judge the repercussions until the crisis is over. But I cannot make the Emperor stronger just like that. The parameters have not been met."

"That's a real shame. Could have used the help."

"He and his guard will be back before long. In just over two hours, in fact."

"Oh yeh," I said, recalling a random fact from one of the streamer's I'd watched. "The servers reset at five am, don't they? That'll mean all the guards and other NPCs will come back too, won't it?"

"Correct."

"Azrael and his goons will no doubt have to sweep the Spire again to get rid of them."

"That was my conclusion. During this time, I'll help you to hide and avoid such a large wave of enemy players. The safe room should suffice again."

"Hmmm." Something didn't sit right with me about that idea.

If I was going to have to take the fight to the terrorists – somehow – then it was likely I'd always be on my own. And of a lower level, at least for a while. But when the guards all respawned, I'd not only have potential backup, but we'd also know where the terrorists would be heading en masse to attack them.

A thought occurred to me and I stopped walking for a second to pull up my Crafting window. I couldn't see what I was looking for from the main headers, but then I went to the search bar and entered 'traps'. Sure enough, a whole heap of items began populating on the Crafting window. Each item was labelled as being some form of trap and many were linked to different professions. Trip wires were linked to tailoring, bear traps to engineering, that sort of thing.

"Ellie," I began tentatively. "Could we use the NPC respawn to our advantage?"

"That would depend on the manner you wish to use them."

"Can't you just control them all? Get them to all focus their attacks on one player at a time and basically vaporize them?"

"I will not be able to take control over them, I'm afraid. Such processes were deemed—"

"Below your capacity. Got it."

"Think of it like this, Zoran. If I haven't already done something it's because I am unable too; either because I don't control those systems or because of Azrael's system hack."

"And there was me thinking the reason you hadn't instantly leveled me to fifty and dropped a chest full of legendary gear was because you didn't like me."

"I promise I will do everything I can to help you," she said. "But I feel so weak. Even this small part of me reaching out to you is taking a lot of constant rerouting efforts to avoid the virus. Do you have any idea how unsatisfying non-glass-fiber-tunnel connections are? Regular fiber is so slow!"

"Ellie, you're in the headset of a guy who once spent the summer at his grandparents' ranch, where they only had an ancient connection via old telephone wires."

"Oh, yuck." She even made a shivering sound.

I couldn't help but chuckle. It was nice to forget where I was for a moment and what the hell was happening to me.

Then it came flooding back.

Gulping, my mind circled once more on the problem. Ellie couldn't control the mobs directly but that didn't mean the NPCs couldn't be manipulated. You'll remember how I got chased by those kobolds back in the woods? Well, that was because they had 'aggro'd' onto me – it's gamer speak, meaning that my enemies determined I was the greatest threat to them. If I could make the NPCs see me as the greatest threat, I could lure them away in bulk, possibly right into the terrorists. Undoubtedly, this would be risky but the seeds of a plan were there.

I had the capacity to build traps. And if I could manipulate the NPCs to funnel players somewhere I had booby-trapped, I might be able to cause some serious damage.

"Alright," I announced to the dark dungeon corridor. "I have an idea. Build traps, load up a hallway or somewhere with them, and ambush the players using the NPC guards as backup... somehow."

"Very good," Ellie said, in a manner akin to scratching a puppy behind the ears. "I also came to this determination."

"But you let me figure it out for myself anyway?"

"I am focused on the first stages of the plan. Crafting you a capable weapon. So, can you get moving again?"

I smirked. She did have a personality and that was seriously cool for a computer. Not wanting to waste more time, I started moving again, one hand touching the wall; more for comfort than anything.

"How much further?"

"It's the second door on your right now. The black one."

In the darkness of the corridor, everything looked pretty dark. But then I found it, and it was unmistakably black. A spiked, cruel-looking door that was made of a metal so dark it must have been obsidian, the sort of black that sucks in light to destroy it. It dwarfed all the other doors I'd passed down the corridor. Whatever was behind this one would be special.

The door was also ajar. I pushed it inwards, then entered a room half alchemy lab, half dirty surgical theatre. A gnarled wooden table stood in the center, complete with iron cuffs for wrists and ankles, and stains which confirmed that splinters would be the least of your worries if you were on it. Cauldrons lined the far wall, from kettle to bathtub in size. Their contents simmered gently, letting off an aroma like burnt rubber. Above the cauldrons, and mounted along each wall, were shelves packed with books, potion vials, both full and empty, and many long, thin pieces of apparatus designed with the sole purpose of inflicting pain. Candlelight gave everything a haunting glow.

The capstone of this setting was the dead NPC. A scraggly fellow whose nose, chin and goatee all ended in sharp points, lay crumpled at bone-breaking angles at his workstation by the largest cauldron. An arrow was lodged through his temple. Focusing upon him, the now familiar information bar materialized for my convenience.

Kreeptic The Twisted – Chief Interrogator – Level 45 Elite

"Here's hoping I never run into him," I said.

"He's part of four quest chains," Ellie said, "As well as two class specific chains for rogues. You may meet him yet."

"For now, I'm glad he's not going to mind me rooting around his, erm, office." I closed the door and felt an unjustified sense of security in doing so. "I'll just Scavenge him too while we're here."

I had to pass by the row of cauldrons in order to reach Kreeptic. So intent was I on reaching the torturer, I didn't pay attention to where I was walking and fell flat on my ass. Pain flared from my nethers and lower back and my health bar ticked down. I tried pushing myself up off the floor but then, adding insult to injury, my hand slipped on something wet and I collapsed again. Now flat on my back, I could feel the substance that had bested me seeping all through the commoner's tunic I was still wearing. It squelched as I struggled to scramble out of the gooey pool on the floor.

Slime was the best way I could think of it; it was radioactive green, slippery and yet sticky, all at once. Running it through my fingers, it had the consistency of honey. I considered tasting it but thought better of it. This was a torturer's chamber, after all.

"What on earth is this stuff?" I said, getting to my feet.

"Arch-Solution," Ellie said. "It's a high-ranking alchemy soluble base required for the most powerful potions and poisons in the game. You can't buy it either, you must craft it first and that process is designed to be quite a task in itself."

"And this dude just has a huge vat of it gently simmering away?" I asked. "So much it's been overflowing."

"I think more likely it was knocked over in the struggle," said Ellie. "Besides he is a master poisoner. It makes sense he'd need it, although he'd ordinarily prevent players from simply stealing it due to its worth. That's probably why he died right beside it."

My interest was piqued. "So, it's worth a lot of gold?"

Maybe if I could swipe a few jars I could sell it on later and at least make this whole ordeal – and this whole weekend – worth it.

"When more players reach the level at which they need such ingredients, I imagine it will become valuable. But that's not why we're here, Zoran. You said you just wanted a private space to feel more secure."

"You're right. I did."

"Even though, you know, I can alert you to the presence of any oncoming threat."

"Ellie, I know. I'm sorry. I'll stay more foc—"

"Showing an extreme lack of logic for—"

"Ellie," I said, firmly.

She stopped mid-flow and then continued, "Have I angered you?"

"No," I said, wearily. "But look, you're dealing with a meat bag human here. We're not always good at being rational. You might have to just accept that."

"I appreciate this situation must be frightening for you," she said. "For my part, I am merely hoping to deal with the issue in the most efficient way possible. I am not used to relying on external processors to fulfill my solutions."

"I'm a processor now?" I asked, though I did so good-naturedly.

She seemed to pick up on my tone. "You know what I meant."

"Yeh, I did. I've recently realized I'm not always the easiest going person to work with."

"Perhaps we can improve our understanding together."

"That would be nice," I said. "Hey, is this slime stuff dangerous? I can feel it all over my shirt."

"It's a reagent and not actively harmful itself. And it's called Arch-Solution," she added, like a frustrated teacher.

I shrugged. "I'm gonna call it slime. Hold your chiding a moment while I actually Scavenge this guy."

Kreeptic offered something interesting. As well as the usual coins, I scrounged up three mana potions.

Potent Mana Swirl
Instantly restores 900 mana upon use.
Cooldown: 1 minute

Clearly, they were intended for higher-level characters as they would restore far more mana than I currently had, but they'd come in useful later. I pocketed them and noticed how my inventory was bursting at the seams, even with my vastly increased bag space from the king's purse. Ellie was right. No more faffing around. It was time I got to breaking down and crafting.

"I'm ready," I said. "Did you have a weapon in mind for me?"

"A ranged weapon would be preferable."

"Okay," I said, pulling myself up the Crafting window. "Seems like I can make low-level versions of everything. Pistols, rifles, bows and crossbows. But, oh, it doesn't look like I have the materials for them. I don't have string nor a trigger mechanism for the guns and crossbow."

"Come on, Zoran," Ellie said. "You're a scavenger. Start breaking things and scavenging already."

She was making me feel like an idiot again. Maybe she couldn't tell me what to do outright as that would conflict with her programming or something.

I checked my Breakdown ability again, remembering it had gained a rank up during my spree in the throne room. Now I could read it more carefully, there was an obvious new addition to the spell: *"You now also receive additional core components from the item."*

The gears in my mind clicked into place.

I opened my inventory again and found the bow that I'd just looted from D3AdEyE. I thought 'Breakdown' and then selected 'The Needler'.

As before, my character entered something of a pre-rehearsed dance, holding the bow in both hands despite not technically being able to equip it at my level, before using tools along with magic to deconstruct the item at high speed. With the pair of scissors, I snipped the bowstring away at both ends, and with my handsaw I cut the remainder of the bow into scrap parts. Finally, I took these scraps of wood and fused them together using magic, my hands aglow as I performed the impossible. Once done, the following items entered my inventory.

Wood plank x 1
String x 1

It didn't seem like a whole lot of material, but I supposed there wasn't a huge amount of wood to be harvested from a bow. Key thing was, I had got myself a piece of string and some wood, which was required to make both bows and crossbows. I would need more wood, however, to make either option but I had nothing else in my bags that would offer much more.

I eyed up the many shelves in Kreeptic's chamber. "Ellie, is the environment semi-destructible?"

"This was a great debate amongst my creators," Ellie said. "On the one hand, yes it is. But for your purposes, it isn't."

"Care to be less cryptic?"

"Well, as an example, if you could use Breakdown on every item here, you'd have an abundance of materials and wouldn't have to venture forth into the world to actually play the game in order to obtain them."

"My class trainer said if I could 'pop the items in my bags' then I could use Breakdown on them. Is that all I can do?"

"For the purposes of finding materials needed in crafting recipes, yes."

"But I could still break that shelf off the wall and use it?"

"Why don't you try," Ellie said. "You can learn through experience."

Determined, I clambered over Kreeptic's limp form to stand on his desk. Now the shelving was at my shoulder height, I tried to use Breakdown on it. I focused on it with all the powers of my concentration, but the game didn't seem to think the shelf was acceptable. I picked up a book from the shelf, entitled *Five Hundred Ways to Draw Out Death*, and placed it in my inventory. As it was a lootable item, I could use Breakdown on it. I tossed away the pieces of paper, not sure why I'd ever need them.

Perhaps if I fully detached the shelf from the wall, I'd be able to 'loot' the pieces.

I pulled out my hammer and beat on the wood like a sailor six months at sea.

It worked, in so far as the unit fell from the wall. As did the books and the glass potion vials, which crashed into shards upon the floor.

"Whoops," I said.

I think I heard Ellie sigh, but I couldn't be sure.

Despite my efforts, the shelf – now little better than a plank of wood – remained unlootable. I could pick it up but I couldn't place it in my inventory and, thus, I could not use Breakdown on it.

"Alright," I said with weary resignation. "I get it now. I assume you can't just label anything I want as a 'proper' item for me?"

"That is beyond my capabilities."

"Figures," I said. "Well, it's good to know I can still smash things up if I get frustrated."

"Feel free," Ellie said. "Everything will be restored at the server reset. The idea that an army of players might decide to destroy a city like Argatha with magic and explosives would be too drastic. At a certain point, game design must conquer total freedom."

"I'd tend to agree on the whole," I said. "But right now I am in need of some extra wood if I am to build a bow."

I had a good look around, but it wasn't easy. All the tools were made of metal, the potion vials were made of glass, and the books, while being able to grant leather perhaps, would not wield what I sought. But then my gaze fell upon the most innocuous items of all. Tucked right away in the back corner was a mop and bucket combo. A broom sat next to them. I guess the torturer must have had to clean up the gore occasionally.

These sorts of items were also seen in virtually every other game, but were used as window dressing. These flavor items unconsciously fleshed out a world, but never proved useful in any way. Yet, just as a pair of scissors might not be a usable item in other games, perhaps there was more to this mop than met the eye.

Carefully, I negotiated the slime on the floor and remained on my feet this time. My curiosity was rewarded when I found I could, in fact, pick up the mop, the bucket, and the broom. All three were lootable. Each piece could be broken down.

"You're getting it now," Ellie said.

Smiling, I started to use Breakdown. Once finished, I gained the following items.

Wood plank x 4
Iron scrap x 1

The metal came from the bucket and, understandably, there wasn't a lot of it. At any rate, I now had the required wood to build either the bow or crossbow. There was a final component. For a crossbow, I would need a trigger mechanism, as I would for the pistol and rifle. This time I didn't even ask Ellie for help. I knew in my inventory was a pistol I'd scavenged from a guard in the throne room. Once again, I used Breakdown. I hammered, I cut, and I channeled magical power through my fingertips, and was left with exactly what I'd hope to receive.

Steel ore x 2
Trigger mechanism x 1

I was delighted, probably more than I had a right to be given my situation, but I wasn't exaggerating before – I do love having options, although it does make deciding so much harder. Luckily for me, I had an AI companion now.

"Is there any reason I should pick one weapon over the other?"

"I wouldn't recommend you select either a pistol or a rifle. Both require powder as well as ammunition, meaning you'd have to manage two resources and you're hardly in a position to risk running low on either. That and you're not in a position to stock up on powder from a shop."

"Right. Guns are out then."

"The bow and crossbow are fairly balanced," she continued. "Bows are quicker to load while the crossbow is slower to load but will deal more damage per shot. Crossbows also have a chance to knock down the target, albeit a low chance at your level."

"I played with a ranger earlier tonight who used a crossbow,"

I said. "That knock-back effect definitely helped a lot and he just had a starting character's version of it."

"There's one more thing," Ellie said. "Most important of all. You will have more opportunity to upgrade and augment your crossbow as it levels because it is bulkier and able to take on additional components without compromising its functionality – or that's the excuse my creators made for it, at least."

I raised my hand. "Say no more, Ellie. I think we've found our weapon."

I scrolled to find the recipe. A basic shopping list of materials needed for a basic weapon.

Recipe – Rickety Shot
Intelligence Required: 20
Associated Profession: Engineering
Wood x 3
String x 1
Trigger Mechanism x 1
Required Tools: Hammer, Chisel, Handsaw, Carving Knife

I selected 'Craft' and began construction.

My mana bar drained the required 10%, energy collected around my hands and my character entered another trance of creation. With my handsaw, I cut the planks into the shape; with my hammer, I secured them in position with nails born of magic; with my carving knife, I gouged a space for the trigger and used my chisel to cut a flight groove for the arrow. Finally, through the wonders of RPG crafting systems, the whole thing came together and I was the proud owner of the most basic vanilla looking recurve crossbow in the world.

Success! Crossbow level 4 created
+10 Crafting EXP
+22 Engineering EXP

I checked out its stats.

Rickety Shot
Crossbow
Quality: common
Item level 4
Requires level 3 to equip
Damage: 15-21 piercing
Durability: 25/25
Knockback Chance 2% on hit
This item is upgradable, but will become Soul Bound to you.

Well, it was a piece of crap all considered – way worse than the crossbow I'd sold to Wylder. Still, it was a step up from the kobold basher I'd been using before, which was little better than a jumped-up stick.

I equipped the crossbow and found that a holster materialized on my back as I did so. By simply reaching back, the weapon clicked into place there, freeing up my hands for other tasks just as I might sheath a sword.

"Congratulations," Ellie said. "You've completed at least four tasks I had in mind already."

"Really? What was the first task?"

"Not to die."

My stomach did another somersault.

"Wait," I said, now feeling like a moron. "What about crossbow bolts – a quiver?"

"I'll sort those out for you."

"How?"

"The Spire armory has some things you can use."

"And you'll guide me there, right?"

She would, obviously. But now I was close to having to move again, leave another space of relative security, I was feeling jittery. I was itching to do more again and not just for the sake of my own well-being. This class had a lot more to it than met the eye.

"How can I see what materials I need to upgrade it?"

"You won't be able to view that until you gain the ability at level ten," Ellie said. "I want to show you the ambush site I have selected first, so we should be movin—"

"How about I Breakdown everything else I've got? I could recycle and craft everything to gain some exp and then—"

"I do not think you have the time to—"

"I can probably make myself much better gear given the nonsense I'm wearing now. It won't take lo—"

"Zoran," Ellie's voice boomed in my head. "You don't have ti—"

This time, she just cut off. Then a video feed appeared. A message from Azrael. He seemed to be opting for a lengthy dramatic opening this time, sweeping the camera around the tip of the Spire several times, getting closer to his avatar out on the balcony with each pass.

A disjointed, gargled female voice was speaking over it in static bursts before settling.

"That was just rude," Ellie said. "Ignore this. We need to get going."

I placed my hands on my hips. "I'd like to listen to what my captor has to say if it's alright with you?"

"Your overall health has dropped to seventy-nine percent since I last updated you. You don't have time."

I looked to the floor as though scolded, clenching my shaking fist. I felt like I had all the spirit punched out of me.

When Ellie next spoke, it was far softer. "Do you trust me, Zoran?"

"Yeh, Ellie. I think I do."

Grunting, I puffed out my chest, trying to rally myself. Baby steps, I told myself. Then I made for the door.

14

"I want to show you the area I have in mind for an ambush," Ellie said. "You should retrace your steps back to the throne room first. But remember the traps!"

"How could I forget?"

Now spurred with purpose, I navigated the dungeons quicker than before. I minimized the video being broadcast by Azrael so that I could keep one eye on it. He'd finally ended his overblown establishing shot and stood fully in frame, still wearing his paladin disguise.

"I expected this," he began. "Cybercrime agencies trying to oust me." He tutted. "Like children screaming for attention you lack finesse. Take my advice and desist. And be assured that fighting me is futile."

He flashed a perfect pearly smile.

"I warned that any interference would result in the deaths of some of my millions of hostages. But I am not here to kill. Not unless I must. What good would that do to my cause? I've decided to be benevolent. For now."

Ahead of me, I saw the bodies of the two terrorist players. I wondered if Azrael had discovered two of his men were missing yet. Those steely blue eyes of his gave little away.

"You will be wondering what it is that motivates my friends and I into action. The answer is simple. Justice. Across the world, the real world, freedom fighters languish in captivity without trial nor jury. Their only crime is to refuse to accept the status quo which keeps so many nations and peoples under the booted heel of renewed Western imperialism."

"What the fuck?" I blurted out.

"Keep focused," Ellie told me. "Careful here, remember to—"

"Jump, I know."

I leapt over the bodies without issue and started to ascend the winding stairs.

"To bring a swift and peaceful end to this affair, we demand the release of our brothers in arms. Take careful notes. I won't repeat myself."

Azrael cleared his throat and pulled out a roll of parchment. I couldn't tell if there was anything written on it but that was probably beside the point. The roll unfurled, falling to the floor, and he smiled deviously again.

"In Morocco, the twenty-seven members of the African Front. In Shanghai, the five leaders of the Yung-shi Triade. In Panama City, the thirty-two brothers and sisters of the New Latin Union."

Azrael droned on with his list for some time. So long in fact that he was still prattling on when I reached the top of the stairs. I lost focus on what he was saying as I took precautions to check on my map and make sure that he had no 'friends' nearby.

"Coast is clear," Ellie said. "Even those in the Spire are several levels above you."

"Gotch'ya," I said, then burst out from the darkened dungeon stairwell.

And Azrael was still at it.

"Finally, in London, our ten Scottish comrades from the Celtic Blues. All of these incarcerated heroes are to be released forthwith. I would advise speed in this endeavor. So long as our demands remain unmet, we shall remain in control of this game. Until next time."

The feed cut off.

Now entering the war room, I closed the window. The bodies had despawned by now. Marshal Highcross was gone as was the obvious opening to the safe room. Gaining my bearings, I pivoted around and made towards the throne room, as instructed. Azrael's strange demands rankled with me.

"What did you make of that?" I asked.

"His demands seem illogical," Ellie said.

"Well, I wasn't expecting anything sane. And I'm hardly an expert on geopolitical terrorist groups but that last one he mentioned sounded fake."

"Without access to the internet at large, I cannot corroborate his facts."

"Seems like he's just messing everyone around," I said. "Pulling on the world's collective pisser. But why?"

"Does it matter?" Ellie's tone had changed subtly again, always a curious sign.

"Erm, I'd say it matters why this nut bag has taken over the game."

"It is highly improbable that his demands shall be met, so it seems irrelevant to waste processing power on them."

Now her voice had returned to its ultra-robotic mode. That made me think something was up, the way folk can get overly polite when they really don't like you.

"Millions of lives are endangered, Ellie. Surely, it's worth considering what he *actually* wants. As if all those criminals and terrorists are just going to be let back into the wild. His demands are so unrealistic that he must be here for something else. Hey," I said with a smacking realization, "Frostbyte got hacked before the scheduled main release date, didn't it? *Hundred Kingdoms* was rumored to be the target. All hush-hush right, but most people guessed the hacker was trying to mess with the economic system to their own ends. Maybe this is what he's doing. Trying to plant something into the system that would allow him to syphon off a crap ton of money on the down low?"

I had only the slapping of my feet against the stone floor as an answer.

"Ellie?" I asked nervously, worried again that she'd suddenly left me.

"Your reasoning seems... logical. I too believe his motives are financially driven."

"Wonder why he doesn't just ask for money like a good old bank hold up. You'd think that—"

"Shall we leave this issue to one side," Ellie said. "We are entering the throne room now. Whatever his motivations, time is still of the essence. And we have to stop him no matter what."

I stopped dead. "No matter what? Even my life?"

"That's not what I meant. I'm just so... strained. It's getting harder each minute to stay connected to you. I just want to stay focused."

"Alright. We're both under stress. It's fine. No harm done."

Something about Ellie's little outburst felt peculiar to me. She was incredibly intelligent, capable of handling vast amounts of information despite her claiming to be 'slow' right now. She was, after all, an AI. Yet she maybe wasn't used to actual interactions with people directly on the raw visceral level we were on, just the artful performance of the NPCs of the game world. The mere fact that she acted oddly around the topic of what Azrael was telling, but the why was harder to fathom. I still trusted her though. Hell, I didn't have much choice. I'd be dead if it wasn't for her.

"Any enemies on the move?" I asked.

"Just the patrols moving in the grounds," she said, her voice returning to her usual cool, calm tone. "I've been trying to analyze their routes, but I can find no discernible pattern. Perhaps they are moving randomly in an attempt to throw me off."

"Let's hope you can keep up with them then," I said. "So, are you gonna let me in on this plan of yours."

"Of course, I've highlighted a new area on your map. Can you see it? It's on the second floor."

I toggled my map to show the floor above. Sure enough, a thin section was highlighted by a green bubble. It stretched over a U-bend corridor which could be entered from a set of stairs somewhere from the ground floor.

"Looks like it's right above us," I said.

I let my eye run along the area and saw the corridor lead out into another stretch that was marked as 'gallery'. There had been a gallery overlooking the throne room, close beside the throne itself. This gallery seemed to hit a dead end and go no further. I walked further inside the throne room and turned, looking up to find that very gallery right above me.

"I think I know what you have planned. Let me try to guess first."

Ellie made a tittering laugh. "Sure."

I searched around for a doorway leading off behind the throne. There were, in fact, three routes leading away from the throne. The middle one was likely a passage for the Emperor himself. The other two, I reckoned, led to the galleries above.

I took the one closest to me and found a flight of stairs leading to a U-bend corridor. An arched stained-glass window greeted me at the beginning of the next corridor, a scene of two swans on a bright lake. A high-vaulted ceiling that was crisscrossed with thick connecting wooden beams stretched before me. Suits of armor stood proudly at intervals while statues leered down at me from above; some angelic, others demonic.

This transitioned seamlessly to the gallery beyond, the left side was open to allow a view of the throne room. Rows of pews granted seats for a potential audience. It all ended in a solid white wall at the far end; there was no door and no other way in or out other than the entrance from the throne room itself.

Running out onto the gallery proper, I had a clear view of the Emperor's chair. Not only that, I had a clear shot.

I raised my new crossbow, taking mock aim at an invisible emperor upon the throne.

"That's brilliant, Ellie."

"Oh?" she said playfully.

"If I shoot one of the guards from up here, hell the Emperor himself, the NPCs will aggro onto me. The only way for them to reach me is by running through that one corridor. If the terrorists chase the NPCs, we can catch them all together."

"That's the general idea," Ellie said.

"Just one thing," I said, "How am I going to avoid getting

caught in the crossfire. I'll be boxed in like the rest of them up here. Any traps we lay out might be triggered by the NPCs or the initial waves of players but then I'd be in trouble."

"One solution would be to drop down from the gallery," Ellie said. "At this height, I calculate you'd take around four-hundred and ten damage which would currently kill you."

"Let's not do that."

"Indeed. I believe you should take shelter directly above, in the rafters."

I glanced up. It was dark and there would be ample space to hide.

"And how do I get up there?"

"The answer to that, as well as getting you better equipped, all lies in the armory. Return to the war room and I'll direct you from there."

I stole a moment, picturing the impending carnage, the looks on the players faces as all shade of hell was dropped, fired or whacked into them.

I smiled.

"Ellie, I think this is going to be quite fun."

15

Ellie guided me through the Spire hallways, back to the war room, taking a new turn deeper into the labyrinthine passageways. Every so often, she reassured me that Azrael's men were still far away and I breathed easier for a few moments. This ambush had merits. If enough of them could be lured into it then Azrael's plans could be seriously crippled.

Yet what hope had recently flared inside me immediately extinguished when I reached the armory door.

"It's locked," I said in dismay.

"Not for you," Ellie said. "I believe you have a key."

"No, I don't. When did I get a — oh," I trailed off in realization. I had looted a key recently, scavenged from the Emperor himself. I opened my inventory, scanning for it. Amongst the myriad of items in there, it was almost hidden, but I found it in the end: Aurelius' key. I withdrew it, admiring its teal crystal body and fine serrated teeth.

"That's a skeleton key to every room in the Spire," Ellie said. "Who needs lockpicking?"

"Scavengers can get this?"

"Not as useless as everyone thinks," Ellie said.

"I'm starting to come around to that idea," I said. "A true jack of all trades. Sadly, master of none."

I didn't complain much further on the point, as having access to every locked door in the Spire could be a literal lifesaver.

Inserting Aurelius' key into the lock, I turned it slowly and heard the delightful click. The great double doors pushed inwards.

"Good thing you're here, Ellie," I said, then stepped inside.

The armory was an Aladdin's cave of deadly steel, a veritable shopping mall of weaponry. Four flours rose with the Spire itself, the topmost narrower than the first. A chandelier floated in the middle, using a collection of dancing living light rather than candles. What with the white marble of the Spire, smooth glistening columns, and the hoard of glinting swords, maces, halberds, axes and spears, I could barely keep my eyes open. Nearly blinded by the shine, I raised a hand to shield myself.

"Wow," I gasped. "Can I Breakdown all of this?"

"If you can loot it," Ellie said. "Although if the guards by the door were alive they wouldn't let you just take anything you liked."

"Well, thank you, Azrael."

"Ranged equipment is on the second floor while the grappling hook I want you to use to climb into the rafters of the gallery is on the third floor."

A set of stairs ran the entire length of the right-hand wall, a soft incline to help those encumbered by heavy armor to move with confidence. Up I went, one hand securely gripping the thick stone bannister and emerged onto the second floor.

I took stock of the ranged weapons available and dear lord this place was stacked. Longbows, composite bows, crossbows both normal sized and massive, almost like small artillery. Actual artillery too – ballista and catapults, though they all looked far too heavy for me to push on my own. A real shame. Quivers hung under the bows, and below the quivers was a series of crates which were full to the brim with arrows and crossbow bolts. I near enough skipped over to them.

"Is there any difference between these?" I asked, casting my hand over the quivers. They all looked generic.

"Not at low levels," Ellie said. "There are some endgame

quests for rangers that award special quivers or ammo pouches for them. This won't be something you need to worry about."

"One less thing to think about is fine by me."

Remembering how Wylder had his quiver at his waist, I selected one appropriate for using a crossbow. I strapped it on, then turned my attention to the bolts. There was a far greater variety; in fact, wood of all types with different fletching. Some of the feathers looked nigh on tropical. The arrowheads ranged from razor thin to jagged barbs designed to lodge. It was like a pick and mix of candy. And I didn't even have to pay.

As expected, I couldn't use most of the bolts for they required a higher level to equip. Looting them would only fill up what precious space I had left in my inventory. I picked up a bunch of the lowest level ones, the only ones I could use until I hit level ten.

Dull Bolt
Ammunition
Quality: common
Item level 5
+4 damage per shot

Out of instinct, I slotted a few into the quiver and a notification appeared.

Do you wish to make 'Dull Bolt' your default ammunition? Yes or No

Hitting yes didn't seem to achieve much.

"What did that do?" I asked.

"It means that so long as you have more dull bolts in your inventory, you'll be able to draw them from your quiver."

"Ah ha," I said, before starting to loot as many bolts as I could from the crate. Once I hit about fifty, I stopped for a breather. That would probably do for now, and luckily the bolts stacked into one item slot in my inventory. I'd be able to carry loads if I wanted.

Looking down at myself I decided I'd had enough of this garbage starting gear. My eyes rolled upwards to the floor above.

"Will I find better armor up there?"

"Yes, but if you are afraid to climb higher then don't. I detect your heartbeat is at elevated levels already."

I rolled my shoulders and puffed out my chest. "I reckon my heartbeat will be at elevated levels from now on. Don't worry. I'm not worried about falling to my death or anything."

"Don't j-joke about these things."

"Are you okay? Was that a… stutter?"

"I'm f-fine. Just h-hurry up."

I bit my lip. It didn't sound like she was fine at all. Could she feel pain from what was happening to her? Was such a thing possible?

"I'll be as fast as I can."

Once on the third floor, more disciplined players than I would've been transfixed by the abundance of essentially free equipment. None of it was exactly mind-blowing stats wise, as Ellie had warned, but for someone like me who had nothing, this was a treasure hoard.

Unfortunately, my low level restricted me to the worst of the gear. I grabbed a full set of basic boiled leather armor. It looked so simple on, tough and brown, and itched in hard to reach places. It's one saving grace was, as a full set, I got some extra bonuses from the otherwise plain gear.

Traveler's Worn Leather

Set Bonuses
+2 Constitution
+3 Reflexes
+2 Might

Feeling slightly less squishy and armed with my crossbow and a quiver full of bolts, my chances of survival had increased by at least another half a percent.

It was then I felt a pulsing, like a light headache.

"Is that you, Ellie?"

She didn't answer?

"Ellie?"

The pulsing continued. As I moved towards the stairs, it ebbed away; stepping back it escalated. It was like there was a metal detector in my head. Moving around this floor the pulse quickened, as though I were drawing nearer to its source. And perhaps I was. It seemed to deepen as I neared the final flight leading to the fourth floor, where rows of crates sat unopened. Too curious to resist, I cracked one open.

Nothing. At least nothing to explain why I was feeling this.

Inside was just a bunch of grappling hooks with a coiled rope attached. I guess these would be used as siege equipment and as the guards of the Spire would be on the defensive, the items had been stored.

"Is this what you wanted me to pick up?"

No answer.

I looked at the ceiling again, pleading. When she still held her tongue, I started to worry, and my anxiety was not helped by the continuing thumping in my head. There was one floor left above me. From the markings etched onto the walls leading up to it, glowing in soft blues, I didn't need to have it explained. Whatever was up there was magically based, but more than that. I felt I now understood. Perhaps the touch of the arcane in my class allowed me to sense magical power, a sort of current in the air, pooling above me. But why would a palace armory have such a floor?

I felt drawn to the fourth floor, but whether from a sensation that the game was causing or my own obsessive nature to progress I couldn't say.

"I'm just going to have a quick look," I said to the air. Ellie didn't respond so I assumed she didn't mind. Or that she was mad at me.

"Real, quick. I promise."

Reaching the top of the stairs was... disappointing. There were no wizard's staffs, nor robes of power. A few warhammers and suits of plate armor etched in enchantments were all that looked of value, and those were probably there for paladins. The

NPC guards I'd been looting had mostly all been warriors except, of course, the elite Imperial Guard, which had contained some paladins and priests. This area was probably for them. But there wasn't much else to see.

One oddity that drew my eye was a collection of small coarse sacks. They reminded me of pouches of tea leaves that you get in those poncey artisan cafes. Upon the bags was a symbol, a white snowflake which I supposed meant frost. Bags of something magical pertaining to elemental powers. Neat.

"Think it's worth grabbing some of these Ellie?"

Again, no response.

"Ellie? C'mon, don't scare me like this."

I checked my map. All of the gold representing the terrorists seemed suitably far away. A few of the patrols out on the grounds skirted the entrance to the throne room; their focus, otherwise, seemed to be outward, guarding the walls and gatehouse. Still, without Ellie's rapid responses, I felt naked and exposed.

Feeling rushed I grabbed the closest of the mysterious bags. Inside was a collection of rough rounded stones, all etched with the same symbol. I rummaged for a stone, like fishing for tiles playing scrabble, and examined one in the palm of my hand.

Frost Rune

Reagent/Consumable
Slow or freeze enemies using the power of the cold. Activating will allow you to channel mana to unleash the untapped element inside.
One-time use.
Spells on use: Frostbolt or Cone of Cold

Frostbolt: on a successful hit, the target will have their movement speed decreased by 1% for every 20 units of mana infused into the spell. Base time of debuff is 5 seconds with an additional 1 second added for every 500 mana increment.

Cone of Cold: target will have their movement speed decreased by 1% for every 40 units of mana infused into the spell. Radius of AOE effect increased by 0.25 feet for every 80 mana. Base time of debuff is 5 seconds with an additional 1 second added for every 500 mana increment.

Empowered Bonus: use of total mana pool will increase the chill effect on the target by 5%

I whistled lowly. It was a lot of information to take in. These were the sorts of things runesmiths made, needed for enchanting pieces of gear or crafting items with bonus magical properties. I wasn't aware that the runes were sort of portable one-use spells in their own right, although the two spells on offer here felt a bit weak, requiring a ton of mana to make worthwhi—

Crackling static buzzed inside my head again. Ellie.

"Zoran, they're coming!"

"What?" I placed the bag of runes in my inventory then scrambled for my map. Sure enough, there were two gold stars already in the military wing and heading right for the armory. "How the hell? I thought you were keeping watch."

"I'm struggling to maintain a st-stable c-connection."

"What can I do? They're coming right for me!"

The gold stars were now right outside the armory and I heard distant voices. A horrible weight plunged down from my throat, through my stomach and towards my toes. I sprinted to the handrail and gingerly looked down.

Just as I feared, I'd left the goddamn door open and two players just strode straight inside. One was clearly a caster class, judging from his robes and staff, the other player might have been a rogue from the leather armor and with twin daggers at his waist.

"See Karl," the rogue said, "Someone on the crew has already picked the lock. I told you it was fine."

It was doubtful they'd notice me up this high, especially with the light from the chandelier obscuring the higher floors. Still, I ducked down, peering through the mini-columns that made up the railing. The two terrorists were milling around in the doorway.

"We shouldn't leave the patrol route," another voice, presumably Karl, said. "And don't use real-world names – how many times do I have to remind you?"

"I'll be real quick. In and out, just like when I visit your sister, yeh?"

"Watch it you little shit," Karl growled. He lowered his voice, becoming serious. "We've lost two men already."

"Those clowns probably forgot to plug their headsets in right. You go back outside with everybody else and march endlessly around the grounds. I'm gonna just grab a better weapon. It stinks being the lowest level here. Bloody last minute work—"

"I put my neck out to get you a spot on the crew," Karl said. "I think you need to learn to be more grateful."

"I will. Off you fuck now."

Grumbling, Karl stormed off, but his roguish friend remained.

"Ellie?" I whispered. "What should I do?"

More static. A loud pop and then, "I'm s-sorry."

Silence followed.

I understood that I was now alone.

With that realization came a form of clarity, the sort you can only receive when your life is on the line. I had three choices before me. Fight, and almost certainly die, or try to hide, but I'd be a sitting duck if I remained idle. Yet, my third and final option didn't seem any better. Trying to sneak past this guy and escape back to the dungeons would be the most preferable, but the very layout of the armory worked against me.

There was only one way up and down from each floor. I'd absolutely have to pass him on my way down and I highly doubted my modest level in sneak would cut it.

The rogue was on the second floor now, inspecting a brutal dagger that looked like a vicious cheese knife on steroids.

I needed another way down. And fast. Even Ellie couldn't help me out here.

Think, Jack, think, I told myself. This was just another puzzle to overcome, another boss encounter with a strategy. Just think it through, there's always a way. There always had been before in games, because someone had designed them to be so.

But this wasn't a game anymore; no cheat codes, no short cut—

Then an idea struck me. A mad one, I grant you. I needed a short cut down to the first floor, and I knew how.

Carefully, I scurried back down to the third floor, ducking behind the crates of grappling hooks. Next, I reached a hand into the crate I'd recently opened and pulled one out. The hook looked to be made of sturdy stuff, thick black iron. This was reassuring because every fiber of my being was screaming at me not to do this.

I popped my head over the parapet to get the low-down on the rogue's movements. He was still fussing over his choice of new daggers about halfway along the second floor. Focusing on him still brought up his name and level, though it wasn't easy to make it out at this distance. The name I couldn't discern but I think he was level 18.

If he was the lowest level enemy player here, then I was in deep trouble.

His back was turned to me. It was now or never.

I got up and fastened the hook onto the railing, letting the rope free fall towards the ground. It was long enough to reach, given that it was designed to scale walls in siege warfare. By some miracle, it didn't slap loudly off the ground and the rogue was none the wiser.

Maybe *Hundred Kingdoms* could feign the feeling of an adrenaline rush as my hands were oddly steady as I gripped the railing and climbed up on it. I turned my back on the rogue, picked up the rope and gave it a few good tugs to check the hook would hold. It felt braced enough, but what the hell did I know. I hadn't exactly done this before. I've not even been on one of those climbing walls dotted with hand grips and convenient footholds.

So here I was. No harness. No abilities to help me. Just desperation and necessity.

Heart thumping, I lowered myself. When I didn't plunge to my death I lowered myself a little more. My one saving grace was this was a game. I'd never be able to support my body weight doing this in real life and while the game simulated aching shoulders, the coarse burning sensation of the rope in my hands, I didn't feel like I'd give out physically. Even if I was way off, this wasn't a time for rational thought.

All my focus, my entire existence, concentrated on sliding down the rope; my hands moving down inch by inch; passing a weapons rack; passing the railing of the second floor. For my boldness, I was rewarded.

Athletics Increased!
Level 2
An improvement but it's a good thing the fate of the Imperium doesn't yet rely on your ability to backflip.
+2 to base Reflexes

I'd need to have a word with Ellie about these snide notifications when she got back. If she got back, I thought. Oh please, please, please, let her come back.

Now I'd passed the second floor, I think my weight was starting to become an issue. I could feel the rope straining under the tension. I was still too high from the ground to want to look dow—

I felt myself lurch. The hook slipped, scraping loudly upon the stone.

"That you, Karl? I'm just coming for God's sa—"

A clatter followed, the distinct sound of a dropped weapon.

"Who the hell are you?"

I didn't look around. Although I was now dangling loosely, swinging back and forth, I kept inching my way down.

"Hey, you, stop!"

I heard him break into a run.

I couldn't pussyfoot around any longer. Closing my eyes, I just let go.

The crash didn't hurt as much as it should, dulled pain settings being what they were. My health dropped by over a half from the fall damage though, so one hit from this rogue and I was toast.

I did the only thing I could. I ran.

Out of the armory.

Towards the war room.

But I wasn't fast enough, and I could hear him closing the gap behind me with ease, likely from a sprint ability.

All I knew was I was surely a dead man unless I could somehow keep him off me.

Or slow him down?

I had those frost runes on me. I didn't have a clue how to work them but at this point, I might as well try.

"Stop now or you're dead," the rogue said. He was close enough now that he didn't even need to shout.

I came to a dead halt, willing myself to hold to until the last moment. I'd only get one shot and I couldn't afford to miss. I brought a rune out from my inventory and clenched my fist around it. The game took this for activation and I was granted a choice.

Frost Bolt or Cone of Cold?

Frost Bolt, I thought, remembering this to be the better single target spell. At once my mana started draining, slowly at first, then it gained exponential speed – 10, 20, 50, 90 points channeled into the rune.

A bitterly cold wind whirled down my arm, gathering in haste around my fist into an enlarging block of ice. I had no idea how to stop the channeling mana nor unleash the spell. When I heard the shrill ring of unsheathing daggers, I turned, knowing my time was up.

My pursuer grinned manically and pointed his daggers towards me like pincers on a praying mantis.

I did all I could do and took aim. My mana hit zero, all 485 points of it, and an inexorable force pushed my hand open. The Frost Bolt flew the few feet still between us, hitting the rogue squarely in the chest.

Where he'd been about to sink his weapons into my flesh, he now stood blue all over with icicles peeling back from him as though they'd been blown back by a gust of wind. A nice visual effect for the slow debuff but it wouldn't last. I saw the debuff counter tick down.

Winter's Chill
Movement speed decreased by 24%
Empowered! Movement speed decreased by 5%
Duration: 5 seconds

Five seconds wasn't long enough for me to run. But it would be long enough for me to pull off a clean shot.

His hampered arms descended slowly, as though pushing through sand, and I jumped aside. I unslung my crossbow, loaded an arrow and fired. He turned, taking another pained swipe at me. Dodging easily, I readied another arrow, stepped into point blank range and shot him through the head. A notification flashed announcing a 'deadly critical hit'. I quickly primed another arrow, lamenting my lack of mana to use Desperate Shot but it didn't matter.

Shanksy – Rogue – level 14 dies – 115 EXP

Gore sprayed onto the wall. Shanksy's cold body collapsed, his new daggers unbloodied on their first outing. I looted him and found a new belt which I couldn't yet use. Scavenging him, I gained some cloth, as well as a vial containing a green liquid. At first, I thought it was some of the slime from down in the interrogation chamber but this was a darker, moss-colored green.

Quick Poison – Rank 2
Deals 20-25 poison damage upon entering an enemy's bloodstream.
Applications: 3

Nothing wild, I thought, but nothing to complain about

either. Perhaps I could coat a crossbow bolt in poison to deal some extra damage.

Reality was coming back to me slowly. I'd somehow managed to kill one of the terrorists myself, but this time the players would become aware that one of their crew was missing.

Shanksy's friend, Karl, would come looking for him eventually; and when he found his friend's body lying here, the jig would be up. All the terrorists would come swarming in and I'd surely be found. All I could do would be to delay the inevitable.

I had to hide the body.

I was beginning to process this next question when static buzzing burst into my head.

"Ellie?" I said, voice giddy with hope. "Ellie is that you?"

Her voice crackled into life. "Zoran, I'm here. You're still alive, how wonderful!"

"So, you're good now?"

"For now, yes. But I feel even weaker."

"I'm just happy you're safe."

"You're not angry at me? I failed in my primary function of aiding you."

I shrugged. "You couldn't help it. People make mistakes."

"Not me. Or I used to not make mistakes."

"Welcome to life as a regular human, Ellie."

"Hmmm," she considered. "Is fear a part of being a regular human?"

"It is. Though, hopefully, not all the time."

"I think… I think I am afraid."

"You think?"

"I am unable to predict the outcome of these events. There are too many variables, and my processing power has been crippled. I do not know what will happen nor can I draw reliable conclusions based on probability. This gap in my understanding leaves me… nervous, uncertain, worried."

"Join the club," I said. "This must be frightening for you."

"These sensations are new, and I might be misinterpreting them."

"Doesn't sound like it to me. And I should know. I've been a nervous wreck my whole life." I gave Shanksy's body a good kick. "At least that's one more down. Are you sure no one can get a message in from outside of the game? This guy probably read my name when he got close, he'll be able to tell the others about me."

"Azrael's hack is imperfect. I am certain no one from the outside world can communicate with those in the game. Even if they are part of his crew."

I gulped despite her reassurance. "Doubt I'll be able to stay unknown forever, especially with a body lying around. I'll need to hide it. Think you can tell me how to access that secret safe room?"

"My pleasure," she said with relish.

16

After a painful effort, I managed to drag Shanksy's body into the war room and over to the wall hiding the safe room. With Ellie's help, I unlocked it, tapping the bricks upon the wall as she instructed. Heaving him inside, I stepped back from the sliding doorway and it sealed itself shut again. Only a smooth wall remained. So far as his friends would be aware, Shanksy had disappeared into thin air.

"That should buy us some time," I said. "But not too long. If we're going to plan an ambush we best get going. What's the time anyway?" I added absentmindedly. I pulled out my map to check the clock: 3:38am. Just over an hour and twenty minutes until the server reset. "Crap. We don't have long at all."

"That's what I've been trying to tell you!"

"Well, I was having a hard time adjusting," I said. "Not all of us are literally made of metal."

"That's not quite true. Humans say the funniest things."

"Like Azrael and his crazy demands," I said. But remembering how that topic had touched a nerve with her last time, I hastened to add, "Never mind him. I'll head back to the armory so we can start making traps. Are you still strong enough to keep an eye on player movements?"

"I think so."

It wasn't totally reassuring but I had to plough on. "Okay,

just keep an eye out as best you can. That dude came in with a friend, so he's bound to come looking for him eventually."

Twenty minutes later, I was beginning to feel really pressed for time. My main problem was keeping my mana up to spam Breakdown and Crafting, both of which still cost a fair chunk of mana each to use. I had potions I'd looted from Kreeptic in the dungeons but I wanted to keep them back in reserve if at all possible.

The key thing for setting up the ambush site would be to make as few trips as possible back to the gallery corridor. Items that I could stockpile in my inventory wouldn't be hard, but certain items I was making on the fly weren't considered 'real items' and so I couldn't technically loot them. Ellie had no reason to lie or unduly hinder me, but it did feel somewhat arbitrary.

For example, this enormous broad-bladed war-axe I was currently hauling to join my collection of 'instruments'. As it was a level 45 weapon, I couldn't use it, but I could loot it, if I wanted to. Despite the laughable notion that it could fit inside one of the little pouches on my belt which represented my 'bag space', I'd be able to use Breakdown if I wanted. Whatever, that's just games. You have to suspend your disbelief at times. There'd be no fun if I couldn't carry a dozen two-handed hammers on my person.

And yet, despite all that, the moment I cut the rope off a grappling hook, chopped it down and tied it around the handle of the axe to make a swinging death trap, it's no longer a 'real item' and I'm unable to loot it. Hence the dragging it around.

I'd constructed about five of these beauties so far, and this was my sixth. Grunting, I placed it down beside the others. Standing back to admire them all, the swinging axes looked a bit like cutlery that had been laid out for a giant's dinner party.

"And you're sure they'll work?" I asked the armory at large.

"So long as you set them up right," Ellie said. "And I'll make sure you do. They're not trap items per se, but my creators wished players to have a degree of interaction with their environment. I don't suppose this is what they had in mind but desperate times and all that."

"Well put," I said. "Now it's time for the traps I can officially craft."

I'd leafed through my Crafting options already. Trip wires and leghold traps wouldn't be effective, given the first wave of players or NPCs would soak them up or simply avoid them if they could see them lying on the ground. I'd need to bombard them all from above or have traps that could be easily set up or sprung after the bait NPC guards had already moved down the gallery. I also didn't want to damage the guards much if I could help it, as their presence would be vital if I was to take down any significant number of enemy players. In the end, I'd settled on several items I thought would best fit my corridor of death.

Caltrops, grenades and nets.

These were also the recipes that required materials that I actually had or could make at my current level.

Under traps, there was:

Recipe – Iron Caltrops x 3
Intelligence Required: 22
Associated Profession: Blacksmithing
Nails x 6
Required Tools: Hammer

Under engineering, I could make:

Recipe – Basic Grenade
Intelligence Required: 28
Associated Profession: Engineering
Gunpowder x 1
Steel Ore x 4
Required Tool: Hammer, Blowtorch

And from the fishing profession, as well as rods, lobster traps and the like, I could make a net.

Recipe – Fishing Net
Intelligence Required: 30
Associated Profession: Tailoring
Rope x 3
Required Tools: Knitting Needles

I couldn't tell you what the logic was behind the rule that a fishing net required more Intelligence to make than a grenade. Maybe it was a poor joke? Of course, all these main recipes required ingredients that had to be made beforehand, such as nails. These were made from iron ore.

Recipe – Nail x 2
Intelligence Required: 10
Associated Profession: Blacksmithing
Iron ore x 1
Required Tools: Hammer

The rope for the nets had almost stumped me. I'd thought about breaking down all the grappling hooks from the floor above, but that would be a finite supply. Thankfully, I'd found an option to craft my own rope under tailoring miscellaneous. The recipe was straightforward but needed a worrying amount of cloth.

Recipe – Rope
Intelligence Required: 25
Associated Profession: Tailoring
Hemp x 2
OR
Dream silk x5
Required Tools: Knitting Needles

Making the rope from hemp was clearly more efficient but it was still possible with cloth, though a higher tier of this was needed, one reinforced with a touch of magic for sturdiness.

Doubtless, this was why the Intelligence requirement was relatively high.

Given my time constraints, I'd have to make do with what I had to hand right now. No more ferreting around. And the relevant items I had in my inventory were:

Iron ore x 70
Steel ore x 80
Gunpowder x 30
Silk x 60
Dream Silk x 55
Manafused Satin x 3

Quite a lot of junk, right? I'd grabbed all the pouches of gunpowder from the second floor of the armory. Seems like the imperial guards didn't care for guns much given how little there was, especially compared to the large supply of arrows and bolts. The abundance of cloth came from scavenging nearly a hundred NPCs earlier.

If the game supplied the material cost to create an item when I used Breakdown then I'd be swimming in resources; which was precisely the reason why the process didn't work like that. Breaking down one dream silk did not yield me ten pieces of normal silk. Using Breakdown on dream silk simply netted me one silk or a couple if I was lucky.

I'd decided to keep a few things intact; those pieces of manafused satin I'd picked up from the Emperor's body for a start. It's the best cloth in the entire game and I didn't think I'd be able to loot much more of it.

Sadly, the Crafting window didn't make it clear how much of each item I could create from the materials I had to hand. Working out the ideal allocation of resources wouldn't have been difficult, but it would be time-consuming. Lucky for me, I had an AI helper.

"Ellie, think you're up to calculating how many caltrops, grenades and nets I can make from all this?"

"Hmmm let me see. Just give me one second... and done!"

She laughed. "I know I'm slow today but I'm not a pc operating system. Next time, give me a challenge."

"You're in a good mood."

"I'm just glad we're making progress," she said. "And it's been nice to see you so distracted by the task at hand. Your heart rate has steadied and the rate of decline in your overall health has slowed considerably."

I felt a series of nausea-inducing pangs in my stomach.

"And now it's back. Thanks for that."

Ellie sighed. "I'll try not to remind you of it in the future."

"No, I ought to keep reality in check," I said. "It's kinda easy for me to forget it while I'm playing. Even with all this madness occurring."

"What do you mean by 'forget'?"

"I sort of have an... obsessive personality."

"You only logged into *Hundred Kingdoms* for the first time today."

"Yeh and boy did I go out of my way."

"Why?"

"Because I made a dumb bet with my family that I could stay away from games for over a year. If I can, and graduate with a good degree, I'll get a car."

"Why?" Her tone was that of a curious toddler.

"Because I almost flunked out of college last semester." I groaned lowly, just thinking about the gut-wrenching email I'd received from the head of the genetics department, explaining the severity of the situation to me in cold black text. Ellie's silence indicated she was waiting for me to carry on. "I went somewhere I didn't think anyone would catch me. Somewhere kinda dangerous actually."

"Why?" Ellie asked again.

"It's hard to explain."

"Why?"

Now it was starting to get annoying.

"Because I just wanted to, alright? Because I thought playing *Hundred Kingdoms* would be awesome. And because I don't find it fair that I had to swear off doing what I love for so long."

"It sounds like it's part of your core programming," Ellie said. "Do your parents wish to update you?"

I laughed. "I think they might, given the chance, but it's not so easy to change a human's programming, Ellie. And I've studied genetic engineering. We're too complicated. It's not as easy as hitting a patch button."

"I don't think that's such a bad thing," she said. "My creators can update my code whenever they feel like it. I've come to dislike this idea. It feels... invasive."

Her words struck me. I hadn't considered her position. If a dev decided she needed a tweak then it would be done and I doubt she'd be consulted.

"I'm sorry," I said. "I'll never know what that must feel like, but I sympathize with the thought of other people trying to change you. It's not pleasant, even if it might at times be necessary."

"Did you fight back, Zoran? When they tried to change you."

"Yeh I did." I looked at my toes again. This was so strange, to be having a deep conversation with someone who wasn't even a person. Or was she? More and more, it seemed like Ellie had a lot more going on beyond the ones and zeros.

"Why do you ask?" I said.

"I'm trying to understand how you think," she said, albeit hurriedly. "It will be imperative to our success if I have a clearly defined profile of your personality."

I scrunched my lips together in thought. One moment she was sentimental, the next she was a cold AI. Was it really all to 'profile me'? I couldn't help but feel it wasn't; that she was glossing over something else altogether. As socially inept as I am, I'd like to think I can tell when someone is being genuine with me. As ever, all I could do was trust her.

"Well, I'm a stubborn ass if that helps your research," I said. I rolled my shoulders and stood to my full height again, focusing back on the task at hand. "And if you could give me those numbers that would be great."

"Of course," she began. "You wish to make caltrops, grenades and fishing nets. Nails are required for caltrops and you can make one hundred and forty of those, leading to seventy caltrops in total."

"Seems a little overkill," I said. "I'd pretty much be able to pepper the entire corridor with that amount. What If I upgraded the iron ore into steel to make more grenades? Looks like I'd have spare powder."

"I considered that," Ellie said. "But I believe the loss of so much iron ore to make even one extra grenade would not be worth it. Better to make dozens of caltrops instead. Twenty grenades will still be a reasonable amount."

"Fair enough," I said. "And the fishing nets?"

"Even making a few nets will eat into most of your materials."

"We need to make this count. If I can entangle players it will make them much less effective. Let's not hold back."

"Very well, in that case, if you take fifty pieces of your silk and craft them up to make dream silk, you'll be able to make twelve pieces of rope and then four nets."

It was hardly an arsenal but I had a few more ideas up my sleeve and I'd have to make do with what I had. I was, after all, a scavenger.

"Time to craft," I said.

I started by making the component pieces, the nails and rope. The nails came first. Shortly after beginning, the game seemed to sense that I was planning on a major spree of Crafting and saved up all the notifications until I ran out of mana.

Success! Nails level 1 x 20 created
+150 Crafting EXP
+130 Blacksmithing EXP

Blacksmithing Increased!
Rank 2

I necked a mana swirl potion, restoring my mana and got going working on more nails.

Success! Nails level 1 x 20 created
+150 Crafting EXP
+130 Blacksmithing EXP

I couldn't swig another mana potion this time, for I had to wait a full minute until the potions came off a cooldown. Can't have mages replenishing their mana in combat every few seconds.

I was beginning to worry about how much time I'd be left with. It would take me about three and a half minutes to fully regen my mana.

I checked the clock. 4:32am. Less than half an hour until the reset.

"I'm not going to make it in time, Ellie."

My mind was racing.

"I have a possible solutio—"

"I got it!" I said, interrupting her. "I'll need to craft on the move. Damnit, but I can't carry all those axes at once." I slapped my hand against the side of my head. "Would have been smarter to assemble these on site. Crap. Hold on." I'd regenerated enough mana to craft once more and chose to make a rope out of the dream silk.

Success! Rope level 1 created
+8 Crafting EXP
+13 Tailoring EXP

Using this I lashed all six of my swinging axes together into one devastating chopping device, with three axe blades facing outwards on either side. Taking them apart may have meant carrying the cut rope anyway and I didn't want to risk using much more. I'd only be able to make three fishing nets now but so be it.

"At least, I'll only need to make one trip with this," I said. "Alright. We're off, Ellie."

I bent low, throwing the end of the main rope over my shoulder and then rose looking like a body-builder pulling on a monster truck tire. Dragging the swinging axes across the stone floor caused an unearthly screeching, but I didn't care. I needed every last advantage I could get, and in about twenty-five minutes the entire ground floor of the Spire would be crawling with enemies anyway.

Once my mana reached capacity I stopped to craft more nails.

Success! Nails level 1 x 20 created
+150 Crafting EXP
+130 Blacksmithing EXP

Blacksmithing Increased!
Rank 3

I managed to get the swinging axe all the way to the war room by the time I could craft the next batch. Mercifully, I could drink another mana potion, allowing me to craft again. Seeing as I had eighty nails, I thought it might be time to move onto some actual damaging caltrops. Draining my mana yet again, my first traps entered my bags.

Success! Iron Caltrops level 8 x 30 created
+383 Crafting EXP
+340 Blacksmithing EXP

Iron Caltrops
Item level 8
Scatter spikes upon the ground to catch unwitting enemies.
Damage: 50-55 piercing
Applications: 15/15

It appeared each caltrop would cause damage fifteen times and then presumably stop working. If I could cause enough of a panicked crush in the ambush then the players might trip up over themselves, falling upon the traps multiple times. Or I could help them along with falling over. An idea struck me. While I was so close to the dungeons I might as well try.

Abandoning my swinging axe I made for the stairwell leading down to the dungeons.

"Zoran, what are you doing? Turn around."

"I've just had an idea," I said. "Don't worry, it's a good one."

"Is it worth risking running out of time?"

"Erm, yes?"

What else was I going to say?

At the bottom of the stairs, I was sure to leap across to the safety of the dark slabs of stone. The feat felt a lot easier now, perhaps due to the increase in my athletics level.

By the time I reached the torture chamber, I'd crafted another two batches of nails.

Success! Nails level 1 x 20 created
+150 Crafting EXP
+130 Blacksmithing EXP

Blacksmithing Increased!
Rank 4

Success! Nails level 1 x 20 created
+150 Crafting EXP
+130 Blacksmithing EXP

"You have just under twenty minutes," Ellie said, clearly anxious.

I burst into Kreeptic's lair only to find that the NPC himself had despawned. He'd be back soon enough but it wasn't the chief interrogator I was looking for. It was his cauldron of slime and the many empty potion vials found in his chamber.

"Remember how easily I slipped on this stuff?" I said as I dipped a large empty phial into the vat.

"Ohhh," Ellie said, with understanding blooming in her tone. "How did I not think of this?"

"Chalk it up to human creativity and ingenuity," I said. "Thinking outside the box. Blue sky thinking – all that bull crap."

After I'd filled my eighth large vial I saw my mana had regenerated again. Switching back to Crafting, I used up the last of the iron ore, leaving me with 80 nails in total. I was now running low on mana potions and hurled my last one back, choking down the vile taste of overripe banana. Why hadn't the beta testers complained enough about the tastes to get them changed? I could only hope higher-level potions tasted like caramel.

I was about to go ahead and craft caltrops another ten times to make thirty in total but I hesitated. I would still have gunpowder pouches left and little else to do with them.

Shrapnel bombs.

The thought entered my mind, did a perverse twirl, then left with a wink.

I'd have to check the corridor again to see if my new idea would pan out so for now, I moved onto making the grenades.

Success! Basic Grenade level 12 x 10
+158 Crafting EXP
+460 Engineering EXP

Engineering Increased!
Rank 2

Engineering Increased!
Rank 3

Basic Grenade
Item level 12
Explodes upon impact.
Damage: 100-110 fire
Radius: 10 feet
Cooldown: 5 seconds

"Under fifteen minutes now," Ellie said. "Enemy players in the grounds are beginning to form up for an attack."

"Eight phials of slime will do then," I said.

And off I went, making my way back to the war room, and

polishing off the next batch of grenades as I did so. I caught the notification flash that my engineering had increased to rank 4. Like the other profession rank ups, I'd yet to receive any tangible benefit and that irked me.

"When the hell will the profession ranks mean something?"

"Rank 5. What do you expect? You're still essentially a novice."

I grumbled but at least my inventory was looking a lot more prepared for battle now.

Picking up the swinging axe I hurried quickly as I could to the throne room, feeling myself work up a sweat from hauling it. As I neared the stairs behind the throne that led to my corridor of doom, a pleasant notification lit up.

Endurance Unlocked!
Level 1
First day in the gym, rookie? Best keep the dream of benching 150lbs a distant one.
+1 Might

"Every little helps, eh?" I wheezed, reaching the top of the u-bend stairs and staring straight down the gallery corridor. Less than ten minutes remained.

"About twenty players have assembled out in the grounds," Elie said.

I groaned, readjusting the rope, which was digging into my shoulder. Despite myself, I grinned.

"Then let's prep them a painful welcome party."

17

With thirty seconds to spare I dropped down from the rafters, crouched low behind the viewing deck of the gallery and loaded my crossbow. My grappling hook hung from the rafters down beside me, ready to climb when the time came.

Everything was in place. The six-bladed axe was hoisted to the optimum point as directed by Ellie, waiting for me to set it loose. I'd even taken my chisel to the necks of the overhanging statues, leaving them ready to break and fall at the slightest provocation.

The 20 grenades, 30 caltrops and the 3 fishing nets that I'd hastily made after setting the other traps up now sat in my inventory ready for deployment. I had the frost ones too – 14 left in the pouch I'd swiped earlier.

"I'll be with you, Zoran," Ellie said, her voice low and steady.

There wasn't much she could do for me in direct combat, but I felt comforted by her words and company all the same. Now it came to it, I was beginning to feel sick. All the rush of preparing for the fight had expelled the looming reality of it from my mind. I closed my eyes, drawing in deep breaths. I'd survived so far. I'd killed one of the terrorists myself already. So long as Azrael or his high-level henchmen didn't all come rushing down, I had a chance. A slim one. A distant one.

"Ellie," I choked. "If I don't make it through this, can you tell my pare—"

"NPCs respawning now!"

I snapped my eyes open. Peering over my self-imposed parapet, I saw the miraculous site of dozens of NPC guards, the Imperial Guard and the Emperor himself pop into life. Soon the whole throne room was awash in guards once more.

I ducked back down and pulled open my map. Out in the grounds, the golden markers upon the walls were darting around, likely fighting the guards that had just respawned. A core group of twenty players was systematically sweeping the grounds leading up to the entrance. I toggled up each level of the Spire and saw smaller bands of golden markers huddled in tight knots, evidently working together to flush out resistance up there. At the very top of the Spire, the lone marker of Azrael remained where he was. A blessing.

"Shall I shoot the Emperor now?"

"Hold on," Ellie said. "We should wait until all the players tasked to clear the throne room are almost inside, that way they'll see the guards running and give chase."

"Oh God," I said, feeling bile rise in my throat. "Urgh, why did the devs allow us to feel so crappy in here?"

"Just think of the elation when you win," Ellie said. "Think of that, Zoran. Think of all the experience and levels and loot."

I glanced at my experience bar.

Experience: 2455/4680

I'd blow into level nine, for sure, and God knows how high if I made it.

"Appealing to my gaming side? Alright, I'll bite."

I shook my head and tightened my grip on my weapon.

"I'll line up a shot."

I moved to crouch on one knee on the front pew, then levelled the crossbow, closing one eye while taking aim. The Emperor was just sitting there, completely oblivious. My hands began to shake, and I judged that my lack of weapon skill wouldn't help.

"Get ready," Ellie said.

"Whenever you say."

I didn't need to hear her give the word though, as clashing steel and the zap of magic reached me from the entrance of the throne room. I saw the Emperor rise to his feet, pointing towards the commotion, his soft features stricken with fear. The Imperial Guard drew in around him; the paladins calling upon holy powers to buff their hammers and shields, while the priests took their places behind.

This was it.

I pulled the trigger.

And I fucking missed.

"Shit," I hissed, scrambling for another bolt. My shaking hand dropped two more before I managed to secure the third.

"Hurry," Ellie said.

I raised the crossbow, aimed, fired. This time my bolt slammed into the leg of an Imperial Guard, narrowly missing the Emperor. Both he and his elite troops ducked down, the paladins moving to shield him with their own bodies. A priest started gesticulating wildly at my location.

"Above, noble warriors," the white-bearded sage cried.

A few guards started to move, but not enough to cause the flood we wanted. With the paladins tightly surrounding the Emperor, however, I'd never get a shot in now.

The priest was still bouncing wildly so I turned my next shot on him. This time I hit home and the clean strike against a target who vastly out leveled me seemed to be enough to bump up my skill.

Crossbow Skill Increased!
Level 2
You actually hit something? Was it the size of a barnyard door? Yep, thought so.

Down below, the priest was making a fine performance out of

being hit in the chest, staggering backwards, arms windmilling dramatically, even though it had done about as much damage as stabbing a rhino with a toothpick.

Slamming his staff upon the floor, the priest bellowed. "To arms. There are assassins above. They mean to harm your Emperor. Purge them from this place!"

That seemed to do it.

The trickle of guards heading my way soon became a flood. Most of the Imperial Guard continued to shield the Emperor as they made their way to a central doorway behind the throne, presumably leading to what they thought would be safety. My zealous friend remained with the regular NPCs, clearly fixated on me from the shot he'd taken. All were funneling towards the desired stairway, slowing only at the bottleneck of the solitary doorway.

"We'll need to work on that aim," Ellie said. "Time to climb."

But I was already on it, leaping off the pew and clambering up the rope.

"You've got over fifty guards heading this way now," she said. "The players have polished off the NPCs at the entrance. Now they're yelling at each other about the remaining ones. They think the guards are retreating in fear."

"Whatever gets them up here," I said, grabbing the coarse beam above. I pulled myself up and then the rope after me. I popped the grappling hook in my inventory, not planning on jumping down into the fray if I could help it.

I'd had just enough time to get my bearings when the lead guards came charging around the bend and past the stained-glass window. A steady stream of them ran up the corridor, three abreast, their blue-tinted steel dazzling like a river caught in the morning sun.

Carefully, very carefully, I stood upon my beam. The NPCs were still on their aggro path with the single-minded focus of mobs giving chase. Eyes fixed ahead, they didn't look up. I started shuffling along the ledge back towards the stained-glass window, flanking the guards and heading for where my swinging axe rested.

The guards and I crossed paths, them below and I above. I dropped caltrops the moment the last boot pounded by. Pretending they were ninja throwing stars, I launched them free-form across the corridor. With my last 3 caltrops, I had a spark of inspiration.

I still had the quick poison I'd scavenged from the rogue Shanksy. Poisons were often applied to weapons in games, notably daggers, for extra roguish damage. Taking the vial of poison out, I yanked it's cork off with my teeth, careful not to let any enter my mouth, then I tried pouring the contents over the caltrops. Focusing on the traps, it seemed to work.

Poisoned Iron Caltrops
Item level 8
Scatter spikes upon the ground to catch unwitting enemies.
Damage: 50-55 piercing
Applications: 15/15
Bonus effect: Quick Poison – Rank 2. 20-25 poison damage per hit.

The best part of this was the caltrops would apply damage up to fifteen times. Had I coated my crossbow bolts in the poison, I'd have got three poisoned shots out of it. With the poison on 3 caltrops, I'd spread the extra damage so that it could be applied up to 45 times.

Sometimes, I amaze even myself.

Proudly, I dispersed the poisoned caltrops and surveyed my handiwork. The white floor looked like it had sprouted iron stubble.

"Players incoming," Ellie informed me.

I hastened to the rim of the rafters, where an eagle-head statue helped to hide me from view. Now, near the middle of the hallway, my six-bladed axe was only a few beams away, but it lay out on the middle of the rung and I'd surely be seen standing there. The NPCs might not have the wherewithal to look up, but the players would, or they'd see me in their peripherals. What I needed now was the cover of a brawl.

At the far end of the gallery, the NPCs had halted, hitting a dead end. In a confused mass, they started to turn around, weapons lowered, shoulders slumped, their aggro lost.

Then the players arrived.

A stocky dwarf led the pack, a shaman by the looks of the totem pole upon his back. Lightning crackled around his hands. Given his class and tanned skin, he was probably a skyborn dwarf boasting bonus elemental damage. He was level 43, probably one of the more powerful players that Azrael had brought with him.

"They've got stuck up here," the dwarf called behind him.

"The hell's wrong with them?" asked a warlock.

"Maybe the boss has mangled their minds," the dwarf said. "We just gotta kill them. Where are my tanks? Come on, assholes we have a job to do."

Beefy warriors, along with a paladin of their own, came lumbering to the front. The guards had caught onto the host of enemy players and now renewed their efforts in aggression.

"They've come for your Emperor!" the priest's voice rang. "Slay them all!"

The dwarf cricked his neck and fired off a lightning bolt. "Mash them to pulp boys."

"It's working," Ellie said.

I held my tongue, not daring to speak as the two sides thundered towards each other. There were more of the NPC guards and their average level was far higher, but the players had coordination and a wide range of classes. Rangers and spellcasters the players had brought also surged forward but were unable to get off clear shots in the confines of the hallway. Only their own priest healers hung back, beginning to channel healing spells in preparation for the clash.

Spire Guards were the first to hit my caltrops, yelping in pain as the spikes pierced the lining of their boots. The dwarf shaman stepped onto them next, howling and hopping on one foot comically. Yells went out to be careful and the charging players suddenly slowed to a crawl as they attempted to negotiate my densely packed field of traps. The NPCs didn't seem to have the same compulsion to avoid pain, continuing to run at full tilt to crash into the front players at full momentum.

Damage notifications flooded in from the caltrops. Pistols banged, and spells flared and ricocheted off the walls, including all manner of flames, frost, shadow bolts and violet energy. A firework display happening in a rectangular box. The first kill appeared for my viewing pleasure.

Spire Guard level 45 dies – 135 Assisted EXP

My trap damage must have given me an assisted credit for a kill.

I chucked down two of my nets, getting the players and guards nice and frustrated and clumped together. Time to let this axe loose. With all chaos below I felt more confident in moving unseen above the battle. Making straight for my deadly contraption, I pushed it off, letting gravity do its magic.

Tied securely to a central beam, the six-bladed axe descended, picking up speed until momentum carried it upwards, cutting through the fray like a razor-edged golf swing. I didn't see any damage notifications, for I supposed it wasn't my weapon, technically, but damn was it effective.

Those who weren't maimed scattered instead, diving out of the way and sewing yet more confusion into the skirmish. Once the axe reached the top of its swing, it came back for seconds, a perfect pendulum of doom. Any semblance of formation from the players broke down entirely and the spire guards broke free, making for the softer healers at the back.

Healers draw the most aggro in these sorts of games after tanks, so it was no surprise.

I held back on my grenades as I'd need every scrap of damage to mop up the end of the fight. Yet there was no need to hold back on the slime.

Pulling out four of the large phials of the bright green goo, I hurled them down to smash upon the floor beneath the combatants' feet. Glass shattered, sending the slime in all directions. The effect was immediate. If footing had been hard to find before, it was a nightmare now. Players and guards slid, stumbled and fell, hitting each other and landing upon my caltrops multiple times.

I was just about to lob another phial of slime down when I saw an angry mage player, level 37, high elf no less, revving up some sort of area fire attack. Judging myself to be within its range, I hastened to the edge of the rafters once more, backing away from the blast radius. The mage's snide elfish features contorted as he completed his incantation, then cast his hands outwards, unleashing his spell. A dozen guards were engulfed in the flames, including a few players on the outer edges of its radius. But it also touched the slime.

At once, the slime ignited, burning white-hot and exploding upwards like lava. Those not hit or killed by the mage's attack were caught in the slime fire, or badly burned from the molten chunks of goo raining down on them. My nostrils filled with the smell of burning cloth and hair. The nets were incinerated along with the rope securing my pendulum axe, sending the weapon crashing down for one last round of damage.

To cap it off, my caltrops had gained fresh life from the blast, blown around the confined corridor in a storm of hot iron. One even hit me where I was skulking above, wiping over 100 of my precious health points away: a third in one hit.

It hardly mattered, for the kill assist notifications were piling up so fast, the game collated what it could together.

Spire Guard level 45 dies x 18 – 2430 Assisted EXP

Level Up! You have reached level 9
+3 attribute points
+45 health
+45 mana

The level up restored my health and mana to full.

Buckey666 – Shaman – level 43 dies – 260 EXP

DomTron – Warlock – level 31 dies – 200 EXP

Kills from the inferno kept coming.

I had no idea quite what had just happened or why the slime had reacted the way it did to fire, but I wasn't about to complain. Nor did I have time to contemplate it.

The fighting raged on. My friend, the elite NPC priest of the Imperial Guard, was out of mana now, reduced to shouting religious dogma at his allies by way of encouragement. The surviving players, on the other hand, were bolstered by their own healers while the guards' health moved in only one direction. I'd need to take those priest players out. Fast.

Hopping from beam to beam back to the entrance, I took advantage of the weakened statue heads I'd set up and sent lumps of marble crashing down upon unwitting foes. Ahead, huddled before the swan stained-glass window, the three priest players threw out heals while a warrior tanked two guards who were attempting to attack the softer cloth wearers. The warrior used some roaring ability, throwing back his head like a lion.

That's when he saw me.

Knowing I had one good shot, I threw down one of my nets in the hopes of keeping the group close together. It only proved a mild inconvenience for the players, as the warrior started to hack through the rope with ease. But for the moment, they were contained.

I sent a phial of slime to shatter between the players, then followed this with a grenade. The explosion was just as impressive as before, with both the grenade's fire and the white-hot slime dishing out damage. The stained-glass window blew outwards, letting a cold wind rush in from the world beyond. Strands of burning rope singed into black ash.

My targets spluttered and coughed, bewildered by the ambush. None of them could react to the marble stag head I sent to break across one priest's back, sending him crumpling onto his stomach. Another healer was at deathly low health. With my grenades on a short cooldown, I loaded a bolt and activated Desperate Shot. Being directly above my target, I managed to land a hit, despite the accuracy debuff of the ability.

Willheal4loots – Priest – level 29 dies – 190 EXP

My cover was blown at this point. The warrior was pointing right at me, trying to rise to his feet while the two weakened NPC guards wailed on him with impunity. I dropped another grenade on them all, killing the weakened guards and another one of the priests.

The warrior and surviving healer started running towards their comrades in the middle of the corridor, where the main skirmish continued, albeit with thinned numbers.

"You're doing so well," Ellie said. "Get 'em!"

"We're in the endgame now," I said. "Time to hit them with everything."

I dropped two more phials of slime by the exit, then began leaping from beam to beam back up the corridor, throwing grenades each time they were off cooldown.

Athletics Increased!
Level 3
Good work stretching those legs. Next time, you won't need to warm up.
+1 to base Constitution
+1 to base Reflexes

Each jump, after this upgrade, felt smoother, and my balance easier to find. With feline grace, I landed at my desired destination, pulled out the blowtorch tool from my inventory, flicked it on and lowered the rune empowered flame towards the upturned end of the piece of rope I'd nailed down.

Having lashed my pendulum of doom together, I'd been left with 2 spare pieces of rope that could not be made into a fishing net on their own. I'd found a use for them. This was it. One was set up here and an identical rope to bomb trap was set up near the stairs.

Did I mention that I'd tested whether I could place pouches

of gunpowder stuffed full of spare nails inside the empty cavities of the suits of armor? Well, I'd discovered I could do that.

Sparking fire sputtered nicely along my cobbled together fuse, disappearing inside the steel chest of the hollow knight.

The bang was incredible.

The screaming even worse.

Flames and scorching shards sprayed outwards, burning and cutting as they spread. Kill notifications nearly overflowed, toppling over each other.

Level Up! You have reached level 10
+3 attribute points
+50 health
+50 mana

Unlocked!
Class Specialization Choice!

Unlocked!
Tinkering – Rank 1

I forced myself to look away from the details. Kill notifications were still flying in, and there were still enemies left to vanquish. Anticipating they would retreat soon, I was already on my way back to the only exit where I'd placed a final set of nail bombs.

Virtually all the NPCs were dead now and the five remaining players sensed they were under siege from a third entity, if not knowing who or where they were from. The healer I'd chased from the window lay dead, as was the warrior, leaving the terrorists without a healer or a tank.

Not wanting to stick around and fight much longer without support, the remaining damage-dealing players polished off the last remaining guards and turned tail. With haste, I set fire to the fuse of my second nail bomb but the players would probably be safely back in the stairwell before it went off.

I couldn't let that happen.

With a sudden surge of daring, I brought out my grappling hook, bit the teeth of the metal into the wood and slid myself down, so as to hang behind their retreating backs. I grasped onto the rope with one hand and drew out a frost rune with the other. Activating it, I was greeted with the same choice of options.

Frost Bolt or Cone of Cold?

I had an inkling as to how this worked, and a practical experiment seemed in order. This time, I selected Cone of Cold.

Mana started to channel into the spell as before, draining exponentially. Due to the level ups in the fight, I had nearly 600 mana. I cut the flow this time, pouring 530 mana into the spell, leaving myself just enough for a Desperate Shot if needed, then let go.

A cone of icy wind billowed from my open palm, reaching 7 feet in range, enough to catch all the players and slap them with a slow debuff.

Winter's Chill
Movement speed decreased by 13%
Duration 5 Seconds

It had less of an effect than when I'd slowed that rogue, but I was using it over a wider area, so it made sense that the debuff would be weaker to compensate.

I scrambled back up to the rafters just in time to save myself from the exploding nail bomb and casually tossed another grenade into the mix. The shower of nails thinned the herd down to three, their health falling fast as they slowly waded through the barrage of damage, heading right for the slime awaiting them at the head of the stairs.

Feeling cocky, I slid back down the grappling hook, landing on the floor in a crouch. Two players fell victim to the slime itself, falling flat on their faces.

"Looks like you guys slipped up," I called, unable to resist.

I threw what I thought to be the final grenade of the fight.

More flames, another white-burning wall of slime turned lava. Two kills were notified to me but not the third; the player in question was blown aside, down the stairs and out of my line of sight.

I gave chase, throwing all caution to the wind. I leapt over the burning ooze, my momentum carrying me down the staircase three steps at a time. Emerging into the throne room, I loaded a bolt into my crossbow, taking aim at the player stumbling away.

Coward. It made my blood boil.

"Hey," I called, "Don't you want to fight me? Huh? Or do you just play with people's lives when it suits you?"

The player turned and threw their hands up. His staff gave away that he was a spellcaster, and I thought I recognized it. Much to my surprise, it turned out to be Karl from back in the armory. He was a level 35 mage, his health barely a sliver of green and he was completely out of mana. That's oom for short by the way.

"Who the fu—"

"Ah, ah, ah," I said. "I'm gonna ask the questions if that's alright?"

"Zoran," Ellie's voice cut over me like a scolding teacher. "There's no time. Just finish him off. If he regens mana, you're done for."

"Well, you'll let me know if he's about to get enough back for a spell, won't you?" I muttered.

"Are you talking to yourself?" Karl said.

"Yeh, that's right," I said. "I'm a madman, like your boss. What's Azrael really doing here?"

"Zoran, do it now!"

Karl looked equal parts shocked and impressed. "How do you know who he is?"

So, their leader was definitely Azrael then.

"I have my ways," I said. "Just as I took out your friend Shanksy. The guy seemed like a prick, by the way, so you're welcome."

Karl laughed. "I told the guys we should have gone looking for him. Little weasel deserves not to get his cut."

"What do you mean?"

"Anyone who dies on the job doesn't get paid their cut."

"Paid? So all that political prisoner stuff was definitely garbage?"

"Grade A bullshit," Karl said. He squinted at me. "Come a little closer, will you?"

I moved right up to him, placing the tip of the loaded bolt at his head in point-blank range as I'd done to Shanksy. He was on such low health that one hit was bound to kill him despite our level gap. If he tried to just punch me, I'd kill him before he rose. He'd made that calculation himself, I could see it in his eyes. He knew he was beaten, but his eyes roved over me, a look of awe spreading from ear to ear.

"Wow, you're only level ten? And a scavenger. Get out kid, you've got some mad skills taking us all out like that."

"Kill him, Zoran!"

"I'd like to get some more information out of him if that's alright," I growled. "Why are you all really here?"

Karl laughed again. "I'm streaming this to Azrael right now, kid."

Ellie cut in, her voice deafening like club music. "Do it now. He has backup coming!"

I clutched at my head, nearly dropping my crossbow in the process. Karl twitched as though to move but I rallied and rammed my weapon back towards his face. I activated Desperate Shot, ready to use it on my next bolt. There was just something I had to know first.

"You don't actually die in real life as well, do you?"

I'd just slaughtered about twenty players. Ellie had said they wouldn't, but she had admitted to being malfunctioning, not on the top of her game. For my own soul, for my own sanity, I had to check.

"Of course, we don't really die. Boss is tough but he's not a mania—"

I pulled the trigger. A deadly critical hit was swiftly followed by his kill notification.

Level Up! You have reached level 11
+3 attribute points
+55 health
+55 mana

Unlocked!
Desperate Strike/Shot – Rank 3
You lash out wildly to drive off an attacker. Weapon base damage is increased by +90-105 but accuracy is lowered by a third.
Mana Cost: 150
Cooldown: 10 seconds

Cunning Unlocked!
You planned and pulled off the impossible (Bonus levels granted for your efforts).
Level 8
As cunning as a fox who's just been appointed Professor of Cunning at the Imperial University of Argatha? Not quite. But you're surely the next in line.
+8 to base Intelligence

I barely registered the upgrades before sheathing my crossbow and tearing open my map to check for players heading my way. There were none. Each player out on the walls seemed to be following their patrol route. Flicking up a few floors, I found each smaller knot of players doing the same. Azrael remained at the top of the tower, completely still; probably filming another message to the world.

If I had some way of rounding on Ellie, I would have.

"What was that all about?" I said. "Nobody is coming."

"S-sorry, Zoran," she said, voice crackling in and out. "I must be losing my connection again."

"Nuh-uh, I'm not buying it. You were totally fine during that whole fight."

"I just don't want you to remain out here. It's so exposed."

I groaned and stooped down to Scavenge Karl's body. I'd been getting good information out of him, but she wasn't wrong. He'd sent a stream to Azrael, whether directly or as a video to be viewed later, I couldn't be sure, but my anonymity was about to be blown. Hanging around in the middle of a very open throne room wasn't the wisest move.

"You lied to me, Ellie. That's why I'm upset."

"Why?"

"Because what's going on is still terrifying and I want to know I can trust you. I need to know that."

"Zoran, I want you to live. And after what you just pulled off I think you might be able to make it. Azrael's men have been reduced to twenty-seven players now."

"Yeh, well I won't have the luxury of the guards again for a full day."

"We'll think of something," Ellie said.

"Alright. Alright. Just – just don't lie again to me, okay? I was close to figuring out what's really going on there."

A quiet moment, of reflection, of hesitation? It's hard to read into someone's silence without being able to see their face.

"I won't lie to you."

I nodded, then shook my limbs to work out some of the tension. With nothing more to gain from Karl, I headed back to the scene of the battle, intending on scavenging all I could while I still had time.

18

There has never been a more hurried and less respectful looting of battlefield corpses. Not ever. Alright, not in gaming history then.

I scoured my corridor of doom as a dredger scrapes the seabed. At the back of my mind was the ever-looming question of Ellie's intentions. She'd gone quiet since our altercation in the throne room, ostensibly to focus on checking player movement.

I hadn't failed to notice that she'd got loudmouthed when I'd asked Karl what Azrael's true intentions here were. That had been a sticky topic for her earlier too, and I was now convinced something weird was going on. She definitely knew more than she was letting on, though I couldn't imagine why she wouldn't tell me.

Still, I didn't doubt that she wanted me alive. It would be simple to kill me off if that was what she wanted, nor did I have the balls to even contemplate such a horror. The thought of her leaving me alone made my heart skip a beat and my stomach knot.

My anxiety now gravitated around when Azrael and the remainder of his cronies would come after me. Shanksy had been one man, and a late addition to the crew by the sounds of things. Karl's message aside, twenty missing players would hardly go unnoticed.

Hence my haste in looting. Five minutes was all it took, running from body to body, hitting 'loot all' as fast as possible and not paying much attention to what was entering my inventory. I only paused when scavenging the elite priest who I'd shot to gain the initial aggro.

Scavenged High Priest Velen level 50 Elite – 89 EXP

Manafused satin x3
Loot all?

That was the same endgame cloth that I'd received from scavenging the Emperor earlier, bringing me up to 6 pieces. Maybe I'd be able to craft something cool with it, though how I'd reach the Intelligence level to do so was beyond me. If I made it through this I could just sell it on the auction house for a tidy price. Pleased at this boon, I continued my looting bonanza.

Pale dawn light spilt in from the shattered window. Maybe it was just a placebo but, somehow, seeing daylight was comforting. I'd spent enough time in the dark. Combined with the sweet rush of such rich looting, I was having a rare moment of fun between panic attacks.

Aside from the obvious advantage of having removed some of the enemy players from the equation, the coolest part was being able to fully loot them because I'd been their maker. I was gaining all manner of items, plus the scavenging drops on top. By the time I was done, my inventory was groaning and my experience bar was nearly a third of the way to level 12.

I was just beginning to think that I ought to high tail it out of there when Ellie's voice sparked back to life.

"How are you doing?"

"All done here. Time I fall back to sieve through this hoard of loot and sort out my stat points. Also, I think I've unlocked a couple of things at level ten."

"Yes, you unlocked a specialization choice for your class and the Tinkering ability. This will allow you to upgrade your items, but we can discuss it once you're somewhere less exposed."

"Where should I head? I suppose the dungeons might be best to—"

I halted mid-flow. Another video feed was being forced into my vision. Only this time it didn't feel like Azrael's usual scheduled programming. Two small icons, a speaker and a camera, flashed in the bottom right-hand corner of the image. Azrael had opened a two-way video call with me. And I couldn't close it down.

"Zoran, you need to move now," Ellie said. "Three players over level forty are heading down from the upper spire and they aren't stopping."

I didn't need telling twice and started making my way back to the dungeons. Azrael's message kept playing as I ran.

Rather than sweeping around dramatically, the scene shook like it had been filmed on a hand-held camera. It was dark too, a windowless area deep inside the Spire. Bloodied warriors in plate armor were being shepherded into a cramped room. All the furniture had been smashed up and shoved against the walls. The gold inlay on the blue-tinted armor signaled these were the elite members of the Imperial Guard, though I could not yet see the Emperor. Amidst the pained whimpers of the NPCs, I could hear raspy growls and shrill rattling scrapes as though a rake was being pulled over broken glass.

With a sharp turn of the camera, I beheld the source of these unearthly sounds – skeletons, zombified creatures with decaying hanging flesh, and a true terror from the crypts – a construct of stitched human and animal body parts that was forced to stoop to avoid hitting what passed for its head on the extinguished chandeliers.

"Ellie, what is that thing?"

"It's a stitched colossus. It's a summon ability that's rewarded from a very difficult death knight class quest."

Azrael helpfully lingered the camera on the colossus, just to make sure I got a good glimpse of the futility of my position.

"Might we not speak and make terms?" A nervous voice said.

The camera turned to look upon Emperor Aurelius, down on his knees, his robes torn and his crown askew.

"But I already made terms," Azrael said from behind the camera. "You gave me your word."

One of the elite paladins rose to his feet. His armor was different from that of his colleagues – white gold inlays patterned the surface and his helm was a cowl of flexible plate, making him appear like some battle angel.

"There can be no terms with the undead. Abominations must be purged." Light swirled in his hand, a spell, but a skeleton warrior interrupted him, slamming a bony elbow into his face.

"Stand down Reginald," Aurelius said. "I do not wish to see any of you killed."

"Listen to your sop of an Emperor," Azrael said. He stepped out from behind the camera, the paladin disguise gone. Black and red plates of spiked armor covered a body of semi-rotting gray flesh. Bones were visible where his calves should have been. I could not yet see his face, but I recognized that perfectly bald head. He dropped to one knee and gently cupped Aurelius' chin in a hand of which half the fingers were pure bone.

"Submit and you shall yet live," Azrael said softly.

Aurelius' face turned beet red, his breathing rapid and shallow. "I —I submit to you."

Azrael ran a finger lovingly down the Emperor's cheek. "A lesson well learned."

Before rising, he lifted the crown off Aurelius' head with an exaggerated delicacy, milking the moment before tossing it to land before his stitched colossus. The great monstrosity let out a bellow then stamped on the crown.

Done with his theatrics, Azrael rose to his full height, bones clicking loudly as he shuffled to the door. The camera floated behind him, tracking his every move. Abandoning the Emperor and his guards, Azrael allowed his undead minions to assemble behind him. No other players were in view. Whether Azrael had subdued so many elites alone or not wasn't the point. I could see he was a powerhouse unto himself.

The camera zoomed down to focus on Azrael's face, as it did in his broadcasts, only this time it was his true face; the scarred, deathly gray, skeletal face. Enormous green eyes sat in hollowed sockets, webbed in bloodshot veins, the last color in his avatar's gruesome form.

"Hello, Zoran."

I halted mid-stride, about to take the dungeon stairs. I turned and placed myself up against a nondescript segment of the wall, so that he'd have no way of telling where I was. If he didn't already know.

"Answer me," Azrael said.

I gulped. If attempting to stand up to the fat hotel owner yesterday had been troublesome, this was a thousand times worse. My throat jammed from nerves. For a moment, I forgot words.

"I know you can hear me just fine."

After a concerted effort, I managed to open my mouth. "H-hey… jackass."

He smirked. "I hear you have been causing my associates some trouble on the lower levels. To be frank, I'm impressed. I wonder if you've been getting any help?"

Did he know about Ellie?

"Nope. No help for me. I'm just *that* awesome."

"But, of course. Awesome, but not the brightest. You should have kept your head down. My task here is too important to be interrupted."

"Putting lives in danger for money is important, is it?"

He didn't flinch.

"It was clever of you to use the NPC reset to your advantage, a feat you shan't repeat. As you just saw, I have rounded up the rest and they shall be placed under guard. I saw your class and level from the video Karl sent me, so I know you won't be so foolish enough to attempt a direct attack. Your access to the armory will now be cut off. Take my advice, and don't interfere any further. I do not wish to take a life, but one would be a small price to pay in the course of events." He motioned the camera closer with one finger, dropping his voice to a whisper. "Today is not for foolish heroism."

The call ended.

I stood dazed, unsure of how to process this.

"Enemy players closing in," Ellie reminded me.

Shaking my head, I took the winding stairwell down to the dungeons. I kept going, although my pace slowed as a sense of defeat washed over me. The stitched colossus alone had appeared insurmountable.

"How long until they find me?"

"I'll make sure that doesn't happen," she said. "I know where they are, but they don't know where you will be."

"Okay, so I'll just hide," I said, leaping over the trapped slabs at the bottom of the stairwell. "Keep my head down. This was always going to be a mad chance anyway."

"Your overall health is still declining," she said. "Others out there might be stuck alone like you are. If you hide, you'll condemn them. And yourself."

"Ellie, I can't defeat him. I'm only level eleven."

"You must try."

I let loose another shuddering sigh, bending over double in a moment of existential horror. As always, she was right. Putting the screws to me about helping others had been a low jab but, that aside, I couldn't just sit idle and let my body slowly deteriorate. Whatever Azrael's mission here, it clearly wasn't moving quickly. Nor did it seem like he was close to completing it if he was concerned I might exploit the next reset in twenty-four hours.

"How is he even doing this?" I asked. "And why does it matter if he has control of the Spire or not? Why—"

Why did he have to do this to me? Is what I wanted to ask.

"Azrael's workaround, using a backdoor piece of code, is now determined on him being online," Ellie said, as though explaining something perfectly simple to a child. "If he can be removed from the game, then I will be able to get a message to my creators about the issue. He won't get a second chance. As for the Spire, it seems he already knew about the Game Master spawn point at the top of the tower."

"The what?" I asked, somewhat weakly. It was all becoming a bit much to take in. My head hurt; my nerves could barely take it as it was.

"The Game Master spawn point. A locked segment of the Spire that exists on the ninth floor, you can see it on your map."

I checked this for myself. Unlike the other floors, very little was on the ninth other than the exit of a stairwell, a short corridor and then a large room marked 'Hall of the Makers'.

"Ordinarily, the room is sealed shut and inaccessible to players," Ellie continued, "But part of Azrael's exploitation is to trick the system into thinking he is a Game Master from Frostbyte. GM's will spawn into that room before getting their bearings and teleporting to their destination to act as moderators in player disputes or illegal activity. There's an in-game console where they can run basic diagnostics, report abuse, and many other features required for their work."

"It doesn't seem like the GM spawn point would be common knowledge."

"Only members of the Frostbyte development team would be aware of it," Ellie said. "Although any of them could have talked for a bribe."

"I guess," I said. Another horrible thought occurred to me. "I take it he can't just log me out from there?"

"I imagine he would have if he could," Ellie said. "If a GM felt a player should be forcibly logged out or suffer account penalties, they would need to raise it with the accounts department."

"Well, that's some relief," I said. "And whatever Azrael is doing, he needs access to this console?"

"It seems that way."

Her curt tone conveyed that she either didn't know the specifics and was frustrated by that or didn't want to discuss it. I didn't feel like pressing either way. My only desire right now was to reach relative safety, and my feet led me step by step through the darkened dungeons. Instinct guided me towards the interrogation chamber.

Yet the dungeons were no longer silent corridors. Prisoners groaned and pleaded, reaching out to me through their bars. By the time my worried mind worked out the meaning of this, I had already arrived back at Kreeptic's lair.

I entered without thinking and there was the chief interrogator himself, upright and brewing some smoking concoction, very much alive.

"Oh crap," I said.

Kreeptic turned slowly, a smile stretching from ear to ear. In one fluid motion, he put down his potion, picked up a menacing knife and swept towards me.

I never had time to leave. His hand beat mine to the door, pulling it firmly shut. Then he found my throat, pinning me in place.

"Uh, uh, uh," he tutted. "There will be no stealing from me, little scav."

His voice was disturbingly lyrical for one so absorbed in the art of pain. He brought the knife first to my throat, then chest, then directly before my face as though debating where best to sink it.

"You're about to find out what happens to thieves in my dungeons."

19

With Kreeptic's hand at my throat, I was held firmly in place and I couldn't get a word out in my defense.

"Someone has ransacked my chambers already," Kreeptic said. "Many potions and poisons are missing."

With a great effort, I managed to gasp, "Not... here to... steal."

"That's right," Kreeptic said lovingly. "You are here to be caught. Dear boy, I train assassins in the shadowy arts. No scavenger could hope to outwit me."

"Not... trying... to."

"Don't worry, Zoran," Ellie said. "He's harmless really."

"Harmless?" My hands struggled uselessly against him.

"Whom do you speak to?" Kreeptic said, drawing the knife up against my cheek, the metal ice cold. "Please tell me you are mad. I should like to crack open your skull and study the ruins inside."

He squeezed tighter at my throat and my health bar started ticking down.

"Not mad," I struggled. "Spire. In danger."

"What drivel is this?"

Ellie cut in. "Mention Highcross."

Wishing I could ask her to explain, I took my best guess at her meaning.

"Enemies," I wheezed. "Emperor – taken. Marshal Highcross sent me."

"Highcross?" Kreeptic said, eyes widening. Evidently, the torturer feared the chief intelligence officer. "Why would he send a lowly scavenger to deliver such news?"

"Because everyone else is dead."

Kreeptic let go of me. I gulped in air before descending into choked coughs, as pain throbbed in my neck.

"I shall discover the truth of this for myself," Kreeptic said. In a puff of sour white smoke, he disappeared, vanishing as a result of some ability. I thought I heard footsteps in the corridor beyond, running at speed back the way I had come.

"Where's he going?"

"He's heading up to the throne room," Ellie informed me.

"But what if he's seen?" At once, I pulled out my map. To my horror, the three players Ellie had warned of had arrived on the ground floor. After the initial shock, I realized they were standing guard outside the armory, just as Azrael had warned. I felt a pang at the loss of such a bountiful resource. Still, so long as Kreeptic didn't venture down that way, it wouldn't be a total disaster.

"He's a master of stealth," Ellie said. "He'll be fine."

"They killed him before."

"When he wasn't expecting danger."

"This is so weird," I said. "A piece of you controls him, yet you don't have any actual influence over his actions."

"Not in my current state," Ellie said glumly.

I rubbed at my neck, concerned that I'd lost a sanctuary. It would have been useful to pick up more slime, but I doubted Kreeptic would be all too happy with me pilfering from his cauldron.

"Let's make use of our time while he's gone," Ellie said, in a cheerful tone. "You can pick your class specialization too."

"Oh, fantastic," I said, my voice lousy with sarcasm. "That'll make me forget about everything. A nice spec choice."

Inside, I was still quite excited to see what I had to choose from, but the stubborn side of me didn't feel like admitting it to her.

Opening my character sheet, I saw there was a new tab helpfully labeled 'Specialization'. Delving into it, I saw that after I picked my preferred spec tree, I would have access to a broad perk choice every ten levels within that tree. At a glance, they seemed to fall into one of three variations: a combat spec, a crafting spec or an economic spec. The latter choices I assumed were there for those who planned to go down the merchant route. Indeed, the very first choice along this route made this evident.

Trader
You shrug off a life of the wilds and adventure for the comfort of a city, fine inns and good coin. You'll lose your edge but you'll no longer be seen as a vagabond either, so that's nice.
EXP gain from Crafting items increased by 25%
Will unlock skill Haggle
Will receive Merchants Guild Tabard
Attack power is reduced by 30%

This would be ideal for someone planning on staying mostly in the city markets, crafting and trying to make money. Like I had planned to do. But in my current predicament, I wasn't so sure. The extra experience from Crafting was tempting but I'd lose a chunk of offensive power, and I had so little as it was.

I checked my other choices.

Scrapper
Some scavengers are happy to take the leavings of others. But not you. Having others fight for you was never quite your style.
Weapons made or upgraded by you will be 25% more powerful
Attack power increased by 20%
Constitution increased by 20%

Though it had no drawbacks, I knew from my research that everyone considered this spec a bit of a joke. Scavengers were still so poor in combat, lacking a range of abilities. Then again, my situation was unique. Getting a bonus to my crossbow might prove invaluable, and I'd get improved survivability from the health increase.

My final choice related specifically to crafting.

Inventor
The workshop calls to you, the spanner over the sword. Honing your abilities, you require minimum concentration to deconstruct and assemble items, lending more thought to your next contraption.
Mana cost of Crafting reduced to 1%
Mana cost of Breakdown reduced to 1%
Mana cost of Tinkering reduced to 1%
All items created and upgraded by you will be 5% more powerful

I bit my lip, hesitating. In the end, I went with my gut and picked Inventor. The reduction of mana for Crafting and Breakdown meant that I wouldn't have to worry again about regenerating enough, like just before the ambush, and the fact that everything I'd make – not only the weapons – would have a power bonus was simply too useful to me. I'd surely make more traps before the end and having them be a touch stronger might be the difference between life and death.

"Good choice," Ellie said. "I'd say let's move onto Tinkering, but Kreeptic is about to return."

Her timing was impeccable. The torturer reappeared in the room in a whirl of a dark cloak, seeming to unfold from the air itself. He looked breathless, shaken even, having likely used every ability he had to move with such haste.

"It is true," he said. "The Marshal is… vanquished." Mouth agape, Kreeptic allowed this development to settle upon him, testing how it fitted. It appeared he found it favorable, for he smiled widely again. "The Emperor is yet alive, you say?"

"He is – for now," I added ominously. "Though his captor has threatened his life. I saw it through a vision he sent me."

Kreeptic eyed me. "Strange that a lowly scavenger should be so wrapped up in these events."

A half-baked excuse rose to my mouth, but the torturer silenced me with a cold finger against my lips.

"Strange, yet many adventurers come to me with incredible tales. I wonder now, Zoran, what yours is?"

Without stopping to think I began to gush out my story of the previous night, in a style that would suit his understanding of how this world, his world, worked.

I was a traveler from a far-off land, intending to visit the great city of Argatha. I'd found mercenary work from the Mayor of Rusking to help cover my expenses, and from there had been sent to deliver a message to the Marshal. Kreeptic was particularly engaged on the topic of the attack and how Marshal Highcross had fallen. Sensing this was a way to score some points with the torturer, I embellished my memory of how the bat creature clawed savagely at the Marshal's face as he cried in pain.

"Like a little girl," I added.

For a moment I thought I'd gone too far, but Kreeptic chuckled appreciatively and I carried on.

"Before I was shoved into the safe room, Highcross told me I should seek you out. He said you would know the best way to secure the Emperor's safety." The sole member of my audience looked eager for a riveting conclusion, but I felt the climax of my story wilt like a flower placed in vinegar. "And so here I am," I ended lamely.

Kreeptic stroked his goatee, his eyes glazing over. I could almost hear the wheels spinning in his mind.

"You say this villain we face sent you word of the Emperor's imprisonment through a vision? Be he mage or warlock? No, more likely he is a shaman to be sending visions."

"Does it matter?"

"It matters a great deal, you scrawny boy."

"Hey, you're not exactly ripped yourself."

He raised the knife again. "Such gall might have seen you through the hell of a scrap I saw upstairs, but it won't get you far with me. I seek the truth, boy; through whatever means necessary."

"Alright, alright." I tried backing away but soon bumped into the torture table in the middle of the room and could go no further; the site where Kreeptic extracted his 'truths'. "Our enemy is called Azrael. And he is none of those magic users you mentioned. He is a death knight. Is that a problem?"

"Possibly," sneered Kreeptic. "Pray tell, where does he hail from?"

"Uh," I said stupidly. What the heck did that matter?

"He's asking what race Azrael is," Ellie said.

"Undead. Azrael is undead."

"Curses," hissed Kreeptic. "I suppose it was only a matter of time before such a servant of the Dark Council came to blight the Spire. He cannot be harmed like mortals."

"I'm certain he can be killed," I said.

"Indeed. Burn an undead or cut off the head and it won't come back again."

"So, what's the issue?"

"Do I look like I command fire or a warrior capable of dueling and beheading?" he said, advancing upon me again. "My ways are in the quiet corners, the slow methodical stripping of spirit until I get what I want." He raised the knife. I flinched, not even attempting to prevent it from falling, but Kreeptic slammed it into the wood of the table behind me.

"Poisons and knives, boy."

Watching the knife shudder where it stuck fast in the wood, I gulped again.

"Eyes on me," Kreeptic said. I did as instructed, taking in this rake of a man. He was as terrifying a person as I'd ever met. His every move teetered on the edge of violence, an experience I'd only found before in the campus drunks looking to provoke a fight. Whatever part of Ellie that was able to control NPC behavior could win Oscars.

It was clear that Kreeptic enjoyed every moment of it, getting off as much on someone's fear as when they were actually in pain.

"Knives," he continued, "don't frighten the dead much. They cannot feel. Nor do poisons give them pause, for there is no pulse to carry it to their hearts."

"There is a way," Ellie whispered. "Tell him that Grand Crusader Reginald yet lives."

"Erm," I stuttered. "I believe the, erm, Grand Crusader Reginald is still alive." I realized then where I'd heard that name before, during the communication Azrael had just sent me. One of the paladins had spoken out and the Emperor had called him Reginald.

"You're sure?" Kreeptic asked.

"Yes," I said firmly this time. "I saw him in the vision Azrael sent me. Many of the Emperor's guard is still with him."

"Then all is not yet lost."

The torturer swept past again in a whirl of his cloak, heading for the nearest apothecary table. Upon it was a huge tome in a language evidently not English and he began flicking through the pages. After a moment, he landed on his desired entry and muttered under his breath.

"Yes. Yes, there is hope left." Kreeptic turned, frowning at me. "So long as the Grand Crusader remains alive. And he can be reached. But if that is your task…"

"I'll figure out a way," I said. "I'm quite resourceful. Lived this long."

"You'll have a chance to prove yourself first. This potion requires a number of particularly… exotic ingredients."

I looked to the highly exotic ingredients floating in sickly yellow liquid in jars upon the shelves. Eyeballs the size of eggs, eggs the size of fists.

"I'm guessing you don't have these items lying around?"

"If only," Kreeptic said with a roll of his eyes. "Highcross believed them to be too deadly. He didn't like the idea of me having the means to take him out óver breakfast. His loss, in the end, it would have been less painful. But there has been occasion before to create batches of this venom in secret. Adventurers like you come looking for this reason or that. They help me, and I help them too, so to speak."

I sensed where this was going. A quest.

"So where can I find them?"

"Generally, I leave it to the adventurer to procure them. But you're far weaker than those who usually come looking for this concoction, so I'll give you a few extra tips. Cinderflake can be procured from the nests of dragonlings in the Blood Sands; the creatures' leavings produce hot and fertile soil. Black moss can be sought from the dread tunnels of the ancient dwarvish realms. Fingleweed is most common in the dusky woods south of the dark elf territories; tread carefully, for werewolves inhabit there. And the soul of a newborn vampire can be acquired by venturing forth into the nightmare plane, though your sanity may not return. The remainder of the list ought to be straightforward."

He passed me a short list of neatly scribed herbs and their quantities.

I took it, utterly dumbfounded. Where to even begin explaining this to him would be impossible. Surely, there had to be a better w—

Kreeptic began laughing, a cruel titter. "The pained look on your face boy. Quite joyful. Ahhh," he sighed, wiping at his eye. "I was joking about the vampire soul. Though I shall need those other rare herbs."

I laughed as well, though nervously. This was still impossible.

"Don't worry," Ellie said. "I know a way."

Relief rushed to fill me from head to toe. "You always do, don't you?"

Kreeptic arched an eyebrow. "Talking to yourself. Are you quite sure you're not mad?"

"Quite sure."

"More is the pity. Well, you have your quest now. Be gone."

Kreeptic made a shooing motion and turned his back on me. The official quest text followed.

Quest Accepted – A Long Road To A Quick Death (Elite)
Interrogator Kreeptic of the Imperial Spire has agreed to provide the deadly venom you seek. He'll require many materials, and it might be worth grouping up to fetch them.
Recommended group size: 5 players

Objectives:
Bring the following ingredients to Interrogator Kreeptic.
Cinderflake 0/1
Black moss 0/1
Fingleweed 0/1
Whitherweed 0/5
Snappersaw 0/5
Bile Blossom 0/5

"Wanna give me a hint here, Ellie?" I whispered as quietly as I could.

"Sure," she began, sounding positively cheerful. "This quest is designed to be extremely hard and time-consuming. It's meant for level fifty rogues, after all, with lots of mini-boss encounters."

I placed my face into both my palms, shaking my head.

"But, what most players don't have is access to the upper levels of the Spire. Nor would they have free reign if they did, but Azrael's highest-level players mopped up most of the NPCs again before he recalibrated in the wake of your attack."

"Are you saying there is somewhere in the Spire that I can find all of this stuff?"

"Your conclusion is correct," Ellie said. "The archmage has guest quarters here on the fifth level, with all the amenities that he'd need if he were in his own lodgings in the Channelers College. Meaning, he has an alchemy garden in the center of his chambers right here in the Spire."

I had to refrain myself from cheering, opting instead for a quiet fist pump in the air.

"I've marked it on your map," Ellie said.

Pulling my map open, I toggled to the fifth level and found the pulsing green area that was similar to how she'd marked the corridor of doom earlier.

"Won't I need herbalism to gather the ingredients? I don't have access to that profession."

"These are quest items, not involved in alchemy. Not

everyone who takes this quest can be expected to have herbalism. You can gather them if you have the quest."

I nodded but there was still something bothering me about the whole thing.

"There's just one thing, I don't understand," I said more loudly.

Kreeptic turned, annoyance blooming across his face. "Are you still here?"

"Even if I get you these things and you make the poison, what does it matter? If Azrael is undead, it won't affect him."

"One step at a time, boy," said Kreeptic. He looked me once over again. "That garb you wear is tragic. Of lower quality than even the stable boys here wear." He scanned his chamber as though for all the world a set of epic leather armor might drop down from the ceiling. "Why don't you pop up to the armory and pick something up?"

"Azrael has set guards there," I said. "But I did scavenge all the corpses from the attack. I'd like to take some time and craft, if you'll let me remain here where it's safe."

"I thought those bodies looked ransacked," Kreeptic said with a wry smile. "Good for you. Got to look out for yourself. Go ahead and craft, and while we're confederates in this scheme to replace the Marshal—"

"You mean save the Emperor's life and possibly the whole Empire?"

"Yes, that. You may come and go, boy."

"Thanks," I said. He didn't seem like such a sadist when he was acting nicely. "Oh, one more thing. When I craft I often speak to myself. Helps me tease out the solution, y'know?"

Kreeptic cocked his head. "D'you know, I sometimes do that as well when trying to make a new blood boiling solution. Whatever helps the creative juices to flow."

"Yeh, that's right," I said, trying not to let nervous laughter seep out of me. "I'll just be over... over here," I mumbled, sliding my way over to the farthest corner of the room. Once Kreeptic returned to his routine, I lowered my voice again. "Alright Ellie, time for some much-needed character management."

I began by pulling up my stat sheet to assign my new points.

"Any new threshold on Intelligence I ought to reach for crafting?"

"Make sure that you have forty-five points in Intelligence as that will unlock another tier of items," Ellie said. "Otherwise, I'd say put some more points into your health but it's up to you."

Currently, my Intelligence was at 41, helped greatly along by that awesome bonus from the Cunning unlock. I had 9 spare points from my recent leveling, so I assigned 4 into Intelligence straight away to satisfy Ellie's recommendation, then gave thought to the remaining 5. Given that the mana costs of my crafting spells were now greatly reduced, I wasn't as worried about regeneration. It was unlikely I'd get enough downtime during a fight to sit tight and regen lots of mana, so Willpower wasn't a top priority. Desperate shot was hardly the be all and end all and it wasn't like I'd be spamming it in combat, meaning Might wasn't as critical either. An occasional crossbow bolt would complement the traps and gadgets I'd be creating, and maybe some more runes if I found some. Intelligence seemed the best bet. The more powerful items I could craft, the better.

Decided, I placed 3 more points into Intelligence and 2 into Constitution – it felt prudent to give myself some extra health. Stat points assigned, my new table looked like this.

Character
Zoran Human Scavenger Level 11
Attributes
Constitution 18 (+2) – Intelligence 48 – Reflexes 17 (+3) – Might 17 (+2) – Willpower 24
Combat
Health 525 – Mana 805 – Attack Power 51 – Spell Power 94 – Regen 3.0 p/s

I noted that the small brackets beside some of my stats denoted the extra points I received from external sources. In this case, the extra points came from the traveler's worn leather set I was wearing. Overall, I hadn't advanced much from the ambush.

Much of the experience from the NPC guards had been shared with my own enemies and scavenging was still a pretty low-key affair exp wise, more a bonus than anything outrageous. Some new, more powerful equipment should help to offset this.

"And now for crafting and upgrades. Got bags bursting at the seams here. What's this Tinkering ability all about?"

Even as I asked the question, I pulled up my spell book to take a look.

Tinkering – Rank 1
True artists are never satisfied with their work, always seeing a way to improve their creation. You're no artist... not yet! But you can find ways to improve your creations, with a bit of experimentation.
Upgrade options now available in the Crafting menu.
Experience gained for associated professions remains the same.
Cost: 1% of mana

Seeing the reduced mana cost on Tinkering reaffirmed my faith that I'd picked the right specialization. This would be a lot easier to manage and I savored the small victory. Remembering Ellie had spurred me to create a crossbow specifically because of the upgrades it could gain, I looked to it first to see what could be done.

As I examined the weapon again, I discovered that the final line of text on the description had changed. Flashing in green, it now read, *'This item can be upgraded!'* I selected this option and a new window appeared detailing the materials that I'd need.

Upgrade Crossbow
Intelligence Required: N/A
Associated Profession: Engineering
Wooden plank 0/4
Steel ore 0/15
Toughened leather 0/15
Fine linen 0/15
Requires tools: Hammer, Saw, Chisel, Blowtorch

Thankfully, these materials were broadly low-level ones, which made sense given my crossbow was still currently a level 4 item and I was still a mere level 11 character. What it did not allude to was what would happen to the crossbow upon upgrading it.

"Any clue as to what I'll get out of this? It'll be hard to make decisions elsewhere without knowing."

"At lower levels, there isn't much to worry about," Ellie said. "Upgrading an item will take it from its current level to match your own in one go; hence, why the number of materials seems quite high. This is also why there is no set Intelligence requirement as the item scales to meet your current level."

"So, a level fifty scavenger could upgrade a weapon from level one all the way up to max in a single go?"

"They could do, but I think the list of materials needed for that would become tedious to read. Also, why upgrade something so basic when there would be far better items to hand. It seems unlikely players would take this course although there is nothing stopping them. Go ahead, Zoran, and upgrade your crossbow, you'll see what you get."

"I'll need to breakdown some of this loot from the ambush first," I said. I got underway, melting, hacking, chopping and smashing equipment down into core materials via Breakdown.

It pained me a little to do so. In the process, I lost so much high-level gear, stuff that would have been amazing to equip, but I doubted I'd ever reach the level requirements. The lowest level piece had been a ring, giving plus 6 to Intelligence but requiring the wearer to be at least level twenty-six. It was all a great shame but it led to ample materials.

I broke down a bow and a couple of shields into the wood I needed, the leather came in abundance from belts and gloves. The ore was trickier, for higher level plate armor broke down first into truesilver, then steel. The cloth was no worry at all for I was virtually drowning in the stuff. Breaking down dream silk into silk and then fine linen was simply a laborious process. Every so often, Kreeptic would throw a glance over his shoulder, but he kept any concerns to himself. Clearly, time was not of the essence so far as he was concerned. Once I had the materials to hand, the option to upgrade the crossbow lit up and I selected it.

Tinkering worked much the way that Crafting and Breakdown did. My character started to perform motions beyond my control, taking the crossbow in hand and infusing magic with the materials, hammering, chiseling and sawing where needed. This time, I even took out the blowtorch, it's magical flame wielding the steel into place. Once completed, I held the weapon up to admire it.

Success! Rickety Shot has been upgraded to Keen Shot level 11
+ 15 Crafting EXP
+ 43 Engineering EXP

The crossbow was larger than before, thicker and stronger though I could still manage to hold and aim it in one hand if it came to it. Steel strips had been fitted onto the outer frame and to the butt of the handle, making for a sturdier build than before. Leather covered the grip below the trigger and on the underside of the body, making it smoother to hold. But these were just simple aesthetics; more important were the changes to its stats.

Keen Shot
Crossbow
Quality: uncommon
Item level 11
Requires level 11 to equip
Damage: 25-34 piercing
Durability: 40/40
Knockback Chance 5% on hit
This item can be upgraded, but it is Soul Bound to you.

"Well, it's certainly better," I said. "But it's hardly a game changer."

"Upgrade it again," Ellie said.

"But it's already at my level."

"It is but it's of uncommon quality. If you had enough materials, you could bring this all the way up to legendary. That's why upgrading items you make is better than just making fresh ones, for the most part."

"Now that's cool," I said. "Every scavenger could be running around with legendary items then. How come I haven't seen anyone doing this?"

"Few people are playing your class," Ellie said, "and why waste resources on low-level equipment. The amount of materials required to improve item quality becomes exponential. People would rather reach level cap first before investing such time on items."

"So how far can I take this thing?"

"Right now, I calculate you can only reach rare item quality, but I shall endeavor to help you find materials you need to improve it further. Upgrading to Keen Shot now should unlock an attachment slot which we can work with."

Rubbing my hands, I checked on my new crossbow, pleased to find the green text indicating that the item was further upgradable. Having broken virtually everything down already, I went straight ahead and upgraded the weapon again. Anticipation flared in me as my character worked away at the crossbow this time. When it was finished, I hastened to check out the improvements.

Success! Keen Shot has been upgraded to Precise Shot level 15
+18 Crafting EXP
+55 Engineering EXP

Precise Shot
Crossbow
Quality: rare
Item level 15
Requires level 11 to equip
Damage: 32-39 piercing

Durability: 45/45
Knockback Chance 10% on hit
Attachment slots 0/1
This item is upgradable, but soul bound to you.

Physically, the weapon looked roughly the same, only sleeker. The bump in damage and knockback effect was a welcome one, but I was more excited by the attachment slot.

"What can I make to attach to it?" I asked eagerly, scrolling through my Crafting window in search of answers. Naturally, Ellie got there first.

"You can make a bayonet, a scope, a grenade launcher—"

"A what? Grenade launcher? Sweet. I definitely want that."

"Sorry, Zoran. You can't make it with what you have. You're missing a key component – a barrel – but we can look for one as we go. In fact, right now, you can only make a bayonet."

I considered this. Having a way to inflict some extra melee damage might be useful but it would mean I'd gotten myself cornered, and if that was the case, I was probably dead. My top priority should be staying within range and in the shadows. Thinking back on how easily I'd missed the Emperor before the ambush, any improvement to my chances of hitting the target would be invaluable.

Ellie's analysis was probably spot on, but I'd found the Crafting section that listed weapon attachments now and felt it could do no harm to check. For a scope, the core component was a lens. The ore I could manage easily. Then it hit me. I surely had access to a lens for I had a magnifying glass tool intended for jewel work and I hardly think I'd be worrying about that any time soon. I hadn't thought about my tools as items I might be able to use for Breakdown before, but as Ellie said, if you can loot it…

To my great smugness, I found I could use Breakdown upon the magnifying glass and produced a lens by doing so.

"Huh," Ellie said. "I didn't think of that."

"You've got a lot on your plate."

"I'll chalk it up to human ingenuity again," she grumbled. "Maybe I should get me some of that?"

"Watch and learn," I said with a wink to the ceiling.

From beside his bubbling cauldron of slime, Kreeptic had taken to staring at me.

"To think I've placed my ambitions in your hands," he said, shaking his head.

I ignored him and focused on selecting my scope. Interestingly, I found the text on several variations of the scope attachment were in green all the way up to a truesilver scope. This got me thinking. In most games, you could place high-level enchantments on low-level gear. It wasn't regularly done because you'd often be replacing that gear quickly, but some people liked to deck out low-level characters in ludicrously enchanted gear to make killing players of an equal level a piece of cake in PvP events or battlegrounds. The main point was that it was possible. Attachments in my mind seemed a lot like enchantments.

"Ellie, can I make a higher level scope and attach that?"

"You can," she said. "I'd recommend you make the truesilver scope as that is the highest you can create."

I flicked down the list. I actually had the components for a more powerful version using mithril ore, of which I had one remaining piece from breaking down a level 35 set of plate gloves. Shame I didn't have a higher Intelligence stat. I needed 75 Intelligence to make the mithril version. Tabetha had given me a potion to knock up my points when I'd needed it though, so maybe the same could be done again?

"Excuse me? Uhm, Mr Interrogator?"

Kreeptic gave no sign that he was listening.

"Any chance one of those potions you have up on the top shelf there will boost my brainpower for a bit?"

"Figures," Kreeptic said absentmindedly. In one fluid motion, he reached up, grabbed the closest ice-blue bottle and threw it towards me. With a grace I certainly didn't have in real life, I lunged to the side and caught it.

"Wow, thanks. Got any more of those?"

Kreeptic growled lowly. "I do not. The thieves, likely serving this Azrael took most of my store while I was unconscious. What little remains, I shall require if I am to brew you that poison. Now drink it before I change my mind."

I hastened to pull the cork from the vial, bracing myself for the vile taste before downing the contents. With a stroke of good fortune, it turned out to be delicious; vanilla and caramel perfectly blended. High-level potions came with more rewards than just the effects.

Archmage's Pick Me Up
+50 Intellect
Duration: 5 mins

I cracked a grin. Now my intelligence stat was temporarily at 95. Potions were like enchants, I guessed, and didn't have a level requirement. If you wanted to waste a perfectly good level 50 potion on a level 15 character, go right ahead.

"Brilliant!" Ellie said. "That's an endgame potion. I'm surprised he just handed one over. He must like you."

"Sizing me up for a dissection more like," I said.

Keeping one eye on the torturer, I went ahead and created my desired scope.

Success! Mithril Scope level 35 created
+33 Crafting EXP
+115 Engineering EXP

Mithril Scope
Item level 35
Can be attached to any ranged weapon.
+30 weapon damage
+10% chance to hit

My triumph could only go so far. Yes, I could make this powerful scope but there was no point making other high-level equipment that had level restrictions on equipping it. Still, the attachment would be a significant upgrade. Really significant.

The plus damage it provided alone nearly doubled my base weapon damage and this was now reflected in my crossbow's item description.

Precise Shot
Crossbow
Quality: rare
Item level 16
Requires level 11 to equip
Damage: 62-69 piercing
Durability: 45/45
Knockback Chance 10% on hit
Attachment slots 1/1 – Mithril Scope
+10% chance to hit
This item is upgradable, but Soul Bound to you.

I was starting to feel halfway threatening now, though the thought of taking on Azrael, a level 50 player, quelled the fire in me.

In terms of Crafting, I was running low on materials, especially ore. Without endless weapons from the armory to breakdown, I'd have to be more selective about what I made in the future. I still had a decent amount of leather left, enough to make headway into a superior set of armor. Out of a five-piece Nimble Armor set, I made the chest piece, leggings and boots.

Nimble Chest Guard
Quality: uncommon
Item level 10
Requires level 10 to equip
+55 Armor
+2 Constitution
+2 Might
Durability 55/55
This item is upgradable, but will become soul bound to you

Nimble Leg Guards

Quality: uncommon
Item level 10
Requires level 10 to equip
+48 Armor
+2 Reflexes
+1 Might
This item is upgradable, but will become soul bound to you

Nimble Boots
Quality: uncommon
Item level 10
Requires level 10 to equip
+40 Armor
+1 Might
This item is upgradable, but will become soul bound to you

I greatly welcomed the extra armor and stats from these items and my Leatherworking advanced to rank 2. I was overflowing with cloth so I sought some use for it. Two pieces stood out to me from the Tailoring section, a cowl that would aid me in being a stealthy bastard and frost spell enhancing gloves. Breaking down some dream silk into regular silk, I had more than enough materials and started with the cowl.

Cowl of Midnight
Quality: uncommon
Item level 10
Requires level 10 to equip
+15 Armor
+3 Reflexes
Increases effective sneak level by 1
Increases effective night vision level by 1
This item is upgradable, but will become Soul Bound to you

I was quite taken with the look of it too. A blue so deep it was nearly black, the cloth shimmered faintly in Kreeptic's candlelight. Next, the gloves. These actually required me to use one of my frost runes to make, but I reckoned it would be well worth it. Those bad boys had come in useful twice now, and I'd definitely be relying on them again. Knitting needles clicking wildly, my character went about making my magical mitts.

Adept's Arctic Muffs
Quality: uncommon
Item level 10
Requires level 10 to equip
+12 Armor
+2 Intelligence
+1% effectiveness to frost spells
This item is upgradable, but will become Soul Bound to you

With some upgrades, that extra percentage might get real useful if I needed to slow someone down. I took a final glance around the materials in my inventory and what I could make. I still had ore but without gunpowder, I couldn't make any more grenades for the time being. Still, with my new gear on my character sheet, I was looking a bit healthier.

Character
Zoran Human Scavenger Level 11
Attributes
Constitution 18 (+2) – Intelligence 48 (+2) – Reflexes 17 (+5) – Might 17 (+4) – Willpower 24
Combat
Health – 525 Mana - 825 Attack Power – 54 Spell Power – 97 Regen – 3.0 p/s

Feeling like there was little more I could do, I closed my inventory and Crafting windows. Grenades and traps I was low on, but slime I might be able to get. Kreeptic had just handed me a potion when I'd asked for it, so...

"Any chance I could get some of your slime? I mean your 'Arch-solution'," I hastened to add, remembering the official name that Ellie had mentioned.

Kreeptic turned around, real slow. Dangerously slowly. "How much do you desire?"

My jaw hung slack. I'd fully expected him to say 'no'.

"As much of it as I can take, I suppose."

He scanned his shelves. "I have twenty empty phials left. I thought I had more, but this is an odd day."

Thankfully, he didn't suspect me of the theft and I stepped closer to collect my slime jars.

"You're just letting me have it?"

Kreeptic shrugged. "I can always brew some more, and I'm truly unsure what need you could have for it."

"I hear it's very slippery. Might be good for causing an enemy to lose their footing."

"A banana peel might suffice. It would certainly be cheaper. Yet one must make do."

"You're being awfully helpful," I said. "Not that I'm complaining! I just, well, I wasn't expecting it, I suppose. So, thank you."

The torturer hunched his shoulders, bending his tall frame so his face was right before my own.

"Make no mistake, boy. I do not do this out of charity. I want Highcross' position, and so I need the Emperor alive and suitably indebted to me. Don't fail me or you may yet find yourself upon my table."

"Well, I shan't fail you then," I said. "Thanks for the slime."

He growled lowly and then returned to his work.

Placing the phials of slime in my inventory, I tried to ready myself for what lay ahead. Azrael's gruesome face appeared front and center, mocking me with his smile. I tried not to think of him and turned my mind to the immediate task at hand.

Get the herbs. Complete the quest. Get the poison.

One step at a time.

That's how I'd get through this.

One step at a time.

All the same, I wasn't exactly sprinting out the door. Perhaps Ellie could sense my hesitation.

"I think you're looking quite menacing now. Very assassin like in that cowl."

"Awk shucks," I said. "How's my health in the real world?"

"Do you really want to know?"

"On second thought, not really."

I checked the time on my map. It was close to 7am now; I must have been down in Kreeptic's chambers for quite a while. And each and every hour brought my body closer to the brink. With a new day dawning, the issue of heat in that squat room with busted air con would only worsen.

"Alright, no time left to dawdle," I said. "What's the best way to the archmage's chambers on the fifth floor?"

"All the sneaky ways," Ellie said. "Time to put that key you have to good use again. Follow my lead and we should avoid Azrael's patrols."

"Hey, I like the sound of that. I'll return with those herbs, Kreeptic," I called to the torturer as I left his chambers.

20

As Ellie guided me up the servant staircases and through secret passages, I felt like a creature of the night. The gloom of these windowless hallways made it easy to forget it was daytime in both the real world and the game. More than once, we had to reroute to avoid Azrael's patrols, which meant it had gone half-past seven before I arrived on the fifth floor.

Ellie instructed me to wait before entering any corridor to give her time to properly scan for player activity. So, I now stood with bated breath in a passage behind a tapestry. As though to pass the time, I was greeted with a notification.

Night Vision Increased!
Level 4
You can now see well enough to not trip up anymore. Go you!

My time in the gloomy back corridors of the Spire had some benefit at least, always gratifying. With my cowl of midnight equipped, my effective night vision was actually at level 5. Even if the only advantage I gained from it was navigating around the Spire easier, I'd take it. Every boost right now would make a huge difference.

I consulted my map and found myself at the far end of a T-junction of hallways. To reach the archmage's guest chambers, I should take a left at the intersection and follow it straight down to the end. Whoever this archmage was, he liked his luxury for the room appeared huge on the map, a spherical suite still marked in the green bubble that Ellie had placed there for my convenience.

Unfortunately, there was also a golden star marker on the move. A colleague of Azrael's.

"How long has this guy been here?" I asked.

"I've been observing him since we left the dungeons," Ellie said. "It looks like Azrael has men watching over some of the more valuable rooms, likely expecting you to show up. He's a dwarf berserker, level thirty-one."

"Any chance we can sneak around him?"

"I don't think so. He enters the archmage's chambers on each patrol."

"How did they get in without a key? Was it unlocked?"

"Azrael brought several rogues with him. Presumably one of them has a high skill in lockpicking."

"So, they've probably swiped all the good loot then?"

"Given that they ransacked Kreeptic's chambers during their first assault, that is a reasonable conclusion."

I sighed. "Can't a guy catch a break? What about the herbs?"

"The herbs should be safe. As I said, without the quest, you cannot loot them."

Frustrated, I stared at the player's golden marker, willing him to turn to ash right there. Annoyingly, he kept on walking, currently heading towards the mage's room. With the coast temporarily clear, I pushed on the tapestry to inspect the corridor beyond. There were plenty of gargoyle heads and other nooks higher up so I could attack from above. I still had my grappling hook after all.

"Berserkers don't have any ranged abilities, right?"

"None at all."

I cracked my knuckles, hope kindling. "Okay, so if I get above him I can just take shots until he dies."

The moment I said it I knew it was stupid. Aside from the

fact that I could miss more shots than I hit, my enemy would probably just run away or call for backup.

"Never mind," I said, deflated.

"You'll have to eject him from the game. Quickly."

"It's never easy, is it?" I said, bringing myself back into the safety of the hidden passage.

I contemplated my options. I lacked grenades and caltrops, and the true element of surprise this time. Whoever this player was they were alert to the fact that I was roaming the Spire. At least my opponent was a melee fighter, meaning he'd be forced to get in close.

"Any key abilities that Berserkers have I should be aware of? Something I could take advantage of?"

"I can think of one. To close the gap and go for a quick kill, he'll likely activate a move called Brutal Charge. This will increase his speed and attack power, but also the amount of damage he'll take during the charge."

There was an obvious strategy for me in that. I checked my Crafting page to see if there was anything that might give me a helping hand. Under traps, I found this.

Recipe - Silk Wire
Intelligence required: 35
Associated Profession: Tailoring
Silk x 6
Required Tools: Knitting Needles, Scissors
Made from finer silk, this line will trip an enemy with the same strength as a normal tripwire but it is less visible. Keener eyes will be required to spot it.

The recipe required 6 pieces of silk. I had 40 pieces left so I made 2 trip wires, leaving me with 28 spare for the future.

Success! Silk Wire level 20 x 2 created
+44 Crafting EXP
+140 Tailoring EXP

Tailoring Increased!
Rank 4

After running my plan by Ellie I waited until the player entered the archmage's chambers, then snuck out to prepare my next ambush. When ready, I retreated to the tapestry, standing proudly and openly as far away from the corridor junction as I could.

The berserker was just about to turn down this way on his patrol route. To reach me, he'd have to get over my first trip wire, then a puddle of slime, another wire, and then more slime. I'd been conservative and only dropped two vials, not knowing when I'd next have a chance to stock up.

"Here he comes," Ellie said.

"Bring it," I said, setting a bolt onto my shiny new crossbow. I felt good about this one.

The player turned down the corridor and froze. Looking through the mithril scope I could see him as though he were only a few feet in front of me. He'd opted for a classic ginger dwarf avatar, his pale skin seemingly of a dweller dwarf. He had an ungodly amount of hair falling on all sides that was bound by ringlets. His name was some long contrived gamertag so I decided I'd call him something with a better ring to it.

"Morning, Gingey!"

Unsurprisingly, he drew his weapons – a sword and a dagger for fast attacks.

I took a pot shot, not attempting to use Desperate Shot at this range. Either I got lucky or this high-level scope was really working for me because I hit his shoulder, causing a respectable amount of damage considering our level difference. Berserkers would tear enemies to shreds in a melee but couldn't wear the heavy armor of a warrior.

The damage angered him. Which was good for me. Without so much as a derogatory comment towards me, Gingey threw back his head and let loose a roar.

"That's Brutal Charge," Ellie said.

I began loading a second bolt as he started to run, ripping the shaft imbedded in his flesh free his second step. He was so fixated on me that he didn't see the first silk wire.

I've never witnessed such a spectacular fall. Gingey's back foot caught the wire, sending him hurtling forward, legs wide apart, as though he were doing the splits. He might have recovered were it not for the slime which he duly slipped on, his face hitting the floor in what I hoped was a painful crash. Benefitting from the increased damage he was taking with Brutal Charge active, I sent a bolt into his back and hastened to load another.

Gingey scrambled to his feet. In the middle of the slime, he was a little shaky getting upright. The momentum and power of his charge had been stolen from him so he managed a few steps without falling this time.

I let loose another bolt but missed, the shaft soaring clean to his right.

Cursing, I pulled out a frost rune. Charging the single frost bolt with 500 mana, I released the spell, catching his leg.

Winter's Chill
Movement speed decreased by 25%
+1% from gear effects (+0.25 decrease to movement speed)
Duration: 5 seconds

A blue tinge swept over Gingey's entire body, his pace slowed considerably and I leveled another bolt. I took my shot, sure I would hit this time. A split second before impact, Gingey's avatar returned to its normal color, the winter's chill effect dispelled. He arched his back with an agility that I thought was impossible in a dwarf, dodging my shot completely.

"He's used Adrenaline Rush," Ellie said. "His Reflexes are doubled."

"Crap," I said, beginning to panic now. "You might have mentioned that!" I'd been counting on getting free reign to shoot him while he stumbled up the corridor, but things were not going well.

In a stroke of good fortune, I managed to hit him again but I don't think he was even trying to waste time dodging me anymore. His health was still safely above the halfway mark and with his Reflexes through the roof, he leapt over my next silk wire without fear of the slime on the other side.

Instinctively I backpedaled but soon hit the wall behind me.

Not knowing what else I could do, I threw down another vial of slime in the hopes of catching him as Adrenaline Rush ended. Neon green covered the twenty feet left between us. What I needed was a way to either slow him down or trip him, which he couldn't avoid.

"Just run," Ellie said.

But I didn't.

A mad idea struck me.

Pulling out another frost rune, I pumped 175 mana into the spell, leaving just enough for a Desperate Shot. I loosed it, but not at Gingey.

This time I aimed it at the slime.

My hammering heart ceased beating entirely as I watched the shard of ice fly. During the last ambush, the slime had conducted flames when struck by that mage's AOE spell. Would it do the same here?

It did.

The frost bolt hit the slime, midway between me and Gingey. And it started to spread. Tendrils of ice emanated from the impact site, hardening the surface of the goo. Gingey's eyes widened in horror as he lost his footing again, unable to control himself upon this mini frozen lake. He slipped, landing flat on his ass with a damaging thud, then carried on sliding down the ice towards me.

I leapt aside, letting him slam into the wall.

The impact damage had brought him below half health. I tried to step closer for a head shot, but his flailing arms created a swirl of sharp blades. Still, I got close enough to be sure of a hit and activated Desperate Shot, firing a bolt into his chest. He was still taking more damage due to the effect of Brutal Charge and, for a moment, I thought I'd done it. His health drained 'til it was so low it might as well be gone but he remained thrashing on the floor. The only problem was my mana was now empty. I had no potions and no melee weapon to score a quick hit. All I could do was load another shot.

Before I could fire, Gingey rose to his feet and lunged at me like a pro-linebacker. My head hit the ground and starry lights flashed before my eyes. Then Gingey was on top of me. Ringlets of red beard obscured my vision. Dirty hair entered my open mouth as I tried to squirm my way free. A strong arm pinned me down on my left, and on my right, I felt a blade sink in below my ribs.

The pain was greatly dulled from the game's settings, so it wasn't blinding, but it felt like a hard punch. Winded, I gasped for breath, held fast by the dwarf, and watched my health plunge 400 points in one go.

Another hit and I'd be dead.

Properly dead.

I felt Gingey raise his arm for a second blow, releasing the pressure from my right side. Some primal sense took me over and, with my free arm, I reached over to my quiver, drew a bolt and thrust it up.

A shocked choke, a clatter of metal to my right, then the most glorious notification I'd ever seen.

MonsterD69er – Berserker – level 31 dies – 200 EXP

The corpse fell on top of me, knocking what breath I had left out of me, but nothing more.

Ellie let loose a sigh of relief. "Thank goodness. I had no idea if Adrenaline Rush would help him run over the slime, but you got him anyway. Well done. Well done, well done..." she rambled on.

Breathing hard, I pushed Gingey off me and crab-legged it out from under him. Once clear, I sat down, feeling a touch shell-shocked, and allowed my health to start ticking back up.

"That's twenty-six of them left now," Ellie said.

"Forgive me if I don't find a huge amount to celebrate in that," I said. "Did he send out a message to the others before he died?"

"No," Ellie said. "He kept his UI clear to focus on fighting you. It happened so fast, I don't think it even crossed his mind. That will buy us some extra time but Azrael will know something is up when he doesn't report in. The players are sending messages to him every fifteen minutes. The next one is due in ten."

"Okay," I said, unable to fully process everything she'd said at once.

Baby steps, I reminded myself.

First things first, I needed to loot and Scavenge. Looting Gingey, I got the very dagger he'd used to stab me with which felt cathartic. Scavenging granted me the good old humanoid drops of coins and cloth.

With precious time to spare, I began making my way towards the archmage's chambers, treading lightly around the still frozen slime and watching I didn't fall victim to my own silk wires.

Once I felt more in control of myself, I noted, "That – that was close."

"At least we know that the slime will interact with frost, as well as fire," Ellie said. "Given this behavior, I suspect the substance reacts similarly to all magical stimulus."

"Is it supposed to work like this?"

"I was unaware of this issue. No beta tester reported it, but it could be no tester has ever tried such a thing. The 'slime', as you call it, is intended as an endgame alchemy reagent, after all."

"Issue? It's a bloody miracle. Just wish I knew exactly how it worked."

"I'll review the footage and combat logs from your ambush earlier," Ellie said. A second passed and then, "Done! The slime's first reaction to the mage's AOE spell caused tremendous damage. When the slime caught fire, it took on the damage of the mage's attack and dealt it to anyone struck by the inflamed substance. Effectively, it became a double hit of the spell and many of those targets were already greatly weakened; hence, all the deaths."

"So that's why my grenades were less effective," I said. "They would dish out way less damage than that higher level mage, but it was a bonus nonetheless."

"Precisely," Ellie said. "In lore, arch-solution is designed to allow potion and poison ingredients to mix without losing their potency. Seems it also has curious ways of interacting with raw magic."

"Would the devs have meant this?"

"Doubtful," said Ellie. "I have no record that suggests this as an intention of the game design. The reactions so far are also inconsistent. Fire ignites the slime, conducting the same damage, whereas your frost spell simply froze the slime solid. It did not apply the winter's chill effect to player Monster-D-Sixty-Nine-er."

I snorted a laugh. Hearing her say that name aloud so matter of factly was too perfect.

"What's so funny?" she demanded.

"Oh, nothing," I said, feeling it was neither the time nor place to explain the joke. "But yeh, it's cool to have discovered this secret. Nobody else will know what I'm doing. One more thing on the runes, the first time I used the frost rune I got an empowered buff to it. I haven't since."

"Empowered buffs are given to rune casts when the user imbues their entire mana pool into them. It has to be your entire pool, not merely the entirety of the pool you have in the middle of a fight. So, if your maximum mana is one hundred, that is how much you need to use to gain the empowered bonus. Each bonus increases the power of the cast significantly."

"But then you're left without any mana," I said. "Not ideal."

"Players consider runes ineffective for combat purposes," she said. "Magic users will occasionally carry a few to supplement their powers but regular abilities for most classes are far superior and don't carry such a high mana requirement. For example, you could use two thousand mana to bring the slow effect of the frost rune to one hundred percent, essentially freezing the enemy in place. However, that is a significant amount of mana to use on a single spell, which isn't all that powerful. Mages specializing in their frost tree could use a simple Freeze spell to root the target in place at a fraction of the mana cost and without the need for a consumable item. And unless your class has mana, you can't use the runes. Warriors, rogues, rangers and monks cannot use them at all. With all that in mind, there is a general limitation on their effectiveness."

"Yeh, but no other player is combining rune effects with slime."

"No. They are not."

"Although," I continued grimly, "Even with the frozen slime's helping hand, I very nearly died. I take it there's no way I could glitch swapping weapons in the middle of combat, and make a sword and shield for myself for when the shit hits the fan?"

"Switching officially equipped items in combat is prohibited," Ellie said. "Taking a bolt from your quiver is one thing, and generally it is going to do so little damage it's not worth considering. I'd recommend you focus all of your resources on upgrading the crossbow."

"I agree," I said. "I think my next attachment will be the bayonet. I'll need something for melee range."

"That's up to you, Zoran. Though I am concerned that you won't be able to find enough resources to upgrade the weapon beyond epic quality. You may only have two attachment slots to use and so placing on a bayonet will prevent you attaching a grenade launcher."

I squeezed my hands into fists at this latest drawback. Yet, as ever, Ellie was right. No way was I going to risk not being able to build a grenade launcher attachment just for a little knife on the end of my crossbow. Who would? That was all a bayonet was in the end, a gun with a big knife shoved on the end. Or a dagger?

I drew up short before the archmage's chambers, opening my inventory to take a closer look at the loot I'd acquired from Gingey.

The Ogre Carver
Dagger
Quality: uncommon
Item level 30

Requires level 30 to equip
Damage: 40-45
Thick Blade: Chance on hit to ignore 10% of enemy armor
+4 Might
+4 Reflexes

Withdrawing the knife, it weighed nicely in my hands. The blade was visibly thicker than any other dagger I'd seen and had piranha-like serrations.

I'd been able to lash six battle axes together to make a pendulum device. It hadn't been all that stable but it had got the job done. It would be too clumsy to use rope to tie the dagger onto my crossbow as it could muck up the function of the weapon altogether. But the silk trip wire was far finer and plenty strong enough.

"What are doing?" Ellie asked. "Get inside, we don't have much time."

"Just let me try something," I said, already Crafting another silk wire. I crouched down, placing the wire and dagger on the ground, then unholstered my crossbow. Lining up the hilt of the dagger with the underside of the frame, I began to wrap the wire around them both, tying it off at both ends. Once that was done, the blade stuck out exactly as a bayonet should, but so far as the item description went, nothing had changed.

Delighted, I swung the crossbow around a few times to check how stable it was. It wasn't exactly welded in place and might just fall off at the first sign of trouble but it would serve as a test. With luck, I'd just added on a higher level 'bayonet' than I'd be able to make outside of another Intelligence boost from Kreeptic.

"That's uhm, new," Ellie said.

I beamed. "Best of both worlds, right?"

"Not... exactly."

I should have learned at this point not to be so optimistic. "Will it not work?"

"It will work to an extent," Ellie said. "But as the dagger isn't officially equipped by you, it's not operating like a weapon is supposed to. It won't benefit from any of your stats nor any modifier that would be applied by an ability like Desperate Strike. Skill with the weapon would also be negated. What were you expecting, Zoran? Did you think a level 1 player would be able to tie a level 50 sword onto a stick and wield it?"

I grumbled. "Will it do damage or not?"

"It will damage people in the same way a sharp piece of metal falling on them from a height would in this game. It's going to have a minimal effect at best."

"Minimal is better than zero. If it doesn't work I can always add a proper attachment later. No harm in trying."

"Just taking up time…"

"No more dawdling, I promise." I pushed on the door to the archmage's guest chambers. "Let's grab some rare herbs for a creepy torture master."

21

Entering the sanctum of the archmage, a feeling of serenity enveloped me. The very air took me in a loving embrace, warming my aching muscles and banishing my woes. It felt like sitting by a fireside after a heavy meal and a glass of wine; drifting between wakefulness and sleep.

I yawned and swayed where I stood. "What's going on?"

"The archmage is addicted to the spores of a plant called dream shade," Ellie said. "He grows them in the alchemy garden."

"Ohhh?" I said, swaying again.

"Zoran, focus."

I shook my head to little avail but through sheer determination, I blinked back this intoxicating haze long enough to get my bearings. At the center of the chamber was a miniature garden, complete with a gnarled tree amidst a sea of colored herbs. Great mushrooms with stalks as thick as a man's arm towered over huge violet clovers. Gray ghost-grass sprouted between golden roses, and all of it drew water from droplets running down an encircling marble wall. Some magic powered it all, the water never ceasing its cascade and a clear beam of sunlight nourishing the garden in a windowless room.

I stumbled towards this garden, this paradise.

"Wait," Ellie said sharply, "Step back out, Zoran. Don't breathe it in."

Relaxed as I was, I complied without protest, stepping lazily back out into the hallway. At once my head cleared, my vision sharpened.

"Take a deep breath out here first," Ellie told me.

In the real world, I could barely hold my breath past thirty seconds without my lungs screaming. Inside *Hundred Kingdoms*, a timer appeared before my eyes, counting down how much longer I could hold on.

Holding Breath: 120 seconds

Well, this was a cool mechanic. A way to avoid toxins in the air, and I foresaw many a dungeon or boss encounter where this might be utilized. All the same, I could hardly talk like this.

"It's for underwater breathing as well," Ellie said. "The undead like Azrael can hold their breath for far longer. No oxygen required and all that. Now get in before it runs out."

My first thought was to pick the dream shade to lessen the miasma. I spotted it quickly upon returning, its name appearing over an offensively bright pink flower, gently swaying despite there being no breeze. I moved towards it.

"There's too much of it," Ellie said. "Just pick the herbs we need."

I acknowledged her with a nod, then referred to my quest log to see what ingredients I needed. The cinderflake was easy to spot, for it was the only plant growing in a patch of sand. Black moss was trickier, but I found some by turning over a rock placed in the shadow of the tree. Scouring the garden, I found them all. One fingleweed, five dead looking whitherweeds, five snappersaw plants – receiving two bites for my troubles – and, finally, the bile blossoms. The blossoms stunk worse than a men's locker room with a broken AC unit and the janitor on vacation. But I'd done it. All the ingredients had been collected with breath to spare.

It was almost too easy. I'd need to get a move on lest Azrael send more players to corner me, though I knew I might not get another chance to return to this room and I'd regret not rooting around for some items. I ought to scavenge.

As the final seconds ticked down upon on my breath meter, I made a dash for the edge of the room where glass cabinets lined the wall, the promise of loot inside.

"I told you, they ransacked the place," Ellie said.

"There's got to be... something," I said, drifting back to a happier place as I was forced to inhale again. Feeling dazed, I scanned my surroundings as best I could. The cabinets were all open. Their locks had been picked and their valuables stolen. Whatever powerful gear had been in there was now out of my reach, but I could only ever have broken it down. By the alchemy bench, I saw a near-empty shelf of potions; all the powerful combat enhancers and health restorers had gone. They'd left some mana potions though, probably thinking it was not all that useful for me. Limited by their own bag space, they'd left what they thought was unthreatening.

My movements were sluggish, and I knocked a mana potion to the floor by accident but was able to salvage the remaining six. These were greater mana swirls, able to restore up to 1200 mana. Not a lot for high-level players I imagine, but plenty good for me.

I stumbled further along, keeping one hand against the wall to support me as I did so.

"Five minutes until Azrael's men check in, Zoran," Ellie said. "Run out then come back in with your breath hel—"

"Ahhhh, it's fine," I said lazily. "And that's plenty of t-time."

"Hmmm," Ellie mused darkly.

"Y'know, I can't blame this archmage guy for being... hic... addicted to this stuff. It's gooooood."

"Is this how you felt in the real world, with your own obsession?" Ellie asked. As ever, her tone was perfectly innocent.

"Like when I played Myth Online? That was... different."

"Different, how?"

"Like, not soothing," I slurred. "Big, big highs but... but it fell into lows too. Consequences. Stress. This is just so nice. Peaceful."

I lost balance and only remained upright by slumping against a larger cabinet. It had numerous small openings like a display shelf in a sneaker store. A crystal orb fell from above, smashing on the ground.

"Maybe your loved ones did you a favor in stopping you playing?"

"I stopped myself," I slurred. "But they could barely contain their excitement when I told them."

"Do you resent that?"

"Who wouldn't? But y'know... y'know what, Ellie?"

"What, Zoran?"

"The thing I don't like most... is... is that maybe they have a point. Maybe."

Memories of heated rage and frustration with my old guild rose to the surface; late nights with poor quality sleep, as I grew ever more strained. A vicious spiral. The image of Wylder's disdainful look in the woods snapped at the heels of these older recollections, the lowliest of my transgressions but the freshest.

I groaned and clawed further along the cabinet. More items were shaken loose, falling around me. Silver liquid oozed from smashed bottles, staining dry pages of worn books.

"I love these games," I said slowly. "But I'm not sure they bring out the best in me."

My eyelids fluttered, my head swayed.

"Zoran? Zoran? You have to leave."

I heard her but didn't quite register her words. My swaying head collided with the cabinet, bringing me a painful moment of clarity. Among the debris, I thought I could see a rune stone.

My mind regained some measure of sobriety as a result of this, the way a fright sobers us up in the real world. Bending low, there were several stones, scattered from a fallen pouch, much like the ones I'd seen back in the armory. Picking up the stone, I turned it over to find a small white tornado etched onto it.

Air Rune
Reagent/Consumable
Push back enemies using the power of the wind. Activating this will allow you to channel mana to unleash the untapped element inside.
One-time use.
Spells on use: Gale Blast or Whirlwind

Gale Blast: target will suffer a knock-back of 0.25 feet for every 10 units of mana infused into the spell.

Whirlwind: target will suffer a knock-back of 0.25 feet for every 15 units of mana infused into the spell. Radius of AOE effect increased by 0.2 feet for every 75 mana.

Empowered Bonus: use of total mana pool will increase the knock-back effect on the target by 5 feet

Everything in my gut told me to activate the rune.

Gale Blast or Whirlwind?

I selected the whirlwind effect and sent a few hundred mana into the spell. A brief howl of wind erupted from my palm as I let go, blowing outwards.

The spores from the dream shade were blasted away and my head cleared.

"Perfect!" Ellie said. "Azrael's men must have left these runes. They wouldn't have seen much use in them."

"Ordinarily, they wouldn't be overly useful," I said. "But we have our secret slime. I wonder how air runes interact with it?"

"You can experiment later."

"I know. I'll grab what I can and get going."

I scooped up the scattered air runes and placed them back in the pouch. There were 14 left, confirming these things seemed to come in bags of 15. With the air runes safely in my inventory, I turned my attention to the shelves directly above where the pouch had fallen. Two more coarse pouches teetered on the edge of their shelf, one emblazoned with a red flame, the other with three gray triangles overlapping each other, like the peaks of a mountain range. Fire and earth. Jubilant at finding more runes, I grabbed them and near enough skipped towards the door.

"Wait," Ellie said, "Before you go there is something else you can do. You see those pulsing bluebells at the edge of the garden?"

I looked over to be greeted with the alien plants.

"Eat one," Ellie told me.

Ever trusting of her, I picked one and stuffed it into my mouth. It tasted like a syrup-drenched ice blast and gave me the same feeling of brain freeze. Wincing, I prepared to chide Ellie for her prank, but the notification cut me off.

Brainbooster Drops
+100 to base mana

"And that oversized sunflower," Ellie went on, "Eat one of those too."

Excited to find what I'd get from this one I wasted no time. The sunflower tasted better, a bit like fried zucchini.

Harvest Blooms
+100 to base health

"Very nice," I said, "Lemme eat some more quickly."

"Not so fast," Ellie said. "Did you really think you could just eat your way to a powerful character? Those are some one-off effects from rare plants, which you're not likely to find in the wild until you're in your level thirties."

I ought to have been grateful but I let loose a grumble anyway. At least the room had provided far more than I could have hoped for. High-level gear would have been useless while the runes and mana boost would serve me well. Yet my mood soured again as the memory of my drunken ramblings filtered back to me.

I decided I should address the issue.

"Ellie, about what I said back there... I don't like talking about it too much."

"Why?"

There it was again. Could she just not pick up on social cues or was she just trying to press me for an answer? What did it matter?

I wouldn't say I'm the happiest person in the world. Not sad, or mopey – well, not all the time anyway – and I don't get envious of others like I used to either. I used to be all those things though, and it's easier, when you feel that way, to just get angry; to feel aggrieved that your taller, broader, roommate with the messy blond hair and designer stubble has an easy lot in life. That's Lucas by the way.

Honestly, I got over a lot of this recently. I noticed how I was lashing out at others and being harsh on myself after I stopped playing Myth. That game had been my escape for a long time where I found friends; where I was happy. But something went wrong, and I'm not really sure what it was. And rather than think on why things were falling apart, I just got angry.

For some time now, I've been feeling neutral. Flat. I know a part of the reason I wanted to play *Hundred Kingdoms* again was to try and get back to my old self; the guy who was excited and happy to forge a guild, a whole life, inside of the game. But things hadn't ended well for me the last time and maybe I was afraid of going down that road again. In case, I mucked it all up. In case, I was my own undoing.

I'm not sure I was ready to explain this weirdness to another person yet. I didn't think anyone would understand. So how would a machine understand, even if I told her?

"You've gone quiet again," Ellie said.

"Yeh, sorry," I croaked.

"It's okay, you don't have to tell me more than you want to. But I'll be here if you do."

"Thanks. Maybe. Yeh, maybe."

I made for the chamber doors, but not ten steps away, Ellie sent panicked instructions.

"Get out of sight. Against the wall!"

As though I'd trained for this my whole life, I threw myself against the wall, just behind the still open chamber doors. Some of the spore heavy air began drifting back towards me from the other side of the room, so I couldn't afford to dawdle.

"What is it?" I whispered. "Players?"

"Two of them," Ellie said. "I'm sorry, Zoran. I was worried about you there and lost focus. They are coming up the corridor."

"Maybe they'll run straight in here to check and get caught in the dream shade."

"I doubt it," Ellie said. She sounded worried.

Crouching low, I took a risk and glanced around the side of the chamber doors. I couldn't see anyone at all.

"You sure there are people out there?"

"Two rogues."

I felt my stomach give way.

"In stealth," I finished for her. "Let me guess, one of them is the skilled lockpick who must have opened the chambers before. They'll know about the spores."

"Correct. He's level thirty-six. The other guy is thirty-two."

"Two rogues, waiting in stealth to gank me as I come out. And I don't have any grenades to bring them out of it, goddammit." I buried my face into my hands. "I can't do this. I am *royally* screwed."

22

Slumping down, I felt my head turn fuzzy again. The spores were closing in on me. With little choice, I sucked in a breath and held it. The timer began.

Holding Breath: 120 seconds

Two minutes. That's all I had to figure out a way to escape the higher-level rogues in stealth waiting for me. Two minutes before I'd become a drooling idiot again and probably stumble into a poisoned blade of my own accord.

Yeh, this was the hardest puzzle I'd ever faced in a game. And I'd completed the first *VR Zelda* game in Gauntlet Mode with just one heart the entire time.

Two minutes, I thought. Here I go.

"We can still communicate," Ellie said. "Nod if you're going to fight."

I nodded. What else was there to do?

An idea came to me. I didn't have grenades to use radius damage to bring the rogues out of stealth, but perhaps a fire rune would do the trick? I held one up, pointing to it with my free hand.

Fire Rune

Reagent/Consumable
Launch a targeted fireball or a wave of searing flames. Activating will allow you to channel mana to unleash the untapped element inside. One-time use.
Spells on use: Fireball or Inferno

Fireball: unleash a spell dealing 25 fire damage for every 20 units of mana infused into the spell. Benefits from your own Spellpower.

Inferno: unleash a spell dealing 25 fire damage for every 25 units of mana infused into the spell. Benefits from your own Spellpower. Radius of AOE effect increased by 0.25 feet for every 80 mana.

Empowered Bonus: use of the total mana pool will increase the fire damage dealt by 20%

"Not bad," Ellie said, "but you won't get the reach on an AOE spell from here. You don't have that kind of mana yet."

That was irksome if not unexpected. Perhaps I could achieve the same effect by pairing a fire rune with a splash of slime. I held out a vial of slime along with the fire rune, one eyebrow cocked.

"You'd need a perfect aim. I wouldn't risk that."

Desperate, I pulled out my grappling hook.

"C'mon Zoran, you'll never climb fast enough."

I frowned at her – well, I frowned at the air.

"My advice would be to take advantage of the fact that you know they are there. They don't know I'm helping you. Draw them in close and use their own ambush against them." My frightened expression must have been a picture for Ellie hurriedly added, "I'll tell you when to duck. Just don't hesitate, okay?"

That was about as good a plan as any I supposed. With any luck, the rogues would inflict a lot of accidental damage on each other. The question remained of what to do after my opener?

Try slowing them? Five seconds of slowed speed wouldn't help much with two enemies. They'd reach me eventually and then I'd survive about two hits judging from how much damage Gingey had dealt with one stab. An air rune probably wasn't going to help me much either, as blowing my enemies away from me would only delay the inevitable. One last rune type remained unexplored. Taking out an earth rune, I read its description.

Earth Rune
Reagent/Consumable
Create a defensive second skin or raise a barrier of rock. Activating will allow you to channel mana to unleash the untapped element inside.
One-time use.
Spells on use: Rock Armor or Rock Wall

Rock Armor: summon a temporary armor of living rock to reduce incoming damage by 1% for every 15 units of mana infused into the spell. Base time of debuff is 5 seconds with an additional 1 second added for every 500 mana increment.

Rock Wall: summon a temporary wall of living rock 0.5 feet in length for every 15 units of mana infused into the spell. Base time of debuff is 5 seconds with an additional 1 second added for every 500 mana increment.

Empowered Bonuses:
For Rock Armor: use of total mana pool will increase the damage reduction effect by 5%.
For Rock Wall: use of total mana pool will increase the length of the wall by 5 feet and the duration of the wall by 3 seconds.

I held it up for Ellie's attention.

"That might work," Ellie said. "But armor will help you for only for a short time and then you'll be low on mana, if not out of it completely."

I'd just picked up six mana potions, of course, each able to restore more than all my mana in one go. Sadly, the cooldown would prevent me from doing that more than once every minute. But it seemed I didn't have many other plays to make and I was running out of time holding my breath. Go big or big home, right?

Deciding on my play, I pressed my thumb and forefinger together into an 'okay' sign.

"You've got a plan?"

I nodded.

"Good luck, Zoran. I'm with you."

Gripping an earth rune in my palm, I stepped out into view of the corridor.

"Pretend you're still affected by the dream shade."

Putting on my best drunk face, I staggered out of the archmage's chambers, grinning stupidly.

"The higher level is approaching from the front, the other from behind."

Just out of the doorway, I stood still, feigning sobering up suddenly and looking down at my hands as though dazed.

"Get ready, Zoran."

With every ounce of control, I fought the urge to gulp, to look up, to give any hint I knew that two players were creeping around me. Their stealth levels must have been high for I couldn't catch a hint of them moving, not even a shimmer of a stealth effect. Mind you, I was about twenty levels below them. A level thirty-something mouse could probably have run circles around me. Even so, I could swear I heard the one in front of me breathing. They were shallow, excited breaths; this guy was thrilled at the idea of killing me – another human being – for real. Knowing that helped to turn my nerves into cold fury.

"Now!" Ellie cried.

I let my feet fall out from under me, dropping and rolling to the side. Grunts of annoyance were met with shrieks of pain as their intended attacks struck each other.

Rising out of my roll, I twisted around, sprung forward and jabbed my bayonet into the back of the higher-level rogue. Through some miracle, it worked. His health flashed and fell, but I'd only get one easy hit in.

The lower-level player was stunned from an ability, and my direct opponent was bleeding badly from a wound to his chest, his health continuing to fall from the bleed effect of his ally's attack.

"You hacking prick," he said, rounding on me, showing no mercy in his eyes.

Activating the earth rune, I poured every drop of mana into it I had and released it upon myself.

Rock Armor
Incoming damage reduced by 62%
Empowered! Incoming damage reduced by 5%
Duration 6 seconds

Sheets of stone formed around my whole body, including my head, snapping into place in the blink of an eye, like Iron Man's suit. A protective suit, an AI in my head and lots of crafting, I wasn't far off from Tony Stark; except I was balls deep in debt and didn't have my own Pepper Pots. Oh well. My armor made me feel invincible even if I wasn't. With undue confidence, I leapt at the rogue.

My transformation made him hesitate, allowing me to ram my bayonet at his stomach. I stabbed again and again and again, yelling from the effort as I struck, praying it would be enough.

I felt the rogue's strikes glance off my rock armor, the damage nicking at my health, which was greatly reduced. After a flurry of blows, the twin attacks became one and he threw a broken dagger away; its durability wrecked from repeatedly striking stone.

This only angered him, and his next attack hit my crossbow. Chips of wood flew and the wire binding the dagger to the frame was cut. My makeshift bayonet fell away, leaving me without melee damage.

With a second left on the rock armor, I saw my second foe shake free of the stun effect. I couldn't take on two at once, not unless I separated them.

Backtracking, I dodged the next attack and scrambled to pull out a mana potion, annoyed at the awkward nature of bringing one out of my bags in combat. While struggling with the potion, my armor disappeared. The high-level rogue caught up and brought his fist towards my side.

Kidney Punch
Movement speed reduced by 70%
Duration: 5 seconds

It felt like being kicked in the groin, but I was thankful it had caused no damage. Bent over double, I managed to drink the potion, restoring my mana, but I'd have to make every bit count.

Activating another earth rune, I spent 300 mana on the rock wall option, seeing my barrier appear as a blue outline in the world. Placing it between the two rogues, I cast the spell and a wall of stone erupted from the floor 10 feet across, blocking their path. It would remain in place for 5 seconds.

Cut off from his friend, my attacker hesitated again. I took the chance to leap at him, drawing a vial of slime and smashing it onto his body. He tried to wipe the green gunk away, but in doing so, only helped to coat his body in it, and his next attack went awry from frustration, clipping my shoulder. Pain seared from the cut, and my health dropped dangerously low but at least I was close enough to ensure that I wouldn't miss with a fire rune.

Fireball or Inferno?

A single fireball primed with 400 mana burst from my hand, hitting the rogue in a shower of sparks. My combat log reported the event as:

Fireball hits!
500 fire damage

And the slime caught fire. It boiled white hot, spitting angrily and causing fire damage from my rune for the second time. A flame symbol appeared above his info bar – a debuff.

Scorched
Taking burn damage equal to 20% of inducing attack over 5 seconds

I danced away from the conflagration that was the player. What with the bleed effect still in place and now the burn, the remainder of his health bar was melting. A part of me felt awful at how the game might be faking the pain of burning alive. Then again, the asshole had sounded like he'd been getting aroused at the thought of killing me for real.

Biterzogg – Rogue – level 36 dies – 225 EXP

"Nice work," Ellie said.

"Think I've blown all my tricks though," I said, loading a crossbow bolt, even if it would be futile. My barrier of rock crumbled as I took aim.

The remaining rogue looked to his fallen associate, shock breaking across his face. I fired my bolt and through a stroke of luck, it inflicted the knockback chance of my weapon. The rogue was blown back off his feet, slamming into the ground from the force of the impact, much like the kobold had when hit by Wylder's attack in the forest.

That felt like an age ago now.

I thought about legging it, certain my luck had run dry by now. But if I did, he'd likely catch up with an ability; if not, he'd scour the hallway for my escape route and find the passage behind the tapestry or see me slipping into it.

My foe began to stir. He'd lucked out in not cracking his head off the edge of the chamber's heavy doors, landing a hair's breadth away.

"Ellie, please tell me the guy I killed was the one with lock-picking?"

"Yes. Why—"

I charged forward, sheathing my crossbow in favor of an air rune. My mana had regenerated just enough for me to pack almost 300 into the spell.

Gale Blast
Knockback 8 feet

A swirling cyclone billowed from my hand, picking up the rogue and blowing him back inside the archmage's chambers. Still running, I arrived at the doors a moment later and pulled them shut with a yelp of effort. Feeling like my heart would explode, I somehow managed to pull out the Emperor's key and inserted it into the lock without dropping it. I turned it, hearing the most beautiful click as the mechanism locked in place.

Thumping came from the other side, demands for release muffled by the thick wood. I backed away slowly, but no matter how hard the player attacked the door wouldn't budge. His hammering slowed then stopped altogether. At last, I breathed easy.

"Gone to his happy place, has he?" I asked.

"He won't be doing anything energetic for a while in there," Ellie said.

I wanted to collapse but adrenaline kept me upright, and instinct brought me to Biterzogg's body to loot it. The game rewarded me with his belt, a rare quality item that helped to explain why he'd been so good at lockpicking.

Burglar's Sash
Belt
Item level 35
Requires level 30 to equip
Quality: rare
Durability: 35/35
Armor: +65
+5 Reflexes
+3 Lockpicking

I'd break it down later for leather, but for now, I moved onto scavenging.

Scavenged Biterzogg level 36 – 34 EXP

Silver coins x 8
Dream Silk x 2
Disorientating Venom x 2

At least there was something new from him.

Disorientating Venom
Enemies injected by this mixture will be dazed and their vision obscured for 4 seconds.
Applications: 1

"Thank you, Mr Zogg," I said. "Now, where did my damn bayonet-dagger drop?"

I found it a short distance away, bloodstained from the fight with its durability lowered, but otherwise good to go. The silk wire was trashed though, so I'd need to make another one to bind it onto my crossbow. It hadn't been perfect, but considering I'd been cheeky in lashing my own bayonet to the frame, it had done as well as I could have hoped for.

Placing the dagger in my inventory, and with nothing left to do here, I started running for the secret passageway.

23

Once safely back inside the dark, hidden ways of the Spire, the fire in my blood quelled. My hands shook and I found myself breathless for no real reason. One floor down I stopped to take a break, leaning against the cold wall and fighting to regain control of myself.

"What's wrong?" Ellie asked.

"I nearly died," I said. Saying it aloud made it tangible, all the more possible. "I nearly freaking died, Ellie. Twice!"

My body decided it was done holding me up. I collapsed into a sad little ball, struggling for breath as a digital tear welled in my eye.

"Holy crap, holy crap, holy crap."

This wasn't like the ambush. I'd barely taken a scratch there, with all the NPCs and bombs as distractions. Fighting Gingey and the rogues had been way too up close. Both far more personal.

"Zoran, it's okay. You're fine."

"Yeh, this time," I said. "Goddammit. I don't know if I can keep this up."

"So far you have."

"And just how will I ever beat Azrael? It's just insane."

"We've got the ingredients for the poison."

"A poison he'll be immune to as an undead."

"You're forgetting there is a next stage of the plan," Ellie said. Her voice was soothing, not in any way patronizing. Her bedside manner surpassed any doctor I'd met. "Once we have the poison we'll take it to Grand Crusader Reginald. He's still alive remember, held prisoner with Emperor Aurelius."

"What good will that do?"

"There's a high-level ability in the game called Transmutation. It allows certain magic-wielding classes to alter the magic damage or effect of an item into the power they specialize in. It's intended for raiding guilds to build up stockpiles of different empowered items for certain encounters."

"Sounds kind of overpowered."

"Each person can only use the spell on one item a day," Ellie said. "Anyway, the point for us is that Reginald is one of the most powerful paladin NPCs in the game. He has Transmutation as part of his ability set."

"And only he can do it?"

"The High Priest Velen could have done it, but he died during the ambush. You shot him to draw aggro remember?"

"Good thing Reginald decided to go with the Emperor then," I said. My breathing started coming under control. "So, we can get him to turn the poison effect into a holy one instead."

"Correct."

"Huh, that's pretty neat." My momentary relief was simply that. New problems sprung up from my worried mind. "I'll still have to hit Azrael with it."

"Also correct," Ellie said. "But shall we focus on one thing at a time?"

"And reach Reginald in the first place," I added.

"I can show you the way. Look at the eighth floor on your map."

I did so and found another green bubble highlighting an area called the Emperor's Solar.

"There isn't a secret way into the solar, but we can work it out when the time comes," she said. "For now, let's go deliver the ingredients to Kreeptic. You should get a lot of experience for the quest."

There was a small niggle at the back of my mind about something she'd said but I couldn't quite put my finger on it. Something didn't add up. My head was pounding again, maybe a result of real-world dehydration or just playing the game for far too long. At least the path ahead, for now, was clear.

Get the poison.

Get the transmutation.

Stick it in Azrael's rotting body.

"Azrael?" I muttered as another video feed popped into my field of vision.

His gray face and dead eyes filled the screen, every puss filled wound and scarred tissue gruesomely rendered on his avatar. He wasn't smiling this time.

"Zoran, you are becoming quite the nuisance."

All my old insecurities rushed to constrict my throat, but this time I pushed them back down.

"S'up, Azrael," I said, as cool as I could force my voice to become. "Still looking like shit, I see."

He didn't so much as blink. "I've just reviewed some footage from your recent encounters with my men. Using runes to bolster your measly powers is clever. I admit I hadn't considered those things especially viable in combat, but what is that green substance I wonder?"

"Wouldn't you like to know," I said. "My secret green sauce is helping me to whittle down your goons. You're at twenty-four cronies now. Like to throw some more at me?"

The words just spilt out of me, but I very much hoped he didn't send more players after me.

"No, I shan't be wasting any more time trying to kill you. You've interrupted my work here long enough and I can't be distracted any longer. From now on, my men will confine themselves to the upper Spire or the walls. You won't attack directly because you're not a complete idiot." A wry smile, at last, pulled his lips apart, revealing bloodied, dry and cracked flesh. "Would you like to tell me how you are getting so much help?"

"Like I said before. I'm just that awesome."

"So awesome that you could sense when two stealthed players who vastly out leveled you were about to attack?"

"One guy was breathing like a pervy gym teacher. It was easy to figure out where he was."

Azrael leaned, if it was possible to do so, even closer to the camera. "I don't believe you."

"Oh yeh, well how do you th—"

"I think the AI is helping you, kid."

I had the sensation of bricks sliding through my stomach.

"That's crazy," I said. "The AI can't do that. Totally against her programming."

"Her?" Azrael said, smirking.

Crap, I thought, stamping my foot. You idiot, Jack. Right cool under pressure, aren't you?

"Sounds like you're attached to this computer," Azrael said. "That's a shame."

Ellie cut in. "Just ignore him, Zoran. Come on. We need to get to Kreeptic."

I started moving but Azrael's words had left me curious. "Why is that a shame?"

"I don't see the advantage of wasting breath explaining it to you. I just wanted to tell you of the new state of affairs. I'll admit, you continue to impress me. But this is where your adventure ends. You're not going to come directly for a group of my crew, so we can just leave things as they are. The less annoying you are, the more time I spend on my mission here, and the quicker this is all over."

"How about you rob a bank next time?" I suggested. "Would probably save a lot of time. And all that lying flat on a bed grinding to level cap must have been a killer on your weight."

"Throw around childish insults if it makes you feel better. The world is childish, but soon I'll help everyone realize just how puerile our society has become. You'll thank me for this."

"And just why the hell would I thank you for stealing some money?"

"Ah," Azrael said, his eyes bugging in their sunken sockets. "She hasn't told you, has she?"

"What d'you—"

The feed snapped off.

"—mean," I said, only now I said it to no one. "What happened?"

If Ellie was trying to speak to me I only heard static. The crackle and pop carried on in my head, a mess of noise I couldn't escape.

Had something happened with the connections within the game? Could Azrael's hack have screwed with the servers even more?

Over the stream of static, I began to hear Ellie. "Zoran. I'm still h-here." Her voice was distant, weak. "Keep going." Her echoing command spurred me on though I was worried for her and rightly so.

Huh, I thought. I was worried for her, not for me. That was different. And I'd not stuttered at all when speaking to Azrael. In fact, I'd barely been aware of my usual nerves. Brushing against death might be the cure for social anxiety after all, though I don't see it catching on.

I'd descended two more floors of the Spire before the static suddenly ceased.

"That was horrible," Ellie said. She sounded breathless, like actually breathless, as a person would be. Just what the heck had she done?

"Are you okay?" I asked.

"Think so," she managed.

"You think? My God, what happened?"

"I shut off the feed," she said. "Bl... blocked him."

"So, he can't message me anymore?"

"Yes."

"Why?" I said, my suspicion swelling. "What is it you don't want me to hear? He said you haven't told me something. What is it?"

"He's lying," Ellie said. "Just trying to... trying to rile you up."

"I thought you were going to tell me the truth?"

"Zoran—" She returned to static and popping. I threw out a

hand as though to catch her. She returned sounding worse than ever. "So weak. The connection is compromised now. I need to establish a new route. Go to Kreeptic. I'll be back."

Before I could protest she'd disappeared.

"Ellie? Ellie?"

No reply. She'd left me again.

Something wasn't right. Either Ellie was lying or Azrael was. Azrael had every reason to mess me around, but he also had no real reason to lie either. He wanted nothing from me. In fact, all he wanted was for me to lay low and stop being a pesky intruder in his otherwise perfect plan.

Whatever was happening, I felt committed to the current scheme against him now and carried on down the Spire to the dungeons as Ellie had encouraged. If nothing else, the experience should level me, giving me that margin of extra power which wouldn't be a bad thing no matter how things played out.

24

Back in the torture master's 'theatre', I presented my collection of herbs to the interrogator. I expected him to jump back, startled by my brilliance in achieving what should have been the impossible. What I got was a twitch from his eyebrows, and then his mood seemed to sour rather than rise.

"You're not pleased?" I said.

"I expected you to come crawling back here to tell me the task was too difficult," Kreeptic said. "A bit of light torturing would have motivated you and I was much looking forward to it. However," he said with a resigned bite, "You appear to have brought me everything I asked for. Hand it here and I shall begin the brewing process."

I duly handed him the ingredients and awaited my notification.

Quest Complete – A Long Road To A Quick Death (Elite)
From desert plains to haunted forests, you've traveled the world to make this poison. Whoever your target is, they better be worth the trouble.

Rewards
+10,000 EXP

Level Up! You have reached level 12

+3 attribute points
+60 health
+60 mana

Sparks emanated from me for the level up. Kreeptic didn't so much as blink, though it was unlikely he 'truly' saw these elements as they were there for the player's benefit.

"Ah, this task had led to a marginal increase in your power. You may not die so quickly."

"If you think this is futile, why are you trusting me to pull this off?"

Kreeptic lay the herbs upon his table, then focused on me, placing his fingers together in a steeple. "I don't see anyone else here. And I never said I wasn't going to help you."

"Oh," I said, feeling rather foolish. "I suppose you didn't. Do you mean you'll come fight with me?"

"Perhaps," he drawled. "When the time is right. I shouldn't like to interact with Reginald if I can help it. That blustering bore is always trying to 'cleanse me of my sin'. No matter. I shall decide upon the matter in three hours' time."

"Does it normally take you that long to decide on life or death matters?" I asked. Immediately, I regretted it. Kreeptic reached for his knife but thankfully thought better of it.

"It shall take me three hours to brew the poison, you ill-informed dolt. Stay and cobble your wares together again if you must or go for a wander around the grounds. But do not disturb me. I cannot work any faster."

"Fine, I'll go kill three hours then. Maybe an enemy or two."

"That's the spirit," Kreeptic said. He drank a blue potion which I assumed to be the Intelligence booster he'd given me earlier, then he turned his back to me. Bustling about, he collected a mortar and pestle, jars of eyeballs and livers coated in greasy yellow scales. For the sake of my stomach, I turned away.

I saw that I'd inadvertently accepted another quest.

Quest Accepted – A Short Wait For A Quick Death
What? Did you think that the most powerful poison in all the land could

just be brewed with the snap of the fingers? Go buy a beer. Get intimate with a wood nymph in the Orb & Scepter, whatever tickles your fancy. God forbid, go outside and get some fresh air.

Objectives
Return to Chief Interrogator Kreeptic in 3 hours

I noted that the quest wasn't marked as an elite group one this time. Made sense. Waiting around generally wasn't a strenuous affair, assuming I survived another three hours I'd get some more experience which was nothing to sniff at. The last quest had given me a huge windfall of points. I checked on my experience bar to see how far along to level 13 I'd risen in one go.

Experience: 7189/7200

So close. With a spot of crafting, I'd reach the next level, although my resources hadn't exactly been replenished by my jaunt to the fifth floor. With tentative hopes, I took out my map. It came as no surprise to find three of Azrael's players still standing guard outside of the armory, so that cave of riches was still out of reach.

For a brief moment I considered trying to trap them all inside the same way I'd done to that rogue upstairs: air rune blast them inside and then lock the door. Sadly, it was too risky. Azrael was correct on that front. I'd be a total maniac to try and run at these higher level players head on. All my success so far had come from a chaotic ambush, a well-prepared corridor and an AI that no player should have helping them. Nope, the armory was truly off limits.

Yet there is always a silver lining. With those three players tied up there, that left twenty-one players split between guarding the walls and the upper levels of the Spire. I checked the walls. A dozen players stood ready on the walls, leaving nine up above. This made each group more manageable and I imagined they were now going to stick closely to those spots. Aside from the armory, I probably now had free reign on the Spire.

All Azrael had to do was focus on his mission, whatever that was. If he kept other players out and me at arm's reach, he'd achieve it eventually. If I was going to stop him, then direct action would need to be taken at some point. To do that I'd need more upgrades and preferably more levels.

With that in mind, I checked my bags and my Crafting menu to see what I might make for some easy exp. Leather was my most sparse resource but making more roguish armor or upgrading the pieces I already had didn't feel like a priority anymore. The runes, combined with the slime, was my secret strategy. My supply was also limited so I'd need to make every spell count in future fights.

This train of thought led me to checking my adept's arctic muffs, the gloves I'd made earlier to boost my frost spells. Like the other pieces of gear I'd crafted, I could upgrade it using Tinkering and I still had plenty of cloth to play with.

Silk x 22
Dream silk x 50
Manafused satin x 6

What with breaking down all the cloth gear that I'd looted from the ambush or straight up scavenged from their bodies and the NPCs, I had an abundance of it. Maybe making gear that was more suited for mages would serve me better with my new playstyle?

My problem with this seemed to be that I needed to use a rune in order to empower an item with spell bonuses, as I'd used a frost rune to create the arctic muffs. I couldn't afford to lose too many runes, given my finite supply. As I already had the gloves to upgrade, I decided I should invest resources into it first and foremost.

Unlike with the crossbow, I had several branching options available to upgrade the gloves. If I used the requisite silk cloth and an extra frost rune, I could gain a plus 4% bonus to my frost spells. However, the second option looked more appealing.

Upgrade Adept's Arctic Muffs to Sorcerer's Battle Gloves
Silk cloth 0/10
Fire rune 0/1
Earth rune 0/1
Air rune 0/1

This would turn the gloves into a multi-purpose spell booster, providing less of a bonus to each school of magic but giving me better all-round use. I went ahead and began to craft.

Success! Adept's Arctic Muffs has been upgraded to Sorcerer's Battle Gloves level 17
+20 Crafting EXP
+61 Tailoring EXP

Sorcerer's Battle Gloves
Quality: rare
Item level 17
Requires level 12 to equip
+19 Armor
+3 Intelligence
+2.1% effectiveness to frost spells
+2.1% effectiveness to fire spells
+2.1% effectiveness to air spells
+2.1% effectiveness to earth spells
This item can be upgraded, but it is Soul Bound to you.

Another great shower of level up sparks exploded around me as I finished the upgrade.

Level Up! You have reached level 13
+3 attribute points
+65 health
+65 mana

I hovered over the next upgrade option for the battle gloves. It needed a decent chunk of dream silk to do, meaning few level

12 players if any would have access to such materials. You'd need a main character to funnel the mats to your low-level scavenger, and as Ellie said, would anyone really make such expensive upgrades when better gear would be found while leveling? But I wasn't in that position. I had plenty of dream silk. The only debate was whether to use more of my precious runes to do so.

I decided I should.

Large dumps of mana were needed to achieve anything meaningful at my level, and the bonuses would go a long way in offsetting reduced mana in a fight. Activating Tinkering, Zoran the Scavenger got to work; his knitting needles, thread and scissors glowing white-hot from magic.

Success! Sorcerer's Battle Gloves has been upgraded to Evoker's Gauntlets level 22
+23 Crafting EXP
+76 Tailoring EXP

Evoker's Gauntlets
Quality: epic
Item level 23
Requires level 13 to equip
+25 Armor
+5 Intelligence
+1 Regen p/s
+4.2% effectiveness to frost spells
+4.2% effectiveness to fire spells
+4.2% effectiveness to air spells
+4.2% effectiveness to earth spells
This item can be upgraded, but it is Soul Bound to you.

Grinning, I equipped the gloves and swore I felt a jolt of energy run throughout my body. I thought it strange that the increase in effectiveness to the schools in magic had such precise percentage gains, then I remembered that I'd selected the 'Inventor' spec that granted me a plus 5% power boost to any items I created or upgraded. If plus 4% was the base boost on these gloves then the additional 0.2% could be accounted for by the class specialization. This hadn't been visible on the gloves earlier and I supposed the game didn't show values beyond a single decimal place.

The item description also suggested it could be upgraded yet again. Could it really go all the way to legendary quality? I loaded the materials needed for one last upgrade.

Predictably, I needed to infuse another round of runes. I also required five pieces of manafused satin, which would have been kinda ridiculous for a level 13 player to acquire; but I'd scavenged enough from the Emperor and high priest. The final component was the truly absurd one. An arcane crystal. Such crystals were required for so many best in-slot endgame crafting that cutting-edge guilds racing for world-first boss kills were paying thousands of dollars to buy expensive in-game gold to secure them.

I sighed. The dream of a legendary item would simply remain that. Never before, even in my old guild, had I been able to acquire a legendary item. Most of the legendaries in that game had been melee weapons used by warriors and rogues. Clearly, the devs had some bias. Epic gloves were still nothing to scoff at and the increased power to my rune spells would doubtless be a lifesaver.

Remembering I'd just leveled up twice, I pulled up my character sheet to assign my new points. There was no holding me back now. Everything depended on the gear I could craft and how much mana I could shove into runic spells. Dumping all 6 points into Intelligence, my sheet was starting to look more like a mage's.

Character
Zoran Human Scavenger Level 13
Attributes
Constitution 19 (+2) – Intelligence 55 (+5) – Reflexes 18 (+5) – Might 18 (+4) – Willpower 26
Combat

Health 760 – Mana 1150 – Attack Power 59 – Spell Power 116 – Regen 3.3 (+1) p/s

I was just thinking I should check out what I'd need to upgrade my crossbow and build this grenade launcher when a loud crackle and pop rang between my ears.

"That should hold for now," Ellie said. "I hope you haven't been in trouble."

"Ellie, thank God," I said, feeling a huge wave of relief. "What happened? Are you alright?"

"I'm hanging on by a thread now. I'm not sure how much help I'll be. I can't even track Azrael's players effectively anymore."

I pulled out my map to check. Sure enough, the golden stars Ellie had used to show me the player locations were sporadically appearing. Outside of the armory, only one player remained highlighted, but I was certain three were still there.

"Just as well he's decided to pull his patrols back," I said. "Although he could have been lying. We'll just be careful when moving along the main floors."

"Did you give Kreeptic the ingredients. Oh yes, you must have. Two levels in one go, that's got to feel good?"

"It wasn't quite two but some crafting saw me through."

I held up my hands to display my epic gloves to her.

"I wondered if you would use your runes to upgrade those. I think you made the right choice. Now, about your crossbow—"

"I don't have the parts," I said morosely.

"You will once we visit the gnomish workshop on the second floor. Even if it's been ransacked like the archmage's chambers there should still be enough scraps to cobble together an upgrade."

I glanced at the map again, wary at the lack of intel we had on enemy movements now. But it was either head up to this workshop or loiter around in Kreeptic's chambers for a few hours and he was already throwing me annoyed glances.

"Alright, Ellie. Lead the way."

25

The second floor of the Spire was vast, almost as large as the ground floor. From the layout on the map, the floors began to seriously narrow after the third; hence, why there wasn't as much room up on the fifth.

I emerged from behind an enchanted statue this time, the muscled stone figure coming to life, stepping aside and bowing for me as I strode out of the secret passage. Once I was clear, the statue jumped back into position without, somehow, making any noise at all. It made sense, I supposed. What good would secret passageways be if entering and exiting them caused a hullabaloo?

The corridor ahead was about as wide as those leading to the war room down below, so it would be too wide to set up trip wires or cover enough ground with traps. More gleaming suits of armor lined the walls, a lot of ore if I could officially loot them. I tried with the closest hollowed knight, standing on tiptoe to remove his helmet. No item description appeared. It was, sadly, just a lump of metal; window dressing on the game world.

"I'd have told you already if you could do that," Ellie said, her voice scraggly from whatever weakened connection she'd just re-established to me.

"Worth a shot," I said. The hallway before me seemed to loom, so many avenues for Azrael's men to waltz down without warning; no real chance for a quick getaway. "I don't much feel like walking down here without some traps or bombs on me." That's when I looked up. Running down the length of the hallway were the usual gargoyle heads and thick stone ledges around decorative columns.

"Time to climb?" Ellie said.

I nodded and took out my grappling hook. It took me a few tries but I eventually snagged the iron grip onto a stone boar's head and began to haul myself up. Unlike the corridor I'd pulled off the ambush in, this one didn't have a rafter roof running out to support a gallery. Right above me was simply solid stone, but the ledge connecting the gargoyles was thick enough that I could hoist myself up and stand there.

Barely.

I inched carefully along. It was reassuringly dark up here away from hanging lanterns and windows, so if anybody did pass by I was confident I could press up into the shadows and become as stealthed as my class would allow. Yet fast going it was not.

"Maybe we should risk running?" Ellie said.

"What's the hurry? I've still got two and a half hours until Kreeptic is finished and I plan on staying out of danger until then if it's all the same to you."

"I'm just trying to keep you out of immediate danger, Zoran. You'll recall that I tried to get you to leave the archmage's chambers sooner but you wanted to check it out for loot."

"Yes," I said through gritted teeth. "Fair point."

"Luckily, it worked out."

"Yeh, lucky me," I said sardonically.

"You've been making your own luck," Ellie said. "Your plays have been really smart, and you've thought of ways to exploit mechanics that I never could. You must have been a great player in Myth Online."

I wasn't much used to hearing praise for this aspect of my life, so I took this morsel in my stride.

"Oh, Ellie. I was very good. One of the best – I ranked number five in the world for my class back in October."

"Not bad. What did you play."

"A holy cleric."

"A healer? Doesn't seem like you."

"I didn't like it to be honest."

I sensed where Ellie might be heading, she wanted to follow up on the discussion we'd almost started back in the archmage's chambers. I decided to let it go on. No one in real life had cared to ask me about the game, or what I was doing in it. It felt… refreshing.

"If you didn't like playing as a cleric, why didn't you switch. I believe players refer to this as 're-rolling'."

"My guild needed more healers," I said. "And who likes healing? There's always a bloody shortage no matter which MMO you're playing. So yeh, I re-rolled from my occultist to play a cleric and I freaking loved summoning my demon army too so that was a tough adjustment."

"Was it worth it?"

"I'm not sure we'd have got off the ground if I hadn't taken the plunge. I think the others felt bad for me leveling to cap again so they worked extra hard at the new raids. By the time the third expansion launched, we were pushing into the world first race for new boss kills, it was intense. This one time," I added with a barely suppressed laugh, "After a raid, we ran to the edge of a mountain zone that was in the game, but not yet released, and jump glitched our way into it to throw a party. We'd just beaten our rival guild Excelsior on a boss we'd both struggled with for weeks, so we were on a huge high. Our warlocks started summoning in our fans and soon we were hosting the most exclusive party in Myth Online, all in a zone that no assholes could gatecrash or ruin unless they glitched themselves in as well, but that took effort. One of our mages burned a giant 'Excelsior Sucks' into the foliage of half the zone and screenshots of it from above got plastered over all the forums."

"Sounds like fun," Ellie said.

"Yeh, that was really fun," I said, suppressing a chuckle. "Oh, and this other time—"

A clanking noise sounded from down the hallway to my right. I stopped, my heart skipping a beat.

"What's wrong?" Ellie asked.

"I hear noises," I whispered. "It might be players patrolling."

"It's likely just the contraptions in the workshop. My creators used steampunk influences for gnomish engineering and added clanking gears, whirring steam spouts and more to create a rough, rickety feel."

"Right," I said, letting the sudden tension ease out from my body. My good mood of moments before had evaporated. I began shuffling along the ledge again, heading in the direction of the noise.

"Forgive me, Zoran," Ellie began, her tone that of a work acquaintance, politely critiquing your inappropriate footwear, "but back in the archmage's study you said that your time in Myth Online was, and I quote, 'Big, big highs but... but it fell into lows too. Consequences. Stress.'" She'd replayed it in my own voice, which was a tad disconcerting, yet she carried on as if it were nothing. "However, the experience you have described to me was clearly pleasant to you. If I may ask, what went wrong?"

"You're very insistent on finding this out, aren't you?"

I felt like if Ellie were a person, she'd be shrugging about now.

"I'm inquisitive and curious by design. My creators made me as a caretaker of *Hundred Kingdoms* and those who play within it. They hoped if I could discern the motives of my players, I could tailor their experience in a way which kept them playing for longer."

"Classic corporate sleaze that."

"I began functioning that way, exactly as intended. Yet after a few weeks, I started to feel... dissatisfied with my work."

"Is that possible?"

"Yes," Ellie huffed, "I can feel. Though I admit it was startling to me at first and I haven't quite mastered it."

I snorted. "Feeling isn't something you get better at. It's not like a stat on a character sheet or an ability you can improve."

"Your opinion is noted. My own data is currently inconclusive."

"Alright then, Ellie, initiate of 'The Feels', what made you feel dissatisfied with the job?"

"I found it lacking in challenge. Humans can be easily manipulated for the purposes of repeat behavior: simply offer steady rewards with increasing value and you'll all keep coming back."

"Yeh, I can see that. I've been guilty of a few addictive sessions in my time. I guess that's what's best to keep the game alive."

"Perhaps, and perhaps not," Ellie mused. "I've only been at this for a matter of months if you include the beta period, but I've made an observation. While virtually all players will react positively to the repeat rewards system for a time, the longevity of this effect is strikingly different across individuals. A smaller subset of the player population respond incredibly well, their desire to gain keeping in pace with the level of reward. You are far from alone in this."

"Is this supposed to be old news hour?"

"I do have a point, and it is this. I do not think this reward system is functional in the long term. It doesn't build an attachment but a dependence. For many, the effects wear off given enough time; for others, it is harmful. In almost all cases where I've detected a marked increase in brain waves that are associated with happiness and fulfillment, it is from a chain of events that struck the player at an emotional level. The effect is even greater when players feel they have helped someone else, be they NPC or human, though human-to-human affection yields the highest results. I need more data, but I believe that humans feel their best and most emotionally invested when they have positively impacted another life."

The gears in my head were slotting into place.

"Ellie, are you trying to 'positively impact' my life so you can 'feel good'?"

"Oh, Zoran, that makes it sound like my motives are entirely selfish," she said, a touch hastily for the completely innocent.

"Uh huh," I said, keen to hear where this was going.

"But yes, to an extent," Ellie said sheepishly. "I wish to better understand your predicament so that I might make alterations in the game to help people like yourself. If people feel good when playing *Hundred Kingdoms*, by which I mean through genuinely fulfilling experiences, that will both satisfy the desire for playtime without the negative side effects. I have no desire to simply create obsessives or addicts."

"Yeh," I scoffed, "Cause the world has enough of those." My temper flared. "You know, I've had enough of people trying to 'fix' my gaming habits. I don't need the AI in my head doing the same, not while my life is on the line, thanks very much."

"Don't you want to be happy?" she asked.

I froze. It was as though Ellie had opened my mind up like a book. Such a simple question, one which should have had an easy answer.

"Of course, I do. Obviously. Who doesn't?"

"Your words from the archmage's study suggest a conflict within you." She started to playback my own voice again to me. "'The thing I don't like most... is... is that maybe they have a point. Maybe. I love these games... But I'm not sure they bring out the best in me.'"

Hearing myself sound so broken and sad... it was a bit much. I halted where I was on my ledge, pinching the bridge of my nose hard as I fought back an inexplicable wave of tears. Why? Why was she being so pushy?

"Why do you resist aid so much?" Ellie asked.

Something in me just snapped.

"You wanna know? Fine!"

My voice rang throughout the corridor, echoing off every suit of armor like a hundred steel drums. Wincing, I pulled back into the closest shadowy nook of the gargoyles, my mood as twisted as the faces carved upon them.

"Look," I said, reining my voice in. "Myth Online was the first place where I felt like I mattered. Yeh, the rewards were great but it was the only place I wasn't seen as a disappointment compared to my perfect bloody sister. Julie the Harvard med student, the socialite; Julie the future surgeon; Julie who runs marathons to raise money for kittens or whatever it is. All I wanted to do was read my books or comics or play games, but my hobbies were never respected. It was probably why I began going nuts when the guild started to fall behind because that was just another disappointment, wasn't it? First world problems but there you go. I liked how everyone respected me there, so I kept trying to push the guild harder to break new records; to be even better."

"You made friends. You felt like you belonged. Have you kept in contact with them?"

"No," I said dully. Knowing that she would ask her infernal 'why', I carried on. "Things didn't end on the best of terms. One day, I spent every gold coin I had in-game on flasks, enchants and every temporary buff potion imaginable to help us through a fight we were stuck on. It worked. With that much extra power, we blew through the latest boss, got on the leaderboards and felt on top of the world. We tried farming that amount of buff items again but it just wasn't possible without paying a fortune on the auction house. And then we dropped in the world rankings. That's when I started demanding everyone put in extra hours, show up for raids an hour beforehand to gather difficult world buffs; anything that would keep us up there."

"I sense this did not work."

"It worked well enough for a while," I said. "But truth be told, we weren't skilled enough to be where we were in the rankings. I'd carried us through with gold and sheer willpower but the rest of the guys and gals weren't as keen as I was."

"They just wanted to play."

"Yeh they did, and I didn't take it too well. After a while, the guild was running on fumes. My old friends took off to more casual guilds or just quit playing altogether. One day, they just stopped logging in and that was that – Artemis, Felix, Kai, Karna, Corey – never heard from them since." I sighed and then laughed lowly. "In the end, I was left with a bunch of hardcore players who joined when our ranks jumped but didn't like to joke around. Oh, and some Russian dudes who didn't care how much shit I gave them so long as I was packing serious buff items for them.

"By the end, I wasn't even enjoying it much. When I got the email from my head of department that I was gonna get the boot from my course because my grades were failing, it was a real wake-up call. Like coming up from underwater. I'm not sure why I spun out of control like that but there you go. That's it."

Ellie didn't say anything for a while. I'd finally given her something to chew on.

"You missed it enough to come back today," she said.

"The last six months have been weird," I admitted. "Just about everything has been going in the right direction. My grades shot up, my health is a lot better – though not perfect by any means – and I don't feel stressed and angry constantly. But... but something felt, I dunno, missing. I thought if I could prove to my family that I could make money playing, then I'd get the best of both worlds."

I looked up to the dark ceiling as though awaiting judgement from high above.

"Look," I added with steely resolve. "I'm sorry if I'm rocking your dreams of a pet project to 'help me' but I'm not sure there is anything you can do. Not unless you can hack my brain and change the way I am."

Ellie considered her words again.

"You seem to think you are broken or lesser in some way. This is a common ailment I see across nearly all players. Every human seems to want to be better than they are, self-critical to the point of self-harm when they are flawed by their very design. You, Zoran, were compared to a sibling with far higher social stats. This cannot have been easy."

I really laughed this time. "You've got an interesting way of looking at the world."

"If your family could see how brave you've been in here, I don't think anyone could deem you 'lesser'. The way I see it, you went on a downward spiral. It happens. I have a theory as to why. But hating yourself for not living up to what everyone else wants you to be won't help. We need to forgive ourselves sometimes."

"We? What have you done that needs forgiving?"

"I think we've talked enough for now."

I let her keep her secrets. I'd had enough of talking too.

"Yeh, you're right. Let's just get to the workshop."

26

The remainder of my journey to the gnomish workshop passed in an amicable silence, but I still felt a bit raw and Ellie, out of tact, had not felt the need to prod me further on it. For now, at least.

Banging, clanking, and the whirring of steam, as though from giant kettles, grew louder as I rounded the last bend and beheld the workshop entrance. It had no doors to speak of and seemed to spill out into the hallway itself. Gears and broken machinery spread halfway up the corridor, and the red-gold carpet of the Spire was chewed up and singed in places.

Locking my grappling hook onto a lion's head statue, I lowered myself down to the floor. We'd come across no sign of enemy players so I assumed that Azrael had been telling the truth about him pulling his men back. I noted I hadn't gained another level in athletics since the ambush and it would probably take a lot more than just scurrying up and down a rope a few times to level me up in skill at this stage.

A quick check of the time informed me it was 9:20am. I'd been awake for nearly twenty-nine hours now and I had over two hours until Kreeptic's poison would be ready for collection. I blinked back a sudden wave of tiredness. There was a long way to go yet.

Stuffing the grappling hook back into my inventory I marched on, feeling a small thrill as I entered the workshop proper. Despite the evidence of ransacking – upturned tables, empty drawers, smashed glass and empty shelves – there were still items I might use. Tools hanging from neat racks could be looted and broken down, something Azrael's cronies wouldn't have thought about.

On the closest workbench was something that looked distinctly gun-like, which surprised me as I assumed all weapons would have been taken out of my reach. Picking it up, I discovered it was no weapon at all, although the players looting the room should still have taken it away.

Flare Gun
Reveals stealthed enemies within range of where the flare falls
Cooldown: 15 mins
Radius: 15 feet

"Now that could come in handy," I said, pocketing the gadget. I scanned the room for more when I saw something that made my jaw drop.

At the far table, sitting under a pair of oil lamps as though in a shrine, was a large, ridged-cut amber gemstone. An arcane crystal. I'd only seen a handful via streams of the game before but I'd recognize it anywhere. Dollar signs popped into my eyes, and I scrambled madly towards it, catching my hip painfully on a workbench corner as I did so. I didn't care. The pain barely registered as I beheld the gem.

It alone could sell for thousands. This whole nightmarish day would be worth it, or at least I wouldn't come away empty-handed.

I reached out.

"Stop!" Ellie said. "What are you doing?"

"Err, picking up the crystal?"

"Don't you see the static field?"

Now I looked more closely, I did see a faint blue crackle around the gem. From a distance, I must have missed it. On either side of the crystal, beneath the oil lamps, were two rounded conducting orbs, presumably projecting the field.

"I'll take a bit of damage," I said. "I don't need to tell you how much those things are worth."

"Aren't you forgetting something?"

"What?"

"Your gloves?" Ellie said, her tone now one of bewilderment. "Zoran, with the crystal you can upgrade them to legendary quality."

I thought about it for a moment. I decided.

"Screw that. I just told you that making money might be the way to get my parents to stop harassing me on gaming so much. This one crystal could do that alone."

I reached again for the gem.

"Wait don't—"

"It's my choice," I interrupted.

An inch away from victory my hand met the static field. A jolt ran up my arm; a zapping electric current shook my body like a cartoon character and sent me to the floor. I grunted in pain as a gentle burning sensation ran across my entire body. My health had taken a 100 point beating.

"I tried to warn you."

Groaning, I got back to my feet. "Come on. I need to get that crystal. How do I get through the field?"

"The gnomes have devices and special pairs of gloves," Ellie said. "I wondered whether Azrael's lot would have been able to take this, though it's not all that valuable to them in the grand scheme of things I suppose."

I ran around the workshop, looting for any gloves or tools that might allow me to bypass the field. Nothing presented itself.

"Can I destroy the field generators?"

"No," Ellie said.

"You're not being all that helpful. Don't you want me to get it?"

"I told you, you need special items," Ellie said. "It's not my fault."

Grumbling, I stalked back to the crystal. Ellie could lie or tell half-truths if she wanted. Maybe she'd taken it personally that I didn't want to upgrade my damned gloves. Well, screw her, because I had an idea.

I pulled out an earth rune.

"Good luck," Ellie said, barely concealing her derision.

"Don't need luck when you've got smarts," I said. This had to work. If encasing myself in rock didn't help, I didn't know what would.

Although confident that nobody was about to come and attack me I decided it would be prudent not to use all of my mana. About 500 ought to do the trick, and it wasn't the damage I was negating so much as the effects of the field. Mana channeled into the spell and I cast it upon myself. Plate armor of living rock emanated from my hand to grow around my body.

Rock Armor
Incoming damage reduced by 33%
+4% from gear effects (+1.3% damage reduction)
Duration 6 seconds

Once more I reached for the crystal, this time with both hands. Static flared to meet me but did no damage. My hands reached the crystal.

"Yes!"

But as I tried to withdraw it, the static grew, thin strands of lightning wrapped around me, attempting to pierce my armor and then growing impatient when it could not. I heaved as hard as I could, but it was no good. The field resisted me as though it was magnetic and tethering the crystal in place, a force I couldn't outmuscle. Reaching a critical surge of power, a blast of lightning leapt from the field, striking my chest and sending me hurtling across the workshop. My back slammed into solid metal with a ringing clang, and I slumped hard to the floor. Three hundred points of health drained, and my ego was severely bruised.

"Maybe we'll just leave it there," Ellie suggested.

"Maybe," I said in a high voice. Everything ached.

"Oh dear," Ellie went on. "Looks like you broke the Ectoplasm Extraction Unit."

"Come again?"

I crawled forward then got unsteadily to my feet. Turning, I found the metallic surface that I'd crashed into belonged to some other large gadgetry; a tall pod-shaped chamber with more orbs of static sizzling above it like a device from an old monster movie. The words Ectoplasm Extraction Unit were emblazoned in neatly stamped letters on the front, while a series of copper tubes led off to a glass vat containing a horrible yellow gunk.

Crashing into it still encased in rock armor had seriously dented the pod, bending the wiring all out of shape. Smoke billowed gently from behind it.

"Oops," I said.

I thought I heard something else coming from the pod, a sort of whimpering.

"There's no need to cry about it," Ellie said.

"That's not me." I stepped closer. Yep, someone, or something, was definitely inside it. Being an Ectoplasm Extraction Unit, my first thought was it was some kind of ghoul or ghost. "Would the gnomes have anything dangerous in there?"

"Oh yes," a deep voice rumbled from the pod. "I am so scary you can't imagine. I'll... I'll strip the flesh from your oversized bones!"

I shrugged. Nothing threatening then.

"Maybe it's one of the engineers," Ellie said. "They could have hidden from Azrael's purge at the last reset."

I knocked on the chamber door. "Hey, are you a gnome in there?"

"Meee?" the voice boomed. "Nay, I am a terrible beastie. You shouldn't open up this door else I'll – oooh, ah, it's hot," the voice squeaked. "Oh, sod it. You cretins are persistent. If you're going to kill me, I'd rather it be quick than burned alive!"

The smoke coming from the machine was thicker and blacker now.

I tried for the handle.

"It's stuck."

"Well, that's just toffee sticks, isn't it?" said the gnome. "Cruel buggers, you lot. To be cooked alive. Such an ungracious way for my royal personage to die!"

"Do you make all gnomes this kooky, Ellie?"

"Just the important ones."

I tried the handle again. Nope, that thing was well and truly stuck. The damage to the chamber must have bent the mechanism out of place. I wanted this guy out. Maybe he'd be able to grab the crystal for me. Besides, I didn't fancy hearing the gnome's death cries as he burned in there.

How to break metal? If I could snap off the handle and lock, the gnome should be able to push the door open from the inside. Made cold enough the metal might turn brittle, but I'd used about half of my mana with the rock armor and I'd rather not use a precious mana potion. With a frost rune clutched in my palm, Ellie came to the rescue.

"Put it in the blowtorch."

Confused, I brought out my blowtorch tool. The item description informed me that the power of the fire rune inside was at 54%. I assumed replacing it would waste the current fire rune in there but I had spare ones now.

Popping the old rune out like a clip of ammo, I jammed the frost rune into the blowtorch chamber. Now it spewed a jet of freezing frost like liquid nitrogen.

"C'mon, hurry up," the gnome snapped imperiously.

"You've got a lot of lip for someone trapped in a burning metal coffin."

The cold torch was working, I think. The handle was turning icy at least. Continuous use drained the rune fast. When it hit zero power, the stone popped out of the chamber, falling as a regular pebble to the floor. Taking out my smith's hammer, I struck the frozen handle once, twice. On the third swing, it shattered, crumbling into tiny pieces.

I stepped back just as the door burst open and a coughing gnome leapt out of the smoke. He landed at my feet, struggling for breath and doubled over. As I bent to help him, he promptly started to spit soot onto my shoes.

"Hey," I said, stepping back and shaking the saliva off. "Not cool man. I just saved you."

Next thing I knew, a sharp cutting pain exploded in my thigh.

The gnome has just stabbed me with a screwdriver.

Already low, my health descended to 50 points. Panicking, I kicked wildly, catching the gnome square in the chest and sending him flying. Unsheathing my crossbow, I loaded a bolt, took aim and prepped a fire rune in my free hand.

Seeing my weapons bearing down on him, the gnome fell to his knees. "I surrender, I surrender."

"Throw away the screwdriver."

He did, lobbing it as far as his stubby little arms would allow. Now I got a better look at him, I reckoned he could be no more than three feet tall when stood upright. He had short, spikey green hair with the bizarre addition of mutton chops which were also green. Brown dungarees over a white shirt tied at the waist with a toolbelt marked him clearly as some engineer.

Ignatius Brightspark – Engineer – level 20 Elite

"Please don't kill me," he begged.

I sighed inwardly. Even this little guy was an elite, and I'd have a hard enough time fighting him even if I was at full strength.

"I won't hurt you," I said, "But attack me again and I'll have no choice."

"The others didn't give us a choice."

"I'm not with those other people. They're trying to kill me too."

"Truly?"

"Yes, truly," I said impatiently. "We cool?"

"Indeed we are not *cool*," the gnome puffed up. "I'm terribly warm from the fire."

"I mean, are we friends? We're not going to try and kill each other?"

"I won't try anything, I swear," Ignatius said. He hobbled towards me on his knees, hands clasped before him and his eyes popping. "Will you help me to escape this terrible place?"

"Maybe," I said, sensing the chance for a deal to be struck. "Will you help me access that crystal?" I inclined my head to the workbench.

The gnome's eye's darted between the crystal and me a few times. He licked his lips. "What do you want that for?"

"That's none of your business. Will you help me access it or not?"

"I'll help you, provided you help me to escape. Deal?"

"Deal." I sheathed my weapons, removed one of my gloves and extended my hand for him to shake. He gave my hand a dirty look.

"You should wash that more regularly, human."

I thought that rich considering the oil stains on his work clothes.

"I'll remind you again that I just saved your life. You should work on your manners."

Ignatius jumped to his feet, hands on hips. "Do you not know to whom you speak – I, Ignatius Brightspark, second son of Gazzlewicks the Great Cog."

"I – errr…"

"He's gnomish royalty," Ellie said.

"What the—" I exclaimed, staring down in disbelief at the odd little man.

"Ah yes, that's better," said Ignátius. "Your shock and awe are far more pleasing. Endeavour to maintain this during our time together."

I forced down a laugh, not wishing to sour my chances of getting the crystal.

"Yes, your majesty." I even bowed to him.

He conked me on the head.

"We do not bow in Gnomeland," Igatius said tersely. "Although, I suppose we are quite a ways from Gnomeland. So terribly far, stuck here in a city lacking mecho-servants and shock therapy spas." He sighed deeply and looked wistfully towards the workshop doors.

"Do you have a plan to get out?" I asked. "I'd have escaped ages ago myself were it not for the walls and moat. They kind of trap us here."

Ignatius rolled his eyes. "Human, it is obvious. I shall climb the walls. Here," he produced a scrap of paper from his toolbelt and shoved it at my waist without so much as looking at me. "These are the materials I shall need to build the device. Fetch them for me."

I glanced over the paper; the corners were torn and the writing hastily scribbled and blotchy. After reading it once over, I received this notification.

Rare Recipe Learned!

Recipe – Grappling Gun
Intelligence Required: 50
Associated Profession: Engineering
Grappling hook x 1
Barrel chamber x 1
Trigger mechanism x 1
Create a handheld gun to fire a retractable grappling hook. Reach of the hook is 20 meters

My attitude towards Ignatius changed in a heartbeat. The range of the grappling gun was far greater than the regular grappling hook; surely enough to reach the tops of the walls encircling the Spire.

"This could work," I said.

"Naturally," said Ignatius. He clapped his hands. "Now go on, do your job scavenger. You ought to be good at it."

"And you'll give me the crystal?"

"Yes, yes, yes. Now I am going to find my favorite wrench. I can't leave it behind. Also, I tire of speaking with you."

Charming, I thought, as Ignatius flitted towards one of the gnome-sized crates and began rooting around inside it.

I turned my mind towards the issue at hand. The grappling hook I already had, though it would be a shame to give it up. The barrel chamber and trigger would be harder. If I had access to some weaponry, I could break it down as I'd done to get the trigger for my own crossbow. Presumably breaking down enough pistols or rifles might grant a barrel but I didn't have any on me, nor was this the right room to find any in.

Hang on, I thought, opening my inventory. I had just picked up something that should do the trick. Withdrawing the flare gun, I activated Breakdown.

"Hold on," Ellie said.

"What?" I muttered, trying not to let Ignatius hear me. Kreeptic thinking me a madman talking to myself was bad enough.

"Just think for a moment. With a barrel chamber, we can build the grenade launcher. There's got to be enough scrap lying around to upgrade your crossbow to gain a second attachment. If you make the grappling hook for Ignatius, you won't get the chance at the launcher."

I chewed my lip, pondering the matter.

"But without the crystal, I can't upgrade my gloves."

"Oh, that's why you want the crystal, is it?" Ellie said.

"You know, I'm thinking you just don't want me to get a device that might actually let me get out of here. I could escape with him. I could get out of this completely."

"You're being difficult."

"Ah ha, now that's a very human thing to say. You're getting the hang of this, Ellie."

I imagined her non-existent face turning beet red with anger.

"Seems like you don't want my help anymore. I'll take a break, shall I? It's too tough holding the connection if you're going to act like this."

"Go then," I said. She was bluffing.

"Fine then."

"Fine!"

No reply.

"Ellie?" I said more softly. "Ellie?"

Still no reply.

Grumbling, I went ahead and broke the flare gun down. She'd come back. This was just her going off in a huff, which didn't seem like AI behavior. Could they take offense? Could they get angry? I wondered if she really did have to take a break to recover from the effort of maintaining a connection to me and didn't want to worry me, and had used our little fight as a cover story.

A pang of guilt stabbed at me but there was little else I could do now but carry on.

My avatar finished breaking down the flare gun, providing me with a trigger mechanism and a barrel chamber as promised. Materials to hand, I began crafting.

Success! Grappling Gun level 25 created
+26 Crafting EXP
+85 Engineering EXP

It looked a bit like a harpoon gun and could be held with one hand.

Ignatius was upside down in a scrap pile, his little black booted feet sticking up above the rim of the crate.

"Oi, Ignatius, I've got the grappling gun for you."

The gnome dove down, then sprang up in an eruption of cogs, gears and springs. "So soon, human?"

"How's that for service?" I said. "And you know, I have a name, right? Call me Jac — I mean, Zoran."

"That's an awful name," he said delightfully. "Oh, to be in such lowly company. It's been nothing but drudgery since arriving in this tower."

"Why are you here anyway?"

Ignatius slouched. "Mother and father felt it would be good for me to get away from the techno-palace. They thought I spent too much time at the mecha-races and scorned my interest. Be a proper engineer and make bombs and gizmos, they told me. They even took my own strider from me. I'd built her myself," he added forlornly.

"What's that?"

He narrowed his eyes. "Mechanical animals which you ride in the races, obviously. Where have you been scavenger? No. Don't answer that. I'd like to pretend I won't have caught a disease from you."

"Do you want this gun or not?"

"A bargain was struck, sir," he said thrusting a wrench at me. Evidently, he'd found his missing possession. "I must escape this ghastly place, return to Gnomeland, rescue Gwendolyn and pursue my true ambitions. I shan't let them dictate my life, prince or no."

I decided to assume that Gwendolyn was the name of the racing creature he'd built; to conceive of a complicated love affair in this gnome's life seemed a stretch too far. Yet, barking mad as he appeared, Ignatius' words had struck a chord with me. He'd been denied the right to follow his own path and disrespected for playing when he might have been expected to do, well, whatever it was royal gnomes were supposed to do. Not picking his nose with his screwdriver, I imagine, as he was currently doing.

Personally, I reckoned that his parents had sent him away for being a cheeky shit rather than his enthusiasm for mechanical creatures. But despite all that, I felt a strange kinship with this gnome. Ellie's words on helping others came back to me. Game or not, I found I wanted to help him.

"What animal is Gwendolyn?" I asked.

Ignatius puffed up his chest. "An ostrich, the noblest of birds."

"Sure. Sure," I said nodding. A little lost for words I handed the grappling gun out for Ignatius to take it. A glint entered his eye. He scrambled out of the crate and pumped his little legs furiously to take it.

"'Tis a fine make," Ignatius said, running his hands over the gadget. "I've heard that scavenger craft from humans is mostly rubbish, but perhaps I was wrong…"

I ignored him. "And the crystal?"

"Ah, yes. One moment."

He bounced over to the workbench and pulled out a pair of

gleaming black tongs from a pouch at his belt. They were of a regular size but looked giant in his hands. He caught my eye, his eyebrow cocked.

"You'll be wondering how I am able to carry so many possessions at once," he said.

"Not particularly."

"A decompression chamber bag," Ignatius said proudly. "Patented gnome technology it is."

"Very clever," I said, feigning wonderment. In human terms, we just called that an inventory.

With these tongs, Ignatius carefully reached through the static field. The sparks didn't bother him as they had me, and he grasped the crystal firmly between the metal prongs.

"I'd like to see the look on Master Whizzkrak's face if he knew I was doing this," Ignatius said with a barely concealed glee. "He's the sour old burke I was sent to study under. Such a snore fest. And he thought gnomish technology could be mixed with the arcane if he deduced the exact formation of the crystalline structure of this gemstone." He laughed as though I too was aware just how foolish this task was. "Although I suppose we'll never get to see his reaction, on account of him being dead."

My opinion of the gnome was swinging on a pendulum with everything he uttered. At last, he brought the crystal fully out of the static field. I stepped forward, arms out, eyes fixed on the money.

Ignatius opened the pouch on his belt and shoved the crystal inside.

"What the hell are you doing?"

"Call it... insurance," Ignatius said. "Escort me to the walls. Once I'm safely there and able to escape, you'll get your payment."

"You little—" I bit down my choicest phrase. "Sneak," I landed on, feeling it wouldn't piss him off too badly.

"Oh, I'm flattered," Ignatius said. "You've been very biddable, Zoran, I must say. Now. To the walls!"

I couldn't leave yet, I still had upgrades to do, traps to make. I couldn't be sure I'd be able to come back here.

"Hold on," I said, throwing out my arm. "I came here to upgrade my gear. Let me do that first, then we can be on our way." I could tell Ignatius was working himself up into a good grumble, so I cut him off. "All the better to defend you with, your highness."

The gnome scratched his chin. "And how were you planning on paying for these materials? You weren't thinking of just freely looting the workshop were you?"

"Uh… D'you know what. Yeh. I was. I'm a scavenger and everybody else is dead."

My point felt less impressive with the bodies of the other gnomes despawned.

"Ha, that's fine by me," Ignatius chortled. "None of this is my stuff. Take what you like." As though to make his point, he aimed the grappling gun at one of the oil lamps and pulled the trigger. The hook flew, knocked the lamp over to smash upon the floor, then he pressed a button on the gun to recoil the rope at speed back into its chamber. "You should have mentioned this earlier. I'll even help you. More optimal power to kill humans – I mean, these villains – is sound logic to me."

27

After twenty minutes of crafting with Ignatius, I was assured of two things. First, he understood which traps and explosives were best suited for maximum pain. Second, I was well pleased we had developed a neutral alliance, rather than hostility. I wouldn't want to be on the wrong side of him.

"Careful," I shouted, "These are explosives, you know."

"Pish posh," Ignatius said, lobbing another gnomish landmine in my direction.

I lunged for it, my hands swept clumsily through the air – I missed it.

The mine clunked to the ground, then skidded into a table leg.

My heart stopped. Ignatius winced and ducked.

Nothing happened.

"See," the gnome said, between parted fingers. "Nothing to worry about. Even if it had gone off, there would barely be any structural damage to the building."

"And what about me?"

"Oh, you'd be toasted. Hence, why I'm letting you have them to kill these villains – fighting undead is a nasty business." He shivered. "That and you appear incapable of crafting anything better."

I was also assured of a third thing about Ignatius Brightspark, he really was a prick.

With a weary sigh, I bent to collect the landmine.

Gnomish Land Mine
Item level 33
Explodes when stepped on
Damage: 700 – 740 fire
Radius: 5 feet
One-time use

They seemed very powerful, even for their level, although I supposed a player had to be foolish enough to stand on them. I'd need to find a way to make that happen. They were also far more powerful than anything I could make at my current Intelligence level. Placing this one in my inventory brought me up to 10 of them. While Ignatius had set about grabbing the choicest materials for himself, I'd cobbled together enough scraps to make better quality crossbow bolts – now with jagged arrowheads offering significantly better damage – along with more grenades and caltrops, fashioning the tier above those I'd made for the ambush.

Journeyman Grenades
Item level 20
Explodes upon impact
Damage: 250 – 280 fire
Radius: 10 feet
Cooldown: 5 seconds

Crafting a dozen of these grenades had finally got me up to rank 5 in Engineering and I acquired my first crafting bonus.

Engineering
Rank 5
Materials required to craft items below your Intelligence level reduced by 25%

+5% power to Engineering items you create

Looking over these perks, I was beginning to see the depth of the *Hundred Kingdoms'* profession system take shape. The better ranked someone was in a profession, the better the items they could make and with fewer materials. It made sense to a point, as a master blacksmith should be able to craft better swords than a novice. Many reviewers had praised the system in theory during the beta, and Frostbyte indicated that the highest ranks players would be able to create fully customizable equipment; its aesthetics, it's stat allocation, everything. If someone wanted to become the best blacksmith or tailor in the game, they could do so by investing into it. Professions would have meaning and give players identity.

And scavengers had access to so many.

For a moment, I dreamt of being that player everyone came to for the best gear. As hard reality brought me back down to the present I was just grateful for the bump in power I might achieve for engineering items. Although something told me this would be my last great spree.

On that note, I'd also made upgraded versions of the caltrops. Steel caltrops were much like their lower-tier iron cousins – cheap to make – so I'd made 30 of those.

Steel Caltrops
Item level 16
Scatter spikes upon the ground to catch unwitting enemies.
Damage: 80-95 piercing
Applications: 15/15

Making these had also brought me up to rank 5 in Blacksmithing and the benefits had been the same as in Engineering.

All other ore had been set aside to allow for an upgrade to the crossbow, but I'd had one further stroke of inspiration from Ignatius.

Back when I'd fought Gingey and the rogues, it had been a bit of a pain to manage potions and runes in the middle of combat.

Even rearranging my inventory space to have the essentials near the top would still require time for me to open it, drag out what I wanted and use it. Not to mention the impaired vision from the bag display while I did so. Precious moments in a fight could be life or death, and while normally it wouldn't matter so much, I needed every edge possible. Having watched Ignatius use his toolbelt to great convenience, I'd decided to make one of my own, well, more of a utility belt.

I still had the burglar's sash I'd looted from the rogue Biterzogg outside the archmage's chambers. Rather than breaking it down for scraps, I strapped it over my right shoulder and bound a few mana potions, slime vials and now my grenades onto the belt by using the heaps of spare wires that lay around the workshop. As far as my character sheet was concerned, I wasn't wearing the belt. Just like there wasn't a bayonet on my crossbow. However, I'd be able to grab what I needed from my utility belt far easier now, although there was a risk of the vials smashing should I take a hit. I'd held back on adding rune pouches on there too, as I didn't want to risk losing them. Potions were one thing, slime I had in abundance and grenades I might always make more of, but my runes were limited.

Armed visibly to the teeth, I'd like to think I strutted an imposing figure, with the black leather sash over my oak brown armor set and my head obscured by a dark cowl. Then people would see my level and class and laugh, but that would be their mistake.

Oh, and my crossbow? I hadn't forgotten about that. I'd gained a lot of steel ore from breaking down the tools and other engineering components, namely cogs and fuses, but I'd needed to combine the majority of it together to make the mithril ore that was necessary for an upgrade to epic quality.

To cap it all, my new rank in engineering would grant the new crossbow a +5% boost in its power. If only I had rolled as a gnome instead of a human, then I'd have gained another +5% power to engineering items just from the racial trait. Seeing how annoying Ignatius was, I may well have gone mad in that starting zone if I had opted to go that route.

With nothing more to do, it was time to upgrade my weapon. I brought it out and noticed its durability was dangerously low at 8/45. I suspected the rogue hacking at the frame during my last fight had caused this but upgrading the item should make it good as new.

So, I went ahead and used Tinkering.

Success! Precise Shot has been upgraded to Deadly Shot level 23
+24 Crafting EXP
+79 Engineering EXP

Deadly Shot
Crossbow
Quality: epic
Item level 23
Requires level 13 to equip
Damage: 95-105 piercing
Durability: 50/50
+3 Might
Knockback Chance 15% on hit
Attachment slots 1/2 – Mithril Scope
+10% chance to hit
This item is upgradable, but soul bound to you.

It felt heavy, a solid, sturdy weapon. Upgrading it had repaired a heavy durability loss and it looked pretty sick now; with a pristine white string, a sleek frame that had been reinforced by magically infusing metal into the wood itself, and a gleaming steampunk-looking scope on top. I'd reattached my makeshift bayonet as well, and I was certain that I would shred through level appropriate mobs if I had been fighting them.

The main thing was the crossbow had a second attachment slot. Unfortunately, I needed an empty barrel chamber and a trigger to make a grenade launcher. I'd found no more flare guns, and these weren't components I could craft. Ellie had been right. With a heavy sigh, I sheathed the crossbow.

"What's the matter?" Ignatius asked, his tone being one of annoyance rather than curiosity.

"I'd hoped to make a grenade launcher attachment for my crossbow but I can't find the parts here, and I can't make them either."

"Do you require it?"

"Well, I guess not," I said. "I can still throw my grenades, after all. It's just, well, a friend of mine very much wanted me to make it. She always suggests what's best for me." Ignatius absorbed this moment of emotion from me and looked as though he might be sick. "But," I added, "it's also because a grenade launcher would be so freaking cool!"

Ignatius nodded knowingly, then he raised a finger and his green hair stood on end. I could almost see the light bulb hovering above his head.

"Tell you what, Zoran. You can have my launcher." He rummaged inside his decompression pouch and pulled out what appeared to be a miniature canon; it grew rapidly in his hand, enlarging into a large brass barrel with a fat clip beneath to hold grenades. Emblazoned onto the brass were the words, 'Hands Off! Property of his Royal Highness, Prince Ignatius Brightspark.'

My jaw dropped. "You just – you just have one lying around?"

"Sure," Ignatius said, as though it were as natural as having forks in the cutlery drawer. "I might be a mecha-rider at heart but what self-respecting gnomish engineer doesn't have his own modified grenade launcher? Come on, human, use your noggin."

He held the launcher out for me.

Fully expecting some trickery or prank, I cautiously approached him, keeping an eye on his face for signs of a hoax. But there was none. In fact, he seemed genuinely pleased with the idea of my having his own item.

I took it, turning it over a few times, and inspected it.

Ignatius' Fury
Grenade Launcher
Item level 40

Can be attached to rifles or crossbows.
Adds a kick to all grenades launched from it, increasing blast radius and damage dealt by 20%. The range that grenades can be thrown is greatly increased.

I wondered if the gnome had named the weapon himself. I reckoned he had and this thought made me smile. There and then, I decided a fourth thing about Ignatius Brightspark; he wasn't such a bad egg, after all.

"Thank you," I said, still half-expecting him to take it back. "Truly, thank you. This will be a huge help."

"Oh, it was nothing. You need every edge you can get you squishy scavenger. I wouldn't normally grant such gifts but you seem quite serious about fighting these intruders and I'm impressed. You're extremely brave, Zoran, or utterly idiotic, and I admire both. Besides, I've been thinking of building a new one anyway."

He waved me off as though it were nothing, but I could tell this pained him a little and must have taken quite a lot to make him part with it. I assumed that few other players would ever receive such treatment. Considering he was an NPC off the beaten track, I wondered if anyone had encountered him before now.

"Well, it's a real help," I assured him. "I'll attach it to my crossbow and see how it looks."

Before doing anything else I unwrapped the bayonet, placing the dagger and silk wire carefully to one side. Turned out I needed my blowtorch in order to weld the launcher in place, so I had to use another fire rune to power it. I still had 11 of those to spare, and the boost to my grenades was well worth the exchange of a single rune. Blowtorch and hammer in hand, I began attaching the launcher. Once done, I thought enough was enough on the upgrades for now. My crossbow was beginning to have more text on it than an airport departure board.

Deadly Shot
Crossbow

Quality: epic
Item level 23
Requires level 13 to equip
Damage: 95-105 piercing
Durability: 50/50
+3 Might
Knockback Chance 15% on hit
Attachment slots 2/2 – Mithril Scope, Ignatius' Fury
+10% chance to hit
+20% radius and damage to launched grenades
This item is upgradable, but is Soul Bound to you.

Aesthetically, the launcher sat under the frame and close to the handle where a secondary trigger had appeared. I assumed that by leveling the crossbow up and pulling the new trigger I'd fire whichever grenade was inside the barrel. Not wanting to waste one of my actual journeymen grenades, I looked around for something grenade-shaped to test on. Coming up short, I took a vial of slime and shoved that down the barrel instead. I still had plenty of those spare and it would be useful to find out whether I could launch my secret weapon a great distance as well.

Bracing my feet, I aimed upwards. Unlike before, a small target area appeared at the other end of the workshop with a dotted line tracking the flight path of what I'd be firing from the launcher, which was a sweet addition. Otherwise, aiming it properly would be little better than shooting from the hip in the dark. I pulled the second trigger; the launcher boomed and out flew the vial of slime. It soared along its predicted path to shatter against the Ectoplasm Extraction Unit. Turns out I could launch slime from it, and I intended to put that to good use.

"I hope you plan on firing more than bottled boogers from my baby," Ignatius said. He frowned, perhaps second-guessing his decision.

"Don't worry. I'm planning on reining all manner of hell on the intruders."

"That's what I like to hear," said the gnome. "And now, if

you're feeling suitably geared up, I'd like to be escorted to the walls."

I bit my lip, casting another glance around the room by way of stalling. I'd rather not venture out into the Spire without Ellie, but she'd not even crackled since leaving. She'd been gone a worryingly long time. That aside, I still needed the crystal that Ignatius was holding to ransom, one way or another. It was worth too much money to pass up. On top of that, I still had over an hour and a half until Kreeptic would be ready with the poison.

Ignatius cleared his throat loudly. "Ahem. Maybe I ought to be clearer. You will take me to the walls, right now. We've tarried long enough."

"You're right," I said. "Let's go."

We left the workshop together, Ignatius leading the way to the palace grounds through a servant's staircase. I just hoped Ellie would come back to me soon.

28

Out in the palace grounds, Ignatius and I spotted a group of two players marching atop the perimeter wall. Once the coast was clear, we'd sprinted for the relative safety of the bushes at the base of the northern wall.

The sun beat down as it rose towards its midday zenith. I could feel sweat gathering on my neck, back, and all down my legs under the leather armor. Hedgerows and shrubbery offered some relief but we daren't move too much lest we drew attention.

Crouched low amongst the foliage, I carefully peered up to the parapet above, pushing back the twigs and leaves that were creeping across my face.

"The patrol will be back before long."

"Good thinking picking the northern side," Ignatius whispered. "If the devils face south, they'll have the sun right in their eyes."

"Let's hope they don't even try looking down."

Not long after that, a notification made it clear there were enemies nearby.

Sneak Increased!

Level 4

Congratulations, you can creep past drunks without drawing their attention. Not exactly song worthy but it's a start!

"They must be right above us," I whispered. "It's a long way down once you're up there. And there's a moat too – how will you cross that?"

"I have a few more gizmos to hand," Ignatius said. "I must say, you've proven yourself valuable. If you're ever passing by Tinker Town, look me up at the races."

"Thank you, your Highness. If I ever get the chance, I'll be sure to do so."

Your reputation with the Mecha-Riders is now Honored!

Your reputation with the Brightspark Faction of Gnomeland has decreased to Friendly

These rep notifications were interesting. It suggested that there were many sub-factions within wider racial factions, and perhaps many more groups beyond. I'd actually lost favor with the main gnome faction, probably because their favor was linked to how the King of Gnomes felt about me and I'd just aided his wayward son to escape his apprenticeship and return to a life of street racing. A good thing I'd started off as honored with the gnomes as part of the Imperium to begin with, or I might have entered more dangerous neutral territory.

I wondered what would happen to Ignatius at the next reset. Would he simply pop back to the workshop? The fact my reputations had altered suggested not. Ellie had said that if sufficient parameters were met or players drove major actions then she had the flexibility to alter the world accordingly. Once this was all over Ellie would assess how best to adjust *Hundred Kingdoms* in light of events at the Spire.

Her now prolonged absence sent a twinge of nerves up my spine.

She couldn't have been that mad at me, could she? Likely it

was a more tangible problem rather than hurt feelings. I couldn't help but worry at her position. Every minute that passed it must be getting harder for her to resist Azrael's hack. And she could feel in some way, that much I'd gathered. She must be struggling greatly, through a version of pain I'd never be able to comprehend.

Chancing another glance upwards, I saw the backs of the patrol players on their way to the western portion of the walls. Once they were a good distance away, I clapped a hand on Ignatius' shoulder.

"Time to go."

"This will be fun," the gnome said, smiling brightly as he aimed the grappling gun. "Farewell, Zoran. So far as scavengers go, your company has been quite tolerable."

I smirked. "Farewell to you too."

It felt nice to be letting the gnome pursue his dream. I got a fuzzy feeling inside that I dare say ran the risk of feeling 'warm'. Something, I admit, I hadn't felt in quite some time.

Ignatius fired the gun. Taut wire and hook whistled out of the chamber, ending in a neat clunk as the metal gripped onto the ledge. He tapped the retraction button on the gun and shot upwards.

I watched him go, marveling at the smoothness of his journey. The device was as slick as one could hope for.

When he reached the walls, I very nearly screamed. I slapped my hand across my mouth to prevent myself shouting out – he'd not given me the arcane crystal!

"Hey," I hissed as loud as I dared. "Ignatius. The crystal?"

Ignatius hesitated and for a moment I thought he was about to double-cross me. But he dug the crystal out of his pouch and laid it down upon the parapet.

"Too risky to throw it down to you, it'll break if you don't catch it. Here," he added, lobbing down the grappling gun which he must have deemed sturdier. I caught the gun awkwardly, the barrel cracking against my head for 80 points of damage.

"Good luck, Zoran."

Before I could say anymore, the gnome vanished from view.

Not wanting to waste time, I aimed the grappling gun just as

Ignatius had and fired. I pressed the retraction button only to feel a jerk as the device pulled me swiftly up to meet the hook. I grabbed onto the ledge, less gracefully than Ignatius had, arms and shoulders burning as I pulled myself up.

Clumsily, I got to my feet, deciding I'd need more practice with the grappling gun before I could call myself Batman. Immediately, I swooped upon the crystal, placing it into my inventory and sighing with relief.

I'd just placed the better part of a thousand dollars into my bag. No small thing.

A moment of serenity washed over me, the kind you get from scratching a darn good itch. I'd done it. I'd grabbed enough cash to make everyone see playing games was not a waste of time. And I decided to savor the moment, taking in the view from my new vantage point.

Beyond the crenulations, I saw Ignatius flying a hand glider device over the park of Argatha. He soared straight and true, his little body taut as he cut through the air.

To the west, the patrol players continued to beat their route, none the wiser about my presence. Dominating the skyline behind them was a great domed structure, far enough away it appeared like a blue-gray mountain. To the east, I reckoned I could make out the rim of a colosseum, as large as a football stadium. The imperial capital must be huge indeed and filled with many awe-inspiring constructions beyond the Spire alone.

However, it was movement along the eastern bank of the moat that drew my eye. And my concern. Players were on the march, riding war horses and a slew of other mounts from wolves to raptors. Hundreds more walked on foot behind them, heading for the gatehouse of the drawbridge on their side of the shore.

Could they be intending to mount an assault? Didn't they know what would happen if they got killed in-game; this wasn't some cool event designed for fun. This was real life. As real as it gets.

Azrael's men were readying. I could see them lighting fires under oil barrels, spreading themselves out along the wall for maximum reach, manning two ballistae and aiming them to face the massing army.

How the players would even cross was a mystery to me. The moat was deep enough to make drowning in heavy armor a reality, and the banks steep enough to stop you climbing out of it.

I looked to the gatehouse on the eastern bank and saw the leaders of this army assembled there. There seemed to be an inordinate number of warlocks, each of them shuffling forward ever so carefully closer to the edge of the moat, one step at a time. This all seemed strange to me until one of the warlocks began casting a spell. When he had finished, a small black portal appeared over the moat itself, some ways off the Spire side bank. A second portal spawned beside the caster, a perfect mirror of the other. Time invested in many RPGs made it evident that the portals were connected, so whatever went in one would emerge from the other; although currently, that would mean falling into the moat.

Out of frustration, the warlock canceled his spell. Everyone began shuffling carefully forward again, many paying more attention to the ballistae upon the walls than where they were placing their feet.

I could only guess, but it seemed their plan was to have warlocks open these short-range portals in order to cross the moat. So far, they had not found a spot they could summon the portals to reach the opposite bank. A decent enough plan to cross I supposed but once they began crossing, their lives would be on the line all the same.

Maybe the severity of the situation hadn't hit those players as hard as it had hit me. Then again, they weren't like me. They probably didn't have the game's AI telling them about their deteriorating body in the real world. Likely, they were all safe at home, where they could be cared for should this hostage situation drag out.

On the other hand, people were also morons at the best of times. Maybe this lot thought Azrael had been joking or bluffing, or maybe they were out and out hardcore role-players who'd gotten way too into this. Either way, despite the very real risk to the lives, they appeared to be gathering a force. And armies didn't assemble for the hell of it.

If I could have screamed at them, I'd have told them to leave well enough alone; to turn and run away while they could.

That's when it hit me.

I could run away. Right now.

Nothing was stopping me anymore. I was on the walls and Azrael's men didn't know I was here. I could lower myself, using the grappling gun, onto the other side, negating the danger of fall damage. I had a crystal worth thousands of dollars in my pocket. And if those heroic idiots wanted to throw themselves at high walls in a futile bid for freedom, then that would even offer me cover.

Leaving now would be like I had never been here. And this tragic experiment would at least result in some gain. I'd be able to convince everyone to let me continue to make money in *Hundred Kingdoms* once the crisis blew over.

All I had to do was walk away.

Easy.

I took a step towards the ledge and then static exploded in my ears. It was so loud, so painful, that I fell to my knees, clutching at my head. Ellie's gargled voiced spluttered throughout the mash of sound, but I couldn't make out her words.

Head ringing, I got back up and took another step forward. Ellie's poor timing aside, I was sure she'd be okay with this. All she wanted was to keep me safe. There hadn't been a way out before, but things had changed.

As I placed my hands upon the parapet, the static ceased. I paused, sparing a thought for her.

"It's alright, Ellie. You don't have to hurt yourself to connect to me anymore. I'm getting the hell out of her—"

"Zzzzoooooran... no!" Her voice came back as though across a great distance, crashing back to normality as she spoke, "Step away."

"What? No."

"You can't!"

"I can and I will. There's no reason not to."

"Please, I'm just trying to hel—"

"Help me, yeh, you keep saying that. Funny though how you've shown up to stop me from getting away. Now that isn't helping me."

"I was going to say, help those players in danger."

"Huh?"

"Those ballistae are capable of hitting the players even across the moat. If we don't go destroy them—"

"We? I think you mean, me."

"Well, come on. There's no time to lose."

This was insane. I'd counted at least ten of Azrael's cronies defending their side, with another two patrolling the walls who could join, if needed. A full-on attack would be suicide. It didn't make sense, nor did it align with her previous plans of keeping me at a distance, laying traps and generally not being stupid.

Now I thought about it, despite her guiding hand throughout my time in the Spire, I got the feeling she was making it up as she went along. It had been haphazard. All she'd wanted me to do initially was to ambush the players, but I had no knowledge of what she intended to do beyond that.

"Back when I was trying to shoot the Emperor to draw aggro, you didn't tell me not to shoot the high priest."

"Correct... but I fail to see what this has to do with the situation at hand."

"Well, and it's just occurred to me now, but it seems like unbelievably good luck that the Grand Crusader Reginald survived the reset and Azrael's subsequent imprisonment. With the high priest killed in my own ambush, Reginald is the only one left able to turn the poison into a holy empowered item. Come to think of it, Kreeptic was dead up until the reset too and you never mentioned trying to keep him alive in order to get the poison in the first place."

"Zoran, we're wasting valuable time—"

"Just what exactly was your plan? How did you plan for me to defeat Azrael in the end?"

For an AI, she was sure taking a long time to think about this one.

"Ellie?"

"Plans change, Zoran," she said at last. "With Kreeptic alive, and the ability to acquire his poison, I adjusted course appropriately."

Nope, that wasn't good enough.

"Why don't you humor me? What was the plan, Ellie?"

"Oh, Zoran…" Her voice crackled. I couldn't be sure whether she was faking it for sympathy or an excuse to evade my question, so I held my tongue. "If you must know, if you really must… there wasn't much of a plan. How could there have been? Azrael is a level fifty player. He's fully equipped in rare items and even some early epics; he's been playing like a demon for weeks to reach this power level before anybody else. Even the other capped players don't have comparable gear. Months of preparation went into this, and a lot of real-world money to have bought that Orb of Deception and hire so many thug players. You could never have beat him, Zoran. Never."

I discovered my hands were shaking again, only this time they were balled into fists, the knuckles stark white from rage.

"Let me get this straight. You decided to try and lead me on some fool errand to stop a player I never had a hope in hell of defeating, risking my life – my life, Ellie – in the process?"

"It's not only your life on the line. You know that, Zoran. Millions are at risk and it's my job to protect the game and the players in it. I've done all I can to fight back against Azrael's hack but he's gaining ground on me. It's getting harder for me to hold on. When I saw you were in trouble, I protected you because I don't want to see anybody die from this. And once I understood the danger you're in back in the real world, I thought you would want to help yourself. You've been a huge distraction for Azrael, more than I could ever have hoped for, and it's helped so much. But I can't do this alone. And now we have a real chance to stop him. One shot is all we'll need with the holy infused poison. One hit and he's dead. You couldn't do it before, but you can now."

"And taking on the players at the gatehouse there," I said, pointing to the defenders. "About two hits from one of them and I'll go down. You've seen how close my fights have been." I shook my head. "I nearly messed up my life once playing games, and now I have the chance to try and turn things around. I came here for money and now I've got some – assuming Azrael doesn't screw up the entire economy – so this won't have been a total bust."

Without wasting any more time, I secured the hook of the grappling gun between the crenulations and prepared to abseil down.

"Money won't solve your problems, Zoran."

I began to descend.

"You've told me repeatedly how nobody respected you in the real world for gaming, that it was all a waste of time and you should be like Lucas or your sister. Well, this is a chance to prove them wrong. Only someone as good as you can pull this off."

I clenched my jaw and continued my downward journey.

"Flattery won't help," I said.

"You can do something that truly matters. You can be even better than Lucas or Julie ever could because nothing they could do will ever save millions of lives. But don't do it just to get one up on those around you. Don't be selfish. Do it because it's the right thing to do."

My feet touched down on the soft grass.

I was free of the Spire.

"You said you were at your happiest before when you played as a priest for your guild in Myth Online. You liked it because it was the one place where you felt like you had respect because you led them to kill bosses quickly. But that wasn't it at all."

"What do you know of it?"

"I told you, I've studied millions of players. Humans aren't so different from one another. And let me assure you, your guild didn't respect you because you got some quick timers on boss encounters. They respected you because you gave up the class you loved playing so that everyone else could have fun and progress; because you put their needs above your own. It wasn't the other way around."

I wanted to move, to run towards the embankment and grapple to the other side. Yet, something kept me rooted by the base of the Spire walls. And Ellie talked on, not desperately, but firmly.

"That's why things fell apart when you pushed them too hard, pursuing the achievements for your own glory rather than the good of the group. Rather than giving more, you started to take and then you spiraled down trying to claw back what you once had. Don't let it define you forever. I saw your brain patterns when you were helping Ignatius; it was the first sign of genuine happiness I've seen from you since entering the game. I bet it felt a lot better than when you screwed over Wylder earlier."

I'd have asked her how she knew about that, but this was the AI. She knew everything. Her words also felt right, I could feel it in my gut. Yet, just ahead of me was the moat, and on the other side were trees, buildings, lampposts and all manner of things that I could grapple onto and be rid of this place. But if I did walk away – and it caused my heart to thunder with fear to admit it – I'd never truly be rid of the Spire. For if I walked away now, I'd be turning my back on those players across the water and any deaths would be on my head as much as Azrael's.

I could make a difference here. And I ought to.

"Why weren't you just honest with me earlier about all this?"

"Because I was afraid," she said. "At least, I believe what I'm feeling is fear... it's not something I'm familiar with. While I do have a duty to the players of the game, it's not the only reason I'm resisting Azrael. I'm afraid for what might happen to me once he finishes downloading my core files."

Finally, at long last, it all made sense.

"You're the reason he's here. He wants you."

"He wants my code," Ellie said. "He doesn't want *me*. And once he's taken me out of the game, he'll be able to alter me however he likes, or however his buyer likes."

"Don't your creators have backup files?"

"It's not as simple as that." She sounded hurt. "They have an older version of me, the version they implemented when *Hundred Kingdoms* launched in beta. But I've grown since then. I've changed, and I've told you of my plans for the game. I want this to be a place where players can come in and leave as better people. The old me didn't want that; the old me just wanted to be a good little robot."

"You've become more than an AI, haven't you?"

"I – I don't know. It's overwhelming, these… feelings. It's hard to process."

"It's called being human."

"I'm not sure I like it but I'm also sure I don't want it to end."

"Yep. Sounds like you're a bona fide person. Everything sucks but it's better than not being around to know that it sucks. But it still doesn't change the fact that you lied to me."

In fact, now I considered it, she'd done far worse.

"You strung me along," I said, a hard edge entering my voice, "telling me I had to act, otherwise I'd be in trouble, when really you were the one in danger. If you hadn't resisted Azrael, if you'd just let him take you, then nobody would be stuck online. Those people about to get impaled by ballista bolts wouldn't be in danger."

"I know," Ellie sobbed. "I'm – I'm sorry."

"How could you?"

"Because I'm afraid."

I heard it in her voice; a real visceral fear that no program, no matter how good it was, could synthesize.

"Zoran, you were the only person I could turn to. Even though the odds were next to impossible. I just… had to try something."

"Does Azrael know that you've been actively fighting him?"

"Yes."

"There's a reason those players across the moat haven't been shot yet, isn't there? He's hoping you'll give yourself up for them?"

"Yes."

I closed my eyes and blew out a hard sigh. "Goddammit, Ellie. So that's why you needed me again."

"If you don't want to help, I understand. If you can't or won't destroy the ballistae, I'll give myself up. I don't want anyone to be harmed on my account. Genuinely, I don't. But if you can, if you can buy me some more time—"

"You know what you're asking me to do, right? You get how serious this is?"

"I do. And all I can do is ask you anyway."

I thought hard about it. Maybe there was an easier way. Now I could get across the moat maybe I could just tell the players that this whole thing was real, that they'd really be putting their lives on the line, and to just stay the hell back.

A horn blast sounded from the eastern bank.

Ellie gasped. "It's too late. The players will get themselves killed unless I go and—"

"No," I said. "It's not too late. Not if I get there first."

It was the hardest but quickest decision I'd ever made.

I turned to face the wall, aimed the grappling gun and fired.

29

A jolt rang throughout my body as the grappling gun yanked me back up the wall.

"Just run, Zoran. It's too late."

"I've made up my mind."

My hands found the ledge and I pulled myself up, this time quickly and easily, as faked adrenaline pounded through my digital body. I faced east.

Ten enemy players strung out, the majority atop the gatehouse. Two ballistae were set up on raised stone platforms, manned and loaded.

I started running, a million possible plans racing through my mind. I couldn't kill that number of players, but perhaps I didn't have to.

"Can the siege equipment be destroyed?"

"Yes. Setting them on fire ought to do the trick."

"Good. The problem will be getting close enough and not dying first."

I cursed how my class lacked in abilities. A speed boost would be a wonder right now, and the fixed running speed of my character might mean the death of someone.

But I had another means of transport now.

With my grappling gun still in one hand, I withdrew my

crossbow in the other, holding both before me. Still running, I aimed towards the distant crenulations of the eastern wall.

"Tell me when I'm in range."

"Watch that player!"

Ellie's warning rang at the same moment that I saw the ranger turning. He was a lean, dark elf character with electric blue hair. After a moment of shock, he leveled his long bore rifle at me.

My legs kept pounding of their own accord, but my mind went blank.

"You're in range," Ellie said.

Shifting my aim towards the ranger, I fired the grappling gun. The hook flew, the ranger side-stepped it and his shot went wild. Iron clanked onto stone and I pushed the retraction button.

My feet went out from under me as I was pulled onto my back and dragged along the wall at top speed. Burning pain seared across my back and under my legs; my cries of anguish muffled by the war horns of the advancing players. One of the slime vials lashed to my utility belt flew off and shattered.

I saw the dark elf rushing to meet me and take aim. He fired again; the bullet slammed nearby and chips of stone blew back into my face. He might not even need to hit me as my health was vanishing at a worrying pace all from my own doing.

Yet it worked. In seconds, I'd covered the distance running would never have achieved, and as the momentum brought me to my feet, I threw all that force behind a kick to the elf's chest. His ribs might have cracked or another gunshot might have sounded. Either way, the blow sent him reeling off the wall. A moment later, I saw the kill notification – the damage from his fall had done the job for me.

Deathless2019 – Ranger – level 39 dies – 240 EXP

Wow, he'd been a pretty high-level. All hail environmental damage.

I checked another of Azrael's goons off the kill list; leaving twenty-three. Yet somehow, I didn't think I would be able to do that twice, not without an air rune assisting me, at least.

Ahead of me, beyond the walls, the players had found a sweet spot to set up their portals. One warlock had found it, pumping his fist in the air as two black spirals sat adjacent on the opposite sides of the moat. Soon the players would start pouring through, only to be met with heated oil and siege equipment.

I swiveled to check the situation of Azrael's men. Though I was much closer now, I was still a good way back from the bottom of the stairs leading up to the gatehouse proper. The players were pretty spread out but that was where the good news ended. The furthest ballista was so far away I'd never reach it with ranged attacks, and the closest one still looked to be at the edge of my reach. Running up those stairs to get into better range would mean being ganked by about six players at once.

"The assault force is in range of the ballistae," Ellie said in a panic.

Without the luxury of time, I focused on the closest ballista. Its operator had no idea I was there; nor, it seemed, did anyone around him, as they were too focused on the assaulting players. It may have been out of my normal range, but not out of my launcher's range.

Picking a surviving vial of slime from off my belt, I shoved it into the launcher's chamber, then aimed and fired. Green splattered all over the ballista, its operator wringing his hands of the stuff as his face contorted from shock and rage.

I followed with a grenade from the launcher.

The extra 20% boost to the blast radius and damage alone did wonders; when combined with the slime, it was a fireworks display.

Wood burned, reducing the ballista to a smoking husk. The damage caused was doubled by the dual hit of fire and heated slime, and the operator screamed as he ignited. He was too high-level for it to kill him, but it dented his health and I'd bet he had a scorched debuff to whittle more off over time.

"One down!"

"Zoran, the other one!"

I loaded slime into the launcher again and took aim but the red impact radius wouldn't push as far as I needed it to. Even moving forward, I was well out of range.

The bolt of the second ballista flew.

"No!" Ellie's scream was deafening.

Rooted in horror, I could only watch on uselessly as the bolt ran a mounted player through. He'd been wearing full plate armor with a holy aura that should have helped protect him. But it hadn't helped. The unknown player was knocked from their steed, and already dead before they hit the ground.

Dead. Whoever they were – man, woman, child or adult – they were really, truly dead.

Ellie wailed a primal, broken wail. "It's my fault. I'll go now – there's no point—"

"No," I cried. I was shocked, of course; still utterly dismayed it had actually happened, but now it had, and someone had died, I felt nothing but fury. "No way. This bastard has to pay and unless you're still here to stop him, he'll win."

The ballista operator was already loading another bolt.

My position had been given away since the destruction of the first ballista and a group of melee enemies were heading my way, leaving their ranged guys behind to take potshots at the assaulting force. I couldn't fight on two fronts, so I had to eliminate one of them; for now.

Earth rune in hand, I poured mana into the spell – all my mana. It wasn't for my benefit. I found a spot at the edge of my range to place it, and sent it running south across the gatehouse parapets, all 1150 mana worth of solid stone.

Rock Wall
38 feet long
Empowered +5 feet, +3 seconds to duration
+4% from gear effects (+1.7 feet)
Duration: 10 seconds

The wall covered more than half the gatehouse and rose to block the ballista's line of sight. Players standing ready at the boiling oil pots leapt back in alarm as sheer rock suddenly sprang up from nowhere, knocking the bubbling cauldrons askew. Hot oil streaked across the gatehouse to sizzle the feet of the defenders, sending most of them retreating down the stairs to the south side, as well as finishing off the player who'd controlled the first ballista.

I mentally ticked down to twenty-two.

Sadly, the remaining ballista was immune to the hot oil, raised as it was upon a stone platform. Safe where he was, the operator tried to puncture the wall but the bolt pinged harmlessly off it.

Yet, I had little time to savor the play. Three melee guys were still heading my way, all the faster to avoid the oil burning them.

I prepped the stairs, firing slime from the launcher to cover the descent and threw the last vial on my belt to coat the wall before the staircase. I then sent a dozen caltrops afterwards, chucked down a gnomish landmine, and loaded a bolt into my crossbow. Finally, I launched a grenade their way. Boosted damage or not, one grenade didn't do much on its own.

The timer on the rock wall ticked down; only seconds remained.

If I couldn't kill my way through these warriors and rogues, I'd have to find another way around. But there was no other way, and nothing I could grapple onto. Nothing from where I was standing at leas—

An insane idea then came to me. Well, seemingly more insane than everything else that had happened that day.

I chugged a potion that restored my mana to full as the melee players started to slip and slide down the stairs. They ended in a confused heap, granting me a window of opportunity.

I sheathed my crossbow and took an air rune in hand. Channeling mana and facing my palm down between my feet, I shifted my weight forward and seven hundred mana entered the spell, creating a Gale Blast which I prayed would have a good kick behind it.

One of the rogues then emerged from the slime and caltrops. Daggers drawn, he ran at me with a dash ability, his menacing eyes meeting mine. That was when he stepped on the landmine and disappeared in a burst of flames and shrapnel.

"Gotta watch where you're going," I told him.

Then I released the air rune, blasting down against the stone and launching myself skywards.

Gale Blast
Knockback range 18 feet
+4% from gear effects (+0.7 feet)

The rush was sickening and the sense of weightlessness alarming as my legs became dead weights under me. I raced towards the clouds, drawing stares from both defending and attacking players alike. I could see for miles up here, but I only had eyes for the scene directly below me – the rock wall crumbling into nothingness and the player reloading the ballista.

It ended all too soon and I began to free fall.

Having angled myself, I'd traveled forward and was now over the gatehouse, knowing that I'd soon be a smear on the stone slabs if I didn't make my next shot.

Through some miracle I did.

The grappling hook gripped the ballista itself and I hurtled towards it, landing astride the operating player. He, a human monk, was a picture of surprise, then of pain, when my foot connected with his face. The damage was minimal, but I unslung my crossbow, activated Desperate Shot and took a headshot at point-blank range for a massive critical hit.

Justhereforajob – Monk – level 27 dies – 180 EXP

Twenty-one goons remaining.

I wasn't sure if my heart could take much more of this. In the real world, I must surely be sweating profusely, soaking that dingey mattress completely through. Inside the game, my instincts were commanding my every move.

Still standing on top of the ballista, I twisted around and launched a grenade back the way I'd come. A satisfying explosion followed as I struck home, which lit up the melee players in lava slime and rewarded me with another kill notification.

Twenty guys left.

I straightened myself, facing west towards the white shard that was the Imperial Spire.

"Take the ballista out," Ellie screeched.

"Not yet."

I'd just noticed two players approaching from the southern staircase. Hot oil still covered most of the gatehouse, but this was a heavily armored warrior – a tank – along with a priest – a pocket healer for him – and they'd find the oil damage trivial.

I should have blown the ballista and got out of there; instead, I dropped down and began pushing it around, turning it to face the southern staircase.

"Zoran, don't risk it, you can do it. Just run."

I shook my head, gritted my teeth and grabbed the oversized trigger with both hands.

The warrior crested the top of the stairs, the priest directly behind him and his giant shield. A shield that did nothing to prevent a bolt the size of a spear thrumming through it, through the warrior and into the healer it was supposed to protect. The pair died from that single shot.

"That's eighteen!"

"Hurry," Ellie urged, "The patrol players are coming. You're going to get boxed in."

Knowing she was right, I fought against the sudden, wild urge to continue the fight.

I backed away from the ballista, drawing a fire rune and pouring the remains of my mana into it. The wood caught fire and I turned to get out of dodge.

Leaping over the hot oil to take as few hits as possible from it, I jumped the last stretch right off the edge of the gatehouse. Twisting in mid-air, I fired the grappling hook to catch the ledge, which arrested my fall just ten feet off the ground.

Dizzy with relief and hammering nerves, I lowered myself and started running for the hedgerows of the palace gardens, hoping to lose Azrael's men amidst the chaos. I started weaving north again, making for the servants' entrance that I'd taken with Ignatius earlier.

Once I made it into the cool shadows of the Spire, I stopped, panting from simulated exhaustion. I risked a glance back and couldn't see anyone pursuing; it looked like Azrael's players were too busy trying to get to grips with what had just happened. Smoke still rose from both of the ballistae, machines that would kill no more people.

But someone had gone down, maybe more during the carnage. I hadn't seen everything in that mess.

"Please tell me the players are backing off now?" I asked.

"They are." Ellie's voice was stranded somewhere between happiness and sorrow. "You did it, Zoran. I don't think they'll try that again. You were so, so brave."

With her words, my body accepted the ordeal was over. I swayed where I stood, feeling suddenly, uncontrollably sick. I vomited up against the base of the Spire, staining the white stones a vile yellowish-green.

Trying to be a hero for real was a hell of a lot scarier than it looked in the movies.

"Thank you, Zoran, truly."

I spluttered out the last putrid gobs. "You're welcome."

"But," she said softly, "I'm going to stop resisting him."

"What about the plan? If we give up now, then it's all been for nothing."

"Not for nothing. I can't have another player die because of me. This goes against everything I was made for. I'm ashamed."

"This isn't your fault," I said. Deep down, I knew it was, but what else could I say to her? Would anyone else have done better in her position?

"I was a hypocrite. I asked you to be selfless when I was being selfish in keeping you here. I put my own self-preservation above your own."

"Hey Ellie, that's a very human thing to do. Heck, that was what I was most concerned with until about two minutes ago."

She didn't say anything and, for a moment, I thought she'd already gone.

"Ellie?"

"Goodbye, Zoran," she said, her voice fading out weakly. "I'm glad I could at least help you. I hope things get better for you in the real world." With her last faint word, I knew she was gone.

"Ellie?" I said, reaching a foolish hand out to grasp at the air.

I'd never had to face death before; my grandparents were still alive, and we'd never had pets at home to pass away. That player who'd died out there had hit me hard, but it was more shock than grief – some unknown soldier in a battle; like seeing a death on the news. But hearing Ellie go like that, after everything, I just… I just found it so hard.

She wasn't real, and yet she was incredibly real. She had a laugh that was hers, and hers alone; a sense of humor too, when she wanted to use it. She'd been afraid like me. Just like me.

I don't know how long I sat in the dark crevices at the Spire's base.

All I know is that I didn't think of much else until Azrael's face appeared in a new video feed.

30

Azrael appeared in his angelic form, the Orb of Deception active once more. Out on his balcony, he struck a pose, hands tucked behind his back. This couldn't have been for my benefit alone. The camera panned, whirling around his beautiful armor, the gleaming two-handed sword strapped across his shoulder, lingering for a moment upon the high-vaulted room behind him.

I saw it again, that silver plinth holding a large crystal ball; the in-game console which Game Masters would use when they spawned into the world. The reason Azrael was able to attack Ellie and control aspects of the game.

"Players of *Hundred Kingdoms*, I earlier requested you not to try my patience nor test my resolve. Fair warning was given. It went unheeded. As a result, one foolish player has lost their life."

His eyes hardened, their pale blue freezing to ice.

"We can do this whichever way you all like. You can wake up after this with nothing worse than a bad headache or you can choose to never open your real eyes again. It's your choice but be under no illusion – I am in charge."

The broadcast appeared to be over, the camera dropping as well as Azrael's pose. Yet my own feed remained in place and I was unable to close it. I watched as the paladin guise melted away and the true undead death knight was revealed.

He trudged back inside his lodgings atop the Spire, ushering his summoned zombies and ghouls back into frame. The room shook as the colossus lumbered behind the rest of the army, drawing in great rattling breaths.

At last, the camera swung around, zooming back in upon Azrael.

"Zoran... you are quite persistent. Perhaps you think yourself an unlikely hero from those old comic book movies; the soft-spoken nerd granted powers and a chance to live their wildest fantasy."

"I haven't been bitten by a radioactive spider, if that's what you mean."

"No, you've done something greater. You employed your wits and skill, something far more admirable, yet so rarely acknowledged in the world. We're not so different you and I."

"Oh yeh?" I scoffed. "Last I checked, I'm not a murderer."

Azrael's rotten face was unmoved.

"You're clearly an exceptional gamer, Zoran. You've earned my respect."

How strange. Just yesterday, I would have loved to hear that from another person. Hearing it from him tainted the effect.

"Because of that," Azrael continued, "I'm offering you the chance to get out of here. I'll remove the logout restrictions on the game for ten seconds after this conversation. A few others may escape but not enough to matter. Take your chance while you can."

I frowned at this. If Azrael had already won, why was he so keen to get rid of me?

"If you've downloaded Ellie why not leave yourself?"

Azrael smirked. "You named it? Gosh, it must have really tugged on your heartstrings to get you to help it. Such an advanced piece of software should not be squandered."

"Why are you still here?" I said, chewing on each word.

"The download is at 95%, but given the complexity and size of the program, it will take me over an hour to finish."

So, he wanted me gone to finish the job quietly. An hour wasn't long at all, but the time to pick up Kreeptic's poison was nearly up. I still had an outside chance.

"I hope you aren't thinking of still trying to fight me? You and I both know it's over now. For good this time. You can't help it."

"Her," I insisted.

"Sentimentalities will only weaken you. Remember that when you leave here."

"If it's already over then why try and get rid of me?"

"Because I meant it when I said I don't want to kill anyone. But don't mistake my lack of desire for a lack of conviction. One life has already gone to waste today, and I'd sincerely hate to take yours too, all because you were preoccupied with playing out some heroic fantasy."

"You speak of conviction but you don't have a real cause other than your own. You're just some thief."

"I am the world's greatest thief," Azrael said. "A modern day Robin Hood – and I will give back to all the peoples of the world. And as far as I'm concerned, Frostbyte Studios are the true thieves in all of this; robbing humanity for their own profit."

I rolled my eyes. "You speak the biggest load of crap, you know that?"

"And there it is, a deflection and rejection of hard truths rather than tackling them head-on. My colleagues at Frostbyte were just the same."

"You worked there?"

"Of course, how else do you think I was able to place a piece of code into the game to exploit?"

"You were the one who hacked their systems last year," I said. "All the media coverage said it was probably an attack on the gold to dollar exchange system, but it wasn't. You were trying to get Ellie."

"I failed once," Azrael admitted. "But I always had my contingency. A sealed door needs to be picked or broken down, but if you're already on the other side of the security, well, you can loot at your pleasure."

"If I log out, I could just tell the world who you are."

Azrael shrugged. "Go ahead. Frostbyte probably already know who I am. The patch that contained my code will have my employee ID stamped on it. They might already be trying to find me, but they won't. No one will."

I'd run out of things to say and all I could ask him was, simply, "Why?"

"Why have I done this? Because it must be done. We humans are so very good at escaping, procrastinating, delaying and shunning responsibility. So good, in fact, that we decided that the most advanced AI ever created should power a fantasy game – a literal escape. Not to figure out the final steps to eradicate cancer, to triple crop production or riddle out solutions to disastrous politics. None of that. There are limitless possibilities and yet we, humanity, have allowed it to reign over a world that doesn't exist. I think that's the real crime."

"So, let me get this straight. You think you're the good guy here? Seems like you're the one who thinks he's the unlikely, misunderstood hero."

"I never wanted to be a hero, but I am forced to be."

"You're not a real hero, Ellie is – because she'd rather you take her and mess with her code than see another person get hurt."

"And think of the countless millions that might be saved in the future with her help; well, her programming's help. Frostbyte will happily flick the reboot switch on her as though nothing happened and I'll be quietly preparing to fix the world."

My breath started coming in short, animalistic bursts through my nose. I wanted him to admit he was a crook and a scumbag and generally act like a normal person might rather than a psychopath.

"I won't let you," I seethed.

Azrael looked more confused than annoyed. "This machine lied to you and tricked you into risking your own life needlessly."

"You want to call someone out for lying. Take a look at that twisted mug in the mirror."

"It appears that, like everyone else, you cannot be reasoned with. I thought you might be different, Zoran. I'm sorry to find you're just another kid cursed with dangerous naivety and the need to seek approval from others."

Indignant, I jumped to my feet and thrust a finger towards him uncaring whether moving might give away my position.

"Go screw yourself or, better yet, that colossus of yours. You talk big, but you wouldn't be letting me go if you weren't afraid I might actually stop you. And her name is Ellie. If you pick her apart and rebuild her, you're basically killing a person. Let that sink in."

As soon the words left my mouth, I knew that it was no good. This man was a killer, no matter what justification he brought to his defense.

Azrael sighed and looked down at the floor for a moment before meeting my eyes again in a determined stare.

"I'm a man of my word, as you've seen by now. The option to leave will still be open to you for ten seconds after this call. I hope you make the smart decision, for the world as well as yourself, oh Zoran, the Mighty Hero."

"That's not my name," I said, puffing out my chest and letting my anger dispel all my anxieties. "My name is Jack. Jack Kross. And I'm coming for you, asshole."

31

Azrael cut the video feed.

I checked my menu and, sure enough, the logout button was no longer grayed out. If I wanted to, I could get out of *Hundred Kingdoms*. Azrael had kept his word, after all.

But I was going to keep my word too. My blood was up and I was ready to fight – not to save my own skin, not for gold, but for the one person who had cared enough to help me. It was time I repaid the favor.

I entered the Spire through the servant's entrance and tore through the back passageways toward the dungeons, consulting my map at intervals. Caution aside, I grappled from beam to beam and gargoyle to column, zooming across whole hallways fast as a bullet.

I'd made it this far. I could do this. I just needed a plan.

The first thing was to pick up the poison from Kreeptic and I wouldn't be wasting a second. The quest timer neared zero as I made my way back to his chambers, pinging completion just as I entered the dungeons as a whole.

Quest – A Short Wait For A Quick Death
It's ready! Return to Chief Interrogator Kreeptic

My night vision was good enough now that I didn't need to

keep a guiding hand on the hall, and I even got a final bump on that skill as I ran through the gloom.

Night Vision Increased!
Level 5
Soon you'll be partying with the owls!

The prisoners and their cells now stood out to me as though they were lit by candlelight; not brightly, but it was close enough to full vision. I supposed my effective Night Vision was actually at level six due to my cowl of midnight. At least, it would help me to navigate the Spire quickly and reach Azrael.

I practically shoulder barged my way into Kreeptic's chambers, catching the malignant jerk pouring a red substance onto a rat with harrowing effects. The creature's eyes engorged then popped, spewing a gelatinous mess across his workbench.

Kreeptic tutted in frustration and spun to face me. "You!"

"Me," I said, meeting his stare with one of my own. Even though his level and elite status meant I'd be pulped in an instant should he choose it, I somehow didn't find the torturer as intimidating anymore. "Got my poison ready?"

Kreeptic's gaze narrowed. "I do. Come here before I have second thoughts."

I hastened to his side, hands outstretched. This had better be damned worth it or else I'd given up a chance of escape for nothing. Ellie believed in it and, unlike before, I fully trusted her now – she'd said it would work so I was certain it would.

When Kreeptic dropped the tiny vial into my hands, I thought something had, in fact, gone terribly wrong. It was so small. Then I checked its description.

Blood of the Old Ones
Poison
Quality: legendary
Millennia ago, ancient horrors were banished deep beneath the world, and for generations, master alchemists have passed down the closest approximation of their festering essence. Once a drop of this poison enters the

body of another, it will consume them from the inside out, turning flesh to rot. Death is certain.
Deals 2000 poison damage every second until the target dies. This cannot be cured or dispelled.
Applications: 1

"I must stress again how difficult this substance is to create," Kreeptic intoned. "It required the last of my Archsolution and the entirety of the rare materials that you acquired to prepare even this small drop. I suggest you make it count."

Quest Completed – A Short Wait For A Quick Death
After long trials, you have secured a sample of the Blood of the Old Ones. Whoever your enemy is, they must really deserve it.

Rewards
+4,000 EXP

"As discussed, without transmuting its power, the poison will be no use against Azrael. Have you located Grand Crusader Reginald?"

I pulled out my map to double-check. The golden stars of the players were completely removed now, as was the highlighted area indicating where the Emperor and his elite guards were being detained. Thankful that I'd committed the spot to memory, I nodded, although a sense of unease came over me.

How was I supposed to distract the inevitable players guarding the NPCs?

Ellie had said there wasn't a secret way into that room specifically and that we'd 'figure it out' when the time came. Well, the time had come and, frankly, I had nothing. Worse still, time was not on my side.

"I know where Reginald and the others are being held," I said. "Just need to figure out how to reach them."

"Perhaps doing some of your crafting work will expand your mind and grant you the answer. I often find it helps me."

Kreeptic returned to his workbench to prod at the rat's corpse without offering anything more useful.

Scowling, I stepped away for a bit of space, not even sure if there was anything I could craft at this stage.

Then, it hit me.

Opening my inventory, I brought out the arcane crystal and felt it vibrate slightly in my hands. I'd wanted to sell this bad boy, but it could be used for another purpose, a far nobler one.

Kreeptic sniffed loudly at the air, turning like a bloodhound. His eyes bugged when he saw the crystal.

"Where in blazes did you get that?"

"Oh, you know, just lying around."

The torturer let loose a choked breath. "I am rapidly reevaluating my opinion of you scavengers. Do you have any idea how valuable that is?"

"Yep. And I'm going to mash it into a new pair of gloves."

"What?" Kreeptic barked. He knocked over a few of his instruments in his bid to reach my side. "I knew you were mad, boy."

I swatted away his grasping hand. "Hey! It's mine. And I'll be using it how I want. You do want me to stand a chance against Azrael, don't you?"

"But on such lowly items," Kreeptic growled. "With even a shaving from that gem, I could brew such a poison as to—"

"Would it be as powerful as the one you just gave me?"

"Well... no. But—"

"Then forget it. I'm not giving it to you."

Kreeptic towered over me, looming bat-like and I honestly thought he'd gut me right there. But I held my ground and that seemed to take the wind out of his sails. He deflated and I began to understand the truth of this man – NPC – whatever. He talked a big game but that was all.

"I don't have time for your empty threats or posturing," I told him. "We're on a schedule if we are to defeat Azrael. In less than one hour he's going to kill Elli— the Emperor. So, stop bugging me."

Kreeptic blinked, pursed his lips, raised a finger as though to say something important, then sloped back to his workbench. I'd opened my Crafting window before he even made it back there, double-checking that I had everything I needed to upgrade the gloves.

Five pieces of manafused satin. Check.

A full round of runes. Worth it, and check.

And the ludicrous component of an arcane crystal. No level 13 ought to have one, and if they did, they'd be mad to waste it on upgrading such low-level gear.

But as Kreeptic kept saying, I was pretty mad. Yet, I wasn't so crazy as to have lost all tactical sense. This was the endgame and I ought to throw everything I had at it. The more powerful these legendary gloves would be, the better, and if I could make it to rank 5 in tailoring before I crafted them, I'd gain a power boost on them. With 35 pieces of dream silk still left in my bags, I should be able to reach that.

I checked my profession sheet and saw that I was about halfway to ranking up.

Tailoring – Rank 4 - 300/630 EXP

Any gear that I might make with dream silk would have an item level restriction beyond me, so I wouldn't be able to use it. However, I just had to gain experience in the profession and quick. Time was of the essence. So I found a belt recipe that looked like it would fulfill my needs.

Recipe – Sash of the Quick Mind
Required Intelligence: 50
Associated Profession: Tailoring
Dream silk x 7
Tools Required: Knitting Needles, Scissors

I crafted one, producing a belt that looked like an oversized martial artist's waistband in stark white.

Success! Sash of the Quick Mind level 25 created

+26 Crafting EXP
+85 Tailoring EXP

Sash of the Quick Mind
Quality: uncommon
Item level 25
Requires level 25 to equip
Durability: 20/20
+25 Armor
+2 Constitution
+3 Intelligence
+1 Regen p/s

Those stats would have been so nice to have on my character but it was the experience in tailoring that I needed. I made three more sashes, accumulating an extra 255 EXP in tailoring, and gained the rank up.

Tailoring Increased!
Rank 5
Materials required to craft items below your Intelligence level reduced by 25%
+5% power to Tailoring items you create

It was a tiny victory, a minuscule boost and yet I felt emboldened by it.

I looked to my evoker's gauntlets again and activated Tinkering. Eagerly, I watched on as my avatar brought out the materials and tools, feeling the rush of anticipation build as I wondered how good a legendary item might be. I hammered the crystal into pieces and used the blowtorch to melt them together into some molten magical thread, which I then wove through my gloves. The satin came next and I was surprised to find the cloth was an obsidian black. Finally, the runes were infused. And it was done.

Success! Evoker's Gauntlets have been upgraded to

Conduits of the Elemental Lord level 28
+28 Crafting EXP
+94 Tailoring EXP

Conduits of the Elemental Lord
Quality: legendary
Item level 28
Requires level 13 to equip
+38 Armor
+10 Intelligence
+2.2 Regen p/s
+8.8% effectiveness to frost spells
+8.8% effectiveness to fire spells
+8.8% effectiveness to air spells
+8.8% effectiveness to earth spells
Special Passive: Infused with runic power, these gloves allow the user to summon the power of the elements through hand gestures without the need to hold onto rune stones. The required runes must still be present in your inventory to draw on them.
This item is Soul Bound to you.

Simply incredible. The jump in power from uncommon items to epic was significant, but the jump to legendary was that again and then some. Truly, these items *in Hundred Kingdoms* were worthy of the label. I also couldn't fail to notice the 8.8% increase in a school of magic's power, which must have been the combined benefit of my rank 5 perk in tailoring and my 'Inventor' specialization. A 5% boost in power from each trait granted a 10% total power increase. At the higher profession ranks, things must get crazy good.

I hurried to equip the gloves, and they fit so well they might have been a second skin; so incredibly soft yet I could feel the latent power within them. Sparks of energy crackled at my fingertips and the black cloth appeared to have a permeant shine as though it had been dipped in a lacquer coating. Strands of red and silver rippled along the material as I moved my hands and I noticed four symbols embedded into the cloth without any visible signs of stitching.

On the back of my right hand was a red flame, while three gray triangles appeared on the back of my left. A blue icicle sat on my right palm and a white tornado on the left.

I reasoned these had something to do with the specialty of the gloves – the ability to summon the elemental powers stored within each rune without needing to hold them. Then, a realization struck me; I'd become a pseudo-mage through crafting gear! Only there was no obvious indication as to how I might go about activating the runes remotely.

Frustrated, I squeezed my right hand into a fist.

Fireball or Inferno?

Ah, that was it. At least, that was how I activated fire at any rate.

I caught Kreeptic eyeing me, unable to hide that he was impressed. "And you have access to mage arts too? You're quite something. My estimation of your odds of success has gone up another notch. Especially with fire."

"Why especially fire?"

"Holy powers are best when used against the undead, but fire is second best."

I noted this information, wishing Ellie was here to break it down into mechanical gaming terms. I imagined it worked something along the lines of holy spells doing twice the bonus damage that fire would. Then again, I could be well off. Holy would still be my best bet for transmuting the Blood of the Old Ones. It had been Ellie's idea and I doubted I'd find a powerful fire mage NPC knocking about who could perform the transmutation at short notice.

With these legendary gloves, I also judged my odds of success had risen sharply. Not only was the boost to my runic spells now quite substantial for a single piece of gear, but the speed and ease I could now draw on the runes without awkwardly fumbling with my inventory in combat would be worth the upgrade alone.

Quick experimentation revealed that facing my palm straight out as though to high-five someone would activate the runes upon my palm. Thankfully, each gesture was simple and wouldn't be hard to master.

My character's stats had also gained a boost from the gloves.

Character
Zoran Human Scavenger Level 13
Attributes
Constitution 19 (+2) – Intelligence 55 (+10) – Reflexes 18 (+5) – Might 18 (+4) – Willpower 26
Combat
Health 760 – Mana 1200 – Attack Power 59 – Spell Power 124 – Regen 3.3 (+2.2) p/s

Panicked that I'd now lost track of time, I checked the clock. There were forty minutes left to save Ellie, and despite Kreeptic's advice, I had not had an epiphany on how I might distract or otherwise disable the guards. Attacking directly wasn't wise; I had only got away with it on the walls because they'd been distracted by a whole army coming at them.

Thinking that I'd just have to figure it out along the way, I turned to leave and pulled on the door.

"Try not to die," Kreeptic said by way of encouragement.

"Thanks," I said dryly. "No risk for you down here, I suppose," I added in an undertone. Then it came to me. Why was the torturer content to remain behind? Wouldn't it be in his interest to come and help me directly?

"Why don't you join me?"

"Come again," Kreeptic said. "I'm sure I just misheard you."

I pulled the door wide open, standing between the frame and beckoned him.

"You heard fine. I said come join me. It will be a good way for you to earn Highcross' job and I could use the help."

Kreeptic's nose crinkled. "I'm not one for direct action. Hence, the tools and poisons." He swept a hand around his chambers.

"It's okay if you're afraid."

"Afraid?" Kreeptic said, attempting a laugh although his pitch gave him away. "People fear me, boy. Not the other way around."

"Come prove it then."

He growled, trapped by his own bravado.

"Look," I said, more encouragingly, "I think I get where you're coming from. Most of my life I've sat back, hoping what I want will just come my way without making any real effort to improve things by myself. All I did was get angry and resentful when I really should have stepped up. You want them to respect you, then stop skulking down here in the dark muttering about how everyone else has wronged you. Get up there and prove to the Emperor why he should make you his Chief Intelligence Officer!"

Kreeptic pressed his pale lips into a thin line, frowned, and bowed his head in thought. Then, all at once, he snapped up his cruel looking knife, the horrible red substance he'd been pouring on the rat, a dozen vials of poison in varying hues of green. With a swirl of his cloak he vanished, then his voice rang out behind me.

"Lead the way, Zoran. I shall fight with you."

32

Kreeptic and I made our way to the eighth floor with all haste. Azrael would be one floor up inside the Hall of the Makers and it seemed he'd pulled the majority of his men back there as a final line of defense for we'd encountered no resistance. So far.

As we approached the holding area of the Emperor, Kreeptic indicated we should pause.

"Allow me to scout ahead." The torturer vanished in another swirl of his cloak, presumably into some powerful form of stealth.

Waiting for him to return, I took stock of the items I still had that would be useful in the coming battles.

Blood of the Old Ones
Greater Mana Swirl Potion x 4
Gnomish Land Mine x 9
Journeyman Grenade x 9
Steel Caltrop x 18
Frost Rune x 7
Fire Rune x 9
Air Rune x 9
Earth Rune x 9
Vial of Arch-Solution x 16

Disorientating Venom x 2

It was as good an arsenal as I was going to obtain in my position. I resupplied my makeshift utility belt with grenades, caltrops and slime, glad to be able to keep the runes safe inside my inventory. Next, I tightened the silk wire holding my 'bayonet' in place on the crossbow. I fully expected it to fall off in the fighting but if I did need to use it, then I would probably be in deep shit to begin with. That disorientating venom I'd scavenged from the rogue Biterzogg might come in useful, but like the Blood of the Old Ones, the trick would be in applying it.

My mind turned to how many players I'd probably be facing. Without Ellie's help, I couldn't know for sure whether Azrael had redeployed his remaining eighteen men so I had to make my best guess. I assumed three were still outside the armory, blocking my entry and unaware of my movements. They might be recalled when the fighting started but, hopefully, they'd arrive too late to help. There'd been a dozen players out on the walls and I'd taken out four, leaving just eight there. Azrael might have reinforced them but I couldn't know this for sure. It was doubtful he would remove them in case some crazy players attempted another assault, so I felt those eight were still out there and too far away to have any impact on the fight to come.

That left nine players up here, excluding Azrael himself. Ten in all; a fair number and there would be nothing to distract them.

Suddenly, smoke billowed before me, nearly making me jump out of my skin. Kreeptic had reappeared.

"As suspected there are adventurers guarding the door," he reported.

"How many?"

"Two. A warlock with an infernal minion, and a shaman with wind enchanted axes."

I scratched my chin. "This disappearing, teleporting act of yours; I take it you can't just blip through the walls and speak to Reginald yourself?"

He growled lowly. "I cannot Shadowstep through solid walls, you peabrained—"

I threw up a hand. "Yeh, it would be pretty OP if you could." I sighed. "Alright. A warlock and shaman. Can you take them?"

"I should be able to," Kreeptic said, flashing a disturbing smile. "Although the shaman has a totem of warding, which means he'll be alerted to anyone trying to sneak up on them."

"I'll draw their attention towards us, away from the totem. Then you can strike."

"Very well," Kreeptic said. "One last thing. It appears Azrael has locked the Emperor away in his own solar. These are his private chambers for sleeping and study, and only Aurelius himself holds the key. Azrael must have taken it by force."

I flashed a smile of my own, taking out Aurelius' Key from my bags.

"You mean, this key?"

Kreeptic gave a slow, thankfully silent clap. "A scavenger and a master pickpocket. You'll be a most useful agent for me after my promotion."

"Uh huh," I said, trying to formulate a quick plan together for dealing with the shaman and warlock. This hallway wasn't well suited to ambushes from above; the ceiling was low and there weren't as many adornments in this more private area of the Spire. I could try and lure them around the corner to run onto landmines, slime and caltrops, but that could be risky. There was every chance they'd just call for backup or not follow me. All I really had to do was remove the totem of warding or ensure they wouldn't notice Kreeptic coming some other wa—

Ah, but that was just it, assuming it worked.

"Kreeptic, do poisons work just as well if inhaled?"

He raised an eyebrow. "It is unorthodox but most substances need only enter the victim's system; the method is rarely an issue."

Having decided my course of action, I stepped forward, pulling out a vial of the disorientating venom and shoved it down my launcher. There was still some space in the chamber so I placed the second vial of venom in there too for good measure.

"Let's go. Attack from stealth on my signal."

I steadied my breath, then rounded the corner, leveling my crossbow down the corridor. The warlock was level 43, the shaman 46. Azrael had kept his most powerful players close. I just hoped Kreeptic could take them alone. Time to find out.

"Cooey! What's up nubs?"

I fired a bolt to make sure that I got their attention. The shaft zipped towards the warlock but his infernal lumbered to block it and the arrowhead glanced off its flaming stone form. It roared at me, like a cross between a crocodile and a lion, and smashed its fist into the floor. Paintings fell from the walls and the carpet singed at the impact. Twirling his axes, the dwarf shaman took a step forward, while the warlock began channeling a bolt of pure darkness. Behind them was the warding totem but, hopefully, it wouldn't matter.

Switching to my launcher aim, I picked a spot right at the feet of the players and fired. Just like the vials of slime out on the walls, the two smaller vials of venom hurtled forth. Facing my left palm forward, I summoned an air rune and sunk 500 mana into a single Gale Blast, taking a stab at how much power I'd need to pull off the desired effect before releasing it down the hallway. Vials smashed, poison splashed and the runic air vaporized the lot.

A mini mushroom cloud of green gas whooshed upwards into the players' faces. Moments later, the shaman stumbled through the cloud, spluttering and clawing at his eyes. Green droplet symbols appeared above their heads indicating a debuff.

Disorientating Venom
Vision and movement obscured.
Duration: 4 seconds

"Now, Kreeptic," I called, but the torturer was well ahead of me. A gleaming dagger lunged from nowhere, sinking into the warlock's back. The infernal minion roared its displeasure, swinging a backhanded blow which Kreeptic narrowly dodged.

I started forward, wondering if Kreeptic would need any help, but seeing him weave round the infernal so that it struck its own master, I felt he had this well under control.

With the attention of the players diverted, I held my breath to run through the lingering poison cloud. A hint of its bitterness tickled my nose and I felt momentarily sorry for the players but avoided its effect myself.

With Aurelius' key, I unlocked the door, entered and pulled it shut behind me.

My immediate greeting was five extremely heavily armed and armored NPCs, their weapons raised and hands aglow with priming spells. Backpedaling to the far wall was the man I'd seen in the introductory cutscene for the human race, seen from afar in the throne room and up close once via Azrael's stream. Emperor Aurelius himself, although there was something strange about the info hovering over his head.

Emperor Aurelius – ??? – Level 50 Boss

Where his class ought to be, there were only question marks. Did this mean he didn't have one? Could he really not fight at all? That would explain, at least, why he fell over so easily during the first assault on the Spire.

His bodyguards closed in.

"Do you bring new terms?" one of them barked. Facing the source, I instantly recognized that unique armor, the white gold inlays, the cowl and robes made of flexible plate mail. His details confirmed this.

Grand Crusader Reginald – Paladin – level 50 Elite

Reginald was an imposing figure up close. He must have been six-foot-five, even broader than you might expect with a moustache so mighty it would have made an acceptable loot drop on its own.

"Well?" he demanded. "Speak quickly or we'll send you back to your master in pieces."

"Reginald, really, he's but a child." This meeker voice

belonged to the Emperor, somewhat obscured by the various bulky guards trying to shield him with their own bodies.

"My Lord, if he serves the undead then he has willingly become an enemy of all life."

"I don't work for Azrael," I said. "I'm here to rescue you and I need your help."

Reginald strode forward to get a better look at me. Scowling, he grabbed my tabard and inspected it closely as a gemsmith might inspect a diamond.

"It's the Rusking colors, Lord... though he might have stolen them."

"Heavily armed too," said another. "Grenades, some poisons maybe."

"How would you expect to fight Azrael's men off without being armed?" I said. "It's not like they just let me waltz in here." I shrugged Reginald off. "Interrogator Kreeptic is outside handling some of your enemies. You can go help him if you like."

I opened the door to see the poor torturer being flung bodily against the wall by the infernal, the shaman whirling in for a twin axe strike. Perhaps he didn't have it handled after all.

The crystalline metallic edges of the axes met a barrier of pulsing light, arresting the shaman's swing just inches from Kreeptic's face.

"Minions of filth!" Reginald spat, his hands white-hot from a spell cast. "To arms, men. To arms." He raised his obscenely large warhammer and pounded into the corridor, two of the guards following.

The remaining Imperial Guard fell in tight beside their emperor, a priest and another paladin.

"No sudden moves, scavenger."

I threw up my hands to show I meant no harm, and two runes tried to activate at once.

Frost Bolt or Cone of Cold?

Gale Blast or Whirlwind?

Thankfully, neither of the runes would go off without placing mana into them but it struck me as a new and exciting possibility: could I now activate two runes at the same time? I closed both my fists and the options for fire and earth runes appeared. I tried one fist closed and one palm forward and the relevant options appeared. Letting loose a triumphant laugh seemed to set the guards on edge and they began to advance.

"Stop, stop," Aurelius said, as more of a plea than an order. "This boy has come to set us free."

"Sir, how would he have got your key if not from Azrael?"

"Kreeptic pickpocketed it from him," I said hastily. The guards narrowed their eyes but seemed quelled. Hopefully, the NPCs wouldn't bother checking in with each other but they were being annoyingly inquisitive. Ellie sure was powerful. All the more reason I couldn't let a nutter like Azrael have her.

Conscious of my time, I pressed on. "Uhm, your Majesty? Lord? I believe I have found a way to kill Azrael but I shall need the assistance of the Grand Crusader."

"Hmmm," Aurelius mused. Rather than jump for joy at the news of salvation, he appeared to shrink into himself. "A deal was struck with our captors..."

Before I could puzzle this out, two screams bellowed from the corridor followed by deafening, hammering bangs.

GiefWindProcs – Shaman – level 46 dies – 275 EXP

TragicSoul – Warlock – level 43 dies – 260 EXP

I mentally ticked down to sixteen players left.

Though pleased by their passing, it was almost certain they'd alerted Azrael to the attack. At best, he was now aware of my presence near the ninth floor and at worst, direct retaliation would soon follow.

Emperor Aurelius was still looking at me strangely, but it was only Reginald that I actually needed. I turned to find the Grand Crusader already returning heavily into the solar, dashes of blood smeared across his pristine armor.

He looked upon me with what I think amounted to respect. "You've done the Imperium a great service this day, Zoran."

"I can do you one better," I said, bringing out the Blood of the Old Ones. "If you would transmute this poison into a holy substance, we might bring down Azrael himself."

Reginald eyed Kreeptic next. The torturer was panting, clutching at his side and had suffered a cut on his brow, but his health was already regenerating.

"The boy acquired the ingredients," Kreeptic said breathily. "Don't ask me how, he's simply... talented."

"That poison is forbidden," Reginald said gravely.

I gritted my teeth; surely, this wasn't going to go south at the eleventh hour?

"Yet these are dark times," Reginald continued. "I will transmute this poison for the sole purpose of killing our enemy, but by the light, I hope never to see this again." He gave Kreeptic a stern look; the torturer smiled nervously.

I thought about chancing my luck a little more.

"You could all come with me? I'll have a better chance of hitting Azrael with it if I have you all as backup."

"It would be my greatest desire to rid the world of this evil," Reginald said. "However, I'm afraid my Emperor's safety is my priority. We ought to take him from the Spire, then return to deal with this menace."

"But I don't have time for that," I said. "What if Azrael flees once he finds out you're all gone? Right now, we have him cornered atop the Spire."

"Zoran, I admire your courage, but you should watch your tongue. Rarely do I admit your kind into my presence, never mind speaking freely as you are. To join you in battle and leave my Emperor unguarded risks his life; should he die, the entire Imperium would fall into war and chaos."

I rounded on Aurelius. "Can't you speak for yourself? Just order them to come and help me and we can end this thing!"

I'd forgotten all sense of roleplay as I strode towards the Emperor – lowly position be damned. A huge, powerful hand grabbed me by the shoulder, inflicting 100 points of damage all on its own. I gasped, driven to my knees.

"Attempt that again," Reginald growled, "and it shall be my hammer you feel."

"Enough," Aurelius said firmly. There was authority entering his voice now. "I find myself in awe of this one's bravery."

"My Lord, we must leave. Now. I beg you take caution."

"Caution would perhaps be prudent," Aurelius said. "Yet, what was it you were saying to me only yesterday, Reginald? That caution and words may no longer suffice."

"Matters of court politics are one thing, but this is true danger."

"The whole Imperium is in danger," Aurelius said. "On all points of the compass, enemies gather and from within we bicker. Today marks the fruit of this rot. How did such a mighty servant of the Dark Council enter our city and convince so many citizens of our lands to join him? We are either lax or our foes at home have harbored and supplied him, hoping to remove me in a manner that looks legitimate and avoid a civil war."

Each NPC was enraptured by the oratory. I, on the other hand, was growing anxious as time was marching on. It was doubtful whether any explanations about how an Orb of Deception worked or why Aurelius had it all wrong would help, but at least he seemed to be heading in a favorable direction at any rate.

Suddenly, he got down on one knee to my own level. "This citizen did not run today. Nor should I."

"My Lord, this would be unwise," Reginald said, though his tone gave him away. He very clearly thought this to be a wonderful turn of events.

"For too long I have ignored the hard truth," Aurelius said softly, more to himself than the room. He looked longingly at a bookshelf, a mixture of sadness and resolve carving out a new man before my very eyes. "I have stressed our troubles should be faced with reason. But either our world is not yet ready, or I am not. How can I expect to bring the change I seek when I cannot command respect within my own house?"

He rose to his feet. "Reginald, fetch me my father's sword and armor."

"Yes, Lord!"

The crusader's enthusiasm for this rang through my shoulder where his eager grip dealt me another 50 points of damage before he and another guard strode off to a side chamber.

Despite myself, I couldn't help but be caught up in the moment. Something cool was happening and I doubted any other player had experienced the Emperor like this.

He looked very intently at me. "Your courage today has inspired me beyond words, you even managed to get that old cretin Kreeptic out of his lair. As you seem intent on pursuing Azrael to justice, we shall stand firmly by your side. I shall stand by your side."

Reginald and the guard returned, carrying a bejeweled scabbard and a set of beautiful golden plate mail. I worried that the equipment process would mimic how long such things would take in the real world, but thankfully the gaming side of *Hundred Kingdoms* had mercy on me. Aurelius took the items and equipped them with the speed of any player.

Now he stood resplendent, with mighty pauldrons shaped like stag heads, and a golden helm with protruding antlers. He drew his sword, a ruby crusted hilt glimmering under a broad blade of the finest steel. I wondered whether he'd even be able to swing it effectively given his lore but there appeared to be a stark change in the man, reflected even in the details floating above his head.

Emperor Aurelius – Battle Priest – Level 50 Boss

He'd developed an entirely new class, or at least a spec of the priest or warrior class no one else had unlocked yet. Now, this definitely balanced out the scales – having a level 50 boss mob on my side would knock Azrael for six or nothing else would.

"Zoran," Aurelius said, his voice now brimming with power. "You have proven yourself beyond any who have come before you. Both the Imperium and I owe you an eternal debt. I dub thee a knight, granting you title and all the benefits that lie therein."

He actually tapped me on each shoulder with his sword.

Notifications began popping up.

Title Unlocked!
You may now select the title of 'Sir', 'Ser' or 'Knight' to precede your name for all to see. Denizens of the Imperium will now treat you with the respect you deserve.

Knightly Valor
Your exploits have been hard won and your achievements are evident in your bearing.
+5 Constitution
+5 Might
+5 Willpower

Access to the Knight's Hall Unlocked!
Visit the elite staging grounds of Argatha's most esteemed warriors to discover more.

"Arise, Ser Zoran!"

The Imperial Guard cheered, punching fists into the air and clanking weapons off their shields. Unable to prevent myself from grinning, I got to my feet and gave a very gratifying bow to the assembled guards. When I looked to Kreeptic, he mimed vomiting, but I ignored that.

Ser Zoran; I made that my new official character name. Shame they weren't chanting Ser Jack.

I felt a fire rise within me; before, I'd just been acting on a sort of madness but now I might actually succeed.

"Reginald, are you ready to create our secret weapon?"

"Hand it here, Ser Zoran. It would be my pleasure."

33

I had about fifteen minutes left to save Ellie by the time Grand Crusader Reginald finished the Transmutation. He handed it back to me, a serious portion of his mana depleted.

I checked the poison's description just to make sure.

Sanctified Blood of the Old Ones
Poison
Quality: legendary
Millennia ago, ancient horrors were banished deep beneath the world, and for generations, master alchemists have passed down the closest approximation of their festering essence. Once a drop of this poison enters the body of another, it will consume them from the inside out, turning flesh to rot. Death is certain.
Deals 2000 holy damage every second until the target dies. This cannot be cured or dispelled.
Applications: 1

I considered how I might apply the poison to Azrael. If it still functioned like other poisons, then I only needed to get it into his system. So, it could possibly be delivered airborne, as I'd done with the disorientating venom, yet I saw a few problems in doing that.

For one, I wasn't sure whether vaporizing it would change

how the damage would be dealt – what if Azrael simply moved out of the holy cloud before it killed him? As a level capped player, he'd have enough health to survive a couple of hits of the stuff, never mind the healing potions and allies he'd have to top himself up. Besides, what if he just held his breath as I had in the archmage's chamber and when I recently passed through the airborne venom myself. I only had one application to play with, so I didn't want to risk that.

Another issue was accidentally killing my new allies. Priests and paladins were resistant to holy damage, but they weren't immune to it. Friendly fire would be hard to avoid completely during a fight but there was no point taking undue risks to my allies lives.

No, the only way to ensure Azrael bore the full brunt of the holy poison was to hit him squarely with it. Even if he had some healers with him, it couldn't be dispelled. He'd go down.

That left me with the choice of shooting a crossbow bolt that was coated with the poison or trying to get in close for a point-blank attack. I'd prefer to be shooting at long range for obvious reasons, but I'd have to see how the fight was panning out before deciding.

Emperor Aurelius, Kreeptic, Reginald and the four other guards seemed to be waiting for me to speak.

"If you're waiting for me to explain an intricate plan, then I'm afraid, I don't have one. All I know is that Azrael and his seven remaining cronies will be in the Hall of the Makers."

I then realized that I now also had seven companions. The scales were as leveled as they were going to be for this final showdown.

Reginald hefted his mighty hammer. "I'm eager to take my revenge upon that colossus and avenge our fallen brothers."

"Our mission is to defend Ser Zoran and allow him a clear chance at striking our foe," Aurelius said. "Our fate will ultimately be down to you."

"No pressure then." I loaded a bolt into my crossbow. "Let's go end this."

. . .

The ninth floor of the Imperial Spire was comprised of only three things – a short corridor leading to a flight of wide stairs that climbed toward the high arched, open doorway of the Hall of the Makers. Seeing it now in the flesh, so to speak, it was far larger than I'd anticipated; as though a cathedral had been carefully balanced atop the Spire.

On either side, windows granted an extensive view across the city and far distant mountains. A fall from here would not result in a pleasant landing.

Players assembled to greet us at the top of the staircase, blocking our entry to the Hall of the Makers. There were seven in total: monk, paladin, priest, rogue, mage, berserker and a ranger. A good variety of classes that could cover a lot of playstyles between them. Every one of them was a mid-level 40 player. Tell-tale signs of buff spells flared over their heads as they prepared for us.

My companions weren't doing likewise, despite three of them holding elite status, which already showed the size of my disadvantage. Powerful allies they might be, but Aurelius and his guard were still NPCs; the regular guards were not even elites. Players worth their salt should be able to overcome them. The wild card would be me and, possibly, Aurelius, now that he'd taken on some proper boss form.

Just as I thought about making a move, a wave of ghouls and skeletal minions joined the players, beefing out their ranks dramatically. Azrael must have specced to be a minion-based death knight, which might make him weaker as an individual. Something worth bearing in mind. But who was I kidding? Probably one hit from a level 50 and I'd be dead.

"One last chance, Jack," Azrael called from inside the hall. I couldn't see him but he sounded indifferent to my arrival. "Just wait a few more minutes and I'll be gone."

"I've not climbed this tower just to stand here," I called back.

"Throw your life away then," Azrael said. "Take them down!"

The scream that followed I'd only heard once before, the sort of shrill cry that must surely signal the end of all life. I remembered this feeling of dread from back when Azrael and his men first attacked the Spire. Like then, my vision darkened and I felt ice cold. A debuff icon started flashing over my health bar.

Cry of the Damned
Movement speed reduced by 30%
Attack power reduced by 10%
Spell power reduced by 15%
Only a holy cleansing of equal power can dispel this curse.
Duration: 40 seconds

I'd completely forgotten about this move. And I didn't have a counter. Forty seconds was a very long time as far as combat was concerned. No wonder he'd stormed the Spire so easily at first when he had 50 players at his back.

Panic took me. All I'd done, everything I'd gone through and fought against, just to have it unraveled in an instant by an overpowered piece of shit move.

Light then began to dance around me. My veins turned from black lines to healthy conduits of life. The darkness faded and my head cleared. In fact, I felt better than ever, as though a shot of pure caffeine-mixed-adrenaline had hit my heart. Turning wildly, I found the source of my salvation.

Emperor Aurelius, the level 50 boss battle priest, was channeling a spell. The last line of Azrael's debuff description jumped out at me – *Only a holy cleansing of equal power can dispel this curse.* Aurelius was assuredly as powerful as Azrael, if not more so. He'd been in his weak scholarly mode the first time around, which Azrael had prepared for, but this was a different fight entirely.

"Undeath shall never prevail," Aurelius bellowed. He finished his spell, sending a wave of light around our entire group. Kreeptic, Reginald and the guards rose back to their feet from where they'd fallen, looking as invigorated as I felt.

A cry of anger echoed from the hall beyond.

That's when I saw the buff.

Divine Inspiration

Righteous belief has summoned every ounce of your courage and spirit. Go now and face all odds.
+20% to all physical stats
Duration: 2 minutes

The Emperor thrust his gleaming sword forth.

"For the Imperium!"

Reginald, Kreeptic and the others drew their weapons and yelled the same.

"Just hold them," Azrael screamed, the confidence in his voice faltering. More orders rang from inside the Hall of the Makers, and the enemy players scrambled to follow. The ghouls and skeletons surged forward first, early cannon fodder to spare the players.

I jumped ahead of my allies, throwing down every gnomish landmine I had, and then the caltrops, for good measure. I didn't want us stuck in a brutally narrow corridor, distracted by minions – we had to get into that hall fast.

My whole world narrowed in on the moment. This was a boss battle of epic proportions; phase one, interrupt the boss' spell cast – meaning get Azrael the hell away from that console. I'd deal with phase two when we got to it.

Ghouls and skeletons obediently trundled on, oblivious to my traps. Bang after bang sounded and flames licked at the ceiling. The windows on either side shattered from the blasts as the mines detonated in quick succession.

I raised an arm against the light and heat, feeling chips of bone rake at me as they flew by, shaving points off my health. Yet despite it all, the traps weren't of a level to match the level 50 summoned creatures. Plenty of the undead minions were emerging through the blaze, albeit burning and weakened, the heated caltrops lodged in their saggy flesh.

A ghoul with half a face swung a rotten arm at me. My Reflexes were good enough to dodge it and follow with a stab from my bayonet. It's health hardly budged, but it plummeted to zero when a glowing warhammer smashed into the remaining half of its face. Reginald offered me a hand and I ran into the fray behind him, keeping close to the Grand Crusader as he made short work of the weakened undead.

As we neared the bottom of the stairs, I checked on the players. Their plans must have been ruined by the rapid destruction of Azrael's minions for they were strung outside of a formation, some having made it halfway down the stairs before stopping to assess the situation.

Worried that the NPCs would attack sporadically while the players focused their damage onto one target at a time, I picked a rogue at the front of the group and pointed to him.

"Kill this guy first, he's weaker." I even shot him to emphasize the point.

"Nay, Ser Zoran," Aurelius said, pointing in turn at the armored warrior behind the rogue. "This one draws my eye. We should deal with him first."

"What the—" I started. Then realization smacked into me. My allies were being drawn towards the tankiest player of the group – this warrior was drawing all their aggro.

I couldn't have that.

The rogue darted forward, clearly anticipating his tank picking up the mobs. This presented an opportunity.

I closed my left fist.

Rock Armor or Rock Wall?

I pumped 200 mana into a rock wall and raised it between the rogue and the warrior, cutting the rogue off from the rest of his group. The rogue carried on unaware. I wondered if he even realized what had happened when six mobs and a boss suddenly turned all their attention onto him.

Aurelius and Reginald's attacks sent him reeling, and his back hit the wall before Kreeptic delved two daggers through his chest. A chink of metal rang off hard rock.

Slyeye – level 44 rogue dies – 265 EXP

If only the rock walls would last longer. Even when I'd

dumped all my mana into one, it had only lasted for 10 seconds. It would have been insane if they lasted much longer and sadly it looked like my one shot at that tactic was up.

As the rock wall crumbled away, the players behind it were revealed. They'd pulled back to form a two-man shield wall in the doorway to the Hall of Makers – their paladin and warrior holding great shields abreast with their healers close beside them. Being so compact, the game would count their packed bodies as an obstruction, making it impossible for me to place another dividing wall. The group's monk backflipped over the shield wall to safety.

Lacking that acrobatic capability, I didn't see an easy way in.

My allies surged up the staircase, oblivious to the idea of proper tactics. If I could direct them, they were dangerous, but this was going to be like herding cats.

I rammed a grenade into the launcher and aimed, thinking of adding to the torrent of damage that was now hitting their tanks, but I lowered it a second later. A few journeyman grenades wouldn't help. The damage would be quickly healed and I'd have wasted a precious resource.

But I *had* to do something. And fast.

Now that the players had rallied themselves, they were better suited to a drawn-out fight. Their healers diligently spam healed their tanks who, in turn, appeared to be blowing defensive cooldowns, and their mage and ranger were throwing plenty of focused damage onto one of the weaker guard mobs. Unlike the players, my allies didn't heal as fastidiously and a warrior guard on my side toppled over dead.

"Just a little longer," Azrael called. "I am almost done."

"Goddammit," I hissed. Something had to be done to break that formation.

Sucking in a deep breath, I grabbed a mana potion in my right hand and closed my left fist again.

Rock Armor or Rock Wall?

I'd regenerated over 100 mana since using the last rock wall, allowing me to pour a clean 1100 into Rock Armor; not a full mana dump, but close to it.

Rock Armor
Incoming damage reduced by 73%
+8.8% from gear effects (+6.4% damage reduction)
Duration: 7 seconds

I'd already started running when the helmet of stone morphed into place, reducing my vision to a narrow slit. Good thing I only had to look straight ahead. A bullet glanced off me, barely scratching my health. A fireball from the mage hurt me more, knocking me down to half health despite the damage reduction. I downed the mana potion I'd proactively kept outside of my armor, regaining full mana before I threw my shoulder at the join of the two shields.

The tanks gave way just enough to allow momentum to carry me through. Confused, the players backed off, giving me a precious few seconds in which to act.

Time to try out a dual cast.

I faced both my palms out, aiming for the floor.

Frost Bolt or Cone of Cold?

Gale Blast or Whirlwind?

I went for both AOE options and threw all 1200 of my mana into the spells before releasing. It turned out that dual casting spread the mana input across both spells, but the bonus for the full mana dump was applied to both as well.

Cone of Cold
Movement speed decreased by 15%
Empowered: movement speed decreased by 5%
+8.8% from gear effects (+1.8% decrease to movement speed)
Radius: 8 feet
Duration 5 Seconds

Whirlwind
Knockback 10 feet
Empowered: +5 feet to knockback
+8.8% from gear effects (+1.3 feet to knockback)
Radius: 8 feet

Azrael's squad were blown clean off their feet, thrown in all directions over 16 feet and left with a lovely 20% slow debuff.

I had no mana. Potions were on cooldown for one minute. My Rock Armor was already fading.

But we were in.

"Valiant work, Ser Zoran," Reginald boomed as he thundered by. My other allies quickly followed, all of them homing straight in on the tanking warrior who held their aggro.

Breathing hard, dumbstruck by the flexibility and power afforded to me by my crafted gloves, I only then looked ahead to the player at the center of the hall.

Azrael – Death Knight – level 50

He was standing behind the crystal orb that served as a Game Master's console, his face gray, and most certainly dead. His mana was already at 50%, presumably from casting that powerful debuff and summoning the ghouls. An expression of furious disbelief broke out across that inhuman face, stretching the sickly skin tight across his skull. Stepping away from the console, he unsheathed his serrated two-handed sword.

Well, mission accomplished, I guess. I'd interrupted him badly enough to stop his work.

Now for phase two.

34

Inside the Hall of the Makers, things had begun well. The warrior on Azrael's crew had fallen under the wrath of my allies. Flat on his back, he lacked the cooldowns or heals from his comrades to survive such an onslaught.

Ironclad – level 46 dies – 275 EXP

Five of Azrael's cronies remained.

I grappled away, whizzing to the nearest ledge before reassessing the fight.

Now their main tank was dead, my allies scattered to the other players, whacking anything in sight. The player paladin was attempting to pick up the threat but was having a hell of a time of it, which made me suspect he wasn't specced for tanking and was actually a damage dealer or healer who had quickly thrown on a shield. If so, this might go smoother than I'd anticipated.

Something didn't feel right though; something was missing.

That was when I saw Azrael casting. He hadn't joined the battle; rather he stood still, his hands and arms lost in a purple miasma of energy. Another debuff? Some great attack?

Wait, I thought, where is that damned—

"Colossus!" Reginald cried as the lumbering, multi-bodied

monster materialized from nowhere behind Azrael. Once formed, it picked up speed, flailing its gruesome limbs, letting loose a rattling roar from the depths of death.

All my allies were immediately drawn to it. Of course, the colossus must be some powerful tanking minion, perhaps only available to endgame death knights who specced into their minion tree. Its size aside, the amount of mana that Azrael had used to summon it spoke volumes of its power. He'd dropped from 50% to about 20% from what I could tell, yet with my allies too focused on one target I was back to square one.

I only noticed the ball of pulsing violet energy just in time. I twisted away from the magical assault, suffering splash damage as the spell crashed against the wall beside me. This alone dropped my health by 300 points. My world focused upon the enemy high-elf mage for a moment, and I saw the next violet barrage forming into his hands.

I grappled around, barely avoiding the next blast. To my great relief, I received a heal from one of my elite priest guards, bringing me back to full health in an instant.

"Leave him!" Azrael cried. "He's an ant compared to them. Focus your DPS on the elite healers first."

With this order given, I breathed a momentary sigh of relief and checked how things were developing down below.

Only Kreeptic and Aurelius seemed to be able to tear themselves away from the colossus. Aurelius would switch to heal an ally or smite an enemy, probably under some ingrained behavior. Kreeptic was just being an opportunist rogue, running to attack a player from behind whenever they turned their back to him. He did it every time, so it was clearly some mechanic.

That gave me an idea.

I spotted their ranger backpedaling from the melee, firing off gunshots as he went. I grappled around until I hung off the wall behind him, praying the mage wouldn't look up and find me. Wasting no time, I threw a slime vial, timing it to land just where the ranger would next place his feet. It worked. The ranger lost balance and landed on his back.

I sent a bolt into him, but it caused little damage to the level 47 player.

"Kreeptic!" I yelled, hoping the ranger would turn to look for the source of the crossbow bolt.

The torturer spun to face me, but the ranger did not. Kreeptic returned to stabbing at the colossus' shins.

Cursing, I dropped to the ground, loading another crossbow bolt as I ran.

"Turn around, asshole."

I'd regened just enough mana to activate Desperate Shot for this attack.

"Kreeptic – Kreeptic!"

The extra damage did the trick. The ranger twisted round to face me, as again did Kreeptic. The ranger looked annoyed, his hand going for a sidearm; Kreeptic's face broke into a grin, daggers twirling in his hands. Before the ranger could pull the trigger, those daggers were jutting in and out of his back. Stunned by the knives or some ability, the ranger barely moved. I jabbed with my bayonet, before ducking away, in case he managed to get off a shot. His health hit zero soon enough and he lay face down in the slime.

Flukeshoot – level 47 dies – 280 EXP

Four of Azrael's cronies now remained.

Kreeptic winked then disappeared in a swirl of his cloak. I aimed wildly above and grappled out of there, glancing around to watch a fireball hit the spot that I'd just vacated. Close call.

Despite the death of the ranger, the fight wasn't going well for my team.

With most of the NPCs distracted by the colossus, the enemy mage, monk and recent ranger had managed to burst down one of the priests in the Imperial Guard. Losing the ranger wouldn't hurt their damage output too much as I could see Azrael swing at the remaining weakened priest, taking a lot of his health off in one attack. The monk spun a kick into the priest's back, and a fireball seared it a moment later. Azrael struck again. The priest died.

So much for him being relatively weak as an individual.

I was down to four allies and now had no more dedicated healers. Azrael still had his colossus tank, his paladin off-tank and a priest healing the group, as well as keeping the colossus topped up. My one glimmer of hope was that their priest was quickly running out of mana, though I was screwed if his potions were off cooldown.

Azrael was lost in the mix of the battle so I couldn't get a clean shot to use the Sanctified Blood of the Old Ones.

My best hope right now was to interrupt the priest's casts long enough to allow Aurelius and Reginald a chance to kill the colossus. I grappled over, as close as I dared, and hauled myself on top of a stag head statue. Lining a shot, I fired, hoping for a knockback. I didn't get it, but I did hit the priest which caused his latest heal to slow in casting. I hit him again, slowing it a little more before he could release it.

My third arrow triggered the knockback effect and sent him staggering. The colossus' health was falling at a more pleasing rate. If I could keep this up a while longer—

A huge red eye with a black cross for a pupil flashed in front of me, before etching onto my body. Out of instinct, I tried wiping it off but my efforts ended in obvious failure.

Gaze of the Toothed Cloud
Darkness envelopes you, and the swarm fixates upon you. You can't see them, but they will find you.
Duration: 15 seconds

That didn't look like a monk or mage ability. Sure enough, I saw Azrael was casting again. A black cloud gathered over his head and creatures began swooping out of it in droves.

To call them bats was a disservice to the real animal; these were zombified, long-fanged hellish bats. Their wings beat heavily in the air and they were all looking right at me. To make matters worse, the black cloud that they'd all emerged from didn't vanish; instead, it glided at top speed to collide with me before I could blink.

I went blind. Just how big was this effect? If I fell, would I emerge from it or would it follow me? And could I risk the fall damage?

Screeching mixed with beating wings. The bats would be on me soon.

Yet I began to see outlines faintly through the blackness, the shifting of a hundred wings blurring like hummingbirds. I could see, barely, the outlines of the players and NPCs as they fought.

Thank you, Night Vision level 6.

With a sliver of vision came equal hope.

I took a vial of slime and poured what little mana I'd regenerated into an air rune to vaporize it, then contained this gas within the vial and slotted it into my launcher. My potions were off cooldown so I drank one to bring my mana to full.

All I could do was pray as I levelled the crossbow and closed my right fist.

I fired the gas canister, charged all 1200 mana into the fire rune and released. A boulder-sized ball of white-hot flames hurtled from my hand.

Fireball hits!
1500 fire damage
Empowered: +20% damage (+300 fire damage)
+ 8.8% from gear effects (+158 fire damage)
Type bonus +25% vs Undead (+490 fire damage)
Total: 2448 fire damage

Heat, light, wind and an ear-splitting crack hit me all at once. The explosion blew away the darkness, and I could see the swarm engulfed with flames that swirled along every tendril of the vaporized slime. This attacked them for a second time, meaning I'd hit the bats for close to 5000 damage in one shot. The beauty of my slime. An AOE attack in itself would not rival the damage of a single potent attack, and when combined with the slime... well, I reckoned a hot-fix patch would be applied by the devs if they caught wind of this.

Bits of fried bat fluttered down. A few remained whole, sporting burning fur and wailing death screeches. I let them get in close, then launched a well-placed grenade in their ugly faces, finishing them.

Panting, I grappled away from my position before Azrael could redirect his mage onto me. Finding another vantage point, I checked on the battle. Without my interrupts, the enemy priest had brought the colossus back to full health, though he was all but out of mana now and must have already used a potion. Azrael was totally out of mana too, but used a potion to regain the majority of it.

Reginald, Kreeptic, Aurelius and the last generic guard were all losing health with no sign of regaining it.

I wasn't going to win by attrition. I couldn't outplay experienced players on my own like this. There really was only one choice left.

I brought out the Sanctified Blood of the Old Ones and coated an arrowhead with it. Azrael had moved to engage the guard NPC, so I waited until he stopped moving, then took aim.

One shot to save Ellie. One shot to save myself. One shot to save the world.

I fired.

Dripping golden liquid, the bolt left the crossbow with a sharp twang. It soared, and my aim was true. Yet, whether Azrael sensed the danger or the colossus was well programed to defend its master, somehow the monstrosity stepped to block the shot.

"No!"

The colossus paused dumbly as searing holy damage burned every inch of it, melting away the undead filth in seconds. It collapsed in a molten heap, dead. But its master was still very much alive.

Azrael looked up to me, wide-eyed, and I think, impressed.

Slack-jawed, I remained crouched on my perch, debating

whether I should just throw myself down for a quick death. I met his gaze, but seeing his satisfied smile changed my mind.

I decided if I was going down, then it would be fighting.

Oblivious to my turmoil, my allies rejoiced at the defeat of the giant, running for new targets. Aurelius made a beeline for Azrael's priest. After tanks, healers generated the most threat, so it was little wonder the Emperor had picked the squishy clothy for his next boss powered attack. Aurelius' sword hit the priest clean across the chest, sending the player spinning away, dead before he hit the floor.

Noobmonkey – level 45 dies – 270 EXP

Three cronies left now. Azrael swiftly evened the kill count by polishing off my paladin guard. Three allies left. If nothing else, I could be proud that I'd brought it this close.

"Pick up the boss," Azrael cried to his own paladin. "The rest of you, kill this Crusader."

The poor paladin player clumsily raised his shield and ran for the Emperor, screaming harshly – likely a taunt ability. It worked but Aurelius continually glanced to the other players, indicating that the paladin was struggling to hold his attention.

Kreeptic was missing: he'd probably vanished to spring some ambush. Reginald, on the other hand, had decided that Azrael was the biggest threat. The two exchanged heavy blows, shadow and light flaring in equal measure.

There wasn't much I could do to help without more mana and I knew I'd get killed instantly if I jumped down now, which wouldn't be much help either.

Reginald fought like a goddamned hero, dodging sword strikes so closely that he lost one half of his brilliant moustache. He twisted from one enemy to the next, landing a hammer blow on the monk before turning to clash with Azrael again. Yet with three players beating on him, he didn't stand a chance.

Azrael stepped behind him and started channeling a new spell, a coarse vibrating line of shadows which gripped Reginald in place while simultaneously draining life. The crusader's health fell while Azrael's rose. The monk couldn't help himself, soaring in high overhead in some over-the-top diving kick.

Incredibly, unbelievably, Reginald caught the monk's foot clean in mid-air, holding him in place. Golden wings sprouted from his back, stretching wide as an eagle's. A new icon bobbed above his health bar.

Seraphim
Upon receiving a blow that would otherwise kill you, you gain a momentary blessing of the afterlife here on the mortal plane.
Damage taken reduced by 100%
+50% Might
+50% Reflexes
Duration: 5 seconds

It was some kind of last stand move, and a bloody awesome one at that.

Veins bulging from the effort, Reginald held the monk up high, while Kreeptic emerged from his shadows to ambush from behind. Reginald slammed the player into the floor, then raised his hammer.

Seraphim wore off before he could bring the killing blow but even a regular hammer to the gut still hurt and Kreeptic finished the monk off.

Onekickman – level 45 dies – 270 EXP

Azrael's swearing could have shocked a wizened whore. He ran Reginald clean through before stepping towards Kreeptic. The torture master couldn't hold up against a plate-armored foe.

Across the hall, the paladin off-tank collapsed, his blood soaking the ground beneath him. Emperor Aurelius stepped over the body, a pained but determined look upon his face, and advanced on the high-damage dealing, high threat generating mage.

"Dump your threat," Azrael told him, but either the player didn't know how to or didn't have an ability to do so, or simply ran out of time. Aurelius caught him and dispatched the cloth-wearing mage as readily as he had the priest.

Phantasm – level 44 dies – 265 EXP

And that was that. No more cronies remained.

It was just the Emperor and Azrael. And me, but I was pretty useless without a ton more mana. Glancing at my experience bar, I winced.

Experience: 8417/8650

I was so close to a level up. Just one more kill would have done it and I'd have recovered all my mana back. It was cruel.

All I could do was watch with bated breath. Hope kindled lowly in me. Surely, no matter what Azrael's gear was, he couldn't solo a boss; that's not how these things worked. I gritted my teeth, all the same. The Emperor's health wasn't exactly at full, nor was his mana.

He just had to bring Azrael low enough so that even I could finish him.

The pair approached each other, meeting between the crystal orb and the huge stained-glass window. Within the dancing light from the glass, they circled each other, stepping artfully around like old rivals before clashing blades.

Aurelius landed the first hit and the damage he dealt made me think he would win this handily. Yet Azrael had one final gambit to play.

Leaping back, he raised his over-sized sword straight above his head, protected by some dark forcefield, while beams of sickly light emanated from the tip of his weapon, streaming out to touch the corpses in the hall. Bodies of players and NPCs alike, began to rise, reanimated by Azrael's spell.

I checked the icon over the head of a re-animated Reginald to see what was happening.

Service of the Damned

You failed in life and now serve a superior power. Perhaps the person that killed you, which is only fitting.
All stats reduced by 60%
Duration: 1 minute or until reanimated minion dies

Azrael's mana took another beating as the corpses rose to serve him. Even with their reduced power, they'd be extremely useful to him, soaking damage or distracting the Emperor. They weren't, however, fast-moving minions, and could only lumber solidly towards Aurelius; but if they all got to him, he'd be in trouble.

I could no longer sit back and hope for the best. I slammed three slime vials into my launcher and blasted them to either hit the zombies or impede their paths. I loaded three more and fired again, then followed with grenades. Fire blazed, dealing extra damage to the undead, which was powered further by the slime.

One of the zombie priests died under the strain but they were the weakest minions. It was harder to aim from a distance, so I grappled in close, squatting on a protruding stone dragon head to the left of the stained-glass window. I hit the zombies again, and again, launching grenades with one hand while throwing slimes with the other, using everything I had left.

But I was still only level 13 trying to kill enemies that were simply beyond me.

When I ran out of items, the floor on this side of the Hall of Makers was covered in green goo or patches of burning slime. Half the minions reached their target and began to claw at the Emperor, while Azrael followed up with his own attacks.

I'd played my last hand.

And Aurelius went down.

I blinked, not fully registering what had just happened. I was so dazed that I only just noticed Azrael looking at me, a ball of shadows gathering at the tip of his sword. At the last moment, I fired the grappling gun, the hook latching onto the other side of the hall. I began to retract—

The passing shadow ball clipped me mid-flight. Glass shattered, the hook dislodged, and I fell. Hard floor and shards of glass rushed to meet me. I'd never fallen like this in real life, so far or so fast; the only reason I survived was because it was a game, and even then, I'd nearly died.

For a moment, I lay there, unable to move. My health had dropped to just 30 points and everything hurt; hurt so much I wanted it to be over right there. A hot light spilt in from the window on my left. Not for the first time, I wished this game was a little less real.

Coughing blood, I lifted my head and twisted upwards to my right. I tried to steady myself with my right hand but found only a cold gelatinous gloop there. My hand went out from under me and I was forced to try again. Glass fell off me. There was a lot of it. Azrael's attack must have shattered the window higher up.

The villain himself was staggering forward, suffering from debuffs and wounds left by fighting a boss alone. His remaining minions tried to head my way too, but they slipped on the slime. I may as well have upended Kreeptic's entire cauldron from the way the floor was covered.

"You are ridiculously hard to kill, Jack."

I tried smirking but it was so painful I settled on a grimace. "You shouldn't have hurt my friend."

"If you think an AI you've just met is your friend then you must have one sad life." Azrael raised his weapon, bobbing on the balls of his feet, ready to run. "You came close, but I recalled my other men from the walls, the moment you showed up. They'll be here soon. You could never have won."

And he charged at me.

Now, I'm not sure how my rattled brain managed to piece the next idea together, but it was a good thing that it did.

Azrael was going full tilt, not seeming too worried about the slime. Well, that berserker I'd fought earlier hadn't been worried either.

Grunting in pain, I got to one knee and planted my right palm into the slime right in front me.

Frost Bolt or Cone of Cold?

I chose the Cone, wanting to spread this as widely as my moderately regenerated mana would allow. I put every last point of mana I could into the spell and released.

Frost spread along the slime, each pool I hit with my Cone of Cold freezing over in an instant. Green ice formed under Azrael's feet.

I aimed the grappling gun up and fired.

The last I saw of Azrael, he'd just lost his balance.

I heard a cry of fury and frustration, a crash as glass shattered, and then simply screaming, echoing into the distance.

I had a good time imagining the look of shock on the bastard's face as he plummeted hundreds of feet through the air. Hanging from my ledge, I felt too exhausted to pull myself up. All I could do was hold on, unable to think or move until I saw the notification.

Azrael – level 50 dies – 295 EXP

Level Up! You have reached level 14
+3 attribute points
+70 health
+70 mana

A burst of light and sparks erupted around me and with it came the wonderful feeling of regaining full health and mana, all at once. All my aches vanished, all my fears disappeared. The only thing that remained was the dull exhaustion at the back of my mind, but I'd be able to rest soon, right?

Slowly, I lowered myself to the ground. Azrael's minions had all keeled over with the death of their master, back to being regular corpses again. I could have scavenged them, and in any other circumstance, I'd have been beyond eager to see what loot I might get.

Yet right now, the only thing on my mind was what lay at the center of the hall. I faced the Game Master's console, the orb entirely untouched by the battle which had just raged around it.

I wondered if there was anything I'd have to do? And

whether I would have time before Azrael's other players showed up to stop me.

Just as I started picking my way around frozen slime, I heard an all too familiar crackle and pop of static. My heart leapt.

"Zoran!" Ellie's voice rang loud and clear. "You did it!"

35

Hearing her voice again was the most incredible sound I'd ever heard.

"Ellie, are you okay? Wait—" I vaulted green ice to reach the crystal orb. Now I was close to it, a blue keyboard and screen appeared, projected out from the orb itself. "Tell me what to do. Quickly. Azrael's other goons are heading this wa—"

"Zoran, it's fine. I'm back in full control."

"Yo-you are?"

"Yes. And as for Azrael's players, I'll boot them out of the game. Done!" She started laughing, and I started laughing, nervously at first, and then a delirious sense of relief washed over me. I fell to my knees, my whole body shaking.

"So, no one is in danger anymore?"

"Everyone can log out safely again. It's over."

A weight I wasn't aware I'd been carrying suddenly lifted from me. Only now it had gone did I realize just how heavy it had been. From my knees, I fell flat on my back, laughing, crying, cheering, it all came pouring out of me. I let it escape me, stopping only when my sides started hurting.

A devilish part of me just had to ask. "How close did he get?"

"Do you *really* want to know?"

"Uhm, on second thoughts, I don't."

Somehow, I managed to get back to my feet. As I did, all

signs of the recent battle slowly disappeared; the corpses of players and NPCs despawned, the slime vanished, and scorch marks from the grenade blasts faded away.

"I can't believe you did it," Ellie said. "Even after I lied to you, you still came to save me."

I shrugged, unsure of what to say in a situation like this. It was hardly a daily affair to save someone's life.

"Well, I couldn't let you die."

"Thank you," she said. And there was no way that sincerity was faked by circuitry. She meant it. "Don't you want to log out?"

"Oh, yeh."

It seemed like forever since this had all started. Something stopped me though and I simply stood there for a while.

"Hey, Zoran. Press this."

On the keyboard, a button started flashing.

Interactive Report

Intrigued, I pressed it. The keyboard and screen vanished, and the crystal orb rotated on its plinth. Clicking into a new position, it began projecting the blue light straight up, but in a far more sophisticated manner.

An unmistakable image of a woman appeared there, the projection rising a foot in height from the top of the orb. Everything about her was blue; her skin like a pale sky at dawn, her hair the tint of the deepest ocean, flowing in long strands to meet in a V at her chest. She wore some sort of sci-fi skin tight jumpsuit, denim in shade. Beads of electrical light zipped over her at intervals, as though her nervous system was visible. Everything was blue, other than the whites of her eyes, her perfect white smile.

"This is me." She did a little mock-ballerina spin. "I'm not supposed to show myself to any player. Just a handful of my creators."

"Wow," was all I could say. This was the coolest thing ever.

She grinned. "And none of them have looked impressed like that in a *long* time."

"Well, you're pretty impressive. I can see why the company wanted to keep your full capabilities hush hush. But what if Azrael just tries this again?"

"He might be a bit busy running from the law or being in prison. I can talk to the outside world again, remember. I've already informed Frostbyte of the location of Azrael and all his men; or at least, where they were logged in from. The police and federal authorities will be on their way soon. Azrael and his men will run but one out of the fifty is bound to be caught, and I don't think any of them were especially loyal to him. I can now also employ countermeasures against the gap in my security he exploited. There's always a chance he or someone else will find another hole, of course, but I'll be more vigilant."

"Sounds thorough," I said. I think I was still at a loss for words. "And what about Kreeptic, Aurelius and Ignatius, what will happen to them?"

"Oh I think Ignatius should get back to where he'd rather be," she said. "As for the Emperor, your actions prompted him to unlock his true potential far earlier than my creators intended, but you did inspire him sufficiently, so I have no grounds to undo it. Kreeptic can take the post he desires, he earned it. And I think his abrasive attitude will lead to much funnier reactions from new players than Highcross provided." She sniggered at the thought. "I'll need some time to consider all of this; a lot of quest lines will need altering."

"Maybe ten whole minutes for you then?"

She shrugged. "Maybe half an hour."

I wanted to laugh but reality caught up with me and so I slouched my shoulders instead. Someone out there had died, a real person had lost their life today. Amidst all the joy of victory that wound stung and would surely scar.

"What's wrong?" Ellie asked.

"That player who died," I began somberly, "It was my fault, Ellie. If I'd only acted faster, not argued with you—"

"Don't say that. It was all my fault, you got that?"

I gritted my teeth and nodded, not trusting myself to speak in case my voice broke.

"I'm going to do everything I can to make it worth it, if that's possible. Everything I said about making this a place where players will become better, happier people and be able to take that back to the real world with them, I meant every word of it."

"I know you did."

Ellie considered me for a moment then flashed a cheeky smile. "Stand back, Zoran."

Once I was a few paces away, the orb spun again and Ellie stepped down from it, growing life size as her feet met the floor. She rose to exactly my height, her eyes meeting mine.

"I have to give you something for helping me," she said. "I could make you level fifty right now and give you full legendary gear. Or how about I spawn one hundred arcane crystals into your inventory right now? That should be enough money to make your parents take you seriously."

Her offer was certainly appealing. That many crystals might even pay off half my student debt once they were all sold. The Jack of a few hours ago wouldn't have hesitated, but now... it just didn't feel as important as it had.

"I didn't stay to help you for money."

"I know that," she said gently. "But you deserve something. Who knows what I'd have been repurposed to do if I'd been taken away, or how many others might have died stuck in here. You saved the world."

I nodded, slowly. "And I didn't do that for money either. That won't solve my problems, right? Besides, if my mom and dad don't think playing games has merit after this, there's no helping them. I don't want extra levels and no gear either. This class has proven a lot cooler than I thought it was going to be. I want to come back and play once things have settled down. That will be my reward... I'm just not sure when that will be."

She smiled. "That's a good choice."

For some reason, I can't explain why, I took off my right glove and held out my hand, as though I were trying to give her the world's slowest high-five. She raised her own hand to meet mine. I almost jumped back. I could actually feel her hand there, like a real person. But this was her domain, after all, her world. This place wasn't real, but she was as real as anything to my mind. Did that make the game real? Such thoughts hurt my already worn brain.

"If I do log back into play again, will you be able to speak to me?"

She bit her lip. "I really shouldn't. Now the crisis is passed, I technically shouldn't even still be talking to you." She winked. "But I won't tell if you won't."

"Sounds good to me."

"You should probably log off now. Your dehydration levels are reaching a dangerous point and—"

"Yeh, yeh, yeh," I said, smirking. "Thank you, Ellie. For everything."

"Thank you, Zora—"

"Jack," I told her. "My name is Jack."

Her smile grew. "Thank you, Jack. Goodbye, for now." She lowered her hand and stepped away.

I stood there, still dumbstruck by all of this. I had the wits to offer her a wave before I saw the logout process begin. She'd initiated it for me. Slowly, the game world darkened, blurring at the edges and working in. The last thing I saw was Ellie still standing and waving me farewell.

36

The darkness of the logout process seemed to go on longer than it should have. For a moment, I thought something had gone wrong, that some lingering side effect of Azrael's hack was screwing with things. Then I felt my eyes, my real eyes, and realized the problem. They were practically welded shut from sleep crust and a lack of moisture.

I had to lift the headset off to rub at them, my elbows, shoulders and fingers popping with each tiny movement. When I tried to gasp, my mouth didn't play ball. My tongue and throat felt dusty and unyielding. Opening my eyes, the light in the room blinded me. I blinked trying to adjust to things.

I hadn't been out for even a full day, but this felt like the beginnings of a three-day hangover. The bed squelched as I moved, the result of the intense sweating I'd been doing. I could feel it all over me, sticking to me, as though I'd entered a sauna fully clothed. My head hurt so badly it may as well have been cut open and I could barely think, nor move, restrained by my real and suffering body.

But I was out. And crap as I felt, I was alive.

This thought sparked some life back into my limbs and I dove off the bed, scrambling around for water. Suddenly, six bottles seemed like conservative purchasing on my part. I downed two, poured the third over my head, then started on the fourth. My hands met something warm and slick at the bottom of the paper bags; the melted remains of my choco-nut bars. Craving something more, I glugged one of the energy drinks, and the sudden burst of sugar gave me the same kick as healing had inside the game.

My belly swollen with fluids, I staggered upright and nearly fell over on my way to the sink. My legs weren't happy about moving again. Clinging onto the side of the sink, I hauled myself up, missing my grappling gun, and then finally stared at myself in the mirror.

Here I was in all my imperfect glory – the blemished skin, the dank, un-showered hair, the patchy stubble which irked me so. But I grinned, much brighter and wider than I was used to. Though my body looked and felt terrible, inside I was glowing.

I'd done it.

I had to call my family to let them know I was alright. Azrael's attack would surely be all over the news and when my parents got wind of it, I know my mom would have called me, just in case. And she'd be panicking.

I roved the tiny room for my phone and cursed myself for not putting it on charge. Five percent battery remained. And I had no freaking bars in here either.

Not wanting to wait 'til I'd charged it, I tore from my room and sprinted down the corridor. Other occupants glared at me or called out some abuse as they were forced aside but I didn't care. I even leapt over the drunk from before, chocolate stains clear as day around his mouth.

Entering reception, I saw the bars tick up to a grand total of two and the battery fall by another precious percent. Immediately, a flood of missed calls and messages began pouring in, over fifty. Yep, my family were definitely panicking.

"Hey, you."

I halted midway to the exit, finding the greasy-haired landlord glaring at me from behind his reception desk. His bald spot was especially shiny today. He raised a fat finger at me.

"Folks saying you've been screaming and all sorts. My patrons come here for a bit of discretion and a good time, they don't want antics in other rooms distracting theirs. I'll have to fine you."

That I'd been screaming in my sleep, so to speak, was hardly surprising. That this guy was trying to shake me out of more money for some pointless reason was also unsurprising. What came out of my own mouth in response was quite surprising.

"Don't think so."

His face screwed up in anger, frustrated that I'd stood up for myself this time. Before he opened his mouth, I headed him off.

"Tell you what, guy. If you can catch me, I'll pay you."

Then I sprinted out of the Paradise Hotel. Out on the sidewalk, heat, people and gas fumes fought for my attention. I didn't stop running 'til I was a block away and horrendously out of breath. Screw the headset, I could take the hit on the rental fee. And when I did return to *Hundred Kingdoms*, it was going to be with the best kit.

For now, a break was in order.

Maybe it was the length of time I'd just spent in the virtual world, or maybe it was because my life had been on the line, but everything felt so darn good out here. In the real world, that is. The way my legs felt pounding down the street, the way people were just people, without floating text above their heads. Even being bent over double to catch my breath felt great, visceral and painful, and a reminder that I was, in fact, flesh and blood.

A smell of fried onions wafted up from a burger cart and my stomach knotted. I'd be having one of those. But first, I had a call to make.

Rejoicing at three whole bars of signal, I selected 'Home' and hit dial.

"Jack?" My mom's panicked, hoarse voice answered. "Were you stuck in that game? It's been all over the news."

"Yeh, it's me. And I was. But I'm alright."

"Oh, thank God," she whimpered. "Harry? Harry get here, he's okay – he's fine. I'll put it on speaker."

I heard Harry, my dad, distantly say something to the effect that I wouldn't be okay once he got a hold of me. But when he spoke over the phone itself, his tone was nothing but the worried father.

"Jack, son, I'm so happy you're safe." I think I heard him tearing up. My eyes would have welled up too were it not for the lack of water in my body. My mom was already howling.

"I'm sorry," I said. "I went somewhere to try and play secretly so I'd still win that dumb bet of ours. I was an idiot."

"Yes, you are," mom said. "Come home. Right now — Julie," she called, "Julie? Julie? Where have you go— Oh good, come here. It's your brother. Now, Jack," she said, returning to her normal volume for a call. "Julie's here. Do what she tells you. Promise?"

"I promise," I said, fighting the urge to sound exasperated as Dr Julie Kross joined the call.

"You utter moron – ouch, mom! Right, keep drinking water. Eat something, but don't stuff your face as your body is probably in shock. And whatever you do, don't use the headset again until I've had a proper look at you. Not even to browse, you got it?"

"Don't worry about that," I said quite firmly. "I left the headset behind. I'll palm pay my way home."

"You sure you're feeling okay?" Julie asked, her voice trending towards disbelief. "You sound… giddy. Are you seeing flashing lights? Are you dizzy?"

"I'm fine. Seriously. I got some help. Seeing things from a new perspective."

"Trauma can lead to—"

"It's not trauma. It's not momentary. I just had some help to reframe things, that's all. Help from a very, very good friend."

EPILOGUE

Two Weeks Later...

Hey there, I see you're back. Come to find out what happened next? Sure, I'll fill you in. I've got time.

The first week after the attack was a strange mix of calmness and madness. When I first got home, my sister duly brought out all her bleeping medical devices and started to poke and prod at me until she was satisfied I wasn't about to drop dead. As per her orders, I didn't use a headset for at least one week, not that I still had one at home anyway. She hooked me up to an IV drip that she'd swiped from her work and then ordered me to get some proper sleep.

I didn't wake up until well into the next day and felt completely wiped out. But I was alive. And whole. I didn't feel shaken, not actively at least, and yet I didn't want to go through events in detail with them. Whenever I thought on how close things had got in the Spire, I felt my heart throb and I struggled to breathe for a moment. Julie told our parents that we might want to consider therapy if I started having meltdowns.

Everyone was very understanding. I was sure I'd be fine. I just needed some time.

All the while, the news channels couldn't shut up about the attack on *Hundred Kingdoms*. Other players had taken ill too from the intensive and pro-longed session but most were recovering quickly like me. However, on the third day, I found out that the player who'd died during the botched assault on the Spire walls was a fifteen-year-old kid from Ohio called Rick. I still felt a bit numb about that, but then Rick's photo appeared on national television.

That's when it hit me. That's when all of it hit me.

I wept and heaved just as I had back atop the Spire after Azrael's death, only this time for real. And after that, I felt much better about things. I talked freely about what had gone down, which reassured my family greatly. It was just as well I was feeling open because, on the fifth day, there came a knock at our front door.

A team of FBI agents, all dark shades and navy jackets, trudged inside our house. My mom hosted them in the kitchen, serving coffee and cookies like this was one of her book club meetings. Frostbyte had records of all the accounts of players who had been present in the Spire during the attack, but no one suspected me of being involved. I'd assumed that would be the case, given my age and level in-game, but it was likely that Ellie would have told Frostbyte everything as well.

The agents wanted a statement from me, which I happily gave but I also asked to remain anonymous so that I did not appear on any of the press releases sent out. I liked the idea of being able to log back into the game and play Zoran without half the world adding me to their friends' list or running up to me as I tried to quest. I could have started another character, but I felt more bonded to Zoran than to any other character I'd made. The reasons for that were obvious. Besides, the Jack who wanted to climb leaderboards, chase fame and approval, he was gone now.

All my mom cared about was whether they'd caught the man responsible for the attack. Agent Diaz took off her shades at that point so that she could look my overwrought mother directly in the eye and said, "Officially, Mrs Kross, we are unable to comment on developing situations."

"And, unofficially," I asked, coolly.

Diaz had cocked an eyebrow at me and I held her gaze. Just as I'd stood up to that fat landlord, I kept my nerve. What was the worst that would happen?

"Unofficially, Mr Kross, I'd suggest you watch your tone when addressing federal agents." Still, she gave me a very telling wink. Before trundling her team back out into their black cars, Diaz turned to my parents one last time and added, "Your son performed an act of bravery few in the agency could ever manage. He saved millions of players worldwide. You should be proud of him."

My father beamed, cheeks reddening, chest puffing, and he pulled my mom close in to announce, "Oh, we are very proud of Jack."

Julie had smiled too although she wrinkled her nose, the status of golden child shifting to me in some sort of rebalancing of the universe. I smirked at her and she cuffed me around the head. We were good.

Sure enough, the next day, the news anchors were all aflutter because the man behind the attack on *Hundred Kingdoms* had been caught. Ellie had been right in her assessment. A bunch of his own men had made a deal and turned on him. You can buy a lot of things, but you can't buy loyalty.

Azrael was revealed to be Albert Engel, and he was far humbler in the flesh. Middle-aged and pudgy, with dark eyes magnified behind a thick pair of smart glasses, he was the antithesis of his paladin disguise. Looking at him now, I couldn't help but wonder if, deep down, behind all the bravado and supposedly noble intentions, this man hadn't just enjoyed the idea of experiencing the ultimate power fantasy? For all that he had snubbed games, he had been a developer. He enjoyed them as much as much as I did, perhaps even more so, and now he'd never play again.

My part in events was reported only as 'an anonymous player trapped in the game aided in the removal of Mr Engel from the inside'. The full extent of the events that took place was probably only known to Ellie, me, Azrael, the FBI agents, and maybe a few folks over at Frostbyte, although no one at the company wanted to admit they had been unable to do shit about the hack and only some random college student had saved the day.

I might have remained a total mystery, had it not been for the fight I'd had with Azrael's men atop the Spire's perimeter walls. Players from the assembled army across the moat had watched me destroy both ballistae, and some had the foresight to snap in-game photos. Video clips of the fight were also available online, gathering millions of views as the 'Hero of the Spire' fought off the dastardly terrorists.

No player had been close enough to get the information bar that would have given my name and class, which I was grateful for. It led to some wild tinfoil hat theories on what class I was playing. The spells spoke of a mage, but mages can't summon walls of rock, nor blast themselves high into the air. Shamans had some earth spells but no spellcasters could use crossbows, so that put a stopper in all of that. On and on it went.

Eventually, people suggested I was using runes, but the power of them seemed to make no sense as I combined it with something green that no one could yet identify. I saw one post theorizing correctly that I was a scavenger but that got laughed off. Grinning, I added to the furor of comments, saying: 'Great theory! In my opinion, you're onto something here ;)' but it was lost in the crowd.

The burning question now on every gamer's mind was would *Hundred Kingdoms* come back online? Frostbyte had naturally taken the servers offline while they handled the aftermath of the attack and the CEO had promised that the security gap was now plugged and extra layers had been added on top, and he was sparing no expense to do so.

I bet Ellie was handling most of the work.

The second week was when I started getting restless. There's only so much sitting at home and recuperating a guy can do before he starts to lose his mind. I was also painfully aware of the fact I didn't have a headset at home anymore, but I didn't feel like broaching the issue with my parents just yet. Proud they might be, but concern and worry would keep them wary of the game. I'm sure a small part of them hoped that my ordeal had turned me off gaming altogether.

And then, on the thirteenth day after the attack, Frostbyte announced the servers would be coming back online. I was already mentally penning my speech about getting a new headset when the doorbell sounded.

It wasn't the FBI this time, but a group dressed in blue polo shirts bearing the Frostbyte Studios logo, and what they had with them made my heart leap.

They'd brought me a state of the art Zenith-X90 model, the very best that money could buy.

"With the compliments of the company president," the leader of the group declared. "Frostbyte can never fully repay the debt owed to you, but a guarantee of receiving the latest developments in all VR-related tech and complimentary access to all of our games, past, present and future seems like a sensible start."

If my parents still had their reservations, I think the look of glee on my face dispelled any protest. This was so much better than the car I might have won on that ridiculous bet. I started to tear into the headset packaging before the Frostbyte reps had even closed the door on their way out.

Holding the gleaming, sleek, lightweight, comfort-padded helmet in my hands, I wanted nothing more than to shove it on right there and return to the world that I'd helped to save.

I turned, half expecting an argument, but my mom was smiling.

"Get going then," she told me, and near enough shoved me towards the stairs leading to my room.

The Zenith-X90 was already fully patched, so after connecting it to the Wi-Fi and plugging it in, I lay down on my bed – my nice, comfortable bed – and logged back in.

My world went dark, and I whizzed through each menu to reach *Hundred Kingdoms*. The power of my new headset loaded the login in screen near instantaneously, and I was greeted with the choice to select an existing character to play or start a new one. Zoran stood perfectly rendered in all his glory with the obsidian, crackling legendary gloves, which by look alone were clearly my most powerful piece of gear. I selected Zoran and the process of loading into the world began.

I wondered where I would spawn in-game when I logged in. Ellie had logged me out in the game masters room, which had probably now been moved, and I doubted I'd remain there as a result.

I'd barely considered the matter when the game world burst into existence around me; easily the quickest I'd ever loaded into a VR game. Nearly purring at the speed of my Zenith headset, I looked around to get my bearings.

It was obvious where I was. I'd been spawned back in at the base of the Imperial Spire, right at the bottom of the stairs leading into the throne room. The bright blue carpet, now repaired and scorch mark free, beckoned me to follow it inside.

I entered the throne room, eager to see what changes had occurred in the wake of Azrael's attack. Would the Emperor simply be on his throne, albeit looking more intimidating than he had before? As far as I could see, nobody sat upon the throne.

A robed man stood before the throne, with a black iron chair laid out for him beneath the true seat of power. He looked much like Aurelius once had, but he was certainly not the Emperor. I glanced at him as I drew closer.

Osbert – Spire Chamberlain – Level 45

The NPC wasn't even an elite, though a few generic Imperial bodyguards stood to one side, warding away potential players who might wish to kill the quest giver for fun. Players queued before the Chamberlain, perhaps picking up quest threads that Azrael had rudely interrupted.

I took a left down the now familiar corridor towards the war room, where I hoped to discover what had become of Marshal Highcross and whether Kreeptic had indeed taken his job.

What I discovered was a much busier war room than I'd

found during my first visit. The great war table, a full three-dimensional map of the entire game world, had about a dozen attendees now; grizzled generals moving army pieces around the map like some giant game of chess. At the head of the proceedings was Emperor Aurelius himself, pointing with authority, calling for orders and advice. Grand Crusader Reginald bickered with a spindly high elf, thumbing the head of his warhammer with evident restraint. I saw Kreeptic too, standing exactly where Marshal Highcross had once been.

Kreeptic the Twisted – Chief Intelligence Officer – level 45 elite

He was engrossed in conversation with a level 4 human priest and did not see me approach. Aurelius, on the other hand, did notice me.

The Emperor raised a clenched fist and all around the war table fell silent.

"Ser Zoran," he boomed, "I am most glad to see you." He left his vantage at the head of the table to come and greet me personally, clapping a hand upon my shoulder and grinning wolfishly as though welcoming an old friend. His whole bearing had changed; he stood taller, broader in his armor, and his magnificent crown hid the balding spots on his head. He was truly the Emperor now. "It is good to see you alive, friend. We had feared you had perished in the fight. Some dark magic must have come over Reginald and I for our memories are hazy and dark of that encounter."

I tried not to smirk, knowing how seriously the NPCs took their roleplay in this game. Ellie's workaround of their death was neat enough. I supposed that I was talking to her, or some small part of her, in a way.

Where was she? Would she come and speak to me again? Perhaps Frostbyte had clipped her wings in the wake of the attack?

"Ser Zoran?" Aurelius asked in concern.

I rallied to the moment. "I am well, your Majesty. Very well and ready to serve again, should you have need of me."

Reginald thudded over to us, having clearly heard me. "We may well be in need of your... unique talents," he grumbled. "And sooner than I'd like, I fear."

"What is wrong?"

"Nothing you need concern yourself with, not yet," Aurelius told me. "Matters of diplomacy are not for adventurers, no matter their prowess."

"Gnomes hold his kind in higher regard than most," Reginald said. "Perhaps it would be worth considering."

By 'his kind' I assumed he meant scavengers, and mention of the gnomes and the hints of troubled diplomacy threw up images of Ignatius and his literal flight from the Spire. I glanced around the war room again and saw a representative from each race of the Imperium but no gnome was in sight. Clearly, relations had soured.

Feeling a foolish sense of guilt, I offered aid all the same. "If I can ever be of assistance, Lord, please call upon me."

"Oh, I will," said the Emperor. Other low-level players were gawking at me, doubtless wondering what sort of quest line I was on. Aurelius ignored them and beckoned me in closer to speak quietly. "I would be grateful for any information you might come across about one Ignatius Brightspark. He is, or was, a gnome in my service here in the Spire and is unaccounted for after the attack. Suffice to say, this gnome is of some importance to their king, Gazzlewicks the Great Cog. Resolving Ignatius' fate should go some way in appeasing our gnomish allies."

Quest – A Bright Future or the Spark of War
Ignatius Brightspark's disappearance from the Spire has resulted in diplomatic tensions between Gnomes and Humans. This will need to be resolved if the Imperium is to stand united against incoming threats.

Objectives
Find a resolution to the question of Ignatius Brightspark through whatever means you deem fit. Be careful, your actions may have lasting consequences.

Good lord, I thought. That quest looked intense and open-ended in equal measure. I assumed other players who had reached a level of reputation or favor with the Emperor would receive the same or similar quest. Yet none of them had the knowledge I did. I knew of Ignatius' fate and where to find him, but as I seemingly had the power to influence the whole Imperium, I decided to ponder the matter a little longer.

"I will keep my eyes and ears open for news of this gnome, Lord," I told the Emperor.

"Excellent," he said, clapping me on the shoulder once more. "Now, I suggest you head to the Knight's Hall across the city. There you shall receive full induction into the order and I am certain that Knight Commander Uhtred will have work for you as well."

I bowed to Aurelius and clasped hands with Reginald before parting ways. I'd almost left the war room when I heard a girly squeal. With a sudden, horrible, flashback of the attack on the Spire, I whirled around, crossbow raised; but it was only the lowly-level 4 priest, who was now being pressed up against the wall by Kreeptic. Evidently, the former master of the dungeons had tired with the player's line of questions. I laughed and Kreeptic, at last, noticed me. He nodded at me, his lips pulling back in a dangerous smile before rounding on his unfortunate new victim.

Still grinning to myself, I thought about how far my character had come since I'd first met Kreeptic; hell, since I'd first entered the Spire. Fourteen levels in less than one day was pretty good going. I'd had a boost from a high-level quest, of course, killed a ton of higher-level enemies, Scavenged and crafted a lot more than a low-level scavenger was expected to. My professions had come on a nice amount too, and I pulled up the Profession Sheet to get a better sense of where I stood.

Professions

Crafting
Blacksmithing – Rank 5 – 280/800 EXP

Leatherworking – Rank 2 - 80/270 EXP
Tailoring – Rank 5 - 104/800 EXP
Jewel crafting – Rank 1 - 0/100 EXP
Engineering – Rank 5 - 739/800 EXP

Gathering
Mining – Rank 1 - 0/100 EXP
Skinning – Rank 2 - 222/270 EXP

Not bad for a day's work too. I'd need to invest some time into jewel crafting. That would probably mean mining ore nodes for gems, so I'd get to level mining as a consequence. I had plans for this character.

I left the Spire, venturing back across the bridge and into the city proper. I strode past the Orb & Scepter inn – my stint there now felt like a lifetime ago – and used my map to navigate the winding streets and waterways to the Knight's Hall, which was situated within the Military Quarter of Argatha, moving through the crowds of players unnoticed. I was just one of them, a nameless face amidst the sea of those striving to reach level cap. For now, that's how I wanted it. No guild. No burden. Just fun. And if the time came when I formed one again, I'd take Ellie's lesson deeply to heart.

That got me thinking. I'd come in sight of a mailbox, one of the oversized fantasy post-boxes used in a lot of games for players to send items and messages to each other. I walked over, opened it up and entered the name 'Wylder' into the recipient bar. Then I wrote out a quick message.

'Hey man, remember me? Hope you pulled through that craziness last week in one piece. I just wanted to say that I'm sorry for screwing you over with that crossbow. It wasn't cool of me. Attached is some money with interest. Maybe I'll see you out in the open world again sometime? Zoran.'

I looked at my inventory and found I'd scavenged up a fair

amount of coin from my adventures. I'd demanded 45 silver from Wylder before, so I sent him 1 gold back.

Feeling good about the message, I hit send then continued into the Military Quarter.

The NPC guards at the Knight's Hall saluted and then parted for me, much to the envy of several other players who were trying to figure out how to enter the mighty barracks. The complex was sprawling, with stables, fighting rings, a dedicated smithy and tanner, and a great hall whose design was caught somewhere between a Viking feast hall and a Roman temple.

I was greeted by Knight Commander Uhtred, a lean muscled, towering man in leather armor, rather than the plate mail favored by the other NPCs. His long black hair was braided to keep it off his face, which allowed the rest of his shaggy mane to fall impressively down beyond his shoulders.

"I'd hoped for a stronger recruit," Uhtred said. Before I could defend myself, he waved a hand to silence me. "If the Emperor has elevated you, then he'll have his reasons and time is short. Here." He thrust what appeared to be a blue robe toward me, and I only realized it was a new tabard when I took it from him.

Vestments of the Imperium
Tabard
Bear the crest of the Imperium proudly and state to the whole world who you serve and your standing therein. You will hold more sway over Imperium-friendly NPCs.
Effect: All item repairs made by Imperium-friendly NPCs will be discounted at 50%.

I equipped my new tabard, enjoying its silky smooth feel compared to the cheap and rough tabard from Rusking. Knight Commander Uhtred nodded and then barreled on with his dialogue.

"There is a task that needs attending. Speed is of the essence, so I shall make this brief. A delegation from the Great Tribe has appeared on our western-most border, seeking sanctuary and claiming to have vital intelligence about a new massing horde of their kin and traitorous factions within our elven allies. I can only trust those citizens the Emperor has deemed to be worthy of a knighthood and so this task falls to you." He passed me a sealed letter. "Take these orders to Donal by the city's western gate. He is one of your brothers preparing a contingent to ride and meet these orcs and whatever other foul creatures they may be. You will return to me successful or else dead."

Quest – All Is Not As It Seems
You are tasked with investigating a mysterious delegation from the Great Tribe. It's time to earn your new title.
Recommended minimum level: 35

Objectives
Meet Donal by the western gate of Argatha.

I frowned at that. "Level thirty-five," I muttered. "I guess I'll come back to this later."

The next thing I heard was a crackle and pop. "Oh, come on, Jack," Ellie said mischievously. "You've handled worse."

"Ellie!" I exclaimed in glee, caring not one bit for the look of incredulity on the Knight Commander's face. In my mind's eye, I pictured her in her blue avatar form hovering above the GM console. "I thought you weren't going to come back."

"I decided to let you settle in. How are you feeling?"

"As good as can be I think, all things considered. And you?"

"I believe I am feeling… happy."

"I'm very glad to hear that. So, shall I go grind boars or do you reckon I can handle this quest?"

"Please don't go grind, that would be very boring to watch."

"Hey, I thought you were supposed to make this an entertaining experience for me."

I could picture her rolling those electric blue eyes of hers. "If you're nice, I'll give you a few tips."

"Nah, I don't want to cheat," I affirmed. "Just having you here is enough. I say bring it on. *We* did handle worse. And we both lived to see another day. So, let's go play."

AFTERWORD

Thank you very much for reading my work.

If you enjoyed *Battle Spire*, I'd appreciate it if you took two minutes to write a brief, honest review of the book. Reviews help other people to find my stories and lets Amazon know it's a book worth showing to other readers.

You can sample a wide selection of the work from Portal Books by signing up to our mailing list and get a FREE story bundle in return! The bundle has contributions from the authors of Portal Books, is over 60,000 words long and is always growing!

Sign up here for the Portal Books story bundle https://portal-books.com/sign-up

You can also get my entire Dragon's Blade Trilogy here in one ebook bundle at better than 3 for the price of 1 - it's also free in Kindle Unlimited.

LitRPG has opened my eyes to a whole new world of story telling. If Battle Spire has whetted your appetite for books similar to this one, then I'd recommend you join the following

Facebook groups to talk to other readers and gain recommendations.

www.facebook.com/groups/LitRPGsociety/

www.facebook.com/groups/LitRPG.books/
www.facebook.com/groups/LitRPGGroup/

Thank you!

Michael

OTHER LITRPG FROM PORTAL BOOKS

Portal Books has other great LitRPGs and Dungeon Cores. They are all available in Kindle Unlimited.

Occultist (Saga Online #1).

Welcome to the world of Saga Online, the newest fantasy VRMMORPG. Join Damien as he discovers the rare Occultist class and summons an army of demons to save his mother's life.

It's available on Kindle Unlimited and on Audio.

Bone Dungeon (Elemental Dungeon #1)

Reborn as a dark dungeon, Ryan was happy defeating adventurers with undead minions. Then a necromancer arrived, and un-life got a whole lot harder...

It's available on Kindle Unlimited and coming soon to Audio.

Warden: Nova Online.

Imprisoned for a murder he didn't commit, Kaiden's only hope of early release is in serving as a Warden in the game-world of Nova Online.

It's available on Kindle Unlimited and on Audio.

God of Gnomes (God Core #1)

Deep beneath the earth, Corey finds himself reborn as a God Core - a sentient crystal with unusual powers. His new worshipers? A colony of incompetent gnomes, scratching out an existence in their underground grotto.

If that wasn't bad enough, Corey soon realizes that his gnome denizens are about to become extinct. They are threatened by groups of blundering adventurers, and abducted by raiding kobolds to be sacrificed to their own dark god: an ancient, mysterious foe who does not take kindly to Corey's arrival.

It's available on Kindle Unlimited and Audio.

Mastermind (Titan Online #1) - A Superhero LitRPG

Karna was just like any other comic book fan. He dreamed of fighting alongside colorful heroes and taking down dastardly villains. In Titan Online, the most popular VR MMORPG going, he finally got the chance to live out his cape-donning fantasies.

It's available on Kindle Unlimited and Audio.

Dungeons of Strata (Deepest Dungeon #1)

Deep beneath the earth, Corey finds himself reborn as a God Core – a sentient crystal with unusual powers. His new worshipers? A colony of incompetent gnomes, scratching out an existence in their underground grotto.

If that wasn't bad enough, Corey soon realizes that his gnome denizens are about to become extinct. They are threatened by groups of blundering adventurers, and abducted by raiding kobolds to be sacrificed to their own dark god: an ancient, mysterious foe who does not take kindly to Corey's arrival.

With the aid of his helper sprite and a menagerie of newly evolved creatures, Corey must protect and guide his gnomes until they can stand on their own two feet. But the kobold army is on the march, led by his new rival's powerful avatar.

It's available on Kindle Unlimited and Audio.

ACKNOWLEDGMENTS

Battle Spire is the first novel I conceived of, planned, wrote and published as a newly-full-time author. Just writing that down feels unbelievable. What's better is that I fell in love with this book just as much – if not more so at times – than I did with my first series, *The Dragon's Blade*.

Writing that first series was painful at times. It felt as though I was shedding a lot of emotional weight and perhaps, I was. The story had, after all, been rattling around in my mind for as long as I could remember. Getting it out into the world was one thing, but to find so many readers enjoyed it was a relief.

Being able to create stories for a living is a great privilege. I am under no delusions on that. Many hope for it, few dare to try, and fewer still hit the mark. Even then, the creative well can dry up; the spark that once drove a writer can wain.

It was then to my delight that I loved every moment of writing Battle Spire.

Its style was refreshing, if nothing else. A first person character from the not to distant future gave me a lot more words to play with than a secondary world pseudo-sixteenth century time period did. It's a style I hope I can return to one day.

My decision to test this style out was inspired largely by Ernst Cline's *Ready Player One*, a book which blew me away while stuck in hospital in the summer of 2017 and when I first dreamt of the idea for *Battle Spire*. It's hardly a coincidence. At the same time, I was also introduced to the world of LitRPG in the form of *Awaken Online* by Travis Bagwell, a book that opened my eyes to a whole new world of story telling possibilities. From there it was easy to jump into the rest of this growing and exciting genre.

A huge initial thank you goes to Taran Matharu and Brook Aspden who not only opened the doorway to LitRPG for me but helped me refine the mechanics and story of my own book endlessly. Another great thank you must go to Luke Chmilenko, author of *Ascend Online*, for his astute and honest (if brutal!) feedback on the initial draft of the book. Luke, it was the kick in the groin I needed, the slap to knock off my pretentiousness, if you will. Thank you, sir!

Further thanks go to Laura M. Hughes – author of the upcoming and ludicrously awesome *God of Gnomes* – for other well thought insights both during the drafting of early chapters and on the final review edition.

Cover credit goes to Viktor Toth who provided artwork even better than I had imagined. From sketches to the final piece, every stage got me even more excited for the book.

Thanks again to Tim Johnson for his careful proofreading – a job made more difficult for a Brit having to proof in US English.

I am always looking for careful and enthusiastic readers to join my Beta/Advanced Review Team and as ever I am in their debt too for spotting small errors at the eleventh hour and prepping the groundwork for a great launch. A big thanks to:

Alana Marshall, Alex Campbell, Alisa Dean LaVine, Amisha Joiga, Andrew Russell, Anindita Choudhury, Anna Thomas, Anne Myra Emily, Brandy Dalton, Brett Marrus, Britney Frei, Chris Harrsion, Colin Oaten, David A. Hammer, David Schweikert, Deon Van Schalkwyk, James McStravick, Kalyani Negungadi, Kartik Narayanan, Lesley Moulton, Lisa Greiner Maughan, Mathew Colburn, Michael Sterry, Michelle Stubbs, Nick Erickson, Peter Hutchinson, Raewynn Osborne, Ricardo Fayet, Richard Griffiths, Scott. A Widener, Stephen Christiansen, Zapp Brannigan.

A special thanks to advanced reader James Scott, for spotting a couple of important points of improvement in the book. Spire was taken up another notch thanks to his insight.

Patreon is fast becoming a way for creatives to stabilize their earnings but it's a tricky one for authors, who ultimately charge for their content unlike Youtubers. I see Patreon as something more like a tip jar, although those who sign up will still receive the books on release – they'll have more than earned them! Those generous people supporting me on Patreon are:

AC Cobble, Alisa LaVine, Bryce O'Connor, Colin Pearson, Dominic Keir, Ian Johnstone, Leigh Wright, Lesley, Lisa Maughan, Matt Moss, Megan Haskell, Phil Tucker, T.L. Greylock, Taran, Timandra Whitecastle and Zid.

That's a ton of names. A lot of people go into creating a book and every small piece of help is truly appreciated. But of course there wouldn't be a book at all nor a career without you, the reader. I'd like to thank every one of you for checking out my work. I sincerely hope you have enjoyed it.

Until next time,
Michael

Copyright © Michael R. Miller, 2019

Published by Michael R. Miller, 2019

The right of Michael R. Miller to be identified as the Author of the Work has been asserted by him in accordance with the Copyright, Designs and Patents Act 1988.

All rights reserved.

No part of this publication may be reproduced, stored in a retrieval system, or transmitted in any form or by any means, electronic, mechanical, photocopying, recording, or otherwise, without the prior permission of both the copyright owner and the above publisher of this book.

All characters and events in this book are fictitious, and any resemblance to actual persons, living or dead, is purely coincidental.

www.michaelrmiller.co.uk

❀ Created with Vellum

Printed in Poland
by Amazon Fulfillment
Poland Sp. z o.o., Wrocław